全新！

外國人天天在用 上班族萬用英文

白善燁 —— 著　許竹瑩 —— 譯

全MP3一次下載

http://www.booknews.com.tw/mp3/9789864543397.htm

此為ZIP壓縮檔，請先安裝解壓縮程式APP，
iOS系統請升級至iOS 13後再行下載。
此為大型檔案（416M），建議使用WIFI連線下載，以免占用流量，
並確認連線狀況，以利下載順暢。

為什麼只要會這 350 個句子，就可以用英文到全世界談生意？

自從我決定要為上班族寫一本英文學習書後，我花了一年時間去拜訪各式各樣的職場、收集各種情報，終於彙整出職場上最常使用的一千多個商務句型。經過在外商企業工作多年的專家與英語母語人士們的嚴格監修，最後精挑細選出最好用的 350 個句型收錄在這本書中。

1. 直接套用可無限延伸幾千幾百句！

- How's **your project** going?
  你的計畫進行進行得怎麼樣了？
- How's **the office renovation** going?
  你的辦公室整修進行得怎麼樣了？
- How's **the staff training** going?
  職員的教育訓練進行得怎麼樣了？

以上三個句子都使用了 "How's...going?"（…進行得怎麼樣了？）這個簡單的句型。卻能造出意義完全不同的三個句子，只要你學會如何反覆套用這些句型，從此不必再思考文法結構與字彙，就能寫出正確的句子。

2. 只要套用可立即反射英文說法

請將以下的句子翻譯成英文。

※ 可以請你代理我的工作嗎？

你可以在 1 秒以內翻譯出來嗎？

你可能會開始思考，「代理」的英文是什麼？該用 be 動詞還是助動詞開頭？這個句子該用什麼時態？

如果你知道以下這個句型，上面的問題，你完全不必考慮。

Can you cover…?

可以請你代理…嗎？

如果懂得套用這個句型，只要在句子後面加上 for me 就行了，完整的句子就是 "Can you cover for me?"。用這個方法來翻譯句子，是不是很簡單呢？句型就像是一個固定的模子，只要搭配單字就能輕鬆造出千百個句子，以下是幾個例句。

- Can you cover for me?
  可以請你代理我的工作嗎？
- Can you cover my shift today?
  今天可以請你幫我代班嗎？
- Can you cover for me while I'm away?
  我外出的時候可以請你代理我的工作嗎？

3. 告別「直譯式」的中式英文

在上面的範例中提到，英語句型 "Can you cover...?" 的意思等於中文的「可以代替我…嗎？」，把中文和英文放在一起的話，就可以看出這樣的對照。

句型
單字・表達事物
Can you cover
for me while I'm away?
我外出的時候 可以請你代理 我的工作嗎？

從上面的對照句可以看出，中文的語序跟英文的語序不太一樣，所以如果你翻譯英文的方式是在腦海裡把中文逐字翻譯，往往會出現奇怪的中式英文。如果你直接將關鍵單字套用句型，就不用擔心這個問題了。

4. 學會本書 350 個句型就是學好英語的捷徑

有很多人認為一定要先學好文法才能開口說英文，所以還在跟複雜的假設語氣、關係代名詞纏鬥。現在，請徹底學會本書所列的句型吧！只要記住最簡單、最常用的 350 個句型，就能輕鬆使用英文來表達自己的想法。尤其是在職場上會用到的英文，通常都有固定的說法，所以用這個方法學英文，其效果更為顯著。

當然，我並不是說英文文法一點都不重要，我想強調的是，對英語初學者來說，透過理解、背誦句型來練習英文會話，絕對是最簡單且最有效的方式。

只要記住本書收錄的 350 個英語會話句型，在工作中因為英語會話能力不足而陷入窘境的機率將會減少 90%，對於工作繁忙且年紀稍長，一直找不出時間來加強自己英語能力的人來說，這絕對是最棒的捷徑。請每天抽出一點時間，用這些句型來練習用英文講電話、寫 E-mail 或開會吧！只要善用這本書，即使你的工作再忙碌，也能夠快速提升你的英文能力與職場戰鬥力。

作者 **白善燁**

學習份量剛剛好，輕鬆掌握句型！

★ 1 次 1 個主題。
★ 1 個主題 5 個句型。
★ 1 個句型 4 個例句。

1 主題 一次學習 1 個主題

2 句型 每個主題學習 5 個句型

Let me give you...	061	讓我來告訴大家…
I suggest that...	062	我建議…
Why don't we...?	063	我們何不…？
What we really need is...	064	我們真正需要的是…
We're expecting...	065	我們預計…

❸ 例句 每個句型學習 **4** 個例句

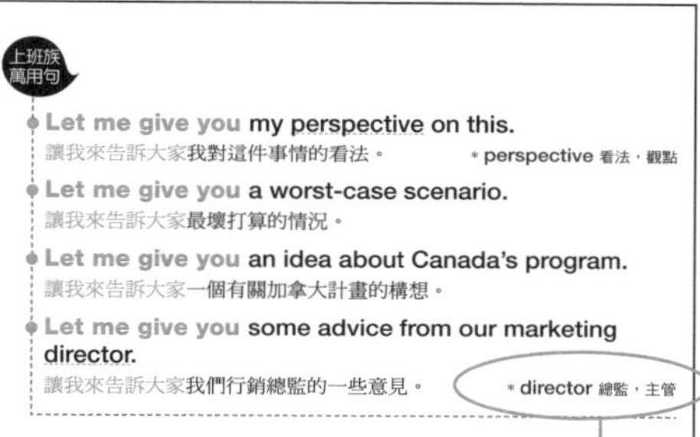
上班族萬用句

Let me give you my perspective on this.
讓我來告訴大家我對這件事情的看法。 ＊perspective 看法，觀點

Let me give you a worst-case scenario.
讓我來告訴大家最壞打算的情況。

Let me give you an idea about Canada's program.
讓我來告訴大家一個有關加拿大計畫的構想。

Let me give you some advice from our marketing director.
讓我來告訴大家我們行銷總監的一些意見。 ＊director 總監，主管

較困難的單字附解說

★特別收錄口語練習 MP3，以「英文－中文－英文」的順序各朗誦一次。

❹ 應用 將句型活用在對話中

1 對話
A We don't understand why this is so difficult.
B 讓我來告訴大家我對這件事情的看法。
A Please.

A 我們無法理解這有什麼困難的。
B Let me give you my perspective on this.
A 請說。

2 練習
我給你一些時間去好好思考這件事。(think something over)
Let me give you ______________________.

★本書共收錄 350 個職場必備英語句型，不但能讓你用流暢的英語應對各大工作場合，還能有效提升生活英語會話能力。從此以後，不論是電話英文、英文Email、英文簡報、海外出差…通通難不倒你！

專為忙碌上班族設計的英文書

★只收錄實際情況下會用到的句子

許多會話書總是號稱收錄了幾千個句子，但要記住「幾千個句子」根本是不可能的。現在，你只需要知道 350 個英文句型，就足夠應付各種場合。

★涵蓋各式各樣的職場商務情境

市面上的書籍都只是將職場商務情境以一個短篇單元帶過，本書不但鉅細靡遺地收錄各種商務情境，更進一步列出適用的句型公式。當你需要使用時，只要透過詳盡的目錄頁面，便能立刻查找到適合的句子。

★附贈「用聽的就能熟記」QR 碼線上音檔

全書內容皆同步錄製在附贈的 QR 碼音檔中，以〔英文－中文－英文〕的順序各朗誦一次。請善用每天早上起床後、往返公司，或是每天睡前的空閒時間，一有空就聽，盡可能地增加自己日常接觸英語的時間。即使不看書只聽音檔，也能熟記書中的常用句型。並用行動裝置隨掃隨聽，輕鬆學習不中斷。

「徹底改造英文基礎」的學習計畫！

平時

一天花一點時間
一次學習 5 個句型

★善加利用時間聆聽音檔，學習更有效率！

回頭複習

一天 15 分鐘
複習 25 個句型

★如果有不熟悉的句型，立刻翻到前面再複習一次！

完整看完

熟悉 350 個句型公式
超越 90% 以上的職場菁英！

目錄 CONTENTS

打電話 · 寫信 · 開會

Unit 1 講電話
不再害怕聽到電話響

Unit 5 發表會
緊緊抓住聽眾的注意力！

和客戶建立好的關係

Unit 6 約定
讓對方再見你一面的祕訣

Unit 8 協商
談成一筆好生意

Unit 9 協議・合約・購買
打動對方的心

職場生活

Unit 12 辦公室交流
與同事打好關係

Unit 13 海外出差 自己一個人也沒問題！

Unit 14 人資檢討
自信說出自己的好表現

Part 1

打電話・寫信・開會

Unit 1
講電話
不再害怕聽到電話響

1-1

打電話與接電話

Good morning. This is... 001 早安。這裡是…

I'd like to speak with... 002 我想要找…

Can I speak to...? 003 請問…在嗎？

Is this...? 004 請問這是…的電話嗎？

This is...from... 005 我是…的…

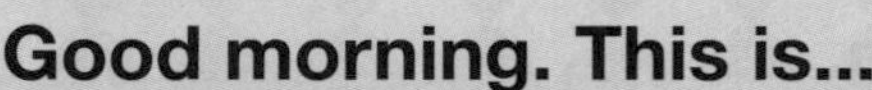

001

Good morning. This is...
早安。這裡是…

　一般來說，接電話時中文會說「喂」，英文會說 "Hello"，但在公司裡會使用較有禮貌的 "Good morning / afternoon!"。問候之後會用 this is 帶出公司名稱、所屬單位、本人姓名等等，有時也可直接省略不說。

- **Good morning. This is Global Enterprises.**
  早安。這裡是全球公司。
- **Good morning. This is Marcus in Legal Affairs.**
  早安。這裡是法務部的馬克斯。 ＊legal affairs 法務
- **Good afternoon. President Ken's office.**
  午安。總裁肯恩的辦公室。 ＊president 總裁，董事長
- **Hello. E-public Company, Julie speaking.**
  您好。E-public 公司，我是茱莉。

1 對話
A 喂，這裡是法務部的馬克斯。
B Hello! Can I speak with Larry?
A Yes. Who's calling, please?

A Good morning. This is Marcus in Legal Affairs.
B 您好！請問萊莉小姐在嗎？
A 在。請問哪裡找？

2 練習
午安！這裡是物流倉庫。(warehouse)
Good afternoon. This is ______________________.

Pattern 002

I'd like to speak with...
我想要找⋯

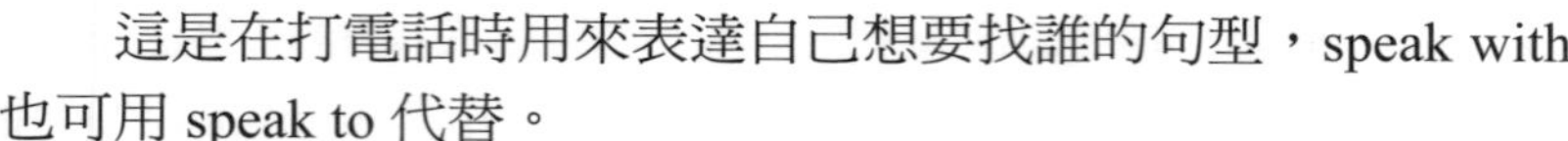

這是在打電話時用來表達自己想要找誰的句型，speak with 也可用 speak to 代替。

- **I'd like to speak with Richard Page.**
  我想要找李察佩吉。
- **I'd like to speak with the manager of the Planning Department.**
  我想要找企畫部經理。 ＊planning department 企畫部
- **I'd like to speak to someone in charge.**
  我想要找負責人。 ＊someone in charge 負責人
- **I'd like to speak to the person I talked to before.**
  我想要找我之前通過話的人。

1 對話 **A** Hello! Cukiz Company, Planning Department.
B 我想要找企畫部經理。
A This is he.

A 您好！這裡是 Cukiz 公司企畫部。
B I'd like to speak with the manager of the Planning Department.
A 我就是。

2 練習 我想要找他的祕書。(secretary)
I'd like to speak with ______________________.

003

Can I speak to...?
請問…在嗎？

跟 I'd like to speak with... 一樣，也是在講電話時用來表達自己想要找誰的句型之一。如果想更有禮貌一些，可以用 Could 或 May 代替 Can。

- **Can I speak to Ms. Smith?**
  請問史密斯太太在嗎？
- **Can I speak to Cohen?**
  請問寇韓在嗎？
- **Could I speak to Ben Johnson?**
  請問班強森在嗎？
- **May I speak to the director of marketing?**
  請問行銷總監在嗎？

＊director 總監，課長，主任

1 對話
A Good afternoon, this is Jina.
B Hi, Jina. 請問寇韓在嗎？
A Cohen's on his lunch break.

A 午安！我是吉娜。
B 吉娜，您好！Can I speak to Cohen?
A 寇韓正在午休。

2 練習 請問海外事業部的負責人在嗎？(in charge of, overseas sales)
Can I speak to ______________________________?

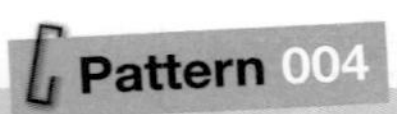

Is this...?
請問這是…的電話嗎？

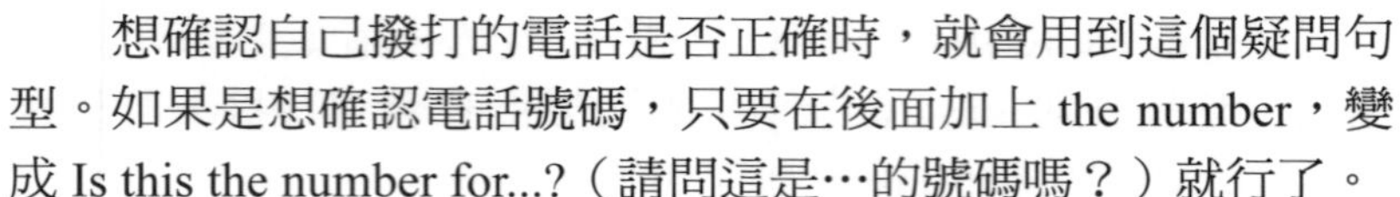

想確認自己撥打的電話是否正確時，就會用到這個疑問句型。如果是想確認電話號碼，只要在後面加上 the number，變成 Is this the number for...?（請問這是…的號碼嗎？）就行了。

上班族萬用句

- **Is this Jim Harrison?**
  請問這是吉姆哈里森的電話嗎？
- **Is this the General Affairs Department?**
  請問這是總務部的電話嗎？　＊general affairs 總務
- **Is this the number for complaints?**
  請問這是客訴的電話嗎？　＊complaint 抱怨，控訴
- **Is this the number for placing an order?**
  請問這是下訂單的電話嗎？　＊place an order 下訂單

1 對話

A Good afternoon. P&B Technology.
B 請問這是下訂單的電話號碼嗎？
A Yes. I can help you.

A 您好！這裡是 P&B 科技公司。
B Is this the number for placing an order?
A 是的，由我來為您服務。

2 練習

請問這是總公司的電話嗎？(headquarters)
Is this ______________________?

Pattern 005

005

This is...from...
我是⋯的⋯

這是在電話中向對方介紹的句型。一般來說不可以用 I'm...，而是用 This is...，句型中的 "from" 後面可以接上自己的公司名稱、所屬部門或居住地區等個人資訊。

- **This is Jane from Global Research, Inc.**
  我是全球研究公司的珍。
- **This is Jim from the Sales Department.**
  我是業務部的吉姆。
- **This is Michael Kim from the Busan office.**
  我是釜山分部的麥可金。
- **This is John from last week's Seoul Conference.**
  我是上週首爾會議的約翰。

1 對話 **A** I'd like to speak with Bill Parsons.
B Certainly. May I tell him who's calling?
A 我是全球研究公司的傑克。

A 請問比爾帕森斯在嗎？
B 他在，請問您哪裡？
A This is Jack from Global Research, Inc.

2 練習 我是他在加州的同事。(colleague, California)
This is ______________ from ______________.

1-2 不方便接聽電話

006

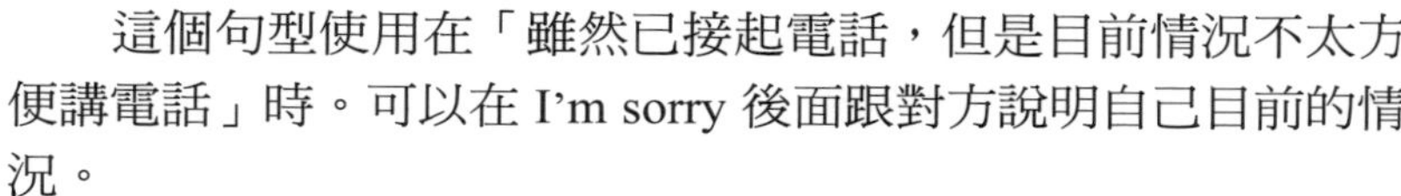

I'm sorry, but I'm...
不好意思，我…

這個句型使用在「雖然已接起電話，但是目前情況不太方便講電話」時。可以在 I'm sorry 後面跟對方說明自己目前的情況。

- **I'm sorry, but I'm unavailable now.**
  不好意思，我現在沒有空。
- **I'm sorry, but I'm in a meeting right now.**
  不好意思，我現在正在開會。
- **I'm sorry, but I'm in the middle of something.**
  不好意思，我正在忙。 ＊in the middle of 正忙於…中
- **I'm sorry, but I'm new to the company.**
  不好意思，我是新來的。 ＊new 新任員工

1 對話

A I'm calling about our new product line. What's the status of it?

B 不好意思，我是新來的。I'll connect you with someone else.

A OK. Go ahead.

A 我想要請教一下關於新產品的事情，請問它的狀況如何？

B I'm sorry, but I'm new to the company. 我幫你轉接給其他職員。

A 好的，請幫我轉接。

2 練習 不好意思，我現在剛好要出門。(go out)

I'm sorry, but I'm ______________________.

Pattern 007

Can I call you...?
我可以…打給你嗎？

當下不方便講電話，想跟對方另外約之後的時間講電話，例如「之後／10 分鐘後再打給你好嗎？」時使用的句型。本句型後面可接上符合當下情況的時間。

- **Can I call you later?**
  我可以待會打給你嗎？
- **Can I call you back in ten minutes?**
  我可以十分鐘後回電給你嗎？
  ＊call back 回電
- **Can I call you this afternoon?**
  我可以今天下午打給你嗎？
- **Can I call you after the meeting?**
  我可以開完會後打給你嗎？

1 對話
A I'd like to talk about my ideas.
B Right now, I'm in a meeting. 我可以開完會後打給你嗎？
A Sure. I'm sorry to interrupt you.

A 我想跟你聊一下我的想法。
B 我現在正在開會。Can I call you after the meeting?
A 好的，很抱歉打擾到你。

2 練習 我可以多蒐集一些資訊後再打給你嗎？(when, information)
Can I call you ______________________________?

Pattern 008

008

I'm afraid he's...
抱歉，他…

當來電者想找的人目前無法接聽電話時，你就可以使用這個句型。I'm afraid 是用來表達遺憾之意，可翻譯為「抱歉」、「不好意思」。

I'm afraid he's on the other line.
抱歉，他正在另一支電話線上。

I'm afraid he's not available now.
抱歉，他現在沒有空。

I'm afraid she's out of the office.
抱歉，她外出了。

I'm afraid she's on vacation.
抱歉，她正在度假中。 ＊on vacation 度假中

1 對話
A 抱歉，他正在另一支電話線上。
B Do you know how long he'll be?
A I guess about a half hour.

A I'm afraid he's on the other line.
B 請問你知道他還要講多久嗎？
A 我想大概還要三十分鐘左右。

2 練習 抱歉，她目前正在出差中。(business trip)
I'm afraid she's ______________________________.

Pattern 009

I think he...
我想他…

當來電者想找的人目前無法接電話時，接電話的你可使用這個句型，跟對方說明自己已知道的資訊或推測。

- **I think he's not here at this moment.**
  我想他目前不在。　＊at this moment 此刻，目前
- **I think he went out for lunch.**
  我想他外出午餐了。
- **I think he's already gone.**
  我想他已經走了。
- **I think she left the documents with our secretary.**
  我想她把文件交給我們的祕書了。　＊document 文件

1 對話
A I'm calling to see if our merger documents are ready.
B All right. Which agent are you working with?
A Nancy Benez.
B Oh, yes. 我想她把文件交給我們的祕書了。

A 我打來是想知道我們的合併資料準備好了嗎？
B 好的，請問跟您合作的專員是哪位呢？
A 南西班茲。
B 喔，是的。I think she left the documents with our secretary.

2 練習 我想他剛進會議室了。(just, leave)
I think he ______________________________.

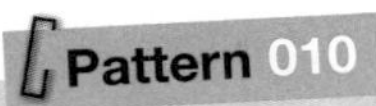

When do you expect he'll...?
請問你知道他什麼時候會…嗎？

如果你想詢問對方「請問你知道他什麼時候會回來嗎？」之類的問題時，可以用 "When do you expect...?" 或 "When do you think...?" 這兩個句型，請參考以下的例句。

- **When do you expect he'll return?**
  請問你知道他什麼時候會回來嗎？
- **When do you think he'll be free?**
  請問你知道他什麼時候會空閒下來嗎？
- **When do you think he'll be available?**
  請問你知道他什麼時候會有空嗎？ ＊available 有空的
- **When do you expect her to call back?**
  請問你知道她什麼時候會回電嗎？

1 對話
A Jim is in Toronto most of this week.
B 請問你知道他什麼時候會回來嗎？
A He'll be back no later than Friday.

A 吉姆這個禮拜幾乎都會待在多倫多。
B When do you think he'll return?
A 他最晚在禮拜五前會回來。

2 練習 請問你知道他什麼時候有空講電話嗎？(have time, take a call)
When do you expect ______________________________?

1-3 留言

Would you like to...? 011 請問您要…嗎？

Please tell him... 012 麻煩轉告他…

Could you tell her...? 013 麻煩請您轉告她…好嗎？

Can I have your...? 014 可以告訴我您的…嗎？

I'll tell him... 015 我會轉告他…

Pattern 011

Would you like to...?
請問您要…嗎？

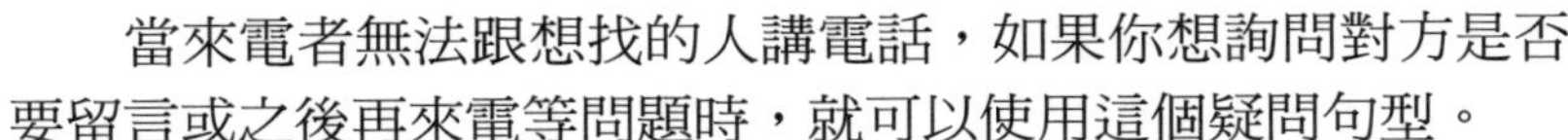
當來電者無法跟想找的人講電話，如果你想詢問對方是否要留言或之後再來電等問題時，就可以使用這個疑問句型。

- **Would you like to leave a message?**
  請問您要留言嗎？　　＊leave a message 留言給他人
- **Would you like to call back later?**
  請問您要待會再打來嗎？
- **Would you like to hold?**
  請問您要在電話線上稍候嗎？
- **Would you like to leave a good time for him to call you?**
  請問您要留下方便他打電話給您的時間嗎？

1 對話
A 請問您要留言嗎？
B Please have Mr. Harrison call me soon.
A I'll let him know as soon as he's out of the meeting.

A Would you like to leave a message?
B 請哈里遜先生盡快回電給我。
A 等他一開完會我就會立刻轉告他。

2 練習 請問您還有其他留言嗎？(another)
Would you like to ____________________?

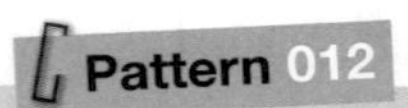

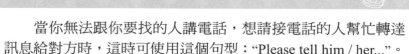

Please tell him...
麻煩轉告他…

當你無法跟你要找的人講電話，想請接電話的人幫忙轉達訊息給對方時，這時可使用這個句型："Please tell him / her..."。

- **Please tell him that I called.**
  麻煩轉告他我打電話來過。
- **Please tell him that I'll call back.**
  麻煩轉告他我會再打來。
- **Please tell her to call me back.**
  麻煩轉告她回電給我。
- **Please tell her that it's urgent.**
  麻煩轉告她這件事很急。

* **urgent** 緊急的

1 對話
A Is Mr. Marvin around today?
B Yes, but he's stepped out of his office.
A 麻煩轉告他回電給我。

A 請問今天馬文先生有上班嗎？
B 有的，但是他現在不在辦公室。
A Please tell him to call me back.

2 練習 麻煩轉告他我有一個問題想要請教他。(question, for him)
Please tell him ______________________________.

 013

Pattern 013

Could you tell her...?
麻煩請您轉告她…好嗎？

這也是當你想請他人幫忙轉達一些訊息給某人時的句型，但是比上一個句型 “Please tell him / her...” 的語氣更為禮貌。這個句型中的動詞 tell 也可以用 ask 替代。

Could you tell her I'm back in my office?
麻煩請您轉告她我回到辦公室了好嗎？

Could you ask her to check my email?
麻煩請您轉告她檢查我的電子信箱好嗎？

* check one's email 檢查某人的電子信箱

Could you tell him to give me a call?
麻煩請您轉告他撥個電話給我好嗎？

Could you tell him I left my wallet in his car?
麻煩請您轉告他我把皮夾留在他的車子裡面了好嗎？

1 對話
A I'd like to speak with Mr. Charles.
B He's out. Can I take a message?
A 麻煩請您轉告他我把皮夾留在他的車子裡面了好嗎？
B Oh, sure. Don't worry.

A 請問查理先生在嗎？
B 他外出了。請問你要留言嗎？
A Could you tell him I left my wallet in his car?
B 沒問題，請不用擔心。

2 練習 麻煩請您轉告他把開會時間延後一小時好嗎？(push back)
Could you tell him ______________________________?

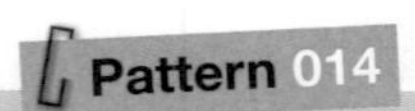

Can I have your...?
可以告訴我您的…嗎？

在講電話的過程中，如果你想詢問對方的姓名、電子信箱、聯絡資料等個人資訊時，就可以用這個簡單的句型：Can I have your...?

- **Can I have your name, please?**
  可以告訴我您的姓名嗎？
- **Can I have your number?**
  可以告訴我您的電話號碼嗎？
- **Can I have your cell phone number?**
  可以告訴我您的手機號碼嗎？
- **Can I have your email address, please?**
  可以告訴我您的電子信箱帳號嗎？

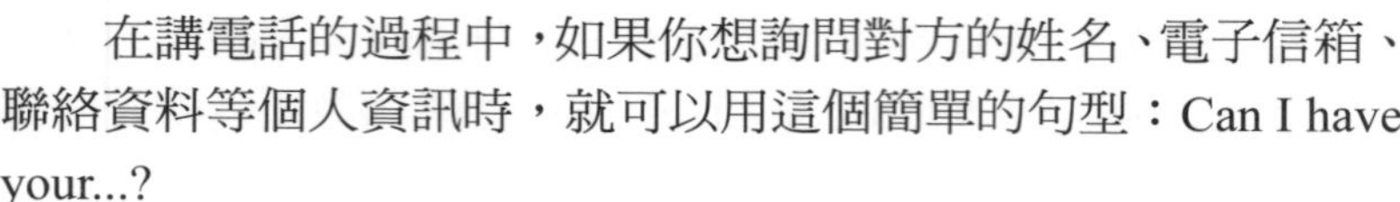

1 對話 **A** Ask Janet to send me the documents by email.
B 可以告訴我您的電子信箱嗎？
A I believe you already have it on file.

A 請叫珍妮特把資料用 Email 寄給我。
B Can I have your email address, please?
A 我想你的檔案裡應該已經有了。

2 練習 可以告訴我您的傳真號碼嗎？(fax)
Can I have your ______________________________?

Pattern 015

015

I'll tell him...
我會轉告他…

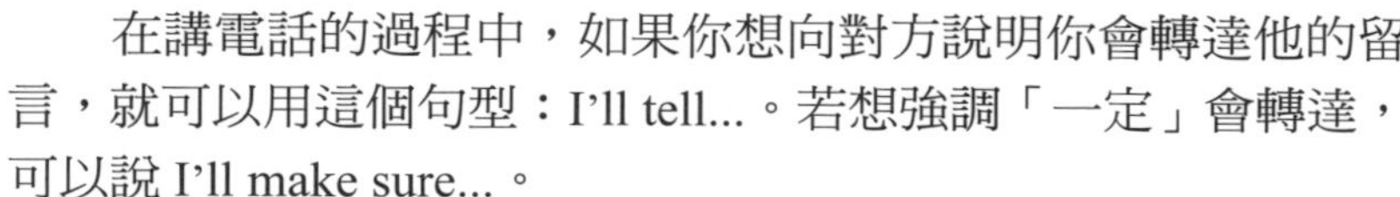

在講電話的過程中，如果你想向對方說明你會轉達他的留言，就可以用這個句型：I'll tell...。若想強調「一定」會轉達，可以說 I'll make sure...。

- **I'll tell him that you called.**
  我會轉告他您打電話來過。
- **I'll tell her that you're expecting her to call you.**
  我會轉告她您正在等她的電話。
- **I'll make sure he gets your message.**
  我會確認他收到您的訊息。
- **I'll make sure he gets back to you as soon as possible.**
  我會確認他會盡快回電給您。　　＊get back to 回電給…

1 對話
A It's very important that Pete calls me today.
B I understand.
A Do you know my home and work numbers?
B Of course. 我會確認他收到您的訊息。

A 今天比特一定要打電話給我才行。
B 我知道了。
A 你知道我家裡的電話和辦公室的電話吧？
B 當然。I'll make sure he gets your message.

2 練習　我會轉告他您急著要跟他聯絡。(be anxious to, speak with)
I'll tell ______________________.

1-4

來電事由：提問與回答

I'm calling to...	016	我打電話來是要…
I'm calling about...	017	我打電話來是為了…
Is this a good time to...?	018	現在方便…嗎？
When do you...?	019	你什麼時候…？
Let me check if...	020	讓我確認一下…是否…

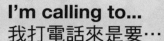

Pattern 016

016

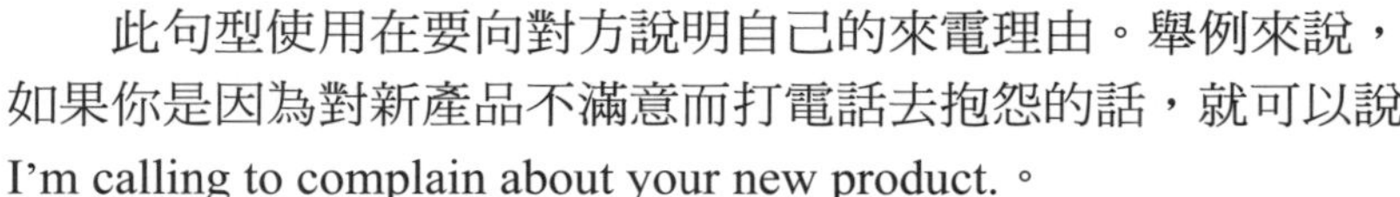

I'm calling to...
我打電話來是要…

　　此句型使用在要向對方說明自己的來電理由。舉例來說，如果你是因為對新產品不滿意而打電話去抱怨的話，就可以說 I'm calling to complain about your new product.。

- **I'm calling to ask you something.**
  我打電話來是要問你一些事情。
- **I'm calling to arrange a meeting for next week.**
  我打電話來是要為下週的會議做安排。　　＊arrange 籌備、安排（會議等）
- **I'm calling to check if you got my email.**
  我打電話來是要確認你是否收到我的電子郵件。
- **I'm calling to notify you that your order has shipped.**
  我打電話來是要通知您，您的訂單已經出貨了。　　＊ship 郵寄，寄送

1 對話　**A** This is Erika from Bangkok Products, Inc.
B Yes. Erika, how can I help you?
A 我打電話來是要通知您，您的訂單已經出貨了。

A 我是曼谷產品公司的艾瑞卡。
B 艾瑞卡您好，請問您有什麼事嗎？
A I'm calling to notify you that your order has shipped.

2 練習　我打電話來是要跟你約定中午會議的時間。(schedule)
I'm calling to ________________________.

Pattern 017

I'm calling about...
我打電話來是為了…

當你為了某特定事項而撥打電話，想要向對方表達自己打電話是「為了…」或「想談一下關於…」的意思時，就可以使用這個句型。

- **I'm calling about your order.**
  我打電話來是為了您的訂單。
- **I'm calling about Mr. Smith's visit next month.**
  我打電話來是為了下個月史密斯先生來訪的事。 ＊visit 參觀，訪問
- **I'm calling about tomorrow's meeting.**
  我打電話來是為了明天的會議。
- **I'm calling about your request for information.**
  我打電話來是為了您所請求的資訊。 ＊request 要求，請求

1 對話
A 我打電話來是為了明天的會議。
B What's up?
A The location has changed.

A I'm calling about tomorrow's meeting.
B 怎麼了嗎？
A 會議地點更改了。

2 練習 我打電話來是為了告訴你付款會延遲。(late payment)
I'm calling about ______________________.

Pattern 018

Is this a good time to...?
現在方便…嗎？

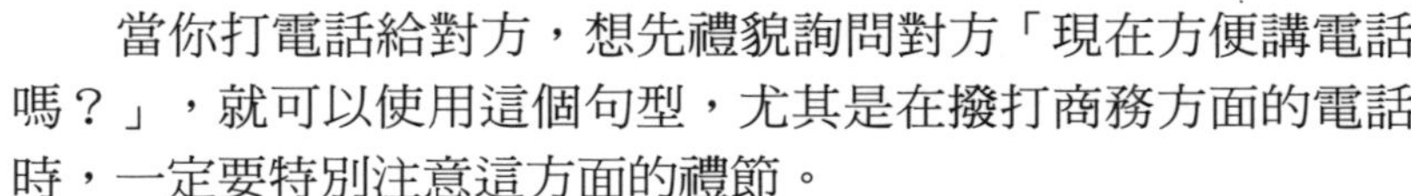
當你打電話給對方，想先禮貌詢問對方「現在方便講電話嗎？」，就可以使用這個句型，尤其是在撥打商務方面的電話時，一定要特別注意這方面的禮節。

- Is this a good time to **talk?**
  現在方便**講電話**嗎？
- Is this a good time for **you?**
  您現在方便嗎？
- Is this a good time to **talk longer?**
  現在方便**長時間談談**嗎？
- Is this a good time to **ask you some questions?**
  現在方便**問你一些問題**嗎？

1 對話
A Oh, hello, Jane.
B 現在方便講電話嗎？
A Actually, I'm in a meeting. Can I call you back?

A 您好，珍。
B Is this a good time for you?
A 其實我現在正在開會。可以晚點再打給你嗎？

2 練習 現在方便討論這件事嗎？(talk about)
Is this a good time ____________________________?

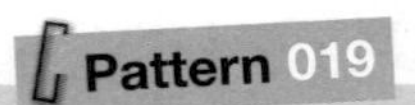

When do you...?
你什麼時候⋯？

這是用來在電話中和對方約定某件事，或確認行程安排時可以使用的句型，非常實用。

- **When do you get off work?**
  你什麼時候下班？　　* get off work 下班
- **When do you take your lunch break?**
  你什麼時候午休？　　* lunch break 午休
- **When do you think you'll be finished?**
  你覺得你什麼時候會完成？
- **When do you fly to Los Angeles for a meeting?**
  你什麼時候飛去洛杉磯參加會議？

1 對話
A 你什麼時候飛去洛杉磯參加會議？
B I fly out on the 23rd.
A Have a good trip.

A When do you fly to Los Angeles for a meeting?
B 我會搭 23 號的飛機。
A 祝你一路順風。

2 練習 你什麼時候需要估價單？(need, estimates)
When do you ______________________________?

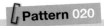

Pattern 020

Let me check if...
讓我確認一下…是否…

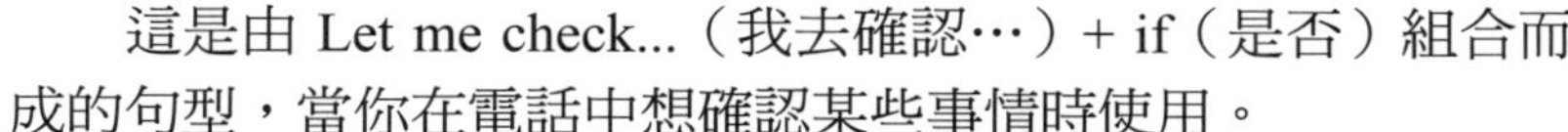

這是由 Let me check...（我去確認…）+ if（是否）組合而成的句型，當你在電話中想確認某些事情時使用。

- **Let me check if she's available.**
  讓我確認一下她是否有空。
- **Let me check if I got everything right.**
  讓我確認一下我的理解是否正確。　＊get~right 對…理解正確
- **Let me check if he got your message.**
  讓我確認一下他是否有收到你的訊息。
- **Let me check if your fax has arrived.**
  讓我確認一下您的傳真是否送達。

1 對話
A Did you leave your phone number?
B Yes, several times.
A 讓我確認一下他是否有收到你的訊息。

A 你有留過你的電話嗎？
B 有的，留過好幾次。
A Let me check if he got your message.

2 練習 讓我確認一下經理是否已經回來了。(manager, arrive)
Let me check if ______________________.

1-5

解決通話過程中遇到的問題

This connection is...	021	這裡的收訊…
I have trouble hearing because...	022	因為…，我聽不太清楚。
Could you speak...?	023	可以請您說…嗎？
Did you say...?	024	您剛剛是說…嗎？
My phone battery is...	025	我的手機電量…

021

Pattern 021

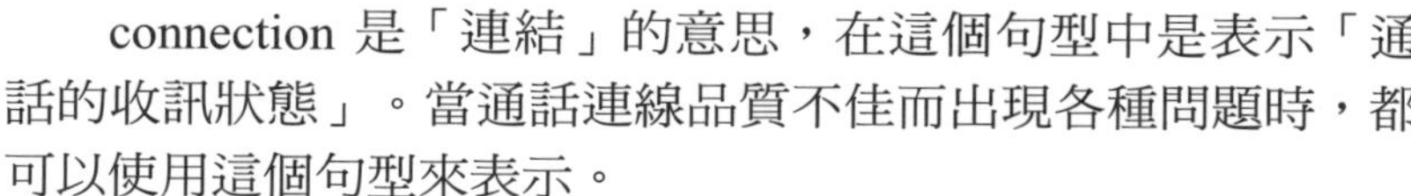

This connection is...
這裡的收訊⋯

connection 是「連結」的意思，在這個句型中是表示「通話的收訊狀態」。當通話連線品質不佳而出現各種問題時，都可以使用這個句型來表示。

- **This connection is confusing.**
  這裡的收訊很混亂。
  ＊confusing 混亂的，模糊的
- **This connection isn't very clear.**
  這裡的收訊不是很清楚。
- **This connection is a problem for me.**
  我這裡的收訊有點問題。
- **This connection is making it hard to understand you.**
  這裡的收訊讓我無法聽到你的話。

1 對話

A Most of the new ad campaigns are very good.
B I'm sorry, what did you say?
A Wait a second. 這裡的收訊很混亂。

A 大部分的新廣告活動都很出色。
B 抱歉，你剛剛說什麼？
A 等一下。This connection is confusing.

2 練習

這裡的收訊不是很好。(good)
This connection isn't ______________.

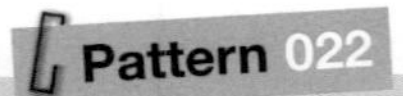

I have trouble hearing because...
因為…，我聽不太清楚。

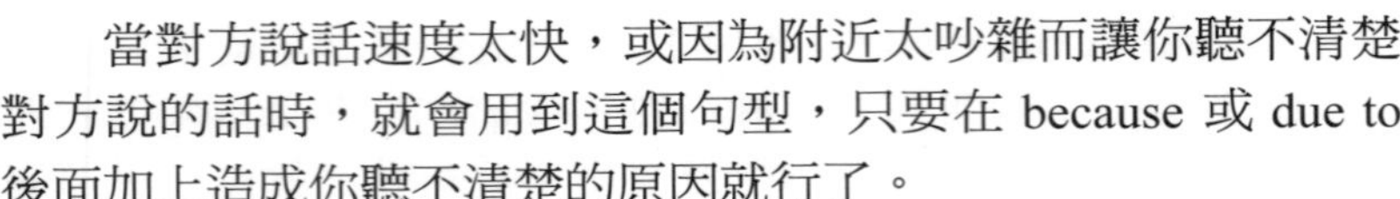

當對方說話速度太快，或因為附近太吵雜而讓你聽不清楚對方說的話時，就會用到這個句型，只要在 because 或 due to 後面加上造成你聽不清楚的原因就行了。

- **I have trouble hearing what you're saying.**
  我聽不清楚你說什麼。
- **I have trouble hearing because you speak quickly.**
  因為你說太快了，我聽不太清楚。
- **I'm having trouble hearing you because this connection is really bad.**
  因為這裡的收訊真的很糟糕，我聽不太清楚。
- **I'm having trouble hearing you because the signal isn't very clear.**
  因為這裡的訊號不是很好，我聽不太清楚。

＊signal 信號，訊號

1 對話

A What? Could you repeat that?
B I said that a sales representative will contact you soon.
A I'm sorry. 因為你說太快了，我聽不太清楚。

A 什麼？你可以再說一次嗎？
B 我是說有一位業務會馬上跟你聯絡。
A 抱歉。I have trouble hearing because you speak quickly.

2 練習 因為影印機太吵了，我聽不太清楚。(due to)
I have trouble hearing ______________________.

Pattern 023

Could you speak...?
可以請您說…嗎？

在電話上用英文談業務方面的事情時，可能會因為國籍不同或發音上的差異而完全誤解對方說的話。當你不太確定對方在說甚麼時，想禮貌地拜託對方重述一遍的話，就可以用這個句型。如果再加上 please，就會顯得更有禮貌。

- **Could you speak louder?**
  可以請您說大聲一點嗎？
- **Could you please speak slowly?**
  可以請您慢慢說嗎？
- **Could you please say that one more time?**
  可以請您再說一次嗎？
- **Could you speak into the receiver?**
  可以請您對著話筒說嗎？

* receiver 話筒

1 對話 A I'm sorry. I'm having trouble understanding you.
B I'm calling from the Moscow office.
A 可以請您說大聲一點嗎？

A 抱歉，我聽不太懂你在說什麼。
B 我這裡是莫斯科辦公室。
A Could you speak louder?

2 練習 可以請您說清楚一點嗎？(clearly)
Could you speak ______________________?

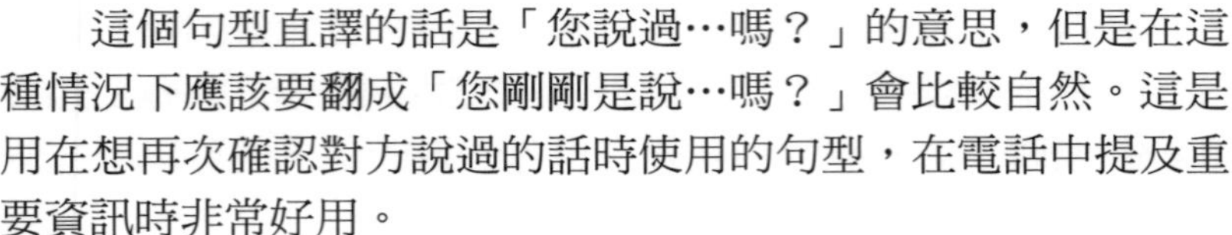

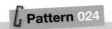

Pattern 024

024

Did you say...?
您剛剛是說…嗎？

這個句型直譯的話是「您說過…嗎？」的意思，但是在這種情況下應該要翻成「您剛剛是說…嗎？」會比較自然。這是用在想再次確認對方說過的話時使用的句型，在電話中提及重要資訊時非常好用。

- **Did you say you're Mike?**
  您剛剛是說您是麥可嗎？
- **Did you say you want to meet on Monday?**
  您剛剛是說您想在禮拜一碰面嗎？
- **Did you say two 5?**
  您剛剛是說了兩個五嗎？
- **Did you say you need more time?**
  您剛剛是說您需要再多一點時間嗎？

1 對話
A Can I have your number?
B Sure. 212-272-5509.
A 您剛剛是說了兩個五嗎？

A 可以跟我說你的電話號碼嗎？
B 當然。212-272-5509。
A Did you say two 5?

2 練習 您剛剛是說您同意這件事嗎？(agree on)
Did you say ____________________________?

 025

Pattern 025

My phone battery is...
我的手機電量…

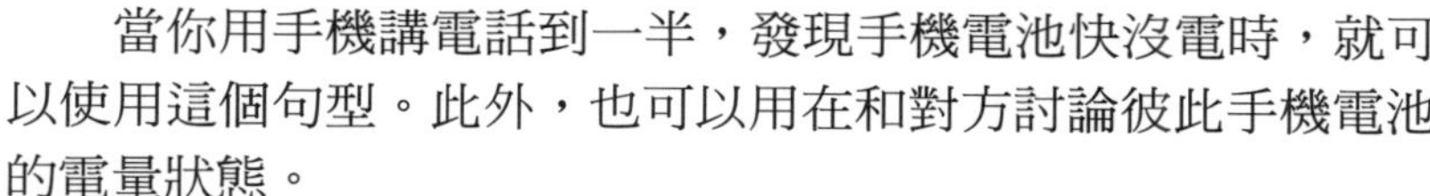

當你用手機講電話到一半，發現手機電池快沒電時，就可以使用這個句型。此外，也可以用在和對方討論彼此手機電池的電量狀態。

- **My phone battery is low.**
  我的手機電量很低。
- **My phone battery is running out.**
  我的手機電池快沒電了。 ＊run out 被用完，耗盡
- **My phone battery is almost dead.**
  我的手機幾乎要沒電了。
- **My phone battery is full-charged.**
  我的手機充好電了。 ＊full-charged 充好電的

1 對話

A Is this a good time to talk longer?
B Sure. 但是我的手機電量很低。
A Oh. Then I'll call you back in 10 minutes.

A 你現在可以聊久一點嗎？
B 當然可以。But my phone battery is low.
A 喔。那麼我十分鐘後再打給你。

2 練習 我的手機電池已經用很久了。(old)
My phone battery is ______________________.

1-1~1-5

黃金複習 15 分鐘！

前面這 25 個句型和 125 個句子全都記熟了嗎？
來驗收一下學習成果吧！如果不能充滿自信地用英文説出以下 40 個句子，請翻到前面再重新複習一次！

01 早安。這裡是全球公司。

____

02 我的手機電量很低。

____

03 請問史密斯太太在嗎？

____

04 您剛剛說您是麥可嗎？

____

05 我想要找李察佩吉。

____

06 可以請您說大聲一點嗎？

____

07 請問這是吉姆哈里森的電話嗎？

____

08 我聽不清楚你說什麼。

____

09 我是全球研究公司的珍。

____

解答 01. Good morning. This is Global Enterprises. 02. My phone battery is low.
03. Can I speak to Ms. Smith? 04. Did you say you're Mike?
05. I'd like to speak with Richard Page. 06. Could you speak louder? 07. Is this Jim Harrison?
08. I have trouble hearing what you're saying. 09. This is Jane from Global Research, Inc.

10 這裡的收訊很混亂。

11 不好意思，我現在正在開會。

12 讓我確認一下她是否有空。

13 我可以待會打給你嗎？

14 你什麼時候下班？

15 抱歉，他正在另一支電話線上。

16 現在方便講電話嗎？

17 我想他目前不在這裡。

18 我打電話來是為了您的訂單。

19 請問你知道他什麼時候會回來嗎？

20 我打電話來是要問你一些事情。

解答 10. This connection is confusing. 11. I'm sorry, but I'm in a meeting right now. 12. Let me check if she's available. 13. Can I call you later? 14. When do you get off work? 15. I'm afraid he's on the other line. 16. Is this a good time to talk? 17. I think he's not here at this moment. 18. I'm calling about your order. 19. When do you think he'll return? 20. I'm calling to ask you something.

21 請問您要留言嗎？

22 我的手機電池快沒電了。

23 麻煩轉告他我打電話來過。

24 您剛剛是說您想在禮拜一碰面嗎？

25 麻煩請您轉告他撥個電話給我好嗎？

26 可以請您慢慢說嗎？

27 可以告訴我您的姓名嗎？

28 因為你說太快了，我聽不清楚。

29 我會轉告他您打過電話。

30 這裡的收訊不是很清楚。

31 早安。這裡是法務部的馬克斯。

解答　21. Would you like to leave a message? 22. My phone battery is running out.
23. Please tell him that I called. 24. Did you say you want to meet on Monday?
25. Could you ask him to give me a call? 26. Could you please speak slowly?
27. Can I have your name, please? 28. I have trouble hearing because you speak quickly.
29. I'll tell him that you called. 30. This connection isn't very clear.
31. Good morning. This is Marcus in Legal Affairs.

32 讓我確認一下我對每件事的理解是否正確。

______

33 請問科恩在嗎？

______

34 你什麼時候午休？

______

35 我想要找企畫部經理。

______

36 您現在方便嗎？

______

37 請問這是總務部的電話嗎？

______

38 我打電話來是為了下個月史密斯先生來訪的事。

______

39 我是釜山分部的麥可金。

______

40 我打電話來是要為下週的會議做安排。

______

解答 32. Let me check if I got everything right. 33. Can I speak to Cohen?
34. When do you take your lunch break?
35. I'd like to speak with the manager of the Planning Department.
36. Is this a good time for you? 37. Is this the General Affairs Department?
38. I'm calling about Mr. Smith's visit next month.
39. This is Michael Kim from the Busan office.
40. I'm calling to arrange a meeting for next week.

Unit 2
電子郵件
五分鐘就寫完一封信

2-1

電子郵件的開場白 (1)

Pattern 026

026

I am...from...
我是…的…

如果是第一次寫信給對方，就可以使用這個句型向對方介紹自己的名字和所屬公司。如果是寫信給很久之前見過的人，可以在此句型前加上 “I hope you remember me...”（不知道你還記不記得我），語氣會更自然。

- **I am Joe Smith from Smith Tech, Inc.**
  我是史密斯科技公司的喬史密斯。
- **I am a senior editor at Login Book.**
  我是羅金出版社的資深編輯。 ＊senior 資深人士
- **I am working as a manager at Sony.**
  我在索尼擔任經理。 ＊manager 經理
- **I hope you remember me, I am Tim Heckler from Jones Textiles.**
  希望您還記得我，我是瓊斯紡織的提姆哈克勒。

1 對話 我是史密斯科技公司的喬史密斯。I'm writing to introduce myself and to tell you a little about my company. We are a technology importer and we have just entered the market within the last five months.

I am Joe Smith from Smith Tech, Inc. 我寫這封信給您是想介紹我自己，以及跟您稍微介紹一下敝公司。敝公司是技術進口業者，剛踏入這個市場五個月。

2 練習 我是麥斯公司的佛朗克・米勒。(Corp.)
I am ______________ from ______________.

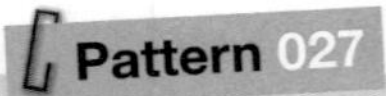

I am in charge of...
我負責…

想要向對方介紹「我負責…／我是…單位（部門）的人」，說明自己負責的工作或所屬單位時，就可以用這個句型：...be in charge of... 或 ...be responsible for...。

- **I am in charge of the Accounting Department.**
  我負責會計部。　＊accounting 會計，結帳
- **I am in charge of human resources.**
  我負責人事部。　＊human resources 人事，人力資源
- **I am in charge of sales in Hong Kong.**
  我負責香港的銷售。
- **I am responsible for conferences.**
  我是負責會議的人。

1 對話　My name is Joanna Lee, and 我負責會計部。I have a few questions regarding your last invoice. I want to make sure our information is correct.

我是 Joanna Lee, I am in charge of the Accounting Department. 我想針對貴公司上次開出的發票向您問幾個問題，我想確認我們的資訊是否正確。

2 練習　我負責所有的出口業務。(imports)
I am in charge of ______________________.

Pattern 028

Let me start off by introducing...
請容我先介紹…

當你想在電子郵件上提及自己的公司、業務或產品等相關訊息時，可以在正式介紹前先用這個句型當作開場白。比起I'll..., Let me... 的語氣較為鄭重。

- Let me start off by introducing **myself.**
  請容我先**自我**介紹。
- Let me start off by introducing **our products.**
  請容我先介紹**我們的產品**。
- Let me start off by introducing **our business.**
  請容我先介紹**我們的公司**。
- Let me start off by introducing **our innovative services.**
  請容我先介紹**我們創新的服務**。

* innovative 創新的

1 對話 請容我先自我介紹。I'm Tom Park. I'm the president and CEO of Dongyang Enterprises. We are a leader in our field, and we would like to do business with you.

Let me start off by introducing myself. 我的名字是湯姆帕克，是東洋企業的社長兼總裁。我們是這個業界的龍頭老大，希望有機會能跟貴公司有生意上的往來。

2 練習 請容我先介紹我們的生產流程。(operation)
Let me start off by introducing ______________.

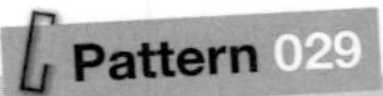

Thank you for...
謝謝您…

當你因為某些原因想向對方表達感謝時，就可以使用這個句型：Thank you for...，請注意此句型中的介系詞 for 後面要接名詞或 V-ing 形態的單字。

- **Thank you for your letter last week.**
  謝謝您上禮拜的信。
- **Thank you for getting back to me so quickly.**
  謝謝您迅速回信給我。
- **Thank you for doing business with our company.**
  謝謝您與敝公司的交易。
- **Thank you for seeing me on short notice.**
  謝謝您在這麼短的時間內就安排見我。 ＊notice 通知

1 對話 Good morning, Mr. Walker. I enjoyed meeting with you yesterday. 謝謝您在這麼短的時間內就安排見我。As I said, I'll send the document to you by tomorrow.

早安，渥克先生。昨天的會議很愉快。Thank you for seeing me on short notice. 如同我之前說的，我最晚明天就會將資料寄給您。

2 練習 謝謝您寄免費的試用品給我。(send, samples)
Thank you for ______________________.

Pattern 030

I'm sorry...
很抱歉⋯

表達歉意的句型為 I'm sorry... .，後面可以接 that ＋子句、for + 名詞或 V-ing、about + 名詞或 V-ing、to + 原形動詞等句型。

- **I'm sorry I couldn't respond earlier.**
  很抱歉我無法早點回信。 ＊respond 回信，回覆
- **I'm sorry I was unavailable to see you.**
  很抱歉我那時沒有時間見您。
- **I'm sorry to have to cancel our account.**
  很抱歉我必須取消我們的帳戶。 ＊account 帳戶，帳目
- **I'm sorry about the damaged shipment.**
  關於損壞的貨物，我很抱歉。

1 對話

Dear Mr. Anderson,
Carla told me you stopped by this morning. 很抱歉我那時沒有時間見您。I have some time tomorrow if you'd like to meet.

親愛的安德森先生，
聽卡拉跟我說您今天早上來了。I'm sorry I was unavailable to see you. 我明天有時間，如果您方便的話我們可以見一面。

2 練習 很抱歉寄錯目錄給您。(send out, wrong)
I'm sorry ______________________________.

2-2

電子郵件的開場白 (2)

We met at...	031	我們在…見過面。
I was referred to you by...	032	…推薦我來找你。
I got your email address from...	033	我從…得知你的電子信箱。
I am the person who + 過去的事件	034	我是之前…的人。
I am responding to...	035	我在此回應…

Pattern 031

We met at...
我們在…見過面。

第一次寫電子郵件給曾見過面的人時，如果在信件裡先以「我們在…見過面…」作為開場白的話，不但較容易喚起對方的回憶，還可以拉近彼此的距離。

- **We met at the annual convention last month.**
  我們在上個月的年度大會上見過面。 ＊annual 每年的，年度的
- **We met at the conference in Los Angeles.**
  我們在洛杉磯的會議上見過面。
- **We met at the seminar on the 21st of September.**
  我們在 9 月 21 日的研討會上見過面。
- **We met at our mutual friend Bill's office.**
  我們在我們共同的朋友——比爾的辦公室見過面。 ＊mutual 共同的

1 對話 My name is Judy Garrison. 我們在上個月的年度大會上見過面。We spoke briefly about collaborating at some point. I've got a new project that I think you might be interested in.

我的名字是茱蒂蓋瑞森。We met at the annual convention last month. 我們稍微聊到了可以一起合作做些事。現在我手邊有一個您可能會感興趣的計畫。

2 練習 我們在上禮拜的發表會上見過面。(presentation)
We met at ______________________.

Pattern 032

I was referred to you by...
…推薦我來找你。

通常在向對方提及自己曾從別人口中聽過對方時，會使用 introduce（介紹）這個單字，但在商務電子郵件中則更常使用這個帶有 refer（提及）這個單字的句型。這個句型直譯為「我曾聽過…提及您」，也就是「…推薦我來找你」的意思。

- **I was referred to you by Fred Jones of Amazon.**
  亞馬遜的佛萊德瓊斯推薦我來找你。
- **I was referred to you by John Houston of Microsoft.**
  微軟的約翰休斯頓推薦我來找你。
- **I was referred to you by my business associate.**
  我的商業夥伴推薦我來找你。
  ＊associate 夥伴，合夥人
- **I was referred to you by my supervisor, Mr. Charles.**
  我的上司查理斯先生推薦我來找你。

1 對話 My name is Bill Thomas. 微軟的約翰休斯頓推薦我來找你。He said that you might be needing some marketing expertise in the near future. I'd like to hear what you're planning.

我的名字是比爾湯瑪斯。I was referred to you by John Houston of Microsoft. 他提到您不久後可能需要一些行銷方面的專業人才。我想了解一下您的計畫內容。

2 練習 愛思銀行的穆雷史密斯先生推薦我來找你。
(Murray Smith, Ace Bank)
I was referred to you by ______________________.

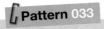

Pattern 033

I got your email address from...
我從…得知你的電子信箱。

第一次寫電子郵件給陌生人時，在進入正題前，禮貌上應該先利用這個句型向對方解釋一下自己是如何得知他的電子信箱會比較好。

- **I got your email address from my co-worker.**
  我從我的同事得知你的電子信箱。　＊co-worker 同事
- **I got your email address from my accountant.**
  我從我的會計師得知你的電子信箱。　＊accountant 會計師
- **I got your email address from the business card you left.**
  我從你留下的名片得知你的電子信箱。　＊business card 名片
- **I got your email address from the company directory.**
  我從公司行號的工商名錄得知你的電子信箱。　＊directory 工商名錄

1 對話　I'm not sure you are the right person to contact. 我從公司行號的工商名錄得知你的電子信箱。Does your company ship to the locations outside the U.S.?

我不太確定自己是否聯絡到對的人，I got your email address from the company directory. 請問貴公司是否有提供配送到美國以外的地區呢？

2 練習　我從貴公司的網頁上得知您的電子信箱。
(company's website)
I got your email address from ______________.

Pattern 034

I am the person who + 過去的事件 我是之前…的人。

這是一個可以幫助對方回想起自己的句型，非常實用，請務必牢記在心。透過以下的例句，好好熟悉一下關係代名詞 who 的用法吧！

- **I am the person who called you about the problem we're having.**
  我是之前打電話來提到關於我們目前問題的人。
- **I am the person who called you yesterday about getting some help.**
  我是昨天打電話來想尋求幫助的人。
- **I am the person who called you about your services.**
  我是之前打電話來提到關於你們服務的人。
- **I am the person who came up with the idea.**
  我是之前提出這個想法的人。　＊come up with（針對問題等）想出，提供

1 對話

我是之前為了我們目前的問題而打電話來的人。I'd like to give you some more details and see if you can help us. We've tried everything, so I hope you have some ideas.

I am the person who called you about the problem we're having. 我會更具體地向您說明細節，看您是否能提供幫助。我們已經嘗試過各種方法了，所以希望您能夠提供一些意見。

2 練習

我是之前為了共同合作計畫而打電話來的那個人。
(collaborate, project)
I am the person who called ________________.

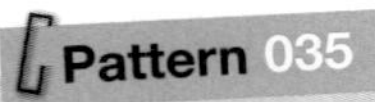

I am responding to...
我在此回應…

當對方公司向你提出的資料要求或其他諮詢事項，你想要透過電子郵件進行回覆時，就可以使用這個句型作為開場白，輕鬆完成一封簡單明瞭的電子郵件。

- **I am responding to your request for information.**
  我在此回應您所要求的資訊。
- **I am responding to your email from June 4.**
  我在此回應您 6 月 4 日的電子郵件。
- **I am responding to your phone call.**
  我在此回應您的來電。
- **I am responding to your inquiry about pricing.**
  我在此回應您的價格詢問。

＊inquiry 詢問

1 對話 我在此回應您所要求的資訊。I have attached some product descriptions and some image files to this email. I hope that they answer your questions. If you need any further information, please contact me.

I am responding to your request for information. 附件為產品的說明書和圖片檔案，希望這些資料能解決您的問題。如果您還需要其他更多資料的話，請再跟我聯絡。

2 練習 我在此回應您之前提出的提案。(proposal)
I am responding to ______________________.

2-3

表達來信目的與傳遞訊息

Pattern 036

I'm writing to...
我寫信來是想要…

在寫電子郵件時，會使用這個句型來說明來信事由或信件的目的與主題。句型中的 to 後面可以接上 inform, express, inquire, request 或 propose 等動詞，以具體說明來信目的。

- **I'm writing to inquire about a product.**
  我寫信來是想要詢問一項產品。 * product 產品，產物
- **I'm writing to request some information.**
  我寫信來是想要要求一些資訊。
- **I'm writing to answer some of the questions you've raised.**
  我寫信來是想要回覆您上次提出的一些問題。
- **I'm writing to check on the availability of a product.**
  我寫信來是想要確認一項產品是否有貨了。 * availability 可利用性

1 對話 我寫信來是想要確認一項產品是否有貨了。The last time we spoke, it was out of stock. The order number is 24601. If you could check on that for us, I would really appreciate it.

I'm writing to check on the availability of a product. 上次跟您提到時，您說目前缺貨中。我的訂單號碼是 24601，如果您能幫我再確認一次，我會非常感激。

2 練習 我寫信來是想要邀請貴公司加入我們的委員會。
(join, committee)
I'm writing to ______________________________.

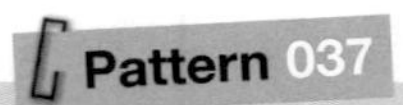

I'm contacting you because...
我寫這封信是因為⋯

當你想要向對方公司提案，或想要取得產品資訊等事宜，就可以用這個句型來表明來信目的，跟前一個句型 I'm writing to... 的意義接近。

- **I'm contacting you because I have a proposal.**
  我寫這封信是因為我有一個提議。 ＊proposal 企畫，提議
- **I'm contacting you because I need some assistance.**
  我寫這封信是因為我需要一些協助。 ＊assistance 援助，幫助
- **I'm contacting you because I'd like some information.**
  我寫這封信是因為我需要一些資訊。
- **I'm contacting you because I want to find out more about your organization.**
  我寫這封信是因為我想要更了解你們機構。 ＊organization 機構

1 對話 我寫這封信是因為我需要一些資訊。I've read about your products. However, I need more details before I decide to place an order. Could you tell me a little more about their features?

I'm contacting you because I'd like some information. 我已經看過你們的產品了，但是在訂購前想要更了解產品的細節內容。請問您能跟我多說一點產品的特色嗎？

2 練習 我寫這封信是因為覺得我們能成為互助的夥伴。
(help, each other)
I'm contacting you because ____________________.

Pattern 038

038

We're pleased to inform you...
我們很高興通知您⋯

在團隊經過積極討論，決定接受對方提出的 offer 或 proposal 等提案，想要透過電子郵件通知對方這個好消息時，就可以使用這個句型。

- **We're pleased to inform you that we have decided to accept your offer.**
  我們很高興通知您，我們決定接受你的提案。 ＊offer 提案 (= proposal)
- **We're pleased to inform you that your order has been discounted.**
  我們很高興通知您，您的訂單已經過折扣。 ＊discount 打折扣
- **We're pleased to inform you that we have decided to extend your contract.**
  我們很高興通知您，我們已經決定延長您的合約。 ＊extend 延長，延續
- **We're pleased to offer you the position.**
  我們很高興提供您這個職位。

1 對話 我們很高興通知您，我們決定接受你的提案。We have looked over the number that you sent us. We think it is fair. Let's meet later in the week to discuss the details of the deal.

We are pleased to inform you that we have decided to accept your offer. 我們仔細查看過您寄給我們的數據資料，我們認為這些數據資料並沒有問題。這週結束前，我們找個時間出來討論細節內容吧。

2 練習 我們很高興通知您，您遺失的物品已經找到了。
(have found, lost product)
We're pleased to ________________________.

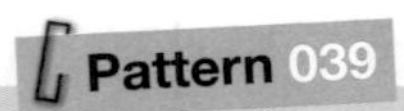

It's great to hear...
很高興聽到…

在聽到對方傳來的好消息後，透過回覆電子郵件表達喜悅之情時，就可以使用這個句型。本句型中的 great 可以依照前後文翻譯成「很好、很高興、很榮幸」等意思。意義相近的句型有 I'm glad to hear...。

- **It's great to hear from you.**
  很高興聽到你的消息。
- **It's great to hear that the project is advancing well.**
  很高興聽到這個計畫進展得十分順利。 ＊advance 進展，進步
- **It's great to hear that you want to do business with us.**
  很高興聽到您想要與我們做生意。
- **It's so good to hear that you're doing well.**
  很高興聽到你做得很好。

1 對話 很高興聽到這個計畫進展得十分順利。Everything is going well at my side, too. We should meet soon to discuss the next step. When will you be available?

It's great to hear that the project is advancing well. 我們這邊也進行得很順利。我們應該要盡快碰面討論下個階段的計畫。請問您什麼時候有空呢？

2 練習 很高興聽到您日益進步的消息。(make progress)
It's great to hear ______________.

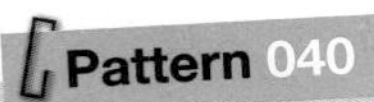

We regret to tell you that...
我們很遺憾地通知您…

這是在要拒絕對方的提議或協商等提案時，想要用電子郵件通報對方這個壞消息時可以使用的句型。

- **We regret to tell you that your order has been lost.**
  我們很遺憾地通知您，您預訂的商品遺失了。
- **We regret to tell you that we have decided against your proposal.**
  我們很遺憾地通知您，我們決定否決您的提案。
- **We regret to tell you that your services are no longer needed.**
  我們很遺憾地通知您，我們不再需要您的服務。
- **We regret to tell you that the item you ordered is not currently in stock.** ＊in stock 有現貨，有存貨
  我們很遺憾地通知您，您訂購的物品現在沒有存貨。

1 對話 我們很遺憾地通知您，您訂購的商品遺失了。We have contacted the shipping company and discovered that they no longer know where the package is.

We regret to tell you that your order has been lost. 我們已經和航運公司取得聯繫，但是他們也不清楚商品的下落。

2 練習 我們很遺憾地通知您，我們無法出席那場會議。
(have decided, participate)
We regret to tell you that ______________________.

2-4

請求和提議

We'd like to...	041	我們希望能⋯
Could you send me...?	042	可以請您把⋯寄給我嗎？
I'd be grateful if you could...	043	如果你能⋯，我會很感激。
As requested, we will...	044	我們會依照您的請求，⋯
I'm attaching...	045	附件資料是⋯

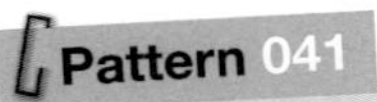

We'd like to...
我們希望能…

當你想向客戶方或某人提出請求或提案時，就可以使用這個句型，直接清楚明瞭地向對方表達你的意圖。

- **We'd like to close the deal by Friday.**
  我們希望能在禮拜五前訂立契約。 ＊close 訂立（契約）
- **We'd like to expand our product line.**
  我們希望能擴展我們的產品線。 ＊expand 擴張，發展
- **We'd like to do business in the future.**
  我們希望能在未來合作做生意。
- **We'd like to invite you to join us.**
  我們希望能邀請貴公司加入我們。

1 對話 We're taking part in a cross-promotion with several firms. Attached is a description of our marketing plan. If executed correctly, it will be quite beneficial to everyone who participates. 我們希望能邀請貴公司加入我們。

我們和幾家公司合作規畫了交叉促銷的活動，附件是關於這個行銷計畫的相關介紹資料，如果計畫順利的話，每位參與者都將會獲得可觀的利益。We'd like to invite you to join us.

2 練習 我們希望能更常與您會面。(more often)
We'd like to _________________________________.

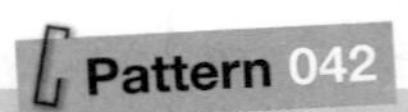

Could you send me...?
可以請您把…寄給我嗎？

當你想用較禮貌鄭重的語氣請求對方公司用電子郵件寄送較為詳細的資訊或新產品目錄給你時，就可以使用這個句型。

- **Could you send me the sample?**
  可以請您把樣品寄給我嗎？
- **Could you send me the reference materials?**
  可以請您把參考資料寄給我嗎？
  ＊material 材料，資料
- **Could you send me the details of your proposal?**
  可以請您把企畫案的細節寄給我嗎？
- **Could you send me the latest version of the contract?**
  可以請您把最新版本的合約寄給我嗎？

1 對話 I'm definitely interested in your proposal. However, before we move forward, I'll need to know a little more. 可以請您把企畫案的細節寄給我嗎？

我當然對您的提案有興趣。但是在我們進行下一步之前，我需要再多了解一下內容。Could you send me the details of your proposal?

2 練習 可以請您把企畫案的大綱寄給我嗎？(outline)
Could you send me ______________________?

Pattern 043

I'd be grateful if you could...
如果你能…，我會很感激。

當你想客氣地拜託對方給你說明書或詳細資料等情報或樣品時，就可以使用這個句型。

- **I'd be grateful if you could give me a fast response.**
  如果你能盡快回覆我，我會很感激。
- **I'd be grateful if you could send me a sample of your product.**
  如果你能寄給我你們商品的樣本，我會很感激。
- **I'd be grateful if you could answer a few questions for me.**
  如果你能回答我一些問題，我會很感激。
- **I'd be grateful if you could provide me with a few more details.**
  如果你能多提供我一些細節，我會很感激。

＊provide 提供

1 對話

如果您能回答我一些問題，我會很感激。I recently came across your company's website and I am interested in doing business with you. Are you prepared to do business with an American company?

I'd be grateful if you could answer a few questions for me. 我最近瀏覽了貴公司的網頁，想跟貴公司合作一筆生意。請問您們是否有打算和美國公司合作呢？

2 練習 如果您能快點做出決定的話，我會很感激。(make, quick)
I'd be grateful if you could ______________________.

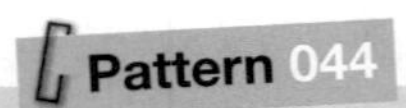

044

As requested, we will...
我們會依照您的請求，…

當對方提出要求時，不論我方是否能接受，都要盡快回覆對方比較好。如果可以接受對方的要求，要給予正面答覆的話，就可以使用這個句型：As requsted, we will...。

- **As requested, we will send you a new toolkit.**
  我們會依照您的請求，寄給您一份新的工具組。　* **toolkit** 工具組
- **As requested, we will increase your order by 50 packets.**
  我們會依照您的請求，將您的訂單增加到五十包。　* **packet** 小包裹，小袋
- **As requested, we will change your address on our computer.**
  我們會依照您的請求，在我們電腦中更改您的地址。
- **As requested, we will fix the errors you found in the contract.**
  我們會依照您的請求，修改您在合約中發現的錯誤。

1 對話 Thank you for letting us know you've moved. 我們會依照您的要求，在我們電腦裡變更貴公司的地址。If you need further assistance, please contact us.

謝謝您通知我們公司搬遷的訊息，As requested, we will change your address on our computer. 如果還有需要幫忙的地方，請再與我們聯絡。

2 練習 我們會依照您的要求，將免費試用品郵寄給您。(mail)
As requested, we will ______________________.

Pattern 045

I’m attaching...
附件資料是⋯

在寫電子郵件時，如果你想告訴對方有跟信件內容相關的附件資料時，就要用 attach 這個單字，表達句型為 I’m attaching... 或 I’ve attached...。此外，「請參考附件資料」的英文為 “Please refer to the attached file.”。

- **I’m attaching the file you requested.**
  附件資料是您所要求的檔案。
- **I’m attaching a copy of the contract.**
  附件資料是合約書的影本。
- **I’m attaching a rough draft of the contract.**
  附件資料是合約書的初步草稿。 ＊draft 草稿
- **I’m attaching our price list file.**
  附件資料是我們的價目表檔案。

1 對話 附件資料是合約書的影本。Our lawyers have already gone over it, and everything looks good from our end. After you have reviewed it, sign it and send it back to us.

I’m attaching a copy of the contract. 我們的律師已經檢查過這份合約，以我方立場看來沒有任何問題。希望等您檢查過這份合約的內容，在上面簽名後，再寄回給我們。

2 練習 附件資料是我們說明書的影本。(a copy, brochure)
I’m attaching ______________________.

2-5

確定日程安排與信件結尾

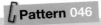

Pattern 046

046

It will take + 時間 + to...
我們要花…的時間來…

在商務情況中，讓對方久等是一件不禮貌的行為。所以當你已經預估出要花多久時間去處理對方的需求時，就可以用這個句型提前通知對方。

- **It will take a few days to go over the data.**
  我們要花幾天的時間來檢查這些資料。
- **It will take a few months to make a decision.**
  我們要花幾個月來做決定。
- **It will take three days to finish the urgent project.**
  我們要花三天的時間來完成這個緊急的計畫。
- **It will take two days to find the relevant documents.**
  我們要花兩天的時間來找到相關的文件。 ＊**relevant** 相關的

1 對話 我們要花幾天的時間來檢查這些資料，I want to make sure the prices are acceptable. After I'm satisfied, I will email you with my decision. Thank you for your patience.

It will take a few days to go over the data. 我想要確認這價錢是否合理。看完後我會寫信告訴你我的決定。謝謝您的耐心等待。

2 練習 我們要花一個禮拜的時間來獲得批准。(approval)
It will take a week ________________.

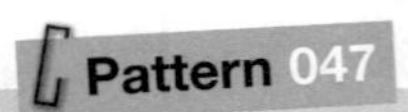

I'll get back to you after...
…之後，我會再跟您聯絡。

這個句型常常搭配表達「檢查、確認」意思的動詞。英文中用來表示「檢查」的單字除了常見的 check 外，還有 go over, review, examine 等，請試著替換練習看看吧！這個句型是用來表達「我會確認你寄來的 proposal / offer 等資料」的意思。

- **I'll get back to you after I complete this rush-job.**
  完成這件緊急任務之後，我會再跟您聯絡。 ＊rush-job 緊急任務
- **I'll get back to you after examining the contract.**
  檢查過這份合約之後，我會再跟您聯絡。
- **I'll get back to you after going over these figures.**
  等我確認過這些金額之後，我會再跟您聯絡。 ＊figure 數字，金額
- **I'll get back to you after I've returned to my office.**
  回到辦公室之後，我會再跟您聯絡。

1 對話 等我確認過這些金額之後，我會再跟您聯絡。I'm sure you understand that I can't make a decision until I know all of the details. I should be emailing you sometime next week.

I'll get back to you after going over these figures. 尚未了解所有細節內容之前，我無法做出決定，相信您一定能體諒。我下個禮拜會再寄信給您。

2 練習 等我和經紀人開完會之後，我會再跟您聯絡。(brokers)
I'll get back to you after ______________________.

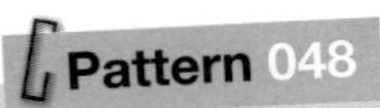

I am still considering...
我還在考慮⋯

當你要晚一點才能答覆某些提案或問題時，就可以使用這個句型。順便提醒一下，你知道 think 和 consider 有什麼不同嗎？think 是表示再進一步「深思熟慮」，consider 則是表示「考慮、認為」的意思，使用時應該要注意兩者的差異。

- **I am still considering your offer.**
  我還在考慮貴公司的提案。
- **I am still considering the decision.**
  我還在考慮這項決策。
- **I am still considering my answer.**
  我還在考慮我的答案。
- **I am still considering ordering more products.**
  我還在考慮是否要訂購更多產品。 ＊order 訂購

1 對話 我還在考慮貴公司的提案。I can see some benefits to the transaction. However, I still have some reservations. I'd like to see some numbers before I accept.

I am still considering your offer. 我能看出這個買賣會帶來利潤。不過，我還是持部分保留意見。所以在決定合作前我想要先看些數據資料。

2 練習 我跟老闆還在考慮貴公司的提案。(boss)
I am still considering ________________.

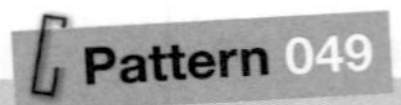

Please feel free to...
隨時都可以…

當你想跟對方表達如果有不了解或疑慮之處，不論何時都能夠毫無顧慮地透過電話或電子郵件跟你聯絡時，就可以使用這個句型。這是一個能向對方表達體貼照顧心意的句型，請牢記在心。

- **Please feel free to call me with any questions.**
  如果有任何疑問，隨時都可以與我聯絡。
- **Please feel free to ask questions at any time.**
  任何時間都歡迎詢問。
- **Please feel free to share any misgivings you have about the project.**
  大家隨時都可以分享對此計畫的任何疑慮。　＊misgiving 擔憂，疑慮
- **Please feel free to get in touch with me if you have any problems.**
  如果你有任何問題，隨時都可以與我聯繫。　＊get in touch 聯繫

1 對話 In the meantime, if you have a chance, look over the information I sent you regarding our services. I look forward to meeting with you next week. 如果有任何疑問，隨時都可以與我聯絡。

這段期間如果您有空的話，希望您可以先看一下我寄給您的資訊，內容與我們的服務有關。期待下週與您的會面。Please feel free to call me with any questions.

2 練習 如果這份文件的措辭有需要修改的地方，隨時都可以與我聯絡。(wording, document)
Please feel free to ______________________.

Pattern 050

050

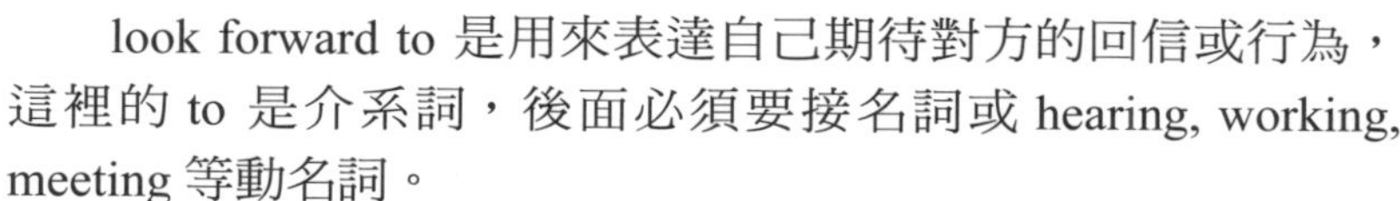

We look forward to...
我們期待⋯

look forward to 是用來表達自己期待對方的回信或行為，這裡的 to 是介系詞，後面必須要接名詞或 hearing, working, meeting 等動名詞。

- **We look forward to hearing from you.**
  我們期待聽到您的消息。
- **We look forward to working with you.**
  我們期待與您共事。
- **We look forward to starting this project soon.**
  我們期待不久後就能開始這個計畫。
- **We look forward to chatting with you about this.**
  我們期待跟您聊聊這件事。

＊chat with 與⋯閒談，聊天

1 對話 I hope you like what you see. Look over the attached documents and let us know what you think. I hope you find our proposal interesting. 我們期待聽到您的消息。

希望您會滿意。請瀏覽附件資料，並提供您寶貴的意見給我們。希望您會對我們的提案有興趣，We look forward to hearing from you.

2 練習 我們期待您早日回覆。(prompt, response)

We look forward to ______________________________.

2-1~2-5

黃金複習 15 分鐘！

前面這 25 個句型和 125 個句子全都記熟了嗎？
來驗收一下學習成果吧！如果不能充滿自信地用英文說出以下 40 個句子，請翻到前面再重新複習一次！

01 我是史密斯科技公司的喬史密斯。

____

02 我們期待聽到您的消息。

____

03 我負責會計部。

____

04 任何時間都歡迎詢問。

____

05 請容我先自我介紹。

____

06 我們還在考慮貴公司的提案。

____

07 謝謝您上禮拜的信。

____

08 完成這件緊急任務之後，我會再跟您聯絡。

____

09 很抱歉我無法早點回信。

____

解答 01. I am Joe Smith from Smith Tech, Inc. 02. We look forward to hearing from you.
03. I am in charge of the Accounting Department.
04. Please feel free to ask questions at any time. 05. Let me start off by introducing myself.
06. I am still considering your offer. 07. Thank you for your letter last week.
08. I'll get back to you after I complete this rush-job. 09. I'm sorry I couldn't respond earlier.

10 我們要花幾天的時間來檢查數據。

11 我們在上個月的年度大會上見過面。

12 附件資料是您所要求的檔案。

13 微軟的約翰休斯頓推薦我來找你。

14 我們會依照您的請求，寄給您一份新的工具組。

15 我從我的同事得知你的電子信箱。

16 如果你能回答我一些問題，我會很感激。

17 我是之前打電話來提到關於我們目前問題的人。

18 可以請你把你企畫案的細節寄給我嗎？

19 我在此回應您所要求的資訊。

20 我們希望能在禮拜五前訂立契約。

解答 10. It will take a few days to go over the data.
11. We met at the annual convention last month. 12. I'm attaching the file you requested.
13. I was referred to you by John Houston of Microsoft.
14. As requested, we will send you a new toolkit.
15. I got your email address from my co-worker.
16. I'd be grateful if you could answer a few questions for me.
17. I am the person who called you about a problem we're having.
18. Could you send me the details of your proposal?
19. I am responding to your request for information. 20. We'd like to close the deal by Friday.

21 我寫信來是想要詢問一項產品。

22 我們期待與您共事。

23 我寫這封信是因為我有一個提議。

24 如果有疑問的話，隨時都可以聯絡我。

25 我們很高興通知您，我們決定要接受您的提案了。

26 我還在考慮這項決策。

27 很高興聽到你的消息。

28 回到辦公室之後，我會再跟您聯絡。

29 我們很遺憾地通知您，我們決定否決你的提案。

30 我們要花幾個月來做決定。

解答 21. I'm writing to inquire about a product. 22. We look forward to working with you.
23. I'm contacting you because I have a proposal.
24. Please feel free to call me with any questions.
25. We are pleased to inform you that we have decided to accept your offer.
26. I am still considering the decision. 27. It's great to hear from you.
28. I'll get back to you after I've returned to my office.
29. We regret to tell you that we have decided against your proposal.
30. It will take a few months to make a decision.

31 我在索尼擔任經理。

32 附件資料是合約的副本。

33 我負責人事部。

34 我們會依照您的請求，將您的訂單增加到五十包。

35 請容我先介紹我們的產品。

36 如果你能多提供我一些細節，我會很感激。

37 謝謝您迅速回信給我。

38 可以請您把樣品寄給我嗎？

39 很抱歉我那時沒有時間見您。

40 我們希望能擴展我們的產品線。

解答 31. I am working as a manager at Sony. 32. I'm attaching a copy of the contract.
33. I am in charge of human resources.
34. As requested, we will increase your order by **50** packets.
35. Let me start off by introducing our products.
36. I'd be grateful if you could provide me with a few more details.
37. Thank you for getting back to me so quickly. 38. Could you send me the sample?
39. I'm sorry I was unavailable to see you. 40. We'd like to expand our product line.

Unit 3
開會
成為會議上的焦點

3-1 會議開始

Thank you for...	051	謝謝您…
We see this meeting as...	052	我們把這次會議當作…
Before we begin, shall we...?	053	在我們開始之前，我們先…如何？
Let's start with...	054	我們從…開始吧！
At our last meeting,...	055	在上次的會議中，…

Pattern 051

Thank you for...
謝謝您…

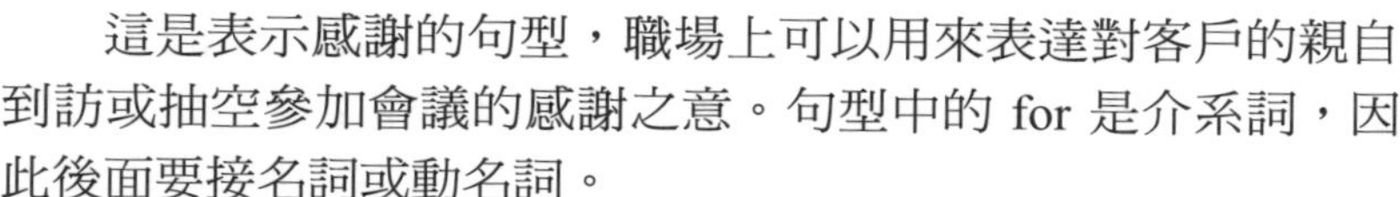

這是表示感謝的句型，職場上可以用來表達對客戶的親自到訪或抽空參加會議的感謝之意。句型中的 for 是介系詞，因此後面要接名詞或動名詞。

- **Thank you for taking the time to see us.**
  謝謝您在百忙之中為我們抽出時間來。
- **Thank you for your visit.**
  謝謝您的來訪。
- **Thank you for meeting us on such short notice.**
  謝謝您在這麼緊急的時間內與我們見面。 ＊short notice 臨時通知
- **Thank you for coming all the way to our office.**
  謝謝您不遠千里地蒞臨敝公司。

1 對話

A 謝謝您在百忙之中為我們抽出時間來。
B You're welcome. We're looking forward to working with you.
A Shall we begin?

A Thank you for taking the time to see us.
B 你太客氣了。我們很期待與你共事。
A 我們現在就開始好嗎？

2 練習 謝謝您的邀請。(invitation)
Thank you for ________________.

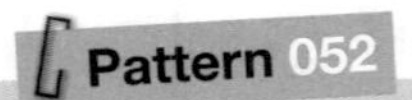

We see this meeting as...
我們把這次會議當作…

在正式進入會議正題之前，你想先向大家闡明召開這次會議的目的以及期待得到的結果時，就可以使用這個句型。多數的情況下，並無法透過一次協商就獲得想要的結果，所以在第一次開會時先說明會議的方向與目標，將有助於會議的進行。

- **We see this meeting as a first step.**
  我們把這次會議當作第一步。
- **We see this meeting as a way to develop our relationship.**
  我們把這次會議當作發展我們關係的方式。
- **We see this meeting as an excellent opportunity for both parties.**
  我們把這次會議當作對我們雙方的絕佳機會。 ＊opportunity 機會
- **We see this meeting as a preliminary negotiation to set up the agenda.**
  我們把這次會議當作擬訂議程的初步協商。 ＊preliminary 初步的

1 對話
A 我們將這次會議視為第一步。
B Are we going to discuss price?
A Only generally.

A We see this meeting as a first step.
B 我們要討論價格嗎？
A 只先討論出大致的價格。

2 練習 我們把這次會議當作達成協議的最後一次機會。
(come to, agreement)
We see this meeting as ______________________.

Pattern 053

Before we begin, shall we...?
在我們開始之前，我們先…如何？

在會議或協商正式展開前，如果你想先簡單地確認一些事項的話，就可以使用這個句型。

Before we begin, shall we go over the proposal?
在我們開始之前，我們先重新看一次企畫案如何？

Before we begin, shall we go over the paperwork?
在我們開始之前，我們先確認一下資料如何？

Before we begin, shall we review the progress we made last week?
在我們開始之前，我們先複習一下上週的進度如何？ ＊review 回顧，複習

Before we begin, shall we introduce ourselves?
在我們開始之前，我們先自我介紹如何？

1 對話 A I'm glad you could all make it today.
B 在我們開始之前，我們先確認一下書面資料如何？
A Please.

A 我高興大家都出席了。
B Before we begin, shall we go over the paperwork?
A 好啊。

2 練習 在我們開始之前，我們先來確立一下方針吧。
(establish, guidelines)
Before we begin, shall we ______________________?

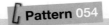

Pattern 054

Let's start with...
我們從…開始吧！

會議主持人可以利用此句型來讓會議氣氛變得更正式，意義相近的句型還有 I'd like to open...。如果你想要正式進入會議正題的話，可以說 "Why don't we get started?" 或 "I think we need to get started" 等。

- **Let's start with a rundown of the schedule.**
  我們從時程表的概要開始吧！　＊rundown 概要，說明
- **Let's start with a roll call.**
  我們從點名開始吧！　＊roll call 點名，點名時間
- **Let's start with a recap of what we discussed last time.**
  我們從整理一下上回討論到的重點開始吧！　＊recap 概括，扼要重述
- **Let's start with a short presentation on the product.**
  我們從簡介這個產品開始吧！

1 對話
A Welcome to the meeting, everyone.
B Good morning, Ms. Smith.
A 我們從點名開始吧！

A 歡迎大家出席這場會議。
B 史密斯小姐，早安。
A Let's start with a roll call.

2 練習 我們從引言開始吧！(introductions)
Let's start with ______________________.

Pattern 055

055

At our last meeting, ...
在上次的會議中，…

在正式進入會議正題之前，如果你想確認上次會議的內容的話，就可以使用這個句型，也可以說 In our previous meeting...。此外，如果想拜託對方簡略說明上次會議內容時，你可以說 "Could you summarize last week's meeting?"。

At our last meeting, we were each given tasks.
在上次的會議中，我們每個人都被指派了任務。 ＊task 職務，任務

At our last meeting, we disagreed on several minor points. ＊disagree 意見相左，不同意
在上次的會議中，我們有幾個小地方的意見不相同。

At our last meeting, we had poor attendance.
在上次的會議中，我們的出席率不佳。

At our last meeting, Mary reported a decline in sales.
在上次的會議中，瑪莉提到營業額下降了。 ＊decline 下降，衰退

1 對話
A Each of you will give a report at this meeting.
B What are we reporting on?
A 在上次的會議中，我們每個人都被指派了任務。

A 這次的會議每個人都要上台報告。
B 我們應該要報告些什麼呢？
A At our last meeting, we were each given tasks.

2 練習 在上次的會議中，我們都同意了這個價格。(agree on)
At our last meeting, ______________________________.

3-2

說明討論議題

Pattern 056

056

We're here today to...
我們今天來到這裡是為了…

如果你在會議中想要控制場面、介紹討論議題的話，就可以使用這個句型。此外，本句型中的 today 後面可以接 to, for, because 等字彙，如果是接 to 時，後面要接 go over, discuss, try, look over 等動詞或動詞片語。

- **We're here today to discuss the merger.**
  我們今天來到這裡是為了討論合併事宜。　＊merger（企業）合併
- **We're here today to try to work together better.**
  我們今天來到這裡是為了設法有更好的合作。
- **We're here today for one reason only.**
  我們今天來到這裡只是為了一個原因。
- **We're here today because we missed the deadline.**
  我們今天來到這裡是因為我們錯過了截止期限。　＊deadline 截止期限

1 對話
A We argue too much.
B 我們今天來到這裡是為了嘗試有更好的合作。
A I hope you have some good ideas.

A 我們好像爭論太多次了。
B We're here today to try to work together better.
A 希望你有一些好點子。

2 練習 我們今天來到這裡是為了檢閱預算。(review, budget)
We're here today to ______________________.

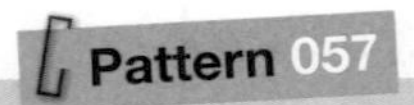

The purpose of this meeting is to...
這次會議的目的是為了…

在正式進入會議正題之前，最好先向出席成員說明這次會議的目的。本句型中的主詞 purpose 表示「目的、意圖」的意思，請找機會利用這個句型吧！

- **The purpose of this meeting is to share our progress.**
  這次會議的目的是為了分享我們目前的進度。 ＊share 分享，共有
- **The purpose of this meeting is to determine the problem.**
  這次會議的目的是為了確認這個問題。
- **The purpose of this meeting is to make budget cuts.**
  這次會議的目的是為了削減預算。 ＊budget cut 削減預算
- **The purpose of this meeting is to go over the market research.**
  這次會議的目的是為了檢視市場調查狀況。

1 對話
A 這次會議的目的是為了分享我們目前的進度。
B I'd like to go first if I may.
A Certainly, Jane.

A The purpose of this meeting is to share our progress.
B 如果可以的話，我想要先報告。
A 珍，那就由你先來吧！

2 練習
這次會議的目的是為了改善我們的行銷策略。(improve, strategy)
The purpose of this meeting is to ____________________.

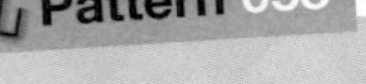

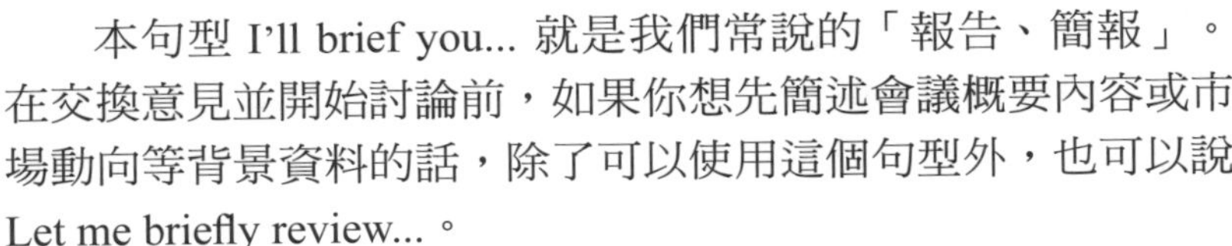

I'll brief you on...
我將為您簡述…

本句型 I'll brief you... 就是我們常說的「報告、簡報」。在交換意見並開始討論前，如果你想先簡述會議概要內容或市場動向等背景資料的話，除了可以使用這個句型外，也可以說 Let me briefly review...。

- **I'll brief you on our progress.**
  我將為您簡述我們的進度。
- **I'll brief you on the recent market trends.**
  我將為您簡述最近的市場趨勢。 ＊recent 最近的
- **I'll brief you on our conversation with my CEO.**
  我將為您簡述我們與總裁之間的會談。
- **I'll brief you on the Korean market's profit margins.**
  我將為您簡述韓國市場的毛利率。 ＊margin 利潤

1 對話

A I'm nervous about the meeting with Starbucks.
B Why? What's there to be nervous about?
A I don't feel like I know much about the coffee industry.
B 我將為你簡述最近的市場趨勢。

A 我有點擔心和星巴克的會議。
B 為什麼？有什麼要擔心的呢？
A 因為我不太了解咖啡這門產業。
B I'll brief you on the recent market trends.

2 練習 我將為您簡述上禮拜研討會的內容。(symposium)
I'll brief you ______________________.

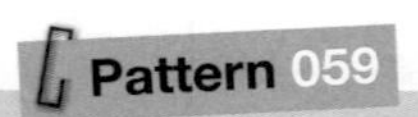

I'll update you on...
我會向您更新…

在正式進入會議正題之前，如果你想要先報告上次的會議內容或變動事項，就可以使用這個句型。除此之外，報告業務內容時也會用到，請一定要熟記。

- **I'll update you on the current situation.**
  我會向您更新目前的情況。 ＊current 當前的
- **I'll update you on the progress with my client.**
  我會向您更新我與客戶之間的進展。
- **I'll update you on how the negotiation is going.**
  我將為您更新談判的進行狀況。 ＊negotiation 談判，協商
- **I'll update you on the whereabouts of the shipment.**
  我將為您更新寄送貨品的下落。 ＊whereabouts 下落，行蹤

1 對話
A Could you summarize last week's meeting?
B Okay. 我會向您更新目前的情況。
A How nice of you!

A 可以請您總結報告一下上週的會議內容嗎？
B 沒問題，I'll update you on the current situation.
A 您人真好！

2 練習 我會向您更新那個企畫案的狀況。(status)
I'll update you on ______________________.

Pattern 060

Allow me to take...to...
請容我花（時間）來…

在正式進入協商事項之前，如果你想要簡單地報告之前討論過的、或是今天想要討論的議題的話，就可以使用這個句型。

- **Allow me to take a few minutes to address this issue.**
  請容我花幾分鐘的時間來說明這個議題。
- **Allow me to take a moment to tell everyone our schedule for today.**
  請容我花一些時間來告訴大家今天的行程。
- **Allow me to take about 10 minutes to review what we've agreed on so far.**
  請容我花大約十分鐘的時間來回顧一下我們目前達成了哪些協議。
- **Allow me to take a few minutes of your time to introduce our new product.**
  請容我花各位幾分鐘的時間來介紹我們的新產品。

1 對話
A 請容我花幾分鐘的時間來說明這個議題。
B We have a lot of concerns.
A But I think we can find a solution.

A Allow me to take a few minutes to address this issue.
B 我們有很多顧慮之處。
A 但我認為我們一定可以找到解決的辦法。

2 練習 請容我花幾分鐘的時間來簡述這個計畫。(outline)
Allow me to take ________ to ________.

3-3

發表意見

Pattern 061

Let me give you...
讓我來告訴大家…

這個句型用來表達自己的意見，如果你想要說明「我想大略報告一些跟…有關的內容」時，就可以使用本句型的擴充句型：Let me give you a run-down on...。

- **Let me give you my perspective on this.**
  讓我來告訴大家我對這件事情的看法。 ＊perspective 看法，觀點
- **Let me give you a worst-case scenario.**
  讓我來告訴大家最壞打算的情況。
- **Let me give you an idea about Canada's program.**
  讓我來告訴大家一個有關加拿大計畫的構想。
- **Let me give you some advice from our marketing director.**
  讓我來告訴大家我們行銷總監的一些意見。 ＊director 總監，主管

1 對話 **A** We don't understand why this is so difficult.
B 讓我來告訴大家我對這件事情的看法。
A Please.

A 我們無法理解這有什麼困難的。
B Let me give you my perspective on this.
A 請說。

2 練習 我給你一些時間去好好思考這件事。(think something over)
Let me give you ______________________________.

Pattern 062

I suggest that...
我建議…

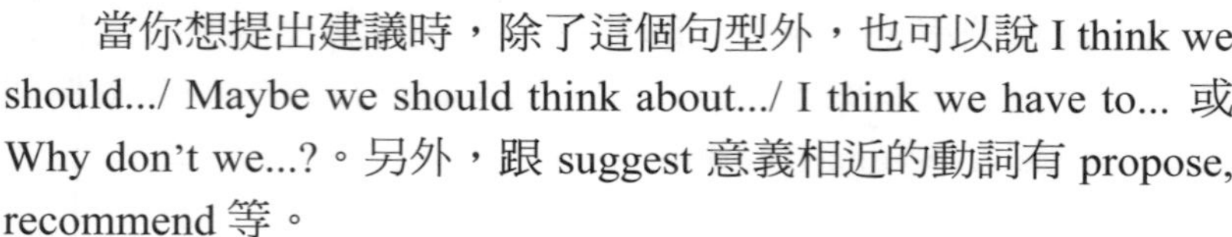

當你想提出建議時，除了這個句型外，也可以說 I think we should.../ Maybe we should think about.../ I think we have to... 或 Why don't we...?。另外，跟 suggest 意義相近的動詞有 propose, recommend 等。

- **I suggest that we divide up the tasks.**
  我建議我們分配一下工作。 ＊divide up 分配
- **I suggest that we leave all questions for the end.**
  我建議我們把所有的問題留到最後。
- **I suggest that we all calm down a little bit.**
  我建議我們大家都冷靜一點。
- **I suggest that we reconsider the project with the facts turned up so far.** ＊turn up 出現，偶然地發生
  我建議我們用目前已發生的事實來重新討論這個企畫案。

1 對話
A Our discussion has become argumentative.
B I don't see how we can resolve this.
A 我建議我們大家都冷靜一點。

A 我們的討論已經淪為爭執了。
B 我真的不知道要如何解決這件事。
A I suggest that we all calm down a little bit.

2 練習 我建議我們在協議時應該更具攻擊性一點。
(aggressive, negotiation)
I suggest that ______________________.

Pattern 063

Why don't we...?
我們何不…？

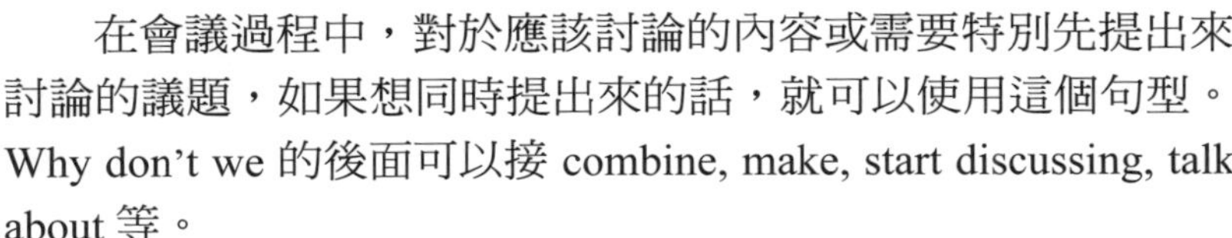
在會議過程中，對於應該討論的內容或需要特別先提出來討論的議題，如果想同時提出來的話，就可以使用這個句型。Why don't we 的後面可以接 combine, make, start discussing, talk about 等。

- **Why don't we ask all staff members for ideas?**
  我們何不問問所有員工的意見？
- **Why don't we combine these two ideas?**
  我們何不結合這兩個意見？ ＊combine 結合，聯合
- **Why don't we do a little research first?**
  我們何不先做一些調查？
- **Why don't we see what our management thinks?**
  我們何不先了解我們的主管是怎麼想的呢？ ＊management 管理部門

1 對話
A I think we should invest in nanotechnology.
B Do we know anything about it?
A 我們何不先做一些調查？

A 我認為我們應該投資奈米技術。
B 我們了解這個領域嗎？
A Why don't we do a little research first?

2 練習 我們何不先把所有的點子列出來呢？(make a list)
Why don't we ______________________________?

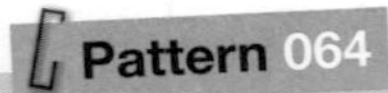

What we really need is...
我們真正需要的是…

當會議進入雙方各自分享提出自己真正需要的條件是什麼的階段時，就可以使用這個句型。此外，本句型中的 need 可以用 look for, want, aim for 等代替。類似的句型為 I'd like to point out... 和 Let me emphasize...。

- **What we really need is a strong leader.**
  我們真正需要的是一位有力的領導者。
- **What we really need is more time.**
  我們真正需要的是更多的時間。
- **What we really need is to contact our customers regularly.**
  我們真正需要的是經常跟我們的客戶們接觸。　＊contact 聯絡，接觸
- **What we really need is your complete cooperation.**
  我們真正需要的是您完全的合作。

1 對話

A Our department is really struggling.
B 我們真正需要的是一位有力的領導者。
A I agree.

A 我們部門的情況真的很糟。
B What we really need is a strong leader.
A 沒錯。

2 練習 我們真正需要的是一個更強硬的業務部門。(tougher)
What we really need is ______________________.

Pattern 065

We're expecting...
我們預計⋯

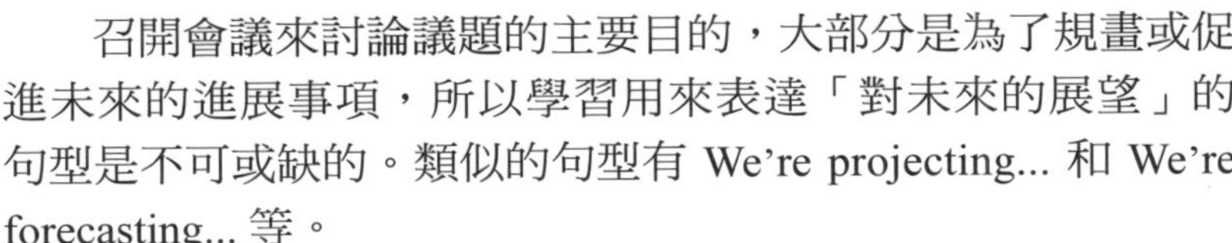

召開會議來討論議題的主要目的，大部分是為了規畫或促進未來的進展事項，所以學習用來表達「對未來的展望」的句型是不可或缺的。類似的句型有 We're projecting... 和 We're forecasting... 等。

- **We're expecting a huge shipment tomorrow.**
  我們預計明天會有一批大量的貨。
- **We're expecting to expand into South America.**
  我們預計擴展到南美洲。
- **We're expecting a huge profit margin from this deal.**
  我們預計這批交易會產生巨大的利潤。 ＊profit margin 毛利，利潤
- **We're expecting to ship 500,000 units of this product.**
  我們預計運送50萬組這項產品。 ＊ship 運送，裝運

1 對話

A Our sales are projected to increase this year.
B That would be great, but how?
A 我們預計明天會有一批大量的貨物。

A 我們預測今年的營業額會提升。
B 這樣是很棒沒錯，但要如何提升呢？
A We're expecting a huge shipment tomorrow.

2 練習 我們預計這條生產線會遭受損失。(see a loss)
We're expecting ______________________.

3-4

表示贊成

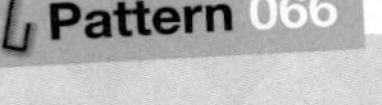

066

That's a great...
那真是個很棒的…

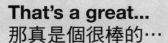

在會議過程中，必須互相分享彼此的看法、點子或計畫，並適時給予好的想法讚美，才能激盪出好的火花。當對方提出一個不錯的 proposal, idea 或 plan 時，就立刻使用這個句型來讚美或鼓勵對方吧！這樣做也有助於提升團隊效益。

- **That's a great idea.**
  那真是個很棒的點子。
- **That's an excellent plan.**
  那真是個出色的計畫。
- **That's an efficient explanation.**
  那真是個有效率的說明。
- **That's a good flow chart.**
  那真是個很棒的流程圖。 ＊flow chart 流程圖

1 對話
A Now I understand our company's structure.
B This flow chart shows all our regional offices.
A 那真是個很棒的流程圖。

A 現在我了解公司的結構了。
B 這個流程圖顯示出我們所有地區的辦公室。
A That's a great flow chart.

2 練習 那真是個很棒的提議。(suggestion)
That's a fine ______________________.

Pattern 067

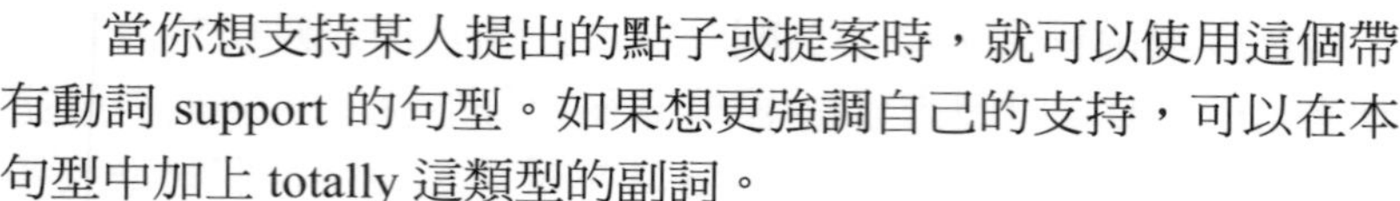

I support that...
我支持…

當你想支持某人提出的點子或提案時，就可以使用這個帶有動詞 support 的句型。如果想更強調自己的支持，可以在本句型中加上 totally 這類型的副詞。

- **I support that business proposition.**
  我支持那項商業提案。 ＊proposition 提案
- **I support that, but I don't know if I can convince my boss.** ＊convince 說服，使信服
  我支持那件事，但我不知道我是否能說服我老闆。
- **I support that, but it'll be hard to sell that to the head office.**
  我支持那件事，但要讓總公司接受很困難。 ＊sell 使接受，使人相信
- **I totally support that suggestion.**
  我完全支持這個提議。

1 對話
A The engineers are asking for more time.
B Why? Is there a problem with the oven's design?
A No. They have found a way to improve it.
B Then, by all means, 我完全支持這個提議。

A 工程師要求能有更多的時間。
B 為什麼？鍋爐的設計有問題嗎？
A 沒有。只是他們已經找到改善鍋爐的方法。
B 那樣的話，當然沒問題，I totally support that suggestion.

2 練習 理論上我是支持的，但就現實面來看我無法確定。
(in theory, practical)
I support that ______________________________.

Pattern 068

068

I can partly agree to that, but...
我在一定程度上同意，但是…

在業務相關的會議上，如果你想表達「部分同意對方的意見或條件，但是自己的意見是…」的話，就可以使用這個句型。這是一個比較進階的句型，請多多練習，配合實際情況好好運用吧！

- **I can partly agree to that, but with one condition.**
  我在一定程度上同意，但是我有一個條件。
- **I can partly agree to that, but first let me check with my boss.**
  我在一定程度上同意，但是讓我先跟我的老闆確認一下。
- **I can partly agree to that, but we have to increase our price.**
  我在一定程度上同意，但是我們必須提高價錢。
- **I can partly agree to that, but there are some elements I have reservations about.**
  我在一定程度上同意，但是在某些要素上面我有異議。

* **reservation** 疑問，異議

1 對話
A 我在一定程度上同意，但是我有一個條件。
B What's that?
A We want the trademark rights.

A I can partly agree to that, but with one condition.
B 什麼條件呢？
A 我們要商標權。

2 練習 我在一定程度上同意，但是我們必須修改那份合約書。
(need, amend)
I can partly agree to that, but ________________.

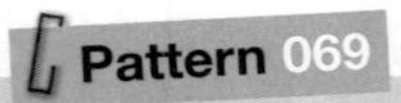

Let me think about...
讓我考慮一下…

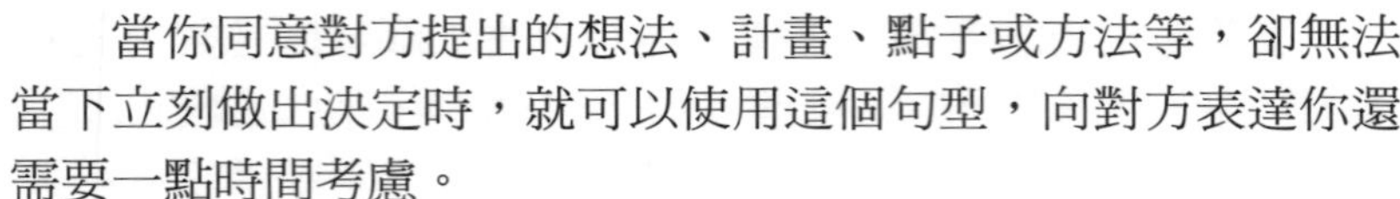

069 考慮提案

當你同意對方提出的想法、計畫、點子或方法等，卻無法當下立刻做出決定時，就可以使用這個句型，向對方表達你還需要一點時間考慮。

- **Let me think about what George said.**
  讓我考慮一下喬治所說的話。
- **Let me think about some ways to make this work.**
  讓我考慮一下解決這件事的辦法。
- **Let me think about some potential problems.**
  讓我考慮一下一些潛在的問題。 ＊potential 潛在的，可能的
- **Let me think about whether I can do this.**
  讓我考慮一下我能不能夠勝任這件事。

1 對話
A We received an old version of the contract.
B So should I contact our lawyer?
A Wait. 讓我考慮一下解決這件事的辦法。

A 我們拿到了舊版的合約書
B 那麼我們現在要聯絡律師嗎？
A 先等等。Let me think about some ways to make this work.

2 練習 讓我考慮一下今天會議中提出的幾個點子。(ideas, from)
Let me think about ______________________.

Pattern 070

I must have + p.p. ...
看來是我（過去做過的事）…

這個句型用來表達「看來是我…了」，是非常重要的商務英語句型。當你誤會對方說的話或犯下失誤時，可以用這個句型來轉換對話的氛圍。

- **I must have misunderstood what you said.**
  看來是我誤會了你說過的話。
- **I must have lost the document.**
  看來是我弄丟了那份文件。 ＊document 文件
- **I must have left the papers in my office.**
  看來是我把資料留在我的辦公室了。
- **I must have forgotten to insert that word in the contract.**
  看來是我忘記把那個字寫進合約裡了。 ＊insert 插入，添加

1 對話
A I'm not happy with the terms of this contract.
B But we gave you 30% ownership of the business.
A I asked for 30% of the profits.
B 看來是我誤會了你說過的話。

A 我不滿意這份合約的條件。
B 但是我們已經給貴公司 30% 的企業所有權了。
A 我們當初要求的是收益的 30%。
B I must have misunderstood what you said.

2 練習 看來是我誤會了合約書中那部分的內容。(part, agreement)
I must have misunderstood ____________________.

3-5 表示反對

Does anyone object to...?	071	有任何人反對…嗎？
I'm sorry to interrupt, but...	072	很抱歉打斷您，但是…
I feel sorry to say this, but...	073	很抱歉這麼說，但是…
I don't think we can...	074	我認為我們無法…
I'm against that because...	075	我反對，因為…

Pattern 071

Does anyone object to...?
有任何人反對…嗎？

當你想要確認是否有人反對自己或其他人提出的意見時，就可以使用這個句型。本句型中的 object 後面常常接 to，表示「對…反對」的意思。

- **Does anyone object to my plan?**
  有任何人反對我的方案嗎？
- **Does anyone object to the merger?**
  有任何人反對合併嗎？
- **Does anyone object to starting early?**
  有任何人反對早點上班嗎？
- **Does anyone object to changing the proposal?**
  有任何人反對更改提案嗎？

1 對話 **A** Tomorrow is going to be busy.
B True. 有任何人反對早點上班嗎？
A No. That's a good idea.

A 明天將會是非常忙碌的一天。
B 沒錯。Does anyone object to starting early?
A 沒有。那是個好主意。

2 練習 有任何人反對我的建議嗎？(suggestion)
Does anyone object to ____________________?

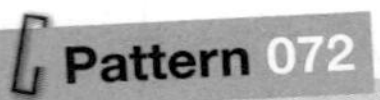

I'm sorry to interrupt, but...
很抱歉打斷您，但是…

在會議或協商過程中，當對方在發表意見時，如果你想在中途打斷並提出自己的意見，就可以使用這個句型，也可以簡單地說 Sorry to interrupt, but...。

- **I'm sorry to interrupt, but could I say something?**
  很抱歉打斷您，但是我可以說句話嗎？
- **I'm sorry to interrupt, but I don't think I agree with what you're saying.**
  很抱歉打斷您，但是我想我不同意你所說的。
- **I'm sorry to interrupt, but I'm not sure I understand why we're discussing this.**
  很抱歉打斷您，但是我不確定我理解我們討論這件事的理由。
- **I'm sorry to interrupt, but could you clarify the final deadline?**
  很抱歉打斷您，但是您可以把最後期限說清楚嗎？ ＊**clarify** 說清楚，闡明

1 對話
A So, are we all in agreement on the product design?
B 很抱歉打斷您，但是我可以說句話嗎？
A Yes, please do, Matthew.

A 那麼，大家全都同意這個產品設計吧？
B I'm sorry to interrupt, but could I say something?
A 馬修，請說。

2 練習 很抱歉打斷您，但是我可以問一個問題嗎？(could, ask)
I'm sorry to interrupt, but ________________________?

Pattern 073

I feel sorry to say this, but...
很抱歉這麼說，但是…

在協商過程中，常常會遇到需要拒絕對方要求的情況，當你想禮貌地拒絕對方時，就可以使用這個句型。類似的句型有 We regert to say we have to... 或 We regret to inform you we can't... 等。

- **I feel sorry to say this, but we can't accept these terms.**
  很抱歉這麼說，但是我們無法接受這個條件。 ＊terms 條件
- **I feel sorry to say this, but we can't accept your offer at this time.**
  很抱歉這麼說，但是這次我們無法接受你們的開價。
- **I feel sorry to say this, but I don't think we can reach an agreement.**
  很抱歉這麼說，但是我認為我們無法達成協議。
- **I feel sorry to say this, but your idea doesn't fit with our plan.**
  很抱歉這麼說，但是你的想法不適合我們的計畫。

1 對話
A 很抱歉這麼說，但是我認為我們無法達成協議。
B I wish you could be more flexible.
A Perhaps we can work together in the future.

A I feel sorry to say this, but I don't think we can reach an agreement.
B 希望你們能再通融一點。
A 也許以後還有合作的機會。

2 練習 很抱歉這麼說，但是我覺得這並不可行。(work out)
I feel sorry to say this, but ______________.

Pattern 074

I don't think we can...
我認為我們無法…

當你無法接受對方的要求，想委婉拒絕對方時，就可以使用這個句型。一般來說，這個句型比 I think we can't... 還常用。

- **I don't think we can sign the contract.**
  我認為我們無法簽訂這份合約。
- **I don't think we can go much higher than this.**
  我認為我們無法出比這更高的價碼了。
- **I don't think we can go any higher than 5 dollars.**
  我認為我們無法出比五美元更高的價碼了。
- **I don't think we can provide more than that kind of service.**
  我認為我們無法提供更多這類的服務了。

1 對話

A What does this paragraph mean?
B It means you agree to take no more than 30% of the profits.
A 我認為我們無法簽訂這份合約。

A 這段內容是什麼意思？
B 這表示貴公司同意不會收取超過 30%的利潤。
A I don't think we can sign the contract.

2 練習 我想我們對這件事愛莫能助。(help somebody with)
I don't think we can ______________________.

Pattern 075

I'm against that because...
我反對，因為⋯

當你不贊成某件提案，並且要說明反對的理由時，就可以使用這個句型。類似的句型有 I can't agree with... / I'm opposed to... / I'd have to disagree with... 等。也可以簡單地直接說 I see things differently 或 I beg to differ。

- **I'm against that because it exposes us to too much risk.**
  我反對，因為這讓我們承擔太高的風險了。 ＊expose 暴露於，接觸到
- **I'm against that because it clearly won't bring in much profit.**
  我反對，因為很明顯地，這麼做獲得的利潤並不多。
- **I can't agree with your proposal of giving a 20% raise.**
  我無法同意你加薪 20% 的提議。 ＊raise 加薪
- **I'm opposed to expanding our business too quickly.**
  我反對太快擴展我們的企業。

1 對話
A Are you suggesting there's a market in Iraq?
B I think we can sell a lot of games in Baghdad.
A 我反對，因為很明顯地，這麼做獲得的利潤並不多。

A 你現在是提議要在伊拉克開發市場嗎？
B 我認為我們可以在巴格達銷售大量的遊戲。
A I'm against that because it clearly won't bring in much profit.

2 練習 我反對，因為這並不實際。(practical)
I'm against that because ______________________.

3-1~3-5

黃金複習 15 分鐘！

前面這 25 個句型和 125 個句子全都記熟了嗎？
來驗收一下學習成果吧！如果不能充滿自信地用英文說出以下 40 個句子，請翻到前面再重新複習一次！

01 謝謝您在這麼緊急的時間內與我們見面。

____

02 我無法同意你加薪 20% 的提議。

____

03 我們把這次會議當作對我們雙方的絕佳機會。

____

04 我想我們無法出比五美元更高的價碼了。

____

05 在我們開始之前，我們先複習一下上週的進度如何？

____

06 很抱歉這麼說，但是我認為我們無法達成協議。

____

07 我們從簡介這個產品開始吧！

____

08 很抱歉打斷您，但是我可以說句話嗎？

____

解答 01. Thank you for meeting us on such short notice.
02. I can't agree with your proposal of giving a 20% raise.
03. We see this meeting as an excellent opportunity for both parties.
04. I don't think we can go any higher than 5 dollars.
05. Before we begin, shall we review the progress we made last week?
06. I feel sorry to say this, but I don't think we can reach an agreement.
07. Let's start with a short presentation on the product.
08. I'm sorry to interrupt, but could I say something?

09 在上次的會議中，我們的出席率不佳。

10 有任何人反對早點上班嗎？

11 我們今天來到這裡只是為了一個原因。

12 看來是我把資料留在我的辦公室了。

13 這次會議的目的是為了削減預算。

14 我支持那項商業提案。

15 我在一定程度上同意，但是讓我先跟我的老闆確認一下。

16 那真是個有效率的說明。

17 讓我考慮一下一些潛在的問題。

18 我們預計這筆交易會產生巨大的利潤。

解答 09. At our last meeting, we had poor attendance.
10. Does anyone object to starting early? 11. We're here today for one reason only.
12. I must have left the papers in my office.
13. The purpose of this meeting is to make budget cuts.
14. I support that business proposition.
15. I can partly agree to that, but first let me check with my boss.
16. That's an efficient explanation. 17. Let me think about some potential problems.
18. We're expecting a huge profit margin from this deal.

19 我將為您簡述我們與執行長之間的會談。

20 我們真正需要的是更多的時間。

21 我會向您更新我與客戶之間的進展。

22 我們何不先做一些調查？

23 請容我花大約十分鐘的時間，來回顧一下我們目前為止達成了哪些協議。

24 我建議我們把所有的問題留到最後。

25 讓我來告訴大家我們行銷總監的一些意見。

26 那真是個很棒的點子。

27 謝謝你們在百忙之中為我們抽出時間來。

28 我反對，因為這讓我們承擔太高的風險了。

29 我們把這次會議當作第一步。

解答 19. I'll brief you on our conversation with my CEO.
20. What we really need is more time. 21. I'll update you on the progress with my client.
22. Why don't we do a little research first?
23. Allow me to take about 10 minutes to review what we've agreed on so far.
24. I suggest that we leave all questions for the end.
25. Let me give you some advice from our marketing director. 26. That's a great idea.
27. Thank you for taking the time to see us.
28. I'm against that because it exposes us to too much risk.
29. We see this meeting as a first step.

30 我認為我們無法簽訂這份合約。

31 在我們開始之前，我們先確認一下資料如何？

32 讓我來告訴大家我對這件事情的看法。

33 我們從時程表的概要開始吧！

34 很抱歉打斷您，但是我想我不同意你所說的。

35 我在一定程度上同意，但是我有一個條件。

36 有任何人反對我的方案嗎？

37 我們今天來到這裡是為了討論合併事宜。

38 看來是我誤會了你說過的話。

39 這次會議的目的是為了分享我們目前的進度。

40 讓我考慮一下解決這件事的辦法。

解答 30. I don't think we can sign the contract.
31. Before we begin, shall we go over the paperwork?
32. Let me give you my perspective on this. 33. Let's start with a rundown of the schedule.
34. I'm sorry to interrupt, but I don't think I agree with what you're saying.
35. I can partly agree to that, but with one condition. 36. Does anyone object to my plan?
37. We're here today to discuss the merger. 38. I must have misunderstood what you said.
39. The purpose of this meeting is to share our progress.
40. Let me think about some ways to make this work.

Unit 4
線上會議
進行會議更順利

4-1

提供或收到開會連結

Pattern 076

Here is the...
這個是…

一般來說開線上會議時，主辦人需要提供參加會議的人線上連結，才可以讓大家都進入會議，這時可以用 Here is the... 這個句型通知其他與會人。若是用 Google meet 或 Zoom 等應用程式進行會議，要分享連結時可以說 Here is the Google Meet link. 或 Here is the Zoom link. 來表達。

- **Here is the Teams meeting link.**
  這個是 Teams 的會議連結。 ＊Teams 是微軟的線上會議應用程式
- **Here is the information for joining the meeting.**
  這個是加入會議的資訊。
- **Here is the meeting call-in information.**
  這個是會議的通話資訊。
- **Here is the video conference ID.**
  這個是視訊會議的識別碼。 ＊ID = identification 識別

1 對話 A 這是 Google Meet 的連結。
B Do you have a call-in number?
A I'll forward that to you.

A Here is the Google Meet link.
B 你有通話代碼嗎？
A 我會轉寄給你。

2 練習 這個是會議的登入資訊。 (details)
Here is the ______________________.

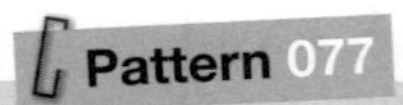

Did you send...?
你有傳送…嗎？

此句型用在詢問參與線上會議的人，通常是主辦人，有沒有傳送線上會議的連結，這時可以用 Did you send the meeting link? 來詢問對方。如果你要特定問某個應用程式的線上連結，可以用這個句子 Did you send the Teams invite to everyone? 來詢問連結網址。

- **Did you send the Google Meet invite to me?**
  你有傳送 Google Meet 邀請給我嗎？
- **Did you send the conference link in a separate email?**
  你有在個別的電子郵件傳送會議連結嗎？ ＊separate 個別的
- **Did you send him the email with the meeting invitation?**
  你有傳送會議邀請的電子郵件給他嗎？
- **Did you send the passcode for the meeting?**
  你有傳送會議的密碼嗎？ ＊passcode（電子設備使用的）密碼

1 對話

A 你有傳送 Google Meet 邀請給我嗎？
B I sent it yesterday.
A I didn't get it. Can you send it again?

A Did you send the Google Meet invite to me?
B 我昨天有傳送。
A 我沒收到，你可以再傳一次嗎？

2 練習 你有傳送會議邀請給萊恩嗎？
Did you send ____________________?

Pattern 078

Use this call-in number for ...
用這個通話代碼來參加…

除了用前面介紹的句型，也可以用此句型 Use this call-in number for… 來邀請同事或客戶參加會議，後面可以加上會議應用程式的名稱和時間等，像是 Use this call-in number for the morning Teams meeting. 如果後面要加上動詞，也可以將介系詞 for 改成不定詞 to，並在後面加上原形動詞。

- **Use this call-in number for our meeting.**
  用這個通話代碼來參加我們的會議。
- **Use this call-in number for the conference call.**
  用這個通話代碼來參加會議通話。
- **Use this call-in number for the video meeting this afternoon.**
  用這個通話代碼參加今天下午的視訊會議。
- **Use this call-in number for your virtual interview.**
  用這個通話代碼參加你的視訊面試。 ＊virtual interview 視訊面試

1 對話 **A** The microphone on my laptop isn't functioning with this platform.
B 用這個通話代碼來參加我們的會議。
A I will. Thanks!

A 這個平台的麥克風在我的筆記型電腦上無法正常運作。
B Use this call-in number for our meeting.
A 我會的，感謝！

2 練習 用這個通話代碼進入線上會議。(access)
Use this call-in number to ______________________.

Pattern 079

I'll forward you ...
我會轉寄給你…

當你要用電子郵件或聊天訊息傳送會議連結時，就可以用這個句型來告知同事或客戶，讓他們知道你有傳送給他們會議相關的資訊，例如 meeting passcode 這種重要訊息，讓大家能夠順利上線參加會議。

- **I'll forward you the online conference information.**
  我會轉寄給你線上會議的資訊。
- **I'll forward you the meeting recording.**
  我會轉寄給你會議紀錄。
- **I'll forward you the agenda for the virtual meeting.**
  我會轉寄給你視訊會議的議程。 ＊agenda 議程
- **I'll forward you the meeting's login details.**
  我會轉寄給你會議的登入詳細資訊。

1 對話 A Tomorrow's meeting is virtual.
B I didn't get the meeting information.
A 我會轉寄給你邀請。

A 明天的會議是視訊進行。
B 我沒有收到會議資訊。
A I'll forward you the invitation.

2 練習 我會轉寄給你會議的所有文件。 (documents)
I'll forward you ______________________.

Pattern 080

Please find the meeting ...
請查看會議的…

此句型是要提醒同事和客戶在哪裡可以找到會議相關的資訊，如果你是用電子郵件通知對方會議資訊在附件中，可以說 Please find the meeting information attached.，用這個句型告訴對方要在哪裡得到資訊。除了用在線上會議，也可以用在一般的電子郵件中。

- **Please find the meeting ID in my previous email.**
  請在我前一封信查看會議的識別碼。 ＊previous 先前的
- **Please find the meeting passcode below.**
  請在下面查看會議的密碼。
- **Please find the meeting agenda and invitation attached.**
  請在附檔查看會議的議程和邀請。 ＊attach 附上
- **Please find the meeting notes in the chat box.**
  請在聊天室查看會議的筆記。

1 對話

A 請在附件查看會議的議程和邀請。
B Can I add an item to the agenda?
A Yes, what do you need to add?

A Please find the meeting agenda and invitation attached.
B 我可以加一個事項到議程裡嗎？
A 可以的，你需要加什麼事項呢？

2 練習 請在群組電子郵件查看會議邀請。 (group email)
Please find the meeting ______________________.

4-2

麥克風、視訊問題

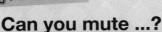

Pattern 081

Can you mute ...?
你可以靜音…嗎？

會議進行時，一定會發生麥克風有雜音的事情，使得討論受到干擾。這時就可以用這個句型使發出噪音的人靜音，可以說 Can you mute your microphone?。另外如果是要讓某人可以順利發言，也可以跟主持人說 Can you mute everyone for a few minutes?。

- **Can you mute the group?**
  你可以靜音群組嗎？
- **Can you mute yourself?**
  你可以靜音你自己嗎？
- **Can you mute whoever keeps talking?**
  你可以靜音一直說話的人嗎？
- **Can you mute everyone?**
  你可以靜音所有人嗎？

1 對話

A Can you mute your microphone, John?
B 好的，現在靜音了。
A 謝謝你。

A 你可以靜音你的麥克風嗎，約翰？
B Yes, muting it now.
A Thank you.

2 練習 你在簡報的時候可以靜音自己嗎？(presentation)
Can you mute ______________________________?

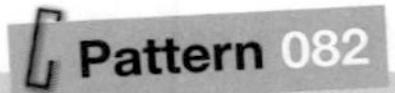

I'm here! I was on ...
我在這裡！我剛剛在⋯

此句型可以用在自己在會議中被其他呼喚的時候，當你在靜音或是剛上線的時候被點名，就可以說 I'm here! I was on mute. 或是 I'm here! I was on another meeting. 等，來告知會議的人自己已經上線或打開麥克風了。

- **I'm here! I was on silent.**
  我在這裡！我剛剛靜音了。
- **I'm here! I was on a call.**
  我在這裡！我剛剛在電話中。
- **I'm here! I was a little late.**
  我在這裡！我來得有點晚。
- **I'm here! I was on a different meeting.**
  我在這裡！我剛剛在不同的會議。

1 對話 **A** I don't think Deb is here.
B 我在這裡！我剛剛靜音了。
A I'm glad you could make it.

A 我不覺得黛柏在這裡。
B I'm here! I was on mute.
A 我很高興你有來。

2 練習 我在這裡！我剛剛靜音但沒有注意到。 (realize)
I'm here! I was on ______________________________.

Pattern 083

083

Your camera keeps ...
你的鏡頭一直…

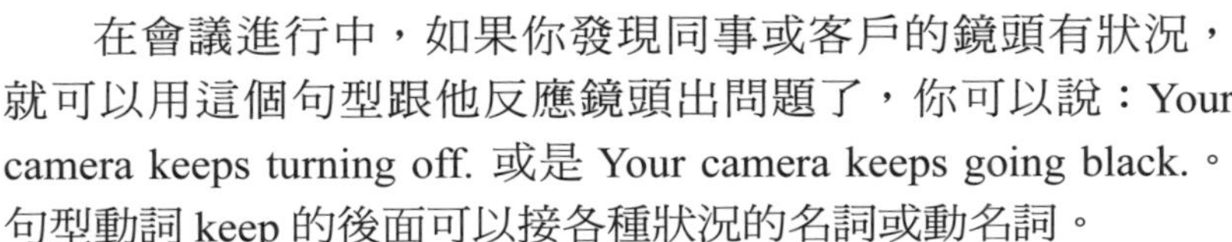

在會議進行中，如果你發現同事或客戶的鏡頭有狀況，就可以用這個句型跟他反應鏡頭出問題了，你可以說：Your camera keeps turning off. 或是 Your camera keeps going black.。句型動詞 keep 的後面可以接各種狀況的名詞或動名詞。

- **Your camera keeps freezing.**
  你的鏡頭一直停頓。
- **Your camera keeps glitching.**
  你的鏡頭一直故障。 ＊glitch 失靈，故障
- **Your camera keeps lagging.**
  你的鏡頭一直延遲。 ＊lag 延遲
- **Your camera keeps blurring your face.**
  你的鏡頭一直讓你的臉模糊。 ＊blur 模糊

1 對話
A Are you there, Bob?
B I'm here. Can you hear me?
A 你的鏡頭一直停頓。

A 鮑伯你在嗎？
B 我在，你聽得到我說話嗎？
A Your camera keeps freezing.

2 練習 你的鏡頭一直關閉。(shut down)
Your camera keeps ______________________.

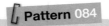

Pattern 084

Is anyone else ...?
有任何人…嗎？

進行線上會議時，想要詢問同事或客戶收聽或收訊狀況如何，就可以用這個句型。關於收聽的問題可以說 Is anyone else having trouble hearing?，而關於電腦的問題也可以說 Is anyone else having computer issues?，用這個句型跟大家確認是否有順利參與線上會議。

- Is anyone else **struggling to hear?**
  有任何人**很難聽清楚**嗎？
- Is anyone else **noticing the problem?**
  有任何人**注意到這個問題**嗎？
- Is anyone else **struggling with the link?**
  有任何人**對連結有困難**嗎？
- Is anyone else **having trouble calling in?**
  有任何人**通話有困難**嗎？

1 對話 **A** 有任何人很難聽清楚嗎？
B The call keeps breaking up.
A Let's try logging out and rejoining the meeting.

A Is anyone else having trouble hearing?
B 通話一直斷斷續續的。
A 我們試試看登出再重新加入會議。

2 練習 有任何人聽到噪音嗎？ (noise)
Is anyone else ______________________________?

Pattern 085

Everyone needs to ...
每個人必須…

如果要跟參加會議的同事指示一些事項，就可以用此句型來提醒，例如：Everyone needs to use the call-in number. 通知大家要開會了，請用這組代碼進入通話，或是 Everyone needs to look at the shared screen. 來提醒大家要看這個分享螢幕。

- **Everyone needs to mute their microphone.**
  每個人必須靜音麥克風。
- **Everyone needs to turn their camera on.**
  每個人必須打開鏡頭。
- **Everyone needs to watch this presentation.**
  每個人必須看這個簡報。
- **Everyone needs to accept the invitation.**
  每個人必須接受這個邀請。

1 對話
A I can't hear the presenter.
B There's a lot of background noise.
A 大家必須把自己靜音。

A 我聽不到簡報者的聲音。
B 有很多背景噪音。
A Everyone needs to mute themselves.

2 練習 每個人必須點擊加入連結。 (join link)
Everyone needs to ______________________.

4-3

分享自己的螢幕

Pattern 086

Can you see ...?
你可以看到⋯嗎

當你正在分享自己的畫面，要跟大家說明文件的內容時，可以用這個句型來確認大家有沒有看到。在動詞 see 的後面接你想要強調的事情，例如可以說 Can you see my shared screen? 或是 Can you see the link?，並用滑鼠指示你正在講述的內容，可以讓大家更知道你要說明的重點。

- **Can you see my screen?**
  你可以看到我的螢幕嗎？
- **Can you see what I clicked?**
  你可以看到我點擊的東西嗎？
- **Can you see how I did that?**
  你可以看到我是怎麼做的嗎？
- **Can you see the chat box?**
  你可以看到這個聊天室嗎？

1 對話
A 你可以看到我的共享螢幕嗎？
B Yes, I can see it.
A Let me show you what I was talking about.

A Can you see my screen?
B 是的，我看得到。
A 讓我展示給你看我講的內容。

2 練習 你可以看到我在做什麼嗎？
Can you see ________________________?

Pattern 087

Could you share ...?
你可以分享…嗎？

想要看同事或客戶所提到的內容，可以用此句型詢問可不可以分享他的畫面，例如：Could you share your PowerPoint / Keynote? 來請同事分享他的簡報內容，或是 Could you share the website with everyone? 來請客戶分享他提到的網站內容。利用這個問句讓會議更有效地進行下去。

- **Could you share your screen?**
  你可以分享你的螢幕畫面嗎？
- **Could you share the documents with the group?**
  你可以分享跟組員們這個文件嗎？
- **Could you share that information with me?**
  你可以跟我分享那則資訊嗎？
- **Could you share this with everyone else?**
  你可以跟大家分享這個內容嗎？

1 對話
A The website they designed is really amazing.
B 你可以跟大家分享網頁的陳列嗎？
A I'll share my screen with you.

A 他們設計的這個網站真的很漂亮。
B Could you share the website layout with everyone?
A 我會分享螢幕畫面給你們看。

2 練習 你可以分享你是如何建立這個會議的嗎？
Could you share ____________________?

Pattern 088

088

I'll share ...
我會分享…

同事或客戶跟你說不太清楚你在報告的內容時，你可以說 I'll share my screen. 來分享你在電腦上操作的畫面，演示要如何操作產品、或是講解你在進行的計畫。或者有人問你該怎麼進入線上會議的時候，你也可以說 I'll share the Zoom invitation. 告知他要如何加入會議。

- **I'll share my screen and show you how I did it.**
  我會分享我的螢幕畫面，並展示給你看我是如何做到的。
- **I'll share the login information.**
  我會分享登入資訊。
- **I'll share my screen, so you can see what I'm doing.**
  我會分享我的螢幕畫面，所以你可以看到我正在做什麼。
- **I'll share the meeting details with you.**
  我會分享會議細節給你。

1 對話

A What are you talking about? I didn't catch it.
B 我會分享我的螢幕畫面，並展示給你看我在做什麼。
A That would be great!

A 你在說什麼？我沒聽清楚。
B I'll share my screen, and show you what I'm doing.
A 那太好了。

2 練習 我會在我們的 Teams 會議期間分享那個簡報。 (Keynote)

I'll share ______________________________.

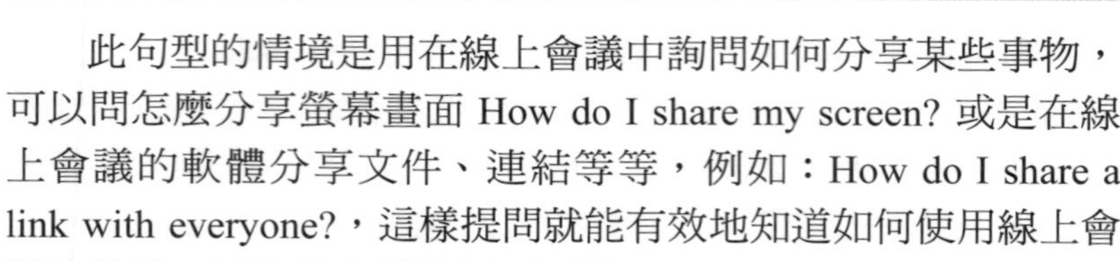

How do I share ...?
我要如何分享⋯？

此句型的情境是用在線上會議中詢問如何分享某些事物，可以問怎麼分享螢幕畫面 How do I share my screen? 或是在線上會議的軟體分享文件、連結等等，例如：How do I share a link with everyone?，這樣提問就能有效地知道如何使用線上會議的軟體，讓你的會議進行更順利。

- **How do I share my screen in Google Meet?**
  我要如何在 Google Meet 分享我的螢幕畫面？
- **How do I share documents during a meeting?**
  我要如何在會議期間分享文件？
- **How do I share the link in the meeting?**
  我要如何在會議中分享連結？
- **How do I share a Zoom invitation with someone?**
  我要如何分享 Zoom 邀請給其他人？

1 對話

A 我要如何在 Google Meet 分享連結？
B Just copy the link into the chat box in Google Meet.
A That makes sense.

A How do I share the link in Google Meet?
B 只要複製連結到 Google Meet 的聊天室就可以了。
A 說得有道理。

2 練習

我要如何在會議中分享我的問題？
How do I share ______________________________?

Pattern 090

Can you see what I'm ...?
你可以看到我在…嗎？

此句型用在跟開會的人確認有沒有看到你所分享的畫面，可以說 Can you see what I'm trying to do? 或 Can you see what I'm talking about?，對方有跟上就會回 yes，若沒跟上就會回 no，可以讓你隨時掌握大家是否有專心聽你說話。

- **Can you see what I'm doing on my screen?**
  你可以看到我在我的螢幕上做什麼嗎？
- **Can you see what I'm clicking?**
  你可以看到我在點擊什麼嗎？
- **Can you see what I'm working on?**
  你可以看到我在做什麼嗎？
- **Can you see what I'm struggling with?**
  你可以看到我在面臨的困難嗎？

1 對話 **A** 你可以看到我在我的螢幕上做什麼嗎？
B No, I can't see anything.
A Let me try again.

A Can you see what I'm doing on my screen?
B 沒有，我沒看到任何東西。
A 讓我再試一次。

2 練習 你可以看到我要求你做的東西嗎？(ask)
Can you see what I'm ______________________________?

4-4 討論會議事項

Let's try to stick to...	091	讓我們試著按照…進行
This item wasn't...	092	這個項目不…
Can I add a point to...	093	我可以新增一點…嗎？
I think we should stay...	094	我認為我們應該維持…
We are getting off...	095	我們脫離…

Pattern 091

Let's try to stick to ...
讓我們試著按照…進行

此句型是要跟參加線上會議的人告知，要按照之前訂定的計畫、想法或是解決問題等來進行會議。如果你想跟對方說按照之前的想法進行，可以說 Let's try to stick to this idea.，使對方不要偏離你們所預定的主題或計畫。

- **Let's try to stick to our agenda.**
  讓我們試著按照議程進行。
- **Let's try to stick to the topic.**
  讓我們試著按照主題進行。
- **Let's try to stick to the plan.**
  讓我們試著按照方案進行。
- **Let's try to stick to the project.**
  讓我們試著按照企畫進行。

1 對話 **A** I have a question about the upcoming project.
B 讓我們試著按照議程進行會議。
A I'll save my question for later.

A 我有個針對即將進行的企畫的問題。
B Let's try to stick to our agenda.
A 我會把問題留到後面。

2 練習 讓我們試著按照時程表進行。(schedule)
Let's try to stick to ______________________.

Pattern 092

This item wasn't ...
這個項目不…

此句型可以用在強調某個項目不是重點的時候使用，例如有人提了不是今日會議的事項，就可以跟他說 This item wasn't on the table for discussion.，來表達現在並不方便說這個項目。

- **This item wasn't on the agenda.**
  這個項目不在議程上。
- **This item wasn't important.**
  這個項目不重要。
- **This item wasn't necessary to discuss.**
  這個項目沒有必要討論。
- **This item wasn't on the docket.**
  這個項目不在議事日程上。

* docket 議事日程

1 對話
A Here's the final report for review.
B 這個項目不是議程的項目。
A Can we add it to the agenda?

A 這個是要審查的最終報告。
B This item wasn't an agenda item.
A 你可以把它加到議程嗎？

2 練習 這個項目沒有排在今天的會議中。 (in the lineup of ~)
This item wasn't ______________________.

093

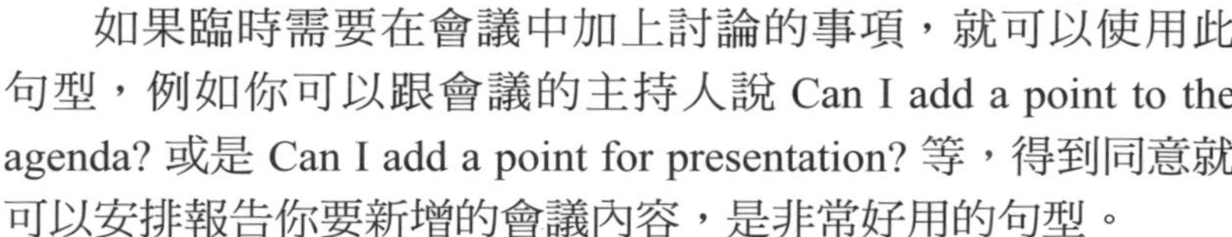

Can I add a point ...?
我可以新增一點來…嗎？

如果臨時需要在會議中加上討論的事項，就可以使用此句型，例如你可以跟會議的主持人說 Can I add a point to the agenda? 或是 Can I add a point for presentation? 等，得到同意就可以安排報告你要新增的會議內容，是非常好用的句型。

- **Can I add a point for discussion?**
  我可以新增一點來討論嗎？
- **Can I add a point to today's agenda?**
  我可以新增一點到今天的議程嗎？
- **Can I add a point to talk through?**
  我可以新增一點來詳細討論嗎？ ＊talk through （做決定前）討論所有細節
- **Can I add a point for clarification?**
  我可以新增一點來說明嗎？ ＊clarification 闡明，說明

1 對話
A 我可以新增一點來討論嗎？
B Sure, what needs to be added?
A It's about the Smith case.

A Can I add a point for discussion?
B 沒問題，有什麼需要新增的嗎？
A 是關於史密斯的案子。

2 練習 我可以新增需要被討論的一點嗎？
Can I add a point ______________________?

Pattern 094

I think we should stay...
我認為我們應該維持…

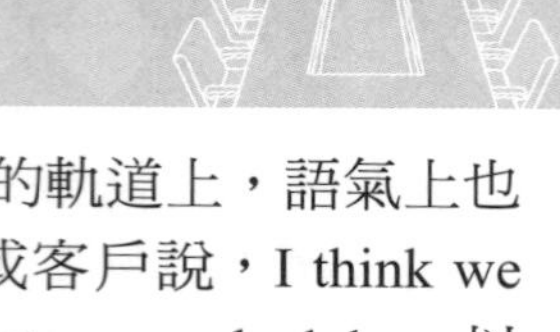

094 維持會議的流程

此句型是用在維持會議的進展在預期的軌道上，語氣上也比較委婉，例如和其他參加會議的同事或客戶說，I think we should stay on topic. 或是 I think we should stay on schedule.，以確保你主持的會議可以維持在預定的進程，而不會被其他事項拖延。

- **I think we should stay on track with the meeting.**
  我認為我們應該讓會議維持在正軌上。 ＊track 足跡
- **I think we should stay on course.**
  我認為我們應該維持在軌道上。 ＊on course 在規定的過程中
- **I think we should stay on target with the meeting.**
  我認為我們應該讓會議維持在進展上。 ＊on target 進展順利
- **I think we should stay on the line to discuss that after the meeting.**
  我認為我們應該維持順序，在會議後再討論那件事。

1 對話
A 我認為我們應該在會議中維持靜音。
B Why?
A I hear a lot of background noise.

A I think we should stay on mute during the meeting.
B 為什麼？
A 我聽到很多背景噪音。

2 練習 我認為我們應該維持在這個主題一分鐘。
I think we should stay ______________________.

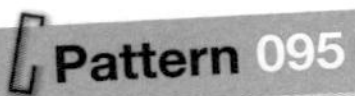

We're getting off...
我們偏離…

此句型用意是要提醒大家，現在的討論偏離會議的主題，要請大家回到會議的主題，你可以說 We're getting off track. 或 We're getting off topic.，如果進度落後，也可以在 getting off 的後面加上 schedule，以提醒開會的人現在要開始趕上進度，以免浪費時間了。

We're getting off track with this discussion.
我們的討論偏離軌道。

We're getting off on the wrong foot.
我們偏離正確的道路。（我們一開始就不順利。）

＊get off on the wrong foot 一開始就不順利

We're getting off the point of the conversation.
我們偏離對話的重點。

We're getting off to a bad start.
我們一開始就偏離正軌。（我們一開始就沒有好的開始。）

1 對話
A 我們偏離主題了。
B I have something I need to say.
A It will have to wait.

A We're getting off topic.
B 我有些需要說的事項。
A 那必須要等等了。

2 練習 我們一開始就順利。(a good start)
We're getting off ______________.

4-5

會議結尾用語

Does anyone have anything to...? 096 有人有任何事項要…嗎？

Are there any...? 097 有任何的…嗎？

Did we cover...? 098 我們有涵蓋到…嗎？

Thank you for...! 099 感謝您…！

Is there anything else we ...? 100 還有任何事項要我們…嗎？

Pattern 096

Does anyone have anything to...?
有人有任何事項要…嗎？

此句型可以當作會議最後的用語，來確認是否有其他項目沒有討論到。當你想要結束會議的時候，可以說 Does anyone have anything to discuss? 或 Does anyone have anything to add?，如果組員都沒有任何事項要補充，接著就可以說 Then, that's it for today.（那麼今天就到這邊。）會議也因而結束。

- **Does anyone have anything to expand on?**
  有人有任何事項要詳談嗎？ ＊expand on 詳談
- **Does anyone have anything to present?**
  有人有任何事項要呈現嗎？
- **Does anyone have anything to share with the group?**
  有人有任何事項要跟團隊分享嗎？
- **Does anyone have anything to add to the conversation?**
  有人有任何事項要新增到對話中嗎？

1 對話
A 有人有任何事項要補充的嗎？
B No, I think you covered it.
A Thanks for joining the meeting.

A Does anyone have anything to add?
B 沒有，我想你都講完了。
A 感謝大家參與這次的會議。

2 練習 有人有任何事項要提出的嗎？(bring up)
Does anyone have anything ____________________?

Pattern 097

Are there any...?
有任何的…嗎？

此句型也是跟大家確認有沒有事項要補充，可以說 Are there any questions? 或 Are there any ideas?，除了用在會議的結尾，也可以用在會議途中，討論事項的時候詢問是否有人有其他想法，藉此為自己要討論的專案提供更多想法，是很好用的句型。

- **Are there any concerns?**
  有任何重要的事嗎？
- **Are there any issues?**
  有任何的議題嗎？
- **Are there any other options?**
  有任何其他的選擇嗎？
- **Are there any other opinions?**
  有任何其他的意見嗎？

1 對話
A 有任何的問題嗎？
B I have a question.
A Go ahead.

A Are there any questions?
B 我有個問題。
A 請說。

2 練習
有任何關於簡報的問題嗎？ (presentation)
Are there any ______________________________?

098

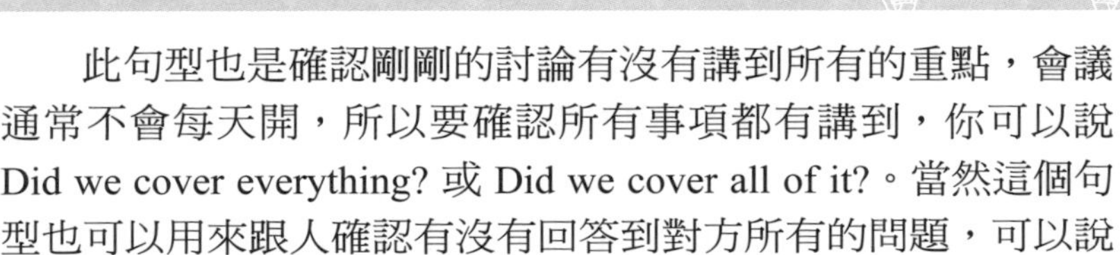

Pattern 098 Did we cover...? 我們有涵蓋到…嗎？

此句型也是確認剛剛的討論有沒有講到所有的重點，會議通常不會每天開，所以要確認所有事項都有講到，你可以說 Did we cover everything? 或 Did we cover all of it?。當然這個句型也可以用來跟人確認有沒有回答到對方所有的問題，可以說 Did we cover your questions?，讓對方回答他還有沒有疑問。

- **Did we cover all the points?**
  我們有涵蓋到所有的重點嗎？
- **Did we cover your concerns?**
  我們有涵蓋到你關心的事嗎？
- **Did we cover the major points?**
  我們有涵蓋到主要的論點嗎？
- **Did we cover that during the meeting?**
  我們在會議期間有涵蓋到那個事項嗎？

1 對話

A 我們有涵蓋到每個事項嗎？
B You missed an important point.
A What did I forget?

A Did we cover everything?
B 你漏掉一個重要的論點。
A 我忘記了什麼？

2 練習

我們有涵蓋你的想法嗎？
Did we cover ______________________________?

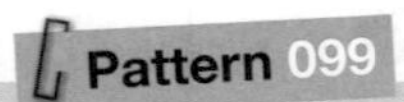

Thank you for...!
感謝您…！

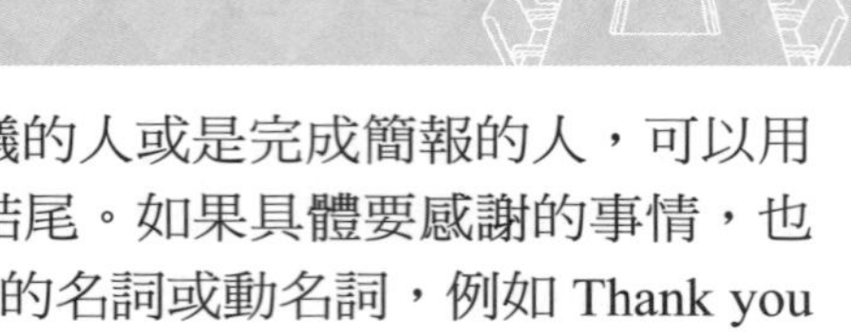

此句型用在感謝參加會議的人或是完成簡報的人，可以用在會議中途的小結或是會議結尾。如果具體要感謝的事情，也可以在 for 後面加上相關事項的名詞或動名詞，例如 Thank you for your help! 或是 Thank you for explaining it again!，來感謝報告的人所做的幫助或解釋說明。

- **Thank you for your time!**
  感謝您的時間！
- **Thank you for the call!**
  感謝您的來電！
- **Thank you for your presentation!**
  感謝您的簡報！
- **Thank you for organizing the meeting!**
  感謝您安排這次的會議！

1 對話
A 感謝您的時間！
B No problem. I enjoyed talking with you.
A Have a nice afternoon!

A Thank you for your time!
B 沒問題，我很享受跟你談話。
A 有個愉快的下午！

2 練習 感謝您安排這次的會議！ (set up)
Thank you for ______________________________!

Pattern 100

Is there anything else we ...?
還有任何事項要我們…嗎？

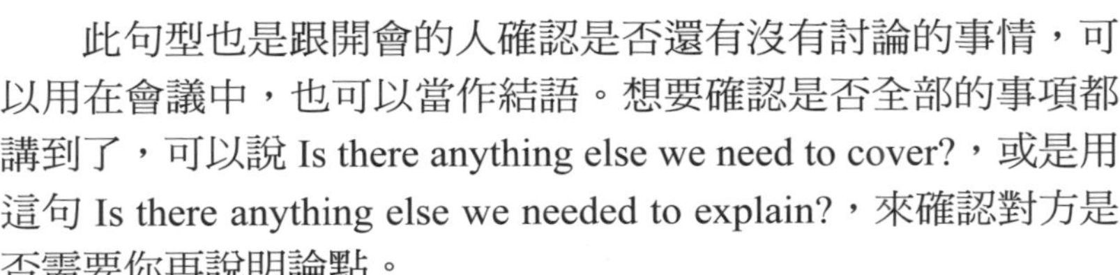

此句型也是跟開會的人確認是否還有沒有討論的事情，可以用在會議中，也可以當作結語。想要確認是否全部的事項都講到了，可以說 Is there anything else we need to cover?，或是用這句 Is there anything else we needed to explain?，來確認對方是否需要你再說明論點。

- **Is there anything else we need to discuss?**
  還有任何事項需要我們討論嗎？
- **Is there anything else we should talk over?**
  還有任何事項要我們討論嗎？ ＊talk over 討論
- **Is there anything else we need to go over today?**
  還有任何事項需要我們今天仔細檢查嗎？ ＊go over 仔細檢查
- **Is there anything else we should talk through?**
  還有任何事項是我們應該討論的嗎？

1 對話
A 還有任何事項需要我們討論嗎？
B I think you covered everything.
A Then we can wrap this up.

A Is there anything else we need to discuss?
B 我想你涵蓋了所有事項。
A 那麼我們可以結束會議了。

2 練習 還有任何事項必須要我們想出來的嗎？ (figure out)
Is there anything else we ______________________?

4-1~4-5

黃金複習 15 分鐘！

前面這 25 個句型和 125 個句子全都記熟了嗎？
來驗收一下學習成果吧！如果不能充滿自信地用英文說出以下 40 個句子，請翻到前面再重新複習一次！

01 請在聊天室查看會議的筆記。

02 我在這裡！我剛剛在不同的會議。

03 你的鏡頭一直停頓。

04 每個人必須靜音麥克風。

05 你可以看到我的螢幕嗎？

06 我要如何在 Google Meet 分享我的螢幕畫面？

07 讓我們試著按照議程進行。

08 這個項目不在議程上。

09 我會分享我的螢幕畫面，並展示給你看我是如何做的。

解答 01. Please find the meeting notes in the chat box.
02. I'm here! I was on a different meeting. 03. Your camera keeps freezing.
04. Everyone needs to mute their microphone. 05. Can you see my screen?
06. How do I share my screen in Google Meet? 07. Let's try to stick to our agenda.
08. This item wasn't on the agenda.
09. I'll share my screen and show you how I did it.

10 我認為我們應該讓會議維持在正軌上。

11 我們的討論偏離軌道。

12 有人有任何事項要詳談的嗎？

13 感謝您的時間！

14 還有任何事項要我們討論嗎？

15 這個是 Teams 的會議連結。

16 你有傳送會議的密碼嗎？

17 用這個通話代碼參加今天下午的視訊會議。

18 我會轉寄給你視訊會議的議程。

19 你可以靜音所有人嗎？

20 我在這裡！我剛剛靜音了。

解答 10. I think we should stay on track with the meeting.
11. We're getting off track with this discussion.
12. Does anyone have anything to expand on? 13. Thank you for your time!
14. Is there anything else we should talk over? 15. Here is the Teams meeting link.
16. Did you send the passcode for the meeting?
17. Use this call-in number for the video meeting this afternoon.
18. I'll forward you the agenda for the virtual meeting. 19. Can you mute everyone?
20. I'm here! I was on silent.

21 你的鏡頭一直故障。

22 我會分享會議的細節給你。

23 你可以看到我在我的螢幕上做什麼嗎？

24 我認為我們應該維持在軌道上。

25 你可以看到我在努力做什麼嗎？

26 我會轉寄給你線上會議的資訊。

27 你可以看到這個聊天室嗎？

28 你可以靜音一直說話的人嗎？

29 你可以分享你的螢幕畫面嗎？

30 讓我們試著按照企畫進行。

解答 21. Your camera keeps glitching. 22. I'll share the meeting details with you. 23. Can you see what I'm doing on my screen? 24. I think we should stay on course. 25. Can you see what I'm struggling with? 26. I'll forward you the online conference information. 27. Can you see the chat box? 28. Can you mute whoever keeps talking? 29. Could you share your screen? 30. Let's try to stick to the project.

31 有人有任何事項要跟團隊分享的嗎？

32 我要如何在會議中分享文件？

33 還有任何事項需要我們今天仔細檢查嗎？

34 你的鏡頭一直延遲。

35 我會分享我的螢幕畫面，所以你可以看到我在做什麼。

36 我可以新增一點到今天的議程嗎？

37 這個項目不在議事日程上。

38 有任何重要的事嗎？

39 感謝您安排這次的會議！

40 還有任何事項需要我們討論嗎？

解答 31. Does anyone have anything to share with the group?
32. How do I share documents during a meeting?
33. Is there anything else we needed to go over today? 34. Your camera keeps lagging.
35. I'll share my screen, so you can see what I'm doing.
36. Can I add a point to today's agenda? 37. This item wasn't on the docket.
38. Are there any concerns? 39. Thank you for organizing the meeting!
40. Is there anything else we need to discuss?

Unit 5
發表會
緊緊抓住聽眾的
注意力！

5-1 開場白

My name is...and I'm responsible for...	101	我的名字是⋯，負責⋯
The topic of today's presentation is...	102	今天發表會的主題是關於⋯
Please interrupt me if...	103	如果⋯的話，請立刻提出來。
After my presentation, there will be time for...	104	發表會結束後，將會安排⋯的時間。
I'd like to begin with...	105	我想先從⋯開始。

Pattern 101

101

My name is...and I'm responsible for...
我的名字是…，負責…

發表會的開場白通常是在說完 Good morning / Good afternoon 等問候語後，就馬上接著自我介紹。自我介紹時只要介紹自己的名字、所屬部門或職務內容就行了。此外，這個句型中的 be responsible for 可以用 be in charge of 替代。

- **My name is Colleen and I'm responsible for human resources.**
  我的名字是蔻琳，負責人力資源。
- **My name is Patrick and I'm responsible for acquisitions.**
  我的名字是派翠克，負責企業收購。 ＊acquisition（企業）收購
- **My name is Mark and I'm responsible for the Overseas Marketing Department.**
  我的名字是馬克，負責海外行銷。
- **My name is Elliott and I'm in charge of product design.**
  我的名字是艾利特，負責產品設計。

1 對話 Good afternoon, everyone! 我的名字是派翠克，負責企業收購。Today I'd like to talk about our government contracts.

大家午安！My name is Patrick and I'm responsible for acquisitions. 今天我想跟大家談的是政府合約書的內容。

2 練習 我的名字是提姆，負責國際通訊。(global)
My name is Tim and I'm responsible for ______________________________.

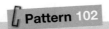

Pattern 102

102

The topic of today's presentation is...
今天發表會的主題是關於…

當你想要點出發表會的主題時，就可以使用這個句型。意義相似的句型為 Today's presentation is about...。

- **The topic of today's presentation is how to improve production.**
  今天發表會的主題是關於如何增進生產量。
- **The topic of today's presentation is expanding the global market.**
  今天發表會的主題是關於擴大全球市場。 ＊expand 擴大
- **The topic of today's presentation is the upcoming exposition.**
  今天發表會的主題是關於即將到來的博覽會。 ＊upcoming 即將到來的
- **The topic of today's presentation is budget allocations.**
  今天發表會的主題是關於預算分配。 ＊allocation 分配

1 對話 今天發表會的主題是關於擴大全球市場。When we think of the global market, we tend to think of the U.S., China, and India. They dominate the global market.

The topic of today's presentation is expanding the global market. 當我們提到全球市場時，傾向想到的是美國、中國和印度。這三個國家控制了大部分的市場。

2 練習 今天發表會的主題是關於我們新設立在東京的分公司。
(Tokyo office)
The topic of today's presentation is ____________________.

Pattern 103

Please interrupt me if...
如果…的話，請立刻提出來。

若你想告知與會者在發表過程中可隨時提出疑問時，就可以使用這個句型，這也是在發表會上必備句型之一。本句型中的動詞 interrupt 可以用 stop 替代，改成 Please stop me at any time if...。

- **Please interrupt me if you can't hear.**
  如果你們聽不清楚的話，請立刻提出來。　　＊interrupt 打斷（講話）
- **Please interrupt me if you're not clear about something.**
  如果對哪個地方不明白的話，請立刻提出來。
- **Please interrupt me if you need further explanation.**
  如果你需要進一步說明的話，請立刻提出來。
- **Please interrupt me if there are any questions.**
  如果有任何問題的話，請立刻提出來。

1 對話 I'm going to run down the budget projections for next year. In an attempt to stay on schedule, I'll do this rather quickly. 如果對哪個地方不明白的話，請立刻提出來。

我現在要帶大家瀏覽一下明年度的預算案。為了配合流程時間，我會瀏覽比較快一點。Please interrupt me if you're not clear about something.

2 練習 如果你需要幫忙的話，請立刻提出來。(assistance)
Please interrupt me if ______________________.

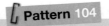

Pattern 104

After my presentation, there will be time for...
發表會結束後，將會安排…的時間。

有些發表者會在發表會結束後直接跳過問答時間，讓這場發表會無法畫下完美句點，為了避免犯下這種失誤，請牢牢記住這個句型。

- **After my presentation, there will be time for questions.**
  發表會結束後，將會安排問問題的時間。
- **After my presentation, there will be time for a discussion.**
  發表會結束後，將會安排討論的時間。
- **After my presentation, there will be time for a break.**
  發表會結束後，將會安排休息的時間。
  ＊break 暫停，休息
- **After my presentation, there will be time for you to check out our products.**
  ＊check out 檢驗，檢查
  發表會結束後，將會安排讓大家檢視產品的時間。

1 對話 I'll be giving a brief presentation of about 20 minutes. We want to introduce our new product line and tell you about some special features. 發表會結束後，將會安排讓大家檢視產品的時間。

現在我要開始進行二十分鐘的簡短發表會。我會介紹我們公司的新產品以及其具有之特色。After my presentation, there will be time for you to check out our products.

2 練習 發表會結束後，將會安排互相交流的時間。(networking)
After my presentation, there will be time for ____________
____________.

Pattern 105

I'd like to begin with...
我想先從…開始。

為了讓發表會更順利，在正式進入發表會前，可以先報告會議前的說明或注意事項，這時就可以使用這個句型，當作發表會的開場。

- **I'd like to begin with a few words about our company.**
  我想先從簡單地介紹一下敝公司開始。
- **I'd like to begin with our new product.**
  我想先從我們的新產品開始。
- **I'd like to begin with an overview.**
  我想先從簡單的概要開始。
- **I'd like to begin with a couple of interesting charts.**
  我想先從幾個有趣的圖表開始。 ＊a couple of 幾個，一些

1 對話 Thank you for coming today. 我想先從簡單地介紹一下敝公司開始。We were founded in 1958 as an auto parts supply company.

謝謝各位今天前來參加這場發表會。I'd like to begin with a few words about our company. 我們是成立於西元 1958 年的汽車零件供應公司。

2 練習 我想先從我們去年的收益比率開始。(earning rate)
I'd like to begin with ______________________.

Please take a look at...	106	請大家看一下…
This slide shows...	107	從這張幻燈片可以看出…
As you can see from this...,	108	大家可以從這…中看到，…
Let's move on to...	109	現在讓我們進入…
For the next + 時間, I'll...	110	接下來的…，我將會…

Pattern 106

Please take a look at...
請大家看一下…

在發表會的進行過程中，當你想請大家觀看相關的投影片或圖表資料時，就可以使用這個句型。此句型中的 take a look at... 是「請看一下…」的意思。

- **Please take a look at these statistics.**
  請大家看一下這項統計數據。 ＊statistics 統計資料
- **Please take a look at the graph up here on the screen.**
  請大家看一下螢幕上的圖表。
- **Please take a look at page three of the catalogue.**
  請大家看一下目錄的第三頁。
- **Please take a look at this picture that I'm passing around.**
  請大家看一下我傳閱下去的照片。 ＊pass around 傳閱

1 對話 This next slide shows our profits margins for the last 5 years. 請大家仔細看一下這項統計數據。It's obvious that our profits have steadily increased in the past five years.

下一張投影片是我們公司過去五年的邊際利潤率。Please take a look at these statistics. 它顯示了在過去五年間我們公司的利潤呈現穩定成長。

2 練習 請大家看一下講義第五頁上的圖片。(on page, handout)
Please take a look at ______________________.

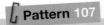

Pattern 107

This slide shows...
從這張投影片可以看出…

107 利用投影片講解

當你採用播放投影片的方式來進行發表會時，就可以使用這個句型。播放投影片的過程中，只要依照投影片的張數來變換本句型中的序數詞就行了，例如 The first slide..., The second slide...。本句型中的 slide 可以用 chart（圖表）替代，後面主要會接 shows, is, demonstrates 等動詞。

- **This slide shows our profit margin.**
  從這張投影片可以看出我們的淨利率。 ＊profit margin 淨利率
- **This slide shows that profits declined last month.**
  從這張投影片可以看出上個月的營收減少了。 ＊decline 下降，減少
- **This second slide shows the project's progress.**
  從第二張投影片可以看出該計畫的進展程度。
- **The last slide shows the sales and earnings to date.**
  從最後一張投影片可以看出目前為止的營業額以及利潤。
  ＊to date 目前為止的

1 對話 Let me show you the current status of our company. 從這張投影片可以看出上個月的營收減少了。We'll have to do our best to increase our profits.

現在讓我們來看一下我們公司的現況。This slide shows that profits declined last month. 我們必須盡全力去提升我們的收益。

2 練習 從這張投影片可以看出公司今年的市佔率又降低了。(shrink)
This slide shows that ______________________.

Pattern 108

As you can see from this...,
大家可以從這…中看到，…

當你用影像資料來說明某件事實或發表見解時，就可以使用這個句型。本句型中的 this 後面可以接 chart, graph, table 等單字。意義相似的句型為 As this...indicates, As shown on..., As indicated on... 等，在發表會上都可以使用。

- **As you can see from this graph, our profit's been increasing steadily.** ＊steadily 穩定地
  大家可以從這張圖表中看到，公司的收益呈現穩定成長。
- **As you can see from these figures, our revenues have been stagnant.** ＊revenue 收益，總收入 ＊stagnant 停滯的
  大家可以從這些數值中看到，我們的收益停滯不前。
- **As you can see from these figures, we made record profits last month.** ＊record 空前的，破紀錄的
  大家可以從這些數值中看到，我們在上個月締造破紀錄的獲利。
- **As you can see from this graph, our main customers are professional women in their 20s.**
  大家可以從這張圖表中看到，敝公司的主要客層是二十幾歲的職業女性。

1 對話 Since expanding our operations in South America, we've done very well. 大家可以從這張圖表中看到，公司的收益呈現穩定成長。This began within a year of building our factories in Peru and Brazil.

自從我們將營運擴展到南美後，公司發展得很順利。As you can see from this graph, our profit's been increasing steadily. 這是我們在祕魯和巴西建廠的一年內開始的。

2 練習 大家可以從這張圖表中看到，公司正處於危機當中。(in trouble)
As you can see from this ____________________.

Pattern 109

Let's move on to...
現在讓我們進入…

當你想進入下一個主題時，就可以使用這個句型。這個句型的作用是連結下個主題，雖然不含任何實際內容，卻能讓你的口頭發表聽起來更為順暢。意義相似的句型為 So, let's now turn to... 和 Moving on... 等，可以交替使用，讓英文詞彙更靈活。

- **Let's move on to the next slide.**
  現在讓我們進入下一張投影片。
- **Let's move on to the next topic.**
  現在讓我們進入下一個主題。 ＊topic 主題
- **Let's move on to the next product description.**
  現在讓我們進入下一個產品說明。 ＊description 說明，描述
- **Let's move on to the final item on the list.**
  現在讓我們進入名單上的最後一項產品。

1 對話 It's clear that there is some disagreement on this issue. Perhaps we should discuss this after the presentation. 現在讓我們進入下一個主題。

顯然有些人對這個議題持反對意見。等發表會結束後我們也許要再討論一下。Let's move on to the next topic.

2 練習 現在讓我們進入下一張圖片。(next)
Let's move on to ______________.

Pattern 110

110

For the next + 時間, I'll...
接下來的…，我將會…

當這場發表會已規畫好各流程的進行時間時，就可以使用這個句型，例如 For the first ten minutes, I... 就是表示「前十分鐘我會…」的意思。

- **For the next forty minutes, I'll** cover our corporate restructuring plan. ＊corporate 公司的，企業的
  接下來的四十分鐘，我將會說明公司的結構調整計畫。
- **For the next ten minutes, I'll** talk about the many advantages we possess over our competitor.
  接下來的十分鐘，我將會談到我們跟其他競爭對手比起來，我們佔有許多優勢。
- **For the next hour, I'd like** everyone's feedback.
  接下來的一個小時，我想要聽聽每個人的看法。
- **For the next twenty minutes, I'm going to** go over our financial report for the year 2011. ＊financial 財政的
  接下來的二十分鐘，我將會跟大家一起看看 2011 年的財務報告書。

1 對話 接下來的四十分鐘，我將會說明公司的結構調整計畫。First, we'll be merging our two Denver branches in August. This will require us to eliminate some upper management positions.

For the next forty minutes, I'll cover our corporate restructuring plan. 首先，我們會在八月時合併兩間丹佛分公司，因此我們需要裁減幾個高階管理職位。

2 練習 接下來的五分鐘，我將會談到投資方面的事。(investments)
For the next five minutes, I'll ________________.

5-3

強調與提出意見

What is really important is...	111	最重要的是⋯
It's essential to...	112	我們必須⋯
I should repeat that...	113	我必須重申，⋯
I'm sure everyone in this room...	114	我相信在座的各位⋯
I think it might be worthwhile to...	115	我認為⋯或許值得⋯

Pattern 111

111

What is really important is...
最重要的是…

當你想在發表會上帶出重要論點或結論，就可以使用這個句型。本句型是在說明具體內容前，先表達「強調」的意味，以此引起大家的注意。

- **What is really important is the market projections.**
  最重要的是市場預測報告。 * projection 預想，預測
- **What is really important is accounting strategies.**
  最重要的是會計策略。 * strategy 策略
- **What is really important is the last part.**
  最重要的是最後一個部分。
- **What is really important is that we uphold the company's image.**
  最重要的是我們要維護公司的形象。 * uphold 維護，維持

1 對話 The company lost several million dollars last year. This was mostly due to some bad investments in the auto industry. 最重要的是市場預測報告。

公司在去年損失了數百萬美元。造成虧損的主要原因就是幾項在汽車產業上的錯誤投資。What is really important is the market projections.

2 練習 最重要的是如何變成全球的領導者。(how to, become)
What is really important is ______________________.

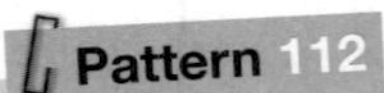

It's essential to...
我們必須…

當你想同時說服聽眾和帶動氣氛，就可以使用這個句型。本句型中的 to 後面可以接各式各樣的原形動詞。

- **It's essential to understand the realities of the market.**
  我們必須了解市場的真實情況。
- **It's essential to understand the buying patterns of our competitors.**
  我們必須理解我們競爭對手的購買行為。
- **It's essential to realize the features of the product we are trying to sell.**
  我們必須了解我們努力販售的商品特色是什麼。 ＊feature 特徵，特色
- **It's essential to emphasize that this item is highly flammable.**
  我們必須強調這項產品的高易燃度。 ＊flammable 易燃的

1 對話 We invested heavily in educational toys for babies. This was a mistake in light of the downturn we saw in the economy. 我們必須了解市場的真實情況。

我們投入了大量資金在幼兒教育玩具上。有鑒於我們看到經濟低迷的情況指出這是一項錯誤。It's essential to understand the realities of the market.

2 練習 我們必須清楚知道要把資源集中在什麼地方。
(where to, resources)
It's essential to ______________________.

Pattern 113

I should repeat that...
我必須重申，…

當你想要強調某件事項時，就可以使用這個句型。動詞 repeat 雖然可以單純表示「重複」，但連同前後文一起看時，翻譯成「強調…／重申…」會比較恰當。

- **I should repeat that these numbers are estimates.**
  我必須重申，這些數據是預估值。　＊estimate 預估（值）
- **I should repeat that there are many options.**
  我必須重申，選擇性還有很多。
- **I should repeat that our company is a leader in the industry.**
  我必須重申，敝公司是這個產業的領頭羊。　＊industry 產業，業界
- **I should repeat that this product has been very reliable.**
  我必須重申，這個產品非常值得信賴。　＊reliable 可信賴的，可靠的

1 對話 If you're unprepared to invest today, that's all right. 我必須重申，選擇性還有很多。This next slide shows a list of the ways you can still take advantage of this opportunity.

如果你還沒準備好要投資也沒關係。I should repeat that there are many options. 從下張投影片大家可以看到可以透過這次機會獲得利益的各種方法列表。

2 練習 我必須重申，這些東西只是樣品，並不是完成品。
(prototypes, final product)
I should repeat that ______________________.

Pattern 114

I'm sure everyone in this room...
我相信在座的各位…

當你希望聽眾能認同你的話並取得共識，就可以使用這個句型。本句型中的 in this room 不可解釋為「在房間裡」，而是應該配合前後語句自然地解釋為「在座的…」。

- **I'm sure everyone in this room is aware of how difficult it can be to make a sale.** ＊make a sale 販售
  我相信在座的各位都知道賣東西是多麼困難的一件事。
- **I'm sure everyone in this room has experienced disappointing sales figures.**
  我相信在座的各位都經歷過慘澹的銷售數字。
- **I'm sure everyone in this room knows that our competitors are doing rather well.**
  我相信在座的各位都知道我們的競爭對手非常優秀。
- **I'm sure everyone in this room wants to improve sales.**
  我相信在座的各位都想改善銷售數字。

1 對話 This graph shows current market comparisons. 我相信在座的各位都知道我們的競爭對手非常優秀。In order to stay competitive, we need to come up with a new product line.

我們可以從這張圖片看到目前的市場比較情況。I'm sure everyone in this room knows that our competitors are doing rather well. 為了維持競爭力，我們必須開發新的產品線才行。

2 練習 我相信在座的各位都知道這件事有多困難。(identify with)
I'm sure everyone in this room ____________________.

Pattern 115

115

I think it might be worthwhile to...
我認為…或許值得…

worthwhile 是「值得…」的意思，常常使用於如同發表會這樣的正式場合中，因此我們可以使用本句型來表達「或許值得…」，來表達講述的內容或許可行。

- **I think it might be worthwhile to list our assets.**
  我認為列出我們的資產清單或許是值得的。 ＊asset 資產
- **I think it might be worthwhile to sell some of our stock.**
  我認為賣掉我們的庫存品或許是值得的。
- **I think it might be worthwhile to take their offer.**
  我認為他們的提案或許值得考慮。
- **I think it might be worthwhile to discuss this in a larger group.**
  我認為這個問題或許值得跟更多人一起討論。

1 對話 GE would like to buy our entire inventory. They have offered us $12 million for everything on this list. 我認為他們的提案或許值得考慮。

GE 願意購買我們所有的庫存，他們說願意支付一千兩百萬美元購買清單上的所有產品。I think it might be worthwhile to take their offer.

2 練習 我認為他的提案或許值得一聽。(proposal)
I think it might be worthwhile to ______________.

5-4 收尾

Pattern 116

Let's briefly go over...
讓我們簡單回顧一下…

這個句型使用在會議或發表會即將邁入尾聲，你想重新檢視之前提過的內容時。本句型的前面還可以加上 Before I finish... 這類的句子，go over 則是表示「回顧，瀏覽」的意思。

- **Let's briefly go over a summary of the presentation.**
  讓我們簡單回顧一下這場發表會的概要。 ＊summary 概要
- **Let's briefly go over the main points.**
  讓我們簡單回顧一下主要的重點。 ＊main point 主要的重點
- **Let's briefly go over the schedule for the next presentation.**
  讓我們簡單回顧一下下一場發表會的行程表。
- **Let's go over the contents of the handout again.**
  讓我們簡單回顧一下講義上的內容。

1 對話 讓我們簡單回顧一下這場發表會的概要。First, our profits declined sharply in the last month. This is due to poor product sales, so we need new product ideas from you.

Let's briefly go over a summary of the presentation. 首先，我們公司的收益在上個月急遽下跌，這都是因為產品銷售不佳，所以我們需要大家提出新的產品構想。

2 練習 讓我們簡單回顧一下因為這件事所產生的問題。(raised by)
Let's briefly go over ______________________.

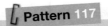

Pattern 117

I'd like to finish by saying...
結束之前，我想說的是：…

當你想要以一句話讓這場發表會畫下句點時，就可以使用這個句型。此外，也可以用來告知聽眾發表會已進入尾聲，要準備散會了。

- **I'd like to finish by saying how grateful I am for your attention.**
  結束之前，我想說的是：感謝大家的專心。
- **I'd like to finish by saying what a great audience you've been.**
  結束之前，我想說的是：你們真的是超棒的聽眾。 ＊audience 聽眾
- **I'd like to finish by saying that I'm excited about our new product.**
  結束之前，我想說的是：我對我們的新產品抱有很大的期待。
- **I'd like to finish by saying that I hope we've cleared up any confusion you have regarding the product.**
  結束之前，我想說的是：我希望我們已經釐清各位對這項產品的疑慮。

1 對話 結束之前，我想說的是：我對我們的新產品抱有很大的期待。I feel it has great potential in today's market.

I'd like to finish by saying that I'm excited about our new product. 我認為它在今日的市場上潛力無窮。

2 練習 結束之前，我想說的是：如果有疑問的話，我隨時都能回答你們。(available, if)

I'd like to finish by saying ______________________.

Pattern 118

I'd recommend that you...
我建議您…

當你想建議對方透過公司的網頁或定期寄送的電子刊物取得公司的產品資訊時，就可以使用這個句型，藉此推廣公司的產品。

- **I'd recommend that you visit our company's website.**
  我建議您瀏覽我們公司的網站。
- **I'd recommend that you look over the information I've given you.**
  我建議您再仔細看看我給你的那份資料。 ＊look over 仔細檢閱
- **I'd recommend that you consider making an order as soon as possible.**
  我建議您考慮一下盡快下訂單。 ＊make an order 下訂單
- **I'd recommend that you not miss this opportunity.**
  我建議您不要錯過這個機會。

1 對話 Information about our products can be obtained from a number of sources. 我建議您瀏覽我們公司的網站。I would also recommend that you subscribe to our listserv.

您可以透過幾種管道取得我們公司產品的情況。I'd recommend that you visit our company's website. 我也推薦您訂閱我們公司的電子刊物。

2 練習 我建議您早一點訂購。(not wait long before)
I'd recommend that you ______________________.

Pattern 119

In closing, I want you to remember...
最後，我希望大家都能記住…

發表會進入尾聲時，你想再叮嚀聽眾一些事情，就可以使用這個句型。請記住我們在結束發表會時常常會使用到 remember 這個單字。

- **In closing, I want you to remember these three points.**
  最後，我希望大家都能記住這三點。
- **In closing, I want you to remember the issues we've looked at.**
  最後，我希望大家都能記住我們已經發現到的問題點。 ＊issue 問題點
- **In closing, I want you to remember the bottom line.**
  最後，我希望大家都能記住基本要求。
  ＊the bottom line 最低限度，基本要求
- **In closing, I want you to remember that the new products will be released in two weeks.**
  最後，我希望大家都能記住新產品將會在兩週內發行。
  ＊release 發行，發表

1 對話 最後，我希望大家都能記住這三點。Teamwork, Hard work, and Smart work are the keys to success. Thank you.

In closing, I want you to remember these three points. 合作、努力工作以及精明工作是邁向成功的關鍵。謝謝大家。

2 練習 最後，我希望大家都能記住這場發表會的目的。(purpose)
In closing, I want you to remember ________________.

Pattern 120

120

Thank you all for...
真的很謝謝大家…

這是當發表會進入尾聲，發表者對每位聽眾表達謝意時最常使用的其中一個句型。本句型只要在 Thank you for... 中加上 all 就行了，所以很好記住。意思相似的句型為 I'm pleased that... 。

Thank you all for coming.
真的很謝謝大家出席。

Thank you all for your attention.
真的很謝謝大家的關注。

＊attention 關注，注意

Thank you all for giving me your attention this afternoon.
真的很謝謝大家今天下午對於這個活動的注意。

Thank you all for taking the time to listen to me.
真的很謝謝大家花時間聽我的說明。

1 對話 It's been my pleasure to present to your group today. I appreciate the time you've taken to hear my sales pitch. 真的很謝謝大家的關注。

我很榮幸今天能向各位做發表，也很感激你們願意花時間聽我推銷產品。Thank you all for your attention.

2 練習 真的很謝謝大家的耐心。(patience)
Thank you all for ______________________.

120 向所有聽眾表達謝意

5-5

提問與回答

Now I'll answer... 121 現在開始，我來回答…

Are there any...? 122 有任何…嗎？

Could you tell us...? 123 可以請您告訴我們…？

That's a...question! 124 這真是個…問題！

As I + 過去式動詞 + earlier,... 125 正如我之前…過的，…

Pattern 121

Now I'll answer...
現在開始，我來回答…

在發表會結束，要開始接受聽眾發問時，就可以使用這個句型，也能用來告知聽眾現在開始是讓大家發問的時間，請台下的各位踴躍發言。

- **Now I'll answer your questions.**
  現在開始，我來回答大家的問題。
- **Now I'll answer questions relating to the presentation.**
  現在開始，我來回答跟發表會有關的問題。　＊ relating to 跟…有關
- **Now I'll answer questions for the next 40 minutes.**
  現在開始的四十分鐘，我來回答大家的問題。
- **Now I'll answer on behalf of the company.**
  現在開始，我代表公司來回答你們的問題。　＊ on behalf of 代表…

1 對話 I see you all have a lot of questions. 現在開始的四十分鐘，我會來回答大家的問題。But, please, raise your hand so that I can address them one by one.

我看到大家好像有很多疑問，Now I'll answer questions for the next 40 minutes. 不過，請大家舉手提問，這樣我才能一一地回答大家的問題。

2 練習 現在開始，我只回答與程序相關的問題。
(relating to, procedure)
Now I'll answer ______________________.

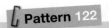

Pattern 122

Are there any...?
有任何…嗎？

當你在問答時間結束前想確認聽眾是否還有其他疑問時，就可以使用這個句型，若沒有問題就可以說結尾語直接結束發表會。

- **Are there any further questions?**
  有任何進一步的問題嗎？ ＊further 進一步的
- **Are there any gray areas that need explanation?**
  有任何曖昧不明的部分需要解釋嗎？ ＊gray area 曖昧不明的部分
- **Are there any volunteers to help me with the demonstration?**
  有任何自願者可以幫我實地示範嗎？ ＊demonstration 實地示範
- **Are there any more handouts?**
  有任何多出來的講義嗎？

1 對話 Now I'd like to demonstrate how this product is used. 有任何自願者可以幫我實地示範嗎？I just need someone to operate the projector.

現在我想示範給大家看如何使用這個產品，Are there any volunteers to help me with the demonstration? 我需要人幫我操作投影機。

2 練習 有任何補充的意見嗎？(additional)
Are there any ________________________________?

Pattern 123

Could you tell us...?
可以請您告訴我們…嗎？

當你想請求對方具體回答你的問題時，就可以使用這個句型。本句型的後面加上 more about 時，是表示要求對方「再多說一點」的意思。

- **Could you tell us what you can offer us?**
  可以請您告訴我們您可以提供些什麼嗎？ ＊offer 提供
- **Could you tell us the new features?**
  可以請您告訴我們有什麼新的特色嗎？
- **Could you tell us more about how our partnership will work?**
  可以請您告訴我們更多關於我們合作的運作方式嗎？
- **Could you tell us more about what you're looking for?**
  可以請您告訴我們更多關於你們要的是什麼嗎？ ＊look for 尋找

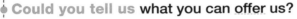

1 對話 We'd love to do business with your company. I think there are several ways we could work together. However, 可以請您告訴我們更多關於你們期待的是什麼嗎？

我們很想要跟貴公司做生意，我認為我們有好幾種合作的方式，不過，could you tell us more about what you're looking for?

2 練習 可以請您告訴我們更多關於您的顧慮嗎？(concerns)
Could you tell us more about ______________________?

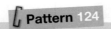

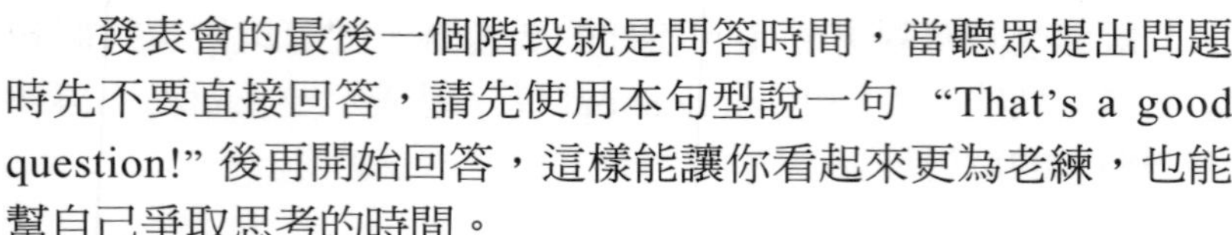

That's a...question!
這真是個…問題！

發表會的最後一個階段就是問答時間，當聽眾提出問題時先不要直接回答，請先使用本句型說一句 "That's a good question!" 後再開始回答，這樣能讓你看起來更為老練，也能幫自己爭取思考的時間。

- That's a **great** question!
  這真是個**很棒的**問題！
- That's a **timely** question!
  這問題問得**正是時候**！
  * **timely** 及時的，適時的
- That's a **difficult** question!
  這真是個**困難的**問題！
- That's a **thoughtful** question!
  這真是個**考慮周到的**問題！
  * **thoughtful** 細心的，考慮周到的

1 對話

The man in the back asked if we'll be laying off any workers soon. 這問題問得正是時候！As a matter of fact, we'll have to lay off 300 workers in February.

後面那位先生剛剛提問我們是否會馬上解雇員工，That's a timely question. 事實上，我們在二月必須解雇三百名員工才行。

2 練習

這真是個相當大膽的問題！(bold)

That's a ______________________________ question!

Pattern 125

As I + 過去式動詞 + earlier,...
正如我之前…過的，…

當你想再次強調之前說過的內容來回答問題時，就可以使用這個句型。本句型中的「動詞過去式」可以用 say, present, mention 等字彙替換。

- **As I said earlier, that will all be cleared up when the final product is released.** ＊be cleared up 解決問題
  正如我之前說過的，這個問題將會全部在最終的產品發行時解決。
- **As I mentioned earlier, that isn't really a short-term concern.** ＊short-term 短期的
  正如我之前說過的，短期內真的不需要擔心這個問題。
- **As I emphasized earlier, it isn't a problem to be concerned about.**
  正如我之前強調過的，這個問題根本不值得擔心。
- **As I noticed earlier, the problem is something for our legal department to worry about.**
  正如我之前提到過的，這個問題就讓我們的法務部門去擔心吧。

1 對話 Whether or not the company will win this lawsuit is irrelevant now. 正如我之前提過的，短期內真的不需要擔心這個問題。It will be years before this case is settled in court.

不論我們公司是否能打贏這次官司，都不會對現在造成影響。As I mentioned earlier, that isn't really a short-term concern. 因為這場官司在法庭上必須花上幾年時間才能結束。

2 練習 正如我之前說過的，這不會成為問題。(say, shouldn't)
As I ________________ earlier, ________________.

5-1~5-5

黃金複習 15 分鐘！

前面這 25 個句型和 125 個句子全都記熟了嗎？
來驗收一下學習成果吧！如果不能充滿自信地用英文說出以下 40 個句子，請翻到前面再重新複習一次！

01 正如我之前說過的，短期內真的不需要擔心這個問題。

02 我的名字是派翠克，負責企業收購。

03 這問題問得正是時候！

04 今天發表會的主題是關於擴大全球市場。

05 可以請您告訴我們有什麼新的特色嗎？

06 如果對哪個地方不明白的話，請立刻提出來。

07 有任何曖昧不明的部分需要解釋嗎？

08 發表會結束後，將會安排討論的時間。

09 現在開始的四十分鐘，我來回答大家的問題。

解答 01. As I mentioned earlier, that isn't really a short-term concern.
02. My name is Patrick and I'm responsible for acquisitions. 03. That's a timely question!
04. The topic of today's presentation is expanding the global market.
05. Could you tell us the new features?
06. Please interrupt me if you're not clear about something.
07. Are there any gray areas that need explanation?
08. After my presentation, there will be time for a discussion.
09. Now I'll answer questions for the next 40 minutes.

10 我想先從簡單的概要開始。

11 真的很謝謝大家的關注。

12 請大家看一下螢幕上的圖表。

13 最後，我希望大家都能記住基本要求。

14 從這張投影片可以看出上個月的營收減少了。

15 我建議您再仔細看看我給你的那份資料。

16 大家可以從這張圖表中看到，敝公司的主要客層是二十幾歲的職業女性。

17 結束之前，我想說的是：你們真的是超棒的聽眾。

18 現在讓我們進入下一個主題。

19 讓我們簡單回顧一下主要的重點。

解答 10. I'd like to begin with an overview. 11. Thank you all for your attention.
12. Please take a look at the graph up here on the screen.
13. In closing, I want you to remember the bottom line.
14. This slide shows that profits declined last month.
15. I'd recommend that you look over the information I've given you.
16. As you can see from this graph, our main customers are professional women in their 20s.
17. I'd like to finish by saying what a great audience you've been.
18. Let's move on to the next topic. 19. Let's briefly go over the main points.

20 接下來的一個小時，我想要聽聽每個人的看法。

21 正如我之前強調過的，這個問題根本不值得擔心。

22 最重要的是會計策略。

23 我們必須理解我們競爭對手的購買行為。

24 這真是個很棒的問題！

25 我必須重申，這些數據是預估值。

26 可以請您告訴我們您可以提供些什麼嗎？

27 我相信在座的各位都經歷過慘澹的銷售數字。

28 有任何進一步的問題嗎？

29 我認為賣掉我們的庫存品或許是值得的。

30 現在開始，我來回答大家的問題。

解答 20. For the next hour, I'd like everyone's feedback.
21. As I emphasized earlier, it isn't a problem to be concerned about.
22. What is really important is accounting strategies.
23. It's essential to understand the buying patterns of our competitors.
24. That's a great question! 25. I should repeat that these numbers are estimates.
26. Could you tell us what you can offer us?
27. I'm sure everyone in this room has experienced disappointing sales figures.
28. Are there any further questions?
29. I think it might be worthwhile to sell some of our stock.

31 真的很謝謝大家出席。

____

32 我的名字是蔻琳，負責人力資源。

____

33 最後，我希望大家都能記住這三點。

____

34 今天發表會的主題是關於如何增進生產量。

____

35 我建議您瀏覽我們公司的網站。

____

36 如果你們聽不清楚的話，請立刻提出來。

____

37 結束之前，我想說的是：感謝大家的專心。

____

38 發表會結束後，將會安排問問題的時間。

____

39 讓我們簡單回顧一下這場發表會的概要。

____

40 我想先從簡單地介紹一下敝公司開始。

____

解答 30. Now I'll answer your questions. 31. Thank you all for coming.
32. My name is Colleen and I'm responsible for human resources.
33. In closing, I want you to remember these three points.
34. The topic of today's presentation is how to improve production.
35. I'd recommend that you visit our company's website.
36. Please interrupt me if you can't hear.
37. I'd like to finish by saying how grateful I am for your attention.
38. After my presentation, there will be time for questions.
39. Let's briefly go over a summary of the presentation.
40. I'd like to begin with a few words about our company.

Part 2

和客戶建立好的關係

Unit 6
約定
讓對方再見你一面的祕訣

6-1 訂下約定

Pattern 126

Is...okay with you?
…你方便嗎？

如果只是想問對方可以見面的時間，只要跟他說 When is good for you? 就行了。若是想更積極地詢問對方是否可以在特定的時間點或地點見面的話，就可以使用這個句型。

- **Is Friday okay with you?**
  禮拜五你方便嗎？
- **Is tomorrow okay with you?**
  明天你方便嗎？
- **Is 4:00 on Monday okay with you?**
  禮拜一四點你方便嗎？
- **Is my office okay with you?**
  在我辦公室你方便嗎？

1 對話
A When is good for you?
B Early in the week is best.
A 禮拜一四點你方便嗎？

A 約什麼時候比較好？
B 能約禮拜一或禮拜二是最好。
A Is 4:00 on Monday okay with you?

2 練習 下個禮拜你方便嗎？(next)
Is ________________ okay with you?

Pattern 127

Can we meet...?
可以約…見面嗎？

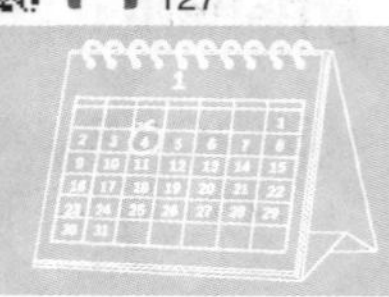

如果你想跟對方約定時間或地點碰面的話，只要在這個句型中的動詞 meet 後面簡單地加上時間或地點就行了。

Can we meet on Thursday at 2:00?
可以約禮拜四兩點見面嗎？

Can we meet earlier in the day?
可以約當天早一點見面嗎？

Can we meet over dinner some evening?
可以約在某天晚上晚餐時見面嗎？

Can we meet at Starbucks?
可以約在星巴克見面嗎？

1 對話

A We really need to go over these figures.
B 可以約禮拜四兩點見面嗎？
A I'll check my calendar to see if I'm available.

A 我們需要好好確認一下這些數據。
B Can we meet on Thursday at 2:00?
A 我會去確認一下我的行事曆看我是否有空。

2 練習 可以約這個月下旬見面嗎？(later)
Can we meet ______________________________?

Pattern 128

I can make it...
…我沒問題。

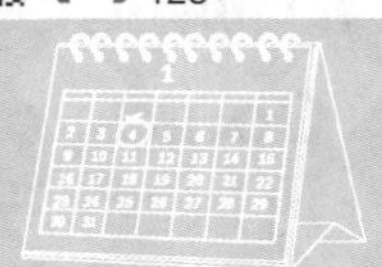

不論是業務上的聚會或一般的訪問，當你想表達「我沒問題」時，都可以使用這個句型：I can make it...。

- **I can make it on Tuesday.**
  禮拜二我沒問題。
- **I can make it by 2:15.**
  兩點十五分之前我沒問題。
- **I can make it on the 22nd.**
  22 號我沒問題。
- **I can make it anytime tomorrow.**
  明天任何時間我都沒問題。

1 對話

A Could you come into the office this week?
B Sure. 明天任何時間我都沒問題。
A Okay. See you tomorrow.

A 你這個禮拜能夠過來辦公室一趟嗎？
B 當然。I can make it anytime tomorrow.
A 好的，明天見。

2 練習 今天下午我沒問題。(afternoon)
I can make it ______________________.

Pattern 129

Could you arrange...?
可以請你安排…嗎？

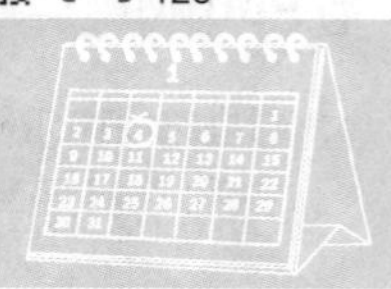

如果你想請對方安排會面的時間，就可以使用這個帶有動詞 arrange 的句型。自己會負責安排會面時間的話，只要回答對方說 I can arrange... 就行了。

Could you arrange a conference call?
可以請你安排一場電話會議嗎？

Could you arrange an appointment to see the manager?
可以請你安排我跟經理見面嗎？

Could you arrange a meeting with Mr. Smith for Monday, please?
可以請你安排我禮拜一跟史密斯先生見面嗎？

Could you arrange a daylong seminar?
可以請你安排進行一日的研討會嗎？

＊daylong 終日的

1 對話
A 可以請你安排一場電話會議嗎？
B That's a possibility.
A Let's try to do this in the next two weeks.

A Could you arrange a conference call?
B 應該可以。
A 往後兩個禮拜都採用這個方式開會看看吧。

2 練習 可以請你安排小組會議嗎？(meeting)
Could you arrange ______________________?

Pattern 130

If it's all right,...
如果可以的話，…

If it's all right 的意思同於 If it's okay，都是表示「如果可以的話」。這句型可以表達體諒照顧對方的心意，十分好用。

- **If it's all right, let's meet at my office.**
  如果可以的話，我們就在我的辦公室碰面吧。
- **If it's all right, we can meet at your office.**
  如果可以的話，我們可以在你的辦公室碰面。
- **If it's all right, I can come over this afternoon.**
  如果可以的話，今天下午我可以順道過去拜訪。 ＊come over 順道拜訪
- **If it's all right, I'll bring my colleague along.**
  如果可以的話，我會帶著我的同事一起過去。 ＊along 帶著…一起

1 對話

A I'd like to meet with you in person.
B That's fine. What time and where?
A 如果可以的話，我們就在我的辦公室碰面吧。

A 我想跟你當面談談。
B 好的。時間和地點呢？
A If it's all right, let's meet at my office.

2 練習 如果可以的話，我想明天跟你見面。(would like to)
If it's all right, ______________________________.

6-2

變更約定

I'm sorry, but I need to...	131	抱歉，我必須…
I don't think I'll be able to...	132	我可能無法…
Can we reschedule...?	133	我們可以改約…嗎？
Is there another...?	134	還有其他…嗎？
Call me if...	135	如果…，請跟我聯絡。

Pattern 131

I'm sorry, but I need to...
抱歉，我必須⋯

當你可能無法配合對方提出的碰面時間，又或是想跟對方改約其他時間時，就可以使用這個句型。本句型是以 I'm sorry 開頭，後面再接你想要表達的事情即可。

- **I'm sorry, but I need to finish this report first.**
  抱歉，我必須先完成這份報告。
- **I'm sorry, but I need to change our appointment time.**
  抱歉，我必須更改我們的會面時間。
- **I'm sorry, but I need to leave the meeting early.**
  抱歉，我必須提早離開這場會議。
- **I'm sorry, but I have another appointment at that time.**
  抱歉，我那個時間另外有約。

1 對話
A We'll be meeting from 3:00 to 5:00.
B Oh... 抱歉，我必須提早離開這場會議。
A No problem. We'll hear your presentation first.

A 我們將會議時間安排為三點到五點。
B 喔⋯ I'm sorry, but I need to leave the meeting early.
A 沒關係，我們可以先聽你的報告。

2 練習 抱歉，我必須取消這個約會。(cancel)
I'm sorry, but I need to ______________________.

Pattern 132

I don't think I'll be able to...
我可能無法…

當你無法遵守約定時，就可以使用這個句型。下面的例句中有一個地方要注意，第一個例句中的動詞 come 不能翻譯成「來」！請記得 come 也能表示「去」的意思。

- **I don't think I'll be able to come.**
  我可能無法去。
- **I don't think I'll be able to make it on time.**
  我可能無法準時完成。　　＊on time 準時
- **I don't think I'll be able to meet tomorrow.**
  我明天可能無法與你碰面。
- **I don't think I'll be able to get there by 5:30.**
  我可能無法在五點半以前到達那裡。

1 對話
A Why don't we meet at 5:30 today?
B I'm sorry. 我可能無法在五點半前到達。
A All right, then. How about 7:00?
B That works.

A 我們約在今天下午五點半，如何？
B 抱歉，I don't think I'll be able to get there by 5:30.
A 沒關係，那改約七點如何？
B 沒問題。

2 練習 抱歉，我可能無法到那裡去。(be)
I don't think I'll be able to ______________________.

Pattern 133

Can we reschedule...?
我們可以改約…嗎？

我們在表達「更改行程」時，常常想要使用 change 這個單字，但是其實在英文裡有個比 change 更適合的單字，那就是動詞 reschedule。之後請試著用 Can we reschedule...? 這個句型吧！

- **Can we reschedule the appointment for 3:00?**
  我們可以更改會面時間到三點嗎？
- **Can we reschedule the date?**
  我們可以改約別天嗎？
- **Can we reschedule the interview?**
  我們可以更改面試時間嗎？
- **Can we reschedule the presentation?**
  我們可以更改發表會時間嗎？

1 對話
A I'm calling about our appointment on Friday.
B Is there a problem?
A 我們可以改約別天嗎？
B Sure, but let's make it soon.

A 我是為了禮拜五的約定打電話來的。
B 有什麼問題嗎？
A Can we reschedule the date?
B 好啊，不過要快點決定日期才行。

2 練習 我們可以更改截止日期嗎？(deadline)
Can we reschedule ______________________?

Pattern 134

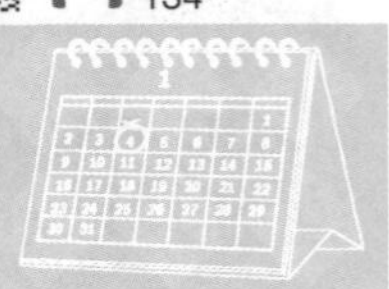

Is there another...?
還有其他…嗎？

當你想要變動約定的時間或地點，又或是想問對方是否還有其他辦法或問題的話，都可以使用這個句型，是個用途很廣的句型。

- **Is there another time that works better for you?**
  還有其他您比較方便的時間嗎？
- **Is there another day of the week that's better?**
  這禮拜還有其他更適合的時間嗎？
- **Is there another location convenient to us both?**
  還有其他對我們雙方都方便的地點嗎？ ＊convenient 方便的
- **Is there another problem with scheduling our meeting?**
  對於安排我們的會議時間，還有其他問題嗎？

1 對話
A I might be late for our meeting on Monday.
B Oh. 這禮拜還有其他更適合的時間嗎？
A Actually, Thursday would be great.

A 禮拜一的會議我可能會遲到。
B 喔。Is there another day of the week that's better?
A 其實，改約禮拜四比較好。

2 練習 還有其他讓我們可以在這禮拜碰面的方法嗎？(way, connect)
Is there another ______________________________?

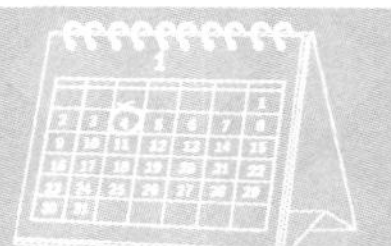

Pattern 135

Call me if...
如果…，請跟我聯絡。

這是一個在行程有更改或有其他的變動事項時派得上用場的句型，商場上往往會遇到對方想變更行程的場合，本句型帶有體貼照顧的心意，請一定要找機會使用這個句型，讓對方感受到你的貼心，使溝通更順暢。

- **Call me if something comes up.**
  如果發生了什麼事，請跟我聯絡。　　＊come up 發生，出現
- **Call me if you need to reschedule.**
  如果您需要更改時間，請跟我聯絡。
- **Call me if you can't find the appointment place.**
  如果你找不到會面的地點，請跟我聯絡。
- **Call me if you get here.**
  如果你到了，請跟我聯絡。

1 對話
A I assume we're still on for a meeting tomorrow.
B Yes, right.
A 如果您需要更改時間，請跟我聯絡。

A 我們明天好像有個會議。
B 對啊，沒錯。
A Call me if you need to reschedule.

2 練習 如果有需要變動的部分，請在那之前跟我聯絡。(before then)
Call me if ______________________________.

6-3

確認約定

Pattern 136

I'm calling to confirm...
我打電話來是想確認…

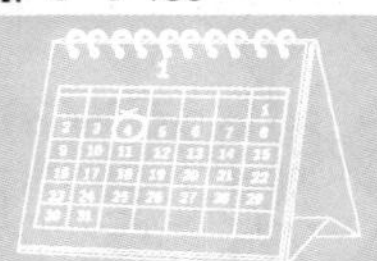

當你想在電話上確認某件事的話，你可以說 I'm calling to confirm...。如果是想在電子郵件上確認某個約定的內容事項，只要改成 I'm writing to confirm... 即可。

- **I'm calling to confirm the location of our next meeting.**
  我打電話來是想確認我們下次會面的地點。
- **I'm calling to confirm that Mr. West will be at the meeting.**
  我打電話來是想確認威斯特先生會出席這場會議。
- **I'm writing to confirm we'll meet promptly at 2:00.**
  我寫這封信是想確認我們在兩點整準時碰面。 ＊promptly 準時地
- **I'm writing to confirm our appointment this afternoon.**
  我寫這封信是想確認我們今天下午的約定。

1 對話
A Hi, Kevin. This is Leonard Nelson at Microsoft.
B Yes, Mr. Nelson.
A 我打電話來是想確認我們下次會面的地點。

A 凱文，你好，我是微軟的李奧納多尼爾森。
B 尼爾森先生你好。
A I'm calling to confirm the location of our next meeting.

2 練習 我打電話來是想確認我們之前約好的行程。(schedule)
I'm calling to confirm ______________________.

Pattern 137

I just want to make sure...
我只是想確認一下…

在約定日前，如果你想再次跟對方確認日期、時間或地點等事項，就可以使用這個句型。此外，也可以使用表示「再度確認」的片語 double check 來替代 make sure。

- **I just want to make sure the meeting begins at 9:00.**
  我只是想確認一下會議是不是九點開始。
- **I just want to make sure I have the correct phone number.**
  我只是想確認一下我這邊的電話號碼是正確的。
- **I just want to make sure whether you need me to bring something.**
  我只是想確認一下您是否需要我攜帶什麼東西。
- **I just want to make sure you have in advance what you need.**
  我只是想確認一下您已事先備妥您需要的資料。 ＊in advance 預先

1 對話 **A** 我只是想確認一下會議是不是九點開始。
B Yes.
A All right. I'll be there.

A I just want to make sure the meeting begins at 9:00.
B 沒錯。
A 知道了，我會出席的。

2 練習 我只是想確認一下我是否已備妥應有的資料。
(appropriate, papers)
I just want to make sure ______________________

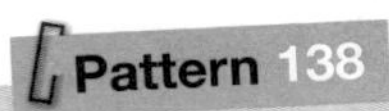

Can you still make...?
您是否還能…？

前面已經有提過利用動詞 make 來表達確定是否能到約定地點的句型。在句型中加入 still，就可以增添「仍然、還是」的意思。

- **Can you still make it?**
  您是否還能來？
- **Can you still make it to the meeting?**
  您是否還能趕上會議？
- **Can you still make our 3:00 appointment?**
  您是否還能趕上我們三點的約定？
- **Can you still make the Friday afternoon appointment?**
  您是否還能遵守禮拜五下午的約定？

1 對話

A Barbara, I'm looking forward to our meeting on Wednesday.
B Oh, is that this week?
A Yes. 你是否還能出席？
B I'm traveling that day, but I will try.

A 芭芭拉，我很期待我們禮拜三的會議。
B 喔，是這個禮拜嗎？
A 對啊，Can you still make it to the meeting?
B 那天還在旅行中，但我會盡可能出席的。

2 練習 您是否還能在十點開會？(meeting)
Can you still make ________________?

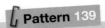

Pattern 139

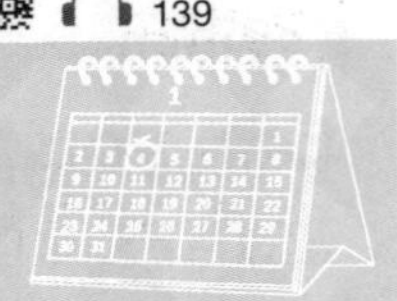

If you need to...
如果你要…

在會議或研討會的過程中，如果體貼對方可能會有其他考量的話，就可以使用這個句型。If you need to 後面可以接 cancel, eat, arrive, leave... 等各種意思的動詞，而 if 後面的子句則是表達這樣做沒關係的意思，試著開口練習看看吧！

- **If you need to cancel the appointment, call Linda.**
  如果你要取消約定，打電話給琳達。
- **If you need to cancel at the last minute, that's okay.**
  如果你要在最後關頭取消，那也沒關係。
- **If you need to eat lunch before the meeting, please do so.**
  如果你要在會議之前用午餐，請便。
- **If you need to ask questions, there'll be time at the end.**
  如果你要問問題，結束時會有時間。 ＊at the end 結束

1 對話
A So, I'll put you down for the 17th of June.
B Okay. 如果你要取消約定，打電話給琳達。
A I'll do that.

A 那麼我就記錄日期為六月十七日囉。
B 好的，If you need to cancel the appointment, call Linda.
A 我會的。

2 練習 如果你要晚一點來也沒關係。(a little, okay)
If you need to ______________________________.

Pattern 140

Please bring your...to...
請帶著你的…來…

想提醒對方要記得攜帶需要的東西時，就可以使這個祈使句。本句型中的介系詞 to 後面可以加上 appointment, meeting 等各式各樣的名詞或場所。

- **Please bring your portfolio to the meeting.**
  請帶著你的作品集來開會。
- **Please bring your quarterly sales sheet to the appointment.**
  請帶著你的季度業績報告書來會面。
  * quarterly 季度的
- **Please bring your laptop to the meeting.**
  請帶著你的筆記型電腦來開會。
- **Please bring your personnel file into the CEO's office.**
  請帶著你的人事資料進總裁的辦公室。

1 對話
A I need someone to take notes during the discussion.
B I can do it.
A Great. 請帶著你的筆記型電腦來開會。

A 開會時，我需要一個人幫忙做會議紀錄。
B 交給我吧。
A 太好了！Please bring your laptop to the meeting.

2 練習 請帶著進展狀況報告書來開第三季的會議。
(status report, quarter)
Please bring your ________________ to ________________.

6-4 與客戶見面

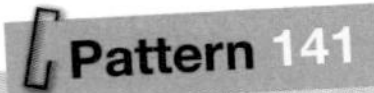

Let me pick you up...
我會去…接你。

這是用來表達自己會親自去迎接的意思的句型。本句型中的 let 和 have, make 等動詞一樣是使役動詞，所以後面要接原形動詞。pick someone up 則是表示「（開車）前往接某人」的意思。

- **Let me pick you up near the taxi stand.**
  我會去計程車招呼站附近接你。
- **Let me pick you up in front of the building.**
  我會去大樓前面接你。
- **Let me pick the client up at the airport.**
  我會去機場接客戶。 ＊client 客戶，委託人
- **Let me pick Janice up on my way to the office.**
  我會去辦公室的路上順道接珍妮絲。 ＊on one's way to 某人去…的路上

1 對話 **A** Will there be someone to meet me?
B 我會去計程車招呼站附近接你。
A Thank you very much.

A 會有人開車來接我嗎？
B Let me pick you up near the taxi stand.
A 非常謝謝你。

2 練習 我會去飯店接演講者。(speaker)
Let me pick ________________ up ________________.

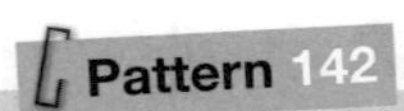

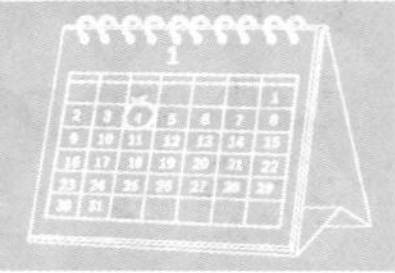

I'll be waiting at...
我會在…迎接你。

在去接對方之前，如果你想告訴對方等候的地點的話，就可以使用這個句型。在這裡 wait 除了「等待」，還能表示「去迎接」的意思。為了讓句子更為通順自然，wait 後面會接 at / in / near，後面再加上地點。

- **I'll be waiting at the Taoyuan International Airport.**
  我會在桃園國際機場迎接你。
- **I'll be waiting at the clock tower in the Plaza Center.**
  我會在廣場中心的鐘樓迎接你。
- **I'll be waiting in the arrival hall.**
  我會在入境大廳迎接你。
- **I'll be waiting near the check-in counter.**
  我會在辦理登機櫃檯附近迎接你。

1 對話
A Mr. Anderson. Where are we going to meet?
B 我會在桃園國際機場迎接你。
A Wonderful!

A 安德森先生，我們要在哪裡會合？
B I'll be waiting at the Taoyuan International Airport.
A 太好了！

2 練習 我會在外面迎接你。(outside)
I'll be waiting ______________________.

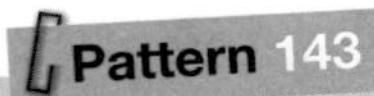

You must be Mr. ...
您是…先生吧？

143 確認對方身分

去迎接從沒見過面的人時，必須要先確認對方身分，此時你可以使用這個帶有 must be 的句型來向對方發問，說 You must be Mr. / Ms. ...。

- **You must be Mr. Robertson.**
  您是羅伯森先生吧？
- **You must be Mr. Nelson and Ms. Littleton.**
  你們是尼爾森先生以及利陶頓女士吧？
- **You must be Mr. Harrison's secretary.**
  您是哈里森先生的祕書吧？
- **You must be Mr. Trump's executive team.**
  你們是川普先生的執行小組吧？

* **executive** 執行的，實施的

1 對話 **A** Nice to meet you. 您是羅賓森先生吧？
B How did you know?
A I received your picture from my secretary.

A 很高興見到您。You must be Mr. Robertson.
B 您是怎麼知道的？
A 我的祕書有將您的照片寄給我。

2 練習 您是米勒先生的夫人吧？(Midler)
You must be Mr. ______________________.

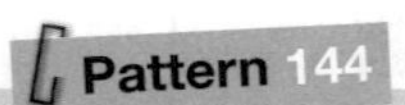

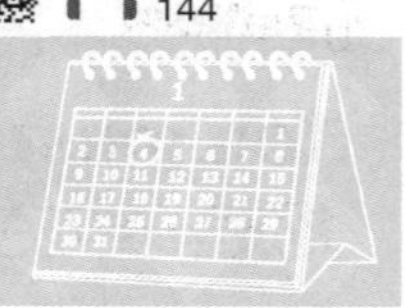

This is my...
這位是我的…

自我介紹後，如果你想要接著介紹同行的人的話，應該要怎麼說呢？這個時候就可以使用這個句型 This is my...。在聽到別人的介紹後，只須回覆對方 Pleased to meet you（很高興認識您）。

This is my partner, Lyle Montgomery.
這位是我的工作夥伴，里爾蒙高梅利。

This is my new assistant, Mindy.
這位是我的新助理，敏蒂。
＊assistant 助理，助手

This is my supervisor, Mr. Chin.
這位是我的主管，秦先生。
＊supervisor 主管，指導者

This is my accountant, Mr. Ingram.
這位是我的會計師，因格朗先生。

1 對話
A I hope we're not too late for the meeting.
B No. Please come in.
A Thank you. 這位是我的新助理，敏蒂。

A 希望這個會議我們沒有遲到太久。
B 沒這回事，請進。
A 謝謝。This is my new assistant, Mindy.

2 練習 這位是我的律師，艾德森先生。(lawyer)
This is my ______________________.

Pattern 145

I'll show you...
我會帶你參觀…

當你要向前來公司拜訪的客戶介紹辦公室或工廠的環境時，就可以使用這個句型。此外，雖然我們常常會使用到 I will 的縮寫 I'll，但其實縮寫的發音不太容易聽得出來。請仔細聽這個單元的音檔，多加練習吧！

- **I'll show you my new office.**
  我會帶你參觀我的新辦公室。
- **I'll show you around our corporate headquarters.**
  我會帶你到處參觀我們的公司總部。 ＊headquarters 總部，總公司
- **I'll show you the city when you visit us.**
  你來拜訪我們的時候，我會帶你到市區逛逛。
- **I'll show you our shoe exhibition.**
  我會帶你參觀我們的鞋展示館。 ＊exhibition 展示館

1 對話
A One day, I'd like to see your Seattle offices.
B Come any time. 你來拜訪我們的時候，我會帶你到市區逛逛。
A I was thinking about later this year.

A 我希望能找一天去參觀你在西雅圖的辦公室。
B 隨時都歡迎你。I'll show you the city when you visit us.
A 我在考慮要不要今年年底去。

2 練習 我會帶你參觀我們工廠在運作時的情況。(at work)
I'll show you ______________________.

6-5

招待客戶

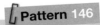

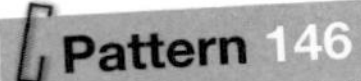

疑問詞 + would you like to...? 您想要…呢？

這是由疑問詞（where / what / when... 等）+ would you like to 組合而成的句型，表示客氣地詢問對方的想法。在招待客戶時，試著用這個句型問對方想要去哪裡、想吃些什麼，以及什麼時候想去吧！

- **Where would you like to go?**
  您想要去哪裡呢？
- **What would you like to eat for dinner?**
  您晚餐想要吃什麼呢？
- **When would you like to meet the rest of the staff?**
  您什麼時候想要與其他的職員見面呢？ ＊the rest of 其他的，剩餘的
- **Which movie would you like to see?**
  您想要看哪一部電影呢？

1 對話
A I want to go out to eat.
B 您想要去哪裡呢？
A Let's try that Mexican place.

A 我想要去外面吃飯。
B Where would you like to go?
A 去墨西哥餐廳好了。

2 練習 您想要聊些什麼呢？(what, talk)
__________ would you like to __________?

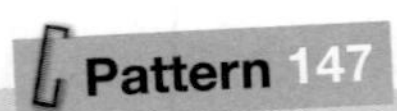

Have you ever...?
你以前有…嗎？

當你想詢問對方過去的經驗時，就可以使用這個現在完成式 “have+p.p.” 的句型。句型中的 ever 表示「曾經」的意思，例句中的 try 則跟 eat 一樣可以解釋為「吃」的意思。

- **Have you ever tried stinky tofu?**
  你以前有嚐過臭豆腐嗎？
  ＊try 嘗試
- **Have you ever tried oyster omelet?**
  你以前有嚐過蚵仔煎嗎？
- **Have you ever been to Hualien?**
  你以前有去過花蓮嗎？
- **Have you ever been there before?**
  你以前有去過那裡嗎？

1 對話

A We’re having Taiwanese food for lunch today.
B That sounds great!
A 你以前有嚐過蚵仔煎嗎？
B I’m not sure. Are there vegetables in it?

A 我們今天中午要吃台灣料理吧！
B 聽起來不錯！
A Have you ever tried oyster omelet?
B 我也不清楚，是裡面有加蔬菜的那道料理嗎？

2 練習 你以前有喝過珍珠奶茶嗎？(bubble tea)
Have you ever ______________________________?

Pattern 148

This restaurant is popular for...
這家餐廳的…很受歡迎。

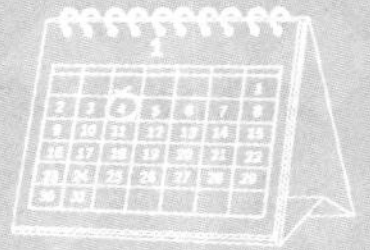

當你想向對方介紹某間餐廳的 speciality（特別料理）時，就可以使用這個句型。這句話也可以讓對方覺得你為了招待他，特別花了很多心思。句型中的 popular 還可以用 famous 或 well known 代替。

- This restaurant is popular for **its lobster.**
  這家餐廳的**龍蝦**很受歡迎。
- This restaurant is popular for **its folk music.**
  這家餐廳的**民俗音樂**很受歡迎。
- This restaurant is popular for **its outdoor patio.**
  這家餐廳的**戶外露台**很受歡迎。　＊patio（在建築物後方的）露台
- This restaurant is popular for **its Korean table d'hôte.**
  這家餐廳的**韓定食**很受歡迎。　＊table d'hôte 桌菜（有別於點菜的）

1 對話
A What a lovely restaurant!
B Yes. 這家餐廳的韓定食很受歡迎。
A I've always wanted to try it.

A 這間餐廳看起來真棒！
B 沒錯。This restaurant is popular for its Korean table d'hôte.
A 我一直都很想吃吃看韓定食。

2 練習 這家餐廳的牛排很受歡迎。(steak)
This restaurant is popular for ____________________.

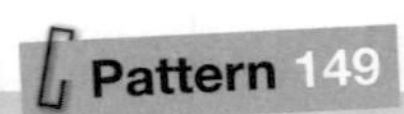

149

Let me show you how to...
讓我為你示範如何…

當我們招待客戶吃中式料理時，想為對方示範如何用餐的話，就可以使用這個句型。Let me show you how to... 是介紹食用方式的萬能句型。

- **Let me show you how to use the chopsticks.**
  讓我為你示範如何使用筷子。
- **Let me show you how to wrap up the meat.**
  讓我為你示範如何把肉包起來。
- **Let me show you how to pour tea.**
  讓我為你示範如何斟茶。
  * pour 倒，灌（液體等）
- **Let me show you how to call the waiter.**
  讓我為你示範如何叫喚侍者。

1 對話
A The Korean tea ceremony is very special.
B I'd like to learn more about it.
A Then, 讓我為你示範如何斟茶。

A 韓國的茶道非常特別。
B 我想要多了解一些。
A 那麼，let me show you how to pour tea.

2 練習 讓我為你示範要怎麼剪泡菜吧。(chop)
Let me show you how to ______________.

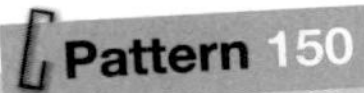

Did you enjoy...?
你喜歡…嗎？

招待完對方，也要跟對方確認是否感到滿意，才算替這次的招待畫上完美的句點。不管你是想問對方是否滿意餐點、剛剛欣賞的表演是否有趣，又或剛剛的談話是否愉快等，都可以使用這個句型 Did you enjoy...?。

- **Did you enjoy National Palace Museum?**
  你喜歡故宮博物院嗎？
- **Did you enjoy the show?**
  你喜歡那場表演嗎？
- **Did you enjoy the small steamed buns?**
  你喜歡小籠包嗎？
- **Did you enjoy your first visit to Taiwan?**
  第一次的台灣行玩得開心嗎？

1 對話

A 你喜歡小籠包嗎？
B Yes, the food is very good here.
A That's good.

A Did you enjoy the small steamed buns?
B 嗯，這裡的食物真的很好吃。
A 太好了。

2 練習 剛剛的對談還愉快嗎？(conversation)

Did you enjoy ________________________________?

6-1~6-5

黃金複習 15 分鐘！

前面這 25 個句型和 125 個句子全都記熟了嗎？
來驗收一下學習成果吧！如果不能充滿自信地用英文說出以下 40 個句子，請翻到前面再重新複習一次！

01 第一次的台灣行玩得開心嗎？

02 明天你方便嗎？

03 讓我為你示範如何把肉包起來。

04 我們可以約當天早一點見面嗎？

05 這家餐廳的民俗音樂很受歡迎。

06 兩點十五分之前我沒問題。

07 你以前有嚐過蚵仔煎嗎？

08 可以請你安排一場視訊會議嗎？

09 您晚餐想要吃什麼呢？

解答 01. Did you enjoy your first visit to Taiwan? 02. Is tomorrow okay with you?
03. Let me show you how to wrap up the meat. 04. Can we meet earlier in the day?
05. This restaurant is popular for its folk music. 06. I can make it by 2:15.
07. Have you ever tried oyster omelet? 08. Could you arrange a conference call?
09. What would you like to eat for dinner?

10 如果可以的話，我們可以在你的辦公室碰面。

11 我會帶你到處參觀我們的公司總部。

12 抱歉，我必須提早離開這場會議。

13 這位是我的工作夥伴，里爾蒙高梅利。

14 我可能無法準時完成。

15 您是哈里森先生的祕書吧？

16 我們可以改約別天嗎？

17 我會在入境大廳迎接你。

18 這禮拜還有其他更適合的時間嗎？

19 我會去計程車招呼站附近接你。

20 如果您需要更改時間，請跟我聯絡。

解答 10. If it's all right, we can meet at your office.
11. I'll show you around our corporate headquarters.
12. I'm sorry, but I need to leave the meeting early.
13. This is my partner, Lyle Montgomery. 14. I don't think I'll be able to make it on time.
15. You must be Mr. Harrison's secretary. 16. Can we reschedule the date?
17. I'll be waiting in the arrival hall. 18. Is there another day of the week that's better?
19. Let me pick you up near the taxi stand. 20. Call me if you need to reschedule.

21 請帶著你的季度業績報告書來會面。

22 我寫這封信是想確認我們在兩點整準時碰面。

23 如果你要在最後關頭取消，那也沒關係。

24 您是否還能趕上會議？

25 在我辦公室你方便嗎？

26 我只是想確認一下我這邊的電話號碼是正確的。

27 可以約在某天晚上晚餐時見面嗎？

28 禮拜二我沒問題。

29 我打電話來是想確認威斯特先生會出席這場會議。

30 可以請你安排我跟經理見面嗎？

解答 21. Please bring your quarterly sales sheet to the appointment.
22. I'm writing to confirm we'll meet promptly at 2:00.
23. If you need to cancel at the last minute, that's okay.
24. Can you still make it to the meeting? 25. Is my office okay with you?
26. I just want to make sure I have the correct phone number.
27. Can we meet over dinner some evening? 28. I can make it on Tuesday.
29. I'm calling to confirm that Mr. West will be at the meeting.
30. Could you arrange an appointment to see the manager?

31 如果可以的話，我會帶著我的同事一起過去。

32 你喜歡小籠包嗎？

33 抱歉，我必須更改我們的會面時間。

34 讓我為你示範如何使用筷子。

35 我明天可能無法與你碰面。

36 這家餐廳的龍蝦很受歡迎。

37 我們可以更改會面時間到三點嗎？

38 你以前有去過花蓮嗎？

39 還有其他對我們雙方都方便的地點嗎？

40 您什麼時候想要與其他的職員見面呢？

解答 31. If it's all right, I'll bring my colleague along.
32. Did you enjoy the small steamed buns?
33. I'm sorry, but I need to change our appointment time.
34. Let me show you how to use the chopsticks.
35. I don't think I'll be able to meet tomorrow.
36. This restaurant is popular for its lobster. 37. Can we reschedule the appointment for 3:00?
38. Have you ever been to Hualien? 39. Is there another location convenient to us both?
40. When would you like to meet the rest of the staff?

Unit 7
詢問產品與介紹產品

這樣推銷產品
反應超熱烈

7-1

介紹公司

Our company is one of...	151	我們公司是…之一。
We specialize in...	152	我們是專門從事…的公司。
We're based in...	153	我們公司位於…
We have a...percent share of...	154	我們在…有百分之…的市佔率。
We have affiliate companies that...	155	我們有關係企業…

Pattern 151

Our company is one of...
我們公司是…之一。

當你想跟對方表達自己公司在眾多同業中是名列前茅時，就可以使用這個句型。「one of + 最高級 + 複數名詞」是表示「最…的…之一」的意思。

- **Our company is one of the largest in the world.**
  我們公司是世界上最大的企業之一。
- **Our company is one of the strongest performers in the industry.**
  我們公司是業界最具有競爭力的公司之一。　＊performer 公司，執行者
- **Our company is one of the most reputable exporters in the region.**
  我們公司是該地區名聲最好的出口商之一。　＊reputable 聲譽良好的
- **Our company is one of fifty automobile parts suppliers.**
  我們公司是五十家汽車零件供應商之一。

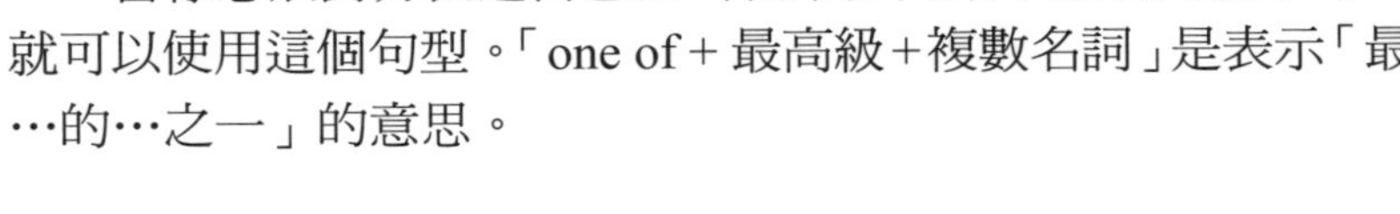

1 對話
A 我們公司是業界最具有競爭力的公司之一。
B Can you show me some numbers?
A Sure. As you can see here, we dominate the market.

A Our company is one of the strongest performers in the industry.
B 你有相關的數據資料可以給我看嗎？
A 當然有。如你看到的一樣，我們公司稱霸整個市場。

2 練習 我們公司是進口業界裡的領頭羊之一。(leaders, imports)
Our company is one of ______________________.

Pattern 152

We specialize in...
我們是專門從事…的公司。

這是介紹公司的專業領域時可以使用的句型。本句型中的 in 是介系詞，後面必須接各個領域事業的名詞或動名詞 (V-ing)。

- **We specialize in textiles.**
  我們是專門從事紡織品的公司。
  ＊textile 布料，紡織品
- **We specialize in electronics.**
  我們是專門從事電子用品的公司。
- **We specialize in exports.**
  我們是專門從事出口貨品的公司。
  ＊export 輸出，出口
- **We specialize in distributing IT products throughout Korea.**
  ＊distribute 分布，分銷
  我們是專門從事將科技產品分銷到全韓國的公司。

1 對話
A 我們是專門從事紡織品的公司。
B Do you have a variety of suppliers?
A Yes, we have sources in several countries.

A We specialize in textiles.
B 你們公司有各式各樣的供應商嗎？
A 有的，我們的供應商遍布好幾個國家。

2 練習 我們是專門從事音響設備的公司。(equipment)
We specialize in ______________________________.

Pattern 153

We're based in...
我們公司位於…

這是介紹公司的所在地或業務範圍時所使用的句型，用來表達「我們公司位於…」或「我們公司的業務範圍是…」的意思。句中的介系詞 in 後面要接特定的產業別或地點。

- **We're based in Detroit.**
  我們公司位於底特律。
- **We're based in the commodities market.**
  我們公司的業務範圍是日用品市場。 ＊commodity 日用品
- **We're based in the financial district.**
  我們公司位於財經區。
- **We're based in five major cities in Asia.**
  我們公司的業務範圍包括五個亞洲主要城市。

1 對話
A We'd like you to visit our New York office.
B Great. Where are you located?
A 我們公司位於金融區。

A 我們希望您能來紐約的辦公室。
B 好的，你們位在哪裡呢？
A We're based in the financial district.

2 練習 我們公司的業務範圍是女性服飾。(clothing)
We're based in ________________.

Pattern 154

We have a...percent share of...
我們在…有百分之…的市佔率。

這是介紹公司目前市佔率時可以使用的句型。市佔率的英文為 market share rate，有時也可省略 rate 不說。

- **We have a 15 percent share of the home appliances market.** ＊home appliance 家用電器
  我們在家電製品市場有百分之十五的市佔率。
- **We have a 12 percent share of the market in the textiles industry.**
  我們在紡織品工業市場有百分之十二的市佔率。
- **We have a 2 percent share of the software market.**
  我們在軟體市場有百分之二的市佔率。
- **We have a 10 percent share of all profits from this deal.**
  我們在此交易中獲取全部收益的百分之十。 ＊profit 收益

1 對話
A 我們在紡織品工業市場有百分之十二的市佔率。
B Not bad.
A And we expect it to increase in the next quarter.

A We have a 12 percent share of the market in the textiles industry.
B 聽起來還不錯。
A 而且我們預測下一季還會更好。

2 練習 我們在國內市場的市佔率為百分之五十。(domestic market)
We have a ________ percent share of ________.

Pattern 155

We have affiliate companies that...
我們有關係企業…

在業務關係中，提及公司規模是取得對方信任的其中一個方法。句型中的 affiliate company 可依照情況解釋為「關係企業、聯營公司、供應廠商」等。

- **We have affiliate companies that use our services.**
  我們有關係企業使用我們的服務。　＊affiliate company 關係企業
- **We have affiliate companies that supply us with products.**
  我們有供應廠商提供我們產品。　＊supply 提供，供給
- **We have three affiliate companies in the fashion business.**
  我們有三家在時尚產業的關係企業。
- **We have five affiliate companies that buy our products.**
  我們有五家購買我們產品的聯營公司。

1 對話
A 我們有供應廠商提供我們產品。
B Do they work with you exclusively?
A Yes. They are under contract with us.

A We have affiliate companies that supply us with products.
B 他們只供應產品給你們公司嗎？
A 是的，他們和我們簽下了獨佔合約。

2 練習 我們有和我們公司簽下獨佔合約的供應廠商。(exclusive)
We have affiliate companies ______________.

7-2

介紹產品

This is the latest... 156 這是最新的…

This product uses... 157 這項產品使用…

This item has... 158 這項產品擁有…

This is designed to... 159 這是…的設計。

It comes with... 160 這項商品會附贈…

156

Pattern 156

This is the latest...
這是最新的…

這是用來介紹產品的版本或型號時可以使用的句型。我們常常用 newest 來表示「最新的、最近的」的意思，但在介紹產品或商品最新的版本或型號時，請改使用 latest 這個單字。

- **This is the latest version.**
  這是最新的型號。　＊version 版本，型號
- **This is the latest trend.**
  這是最新的趨勢。　＊trend 趨勢，流行
- **This is the latest technology.**
  這是最新的科技。
- **This is the latest in cell phone technology.**
  這是行動電話中的最新科技。

1 對話
A What makes this product unique?
B 這是最新的型號。
A Does it offer new features?
B Yes. Here, take a look.

A 這產品有什麼獨特之處？
B This is the latest version.
A 有什麼新功能嗎？
B 有的，請看這裡。

2 練習 這是最新型的通訊裝置。(communication devices)
This is the latest ______________________.

Pattern 157

This product uses...
這項產品使用…

當你想要詳細地介紹產品的材料、生產技術等相關規格資訊時，就可以使用這個句型。另外，請注意名詞 product 的重音在前，動詞 produce 的重音在後。

- **This product uses solar power to get electricity.**
  這項產品使用太陽能發電。 ＊solar 太陽的，利用太陽光的
- **This product uses four AA batteries to power its systems.**
  這項產品使用四個二號電池提供系統動力。
- **This product uses recycled materials.**
  這項產品使用回收再利用的原料。 ＊recycled 再利用的
- **This product uses flour and butter to make dough.**
  這項產品使用麵粉與奶油來製作麵糰。 ＊dough 麵糰

1 對話
A What is your company policy on environmentalism?
B 這項產品使用回收再利用的原料。We're proud of this particular product.

A 貴公司在環境保護方面有什麼樣的政策？
B This product uses recycled materials. 我們對這項獨特的產品感到自豪。

2 練習 這項產品使用水作為冷卻劑。(coolant)
This product uses ______________________________

Pattern 158

This item has...
這項產品擁有…

表示「產品」的意思的單字很多，包括 item, product, model 等。當你想簡單地介紹產品時，就可以使用這個句型。

This item has a lot of versatility.
這項產品擁有許多功能。 ＊versatility 多用途，多功能

This item has the best performance specifications.
這項產品擁有性能表現最佳的規格。 ＊specification 規格

This model has a long shelf life.
這項產品擁有很長的耐儲時間。 ＊shelf life 貨架壽命，耐儲時間

This model has the best sales history.
這項產品擁有史上最佳銷售紀錄。

1 對話
A 這項產品擁有史上最佳銷售紀錄。
B It's done well in foreign markets?
A Exactly.

A This model has the best sales history.
B 在國外市場也有這麼好的表現嗎？
A 當然。

2 練習 這項產品擁有絕佳的耐用度。(durability)
This item has ______________________.

Pattern 159

This is designed to...
這是…的設計。

這是用來介紹產品結構特色的句型，在後面說明使用時的注意事項、可否使用無線網路，又或者是產品使用上的安全性方面等優點，是非常好用的句型。

- **This is designed to repel water.**
  這是防水的設計。 ＊repel 抗，防
- **This is designed to access Wi-Fi.**
  這是連上無線網路的設計。 ＊access 接近，進入
- **This is designed to shut down automatically.**
  這是自動關機的設計。
- **This is designed to keep you organized.**
  這是讓你保持井井有條的設計。

1 對話
A It looks very good.
B Thank you.
A How does the Internet work?
A 這是連上無線網路的設計。

A 這產品看起來很不錯。
B 謝謝。
A 要如何連線上網？
B This is designed to access Wi-Fi.

2 練習 這是為了幫助身障人士的設計。(assist, disabled)
This is designed to ______________________.

Pattern 160

It comes with...
這項商品會附贈⋯

如果銷售商品時有附送贈品，這時就可以使用這個句型。句型後面 with 可以接有形的物品或無形的附加價值（lifetime, membership 等）。

- **It comes with batteries.**
  這項商品會附贈電池。
- **It comes with a free carrying case.**
  這項商品會附贈免費的提箱。
- **It comes with a ten-year warranty.**
  這項商品會附贈十年保固。 ＊warranty 保證，保固
- **It comes with a useful reference guide.**
  這項商品會附贈一份實用的參考指南。 ＊reference 參考

1 對話 **A** Does the product come with any extras?
B 這項商品會附贈一個免費的提箱。
A Oh, that's quite nice.

A 這項商品有附送贈品嗎？
B It comes with a free carrying case.
A 喔，那挺不錯的。

2 練習 這項商品會附贈一個充電器。(charger)
It comes with ______________________.

7-3

介紹服務內容

We can guarantee...	161	我們保證⋯
The warranty is...	162	保固⋯
The limited warranty covers...	163	有限的保固包括⋯
This will provide... to...	164	這可以提供⋯
We run...	165	我們經營⋯

Pattern 161

161

We can guarantee...
我們保證…

我們常常可以聽到廣告說「我們保證…」，而本單元的 We can guarantee... 就是用來表達這個意思的句型，可以用來取得顧客的信任，進而跟顧客成功做到生意。

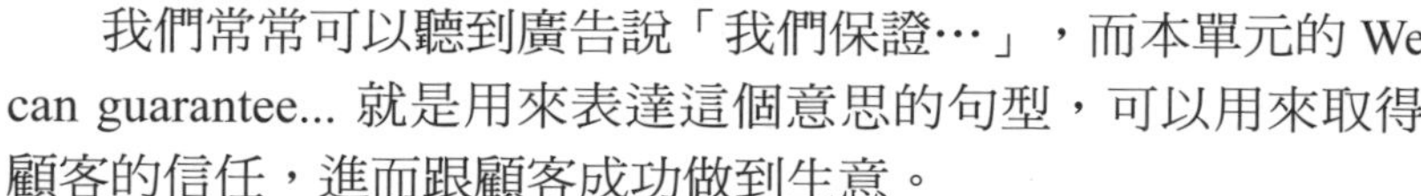

- **We can guarantee this product for five years.**
  我們保固這項產品五年的時間。
- **We can guarantee this product for one year from the date of purchase.**
  我們保固這項產品從購買日起一年的時間。 ＊purchase 購買
- **We can guarantee a full refund if you're not satisfied.**
  如果您對商品不滿意的話，我們保證全額退費。
- **We can guarantee this product against all defects.**
  我們保障這項產品的全部瑕疵。 ＊defect 缺陷，瑕疵

1 對話

A 如果您對商品不滿意的話，我們保證全額退費。
B Are you planning to raise prices?
A We constantly adjust our prices based on the market.

A We can guarantee a full refund if you're not satisfied.
B 請問近期有漲價的計畫嗎？
A 我們一直以來都會依照市場情況而調整價格。

2 練習 我們保證顧客一定會滿意。(satisfaction)
We can guarantee ______________________.

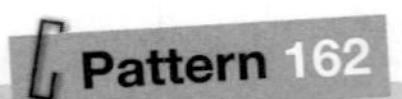

The warranty is...
保固…

「品質保證書」的英文為 warranty 或 guarantee，一般來說比較常使用 warranty 這個單字，guarantee 則主要用來當作句型中的動詞，如 Our company guarantees...。

- **The warranty is good for a year.**
  保固的有效時間是一年。
- **The warranty is quite extensive.**
  保固的範圍相當廣泛。 ＊extensive 廣泛的
- **The warranty is better than most.**
  保固比其他大部分的產品都要好。
- **The warranty has expired.**
  保固已經過期了。 ＊expired 終止，期滿

1 對話
A Is there a warranty?
B Yes, there is.
A What does it cover?
B 保固的範圍相當廣泛。

A 有保證書嗎？
B 有的，在這裡。
A 保固範圍包括哪些呢？
B The warranty is quite extensive.

2 練習 保固內容無法轉讓給他人。(non-transferable)
The warranty is ______________________.

Pattern 163

The limited warranty covers...
有限的保固包括⋯

the limited warranty 指的是有限制的附件保固內容或保固期間，the general warranty 指的則是一般的保證書。句型中的 cover 是用來表達保固的範圍。

- **The limited warranty covers the cost of repairs for six months.**
  有限的保固包括六個月期間的修理費用。 ＊repair 修理
- **The limited warranty covers the cost of a refund or exchange.**
  有限的保固包括退換貨的費用。
- **The limited warranty covers up to $500 in parts.**
  有限的保固包括最多五百美元的零件費。
- **The limited warranty can't cover accidental damage.**
  有限的保固不包括意外的損壞。 ＊accidental 意外的

1 對話
A 有限的保固不包括意外的損壞。
B I see. Are the repairs expensive?
A Not terribly.

A The limited warranty can't cover accidental damage.
B 我知道了。維修費用會很貴嗎？
A 不會很貴。

2 練習 有限的產品保固期有一年。(for)
The limited warranty covers ______________.

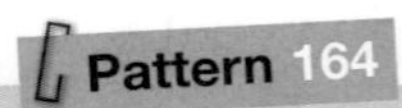

This will provide...to...
這可以提供…

當你想要向顧客介紹公司提供的「產品或服務（包含網路）」時，就可以使用這個句型，是向客戶介紹產品或服務時十分重要的其中一個句型。

- **This will provide a 24-hour service to customers.**
  這可以提供顧客24小時的服務。
- **This will provide high-speed Internet access to your company.**
  這可以提供貴公司高速的網路服務。
- **This will provide another option to buyers.**
  這可以提供買家另一個選擇。
- **This will provide peace of mind to customers.**
  這可以讓客戶感到安心。 ＊peace of mind 心平氣和

1 對話
A How do you like our on-site babysitting service?
B It's a great idea.
A 這可以讓客戶感到安心。

A 你覺得我們的現場托育服務如何呢？
B 這是個很棒的想法。
A This will provide peace of mind to customers.

2 練習 這可以讓客戶省下很多時間。(huge, time savings)
This will provide ________________ to ________________.

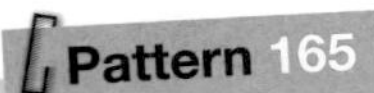

We run...
我們經營…

想要介紹說明公司為客戶提供哪種類型的系統或服務時，常常會使用 run 這個動詞，在這裡是「經營」的意思。

- **We run a 24-hour answering service.**
  我們的客服電話24小時營運。
- **We run a state-of-the-art website.**
  我們經營有提供最新資訊的網站。 ＊ state-of-the-art 最先進的
- **We run daily backups of our email activity.**
  我們每天執行一次備份電子郵件的動作。
- **We run a trained customer support team on a 24-hour basis.**
  我們有訓練完備的客戶支援小組 24 小時營運。

1 對話

A I'd like to know about your appliance line.
B Sure. Why don't you visit our website?
A Is the information there up to date?
B Yes. 我們經營有提供最新資訊的網站。

A 我想了解一下貴公司的家電產品線。
B 好的。您要不要瀏覽一下我們公司的網頁呢？
A 網頁上的資訊都是最新的嗎？
B 是的。We run a state-of-the-art website.

2 練習 我們經營有歐洲最棒的顧客服務中心。
(customer service center)
We run ________________________.

7-4

詢問產品

We're interested in... 166 我們對…有興趣。

I'm looking for... 167 我在找…

We'd like to get information on... 168 我們想知道關於…的資訊。

Please explain the details of... 169 請詳細說明一下…的細節。

I was wondering if you could... 170 不知道您能否…

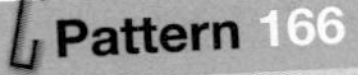

166

We're interested in...
我們對…有興趣。

這個句型常用來表達對於對方的公司或產品有興趣。本句型中的 in 後面要接一般的名詞或 V-ing 動名詞，如 working, finding, helping 等。如果想強調自己「非常」有興趣時，可以在句型中的形容詞 interested 前面加上 very, really, totally, absolutely 等副詞修飾。

- **We're interested in your best deal on handbags.**
  我們對貴公司手提包的最低價格有興趣。 ＊deal 交易
- **We're interested in the toolkit on page 41 of your catalog.**
  我們對貴公司目錄上第41頁的工具組有興趣。
- **We're really interested in your paper products.**
  我們對貴公司的紙製品非常有興趣。
- **We're very interested in placing a large order.**
  我們對大量下訂非常有興趣。

1 對話
A We'd like to do business with your company.
B Fabulous! What kinds of products are you talking about?
A 我們對貴公司的紙製品非常有興趣。

A 我們想跟貴公司做生意。
B 當然好！請問你們對哪個產品感興趣？
A We're really interested in your paper products.

2 練習 我們對貴公司最新的皮製品有興趣。(latest)
We're interested in ____________________.

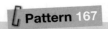

Pattern 167

I'm looking for...
我在找…

這個句型可以用來表達「在尋找某樣特定產品」。本句型的介系詞 for 後面也可以接上物品或人名，在生活和工作上都會接觸到，是相當實用的句型。

- **I'm looking for a laptop in a different color.**
  我在找不同顏色的筆記型電腦。 ＊laptop 筆記型電腦
- **I'm looking for something less expensive.**
  我在找便宜一點的東西。
- **I'm looking for a necktie that looks like this one.**
  我在找跟這個類似的領帶。
- **I'm looking for some alternative to this keyboard.**
  我在找這個鍵盤的替代品。 ＊alternative 替代，替代品

1 對話

A This laptop comes fully loaded.
B I like it, but...
A Is there a problem?
B 我在找不同顏色的筆記型電腦。

A 這款筆記型電腦的功能十分齊全。
B 我滿喜歡的，但是…
A 有什麼問題嗎？
B I'm looking for a laptop in a different color.

2 練習 我在找強力清潔劑。(powerful, cleaning solution)
I'm looking for ____________.

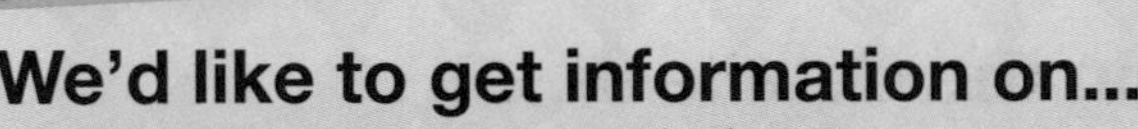

Pattern 168

168

We'd like to get information on...
我們想知道關於⋯的資訊。

get 是萬能動詞，可解釋成「獲得、得到」等。在本句型裡可替換為 receive，另外還可表達 arrive（抵達）、obtain（得到）、become（變成）等意義。

上班族萬用句

- **We'd like to get information on performance.**
  我們想知道關於性能的資訊。　＊performance 性能
- **We'd like to get information on pricing.**
  我們想知道關於價格的資訊。
- **We'd like to get information on how long the shipping takes.**
  我們想知道關於運送時間的資訊。
- **We'd like to get information on green technology.**
  我們想知道關於綠色科技的資訊。　＊green 關心環境的，環境保護的

1 對話
A 我們想知道關於價格的資訊。
B This unit starts at $700.
A That's too much for us right now.

A We'd like to get information on pricing.
B 這項產品的價格是七百美元起跳。
A 這對現在的我們來說太貴了。

2 練習 我們想知道這輛車的哩程數資訊。(gas mileage)
We'd like to get some information on ______________.

Pattern 169

Please explain the details of...
請詳細說明一下…的細節。

當你希望對方針對產品或系統進行更詳細的解說時，就可以使用這個句型。句型中的 explain 表示「說明…」的意思，of 後面則是要接說明對象的內容，如 of the product。

- **Please explain the details of the product.**
  請詳細說明一下這項產品的細節。
- **Please explain the details of the payment plan.**
  請詳細說明一下付款方式的細節。
- **Please explain the details of the return policy.**
  請詳細說明一下退貨規則的細節。
- **Please explain the details of the rental agreement.**
  請詳細說明一下租賃協定的細節。

* rental 出租，租賃

1 對話

A We have a few things to work out first.
B Sure. What do you want to know?
A 請詳細說明一下付款方式的細節。

A 我們想要先弄清楚幾件事情。
B 當然。請問你們想知道些什麼呢？
A Please explain the details of the payment plan.

2 練習 請詳細說明一下電腦上鎖的方法。(how to)
Please explain the details on ______________.

Pattern 170

I was wondering if you could...
不知道您能否…

針對好奇之處提問時常會使用這個句型：wonder（動詞）+ if / whether...，表達「不知道…能否…」的意思。這個提問句型的語氣比較恭敬，在商務場合會很常用到。

- **I was wondering if you could tell me about how this product compares to others.** ＊compare to 跟…做比較
  不知道您能否告訴我這項產品跟其他產品比起來如何？
- **I was wondering if you could tell me about your new rates.**
  不知道您能否告訴我貴公司的新價格？ ＊rates 金額，價格
- **I was wondering if you could tell me about the availability in my area.**
  不知道您能否告訴我在我的區域是否還有庫存？
- **I was wondering if you could tell me about the company's philosophy.**
  不知道您能否告訴我貴公司的經營理念？ ＊philosophy 哲學，理念

1 對話

A We're glad to have you with us.
B Do you have any questions for us?
A 不知道您能否說一下貴公司的經營理念？

A 很高興能跟貴公司合作。
B 請問你對我們公司有什麼疑問嗎？
A I was wondering if you could tell me about the company's philosophy.

2 練習 不知道您能否跟我說明一下這台腳踏車的耐用度？(durability)
I was wondering if you could ____________________.

7-5 行銷

This will appeal to...	171	訴求對象是…
Our main target is...	172	我們主要的目標客戶是…
We focus on...	173	我們會致力於…
Market research shows...	174	市場調查顯示，…
We'll advertise...	175	我們將會…打廣告。

Pattern 171

This will appeal to...
訴求對象是⋯

在宣傳或廣告某樣產品的「訴求對象」時，最常用到的單字就是 appeal（吸引），所以當你想要說明產品會吸引哪些客層時，就可以使用這個句型。

This will appeal to teenagers.
訴求對象是十幾歲的青少年。

This will appeal to single men.
訴求對象是單身男性。

This will appeal to a wide range of people.
訴求對象是廣大階層的人。　＊**range** 範圍，階層

This will appeal to the average American.
訴求對象是一般的美國人。　＊**average** 平均的，一般的

1 對話
A Who is our most likely customer?
B 訴求對象是單身男性。
A Then perhaps we can promote it at sporting events.

A 我們的主要客戶群是誰？
B This will appeal to single men.
A 那麼我們或許可以在體育活動上進行宣傳。

2 練習 訴求對象是媽媽們。(mothers)
This will appeal to ______________.

Pattern 172

Our main target is...
我們主要的目標客戶是⋯

main target 是表示「主要目標」的意思，在提及宣傳廣告某樣產品的目標客戶時，若能使用本句型 Our main target is... 來表達的話，可以展現出自己專業的商務會話能力。意義相近的句型有 Our service is mainly targeted...。

- Our main target is **housewives.**
  我們主要的目標客戶是家庭主婦。
- Our main target is **the elderly.**
  我們主要的目標客戶是老年人。
  * the elderly 老年人，高齡者
- Our main target is **high-income buyers.**
  我們主要的目標客戶是高收入的購買者。
  * high-income 高收入的
- Our main target is **18-to-24-year-old people.**
  我們主要的目標客戶是 18 到 24 歲的群眾。

1 對話

A Whom are you targeting?
B 我們的主要目標客戶是 18～24 歲的群眾。
A How will you reach that market?
B We plan to spend heavily on television advertising.

A 你們的目標客戶是誰？
B Our main target is 18-to-24-year-old people.
A 你們要如何打進這個市場呢？
B 我們打算投入大筆資金在電視廣告上。

2 練習 我們的主要目標客戶是年輕的專業工作者。(professionals)
Our main target is ______________________.

Pattern 173

We focus on...
我們會致力於…

在宣傳或廣告某產品時想要強調某個重點想法的話，就可以使用這個帶有動詞 focus（集中、焦點）的句型，讓對方抓住重點。

- **We focus on maximizing the exposure of the product.**
  我們會致力於最大化商品的曝光度。 ＊maximize 達到最大限度
- **We focus on the youth market.**
  我們會鎖定年輕人的市場。
- **We focus on the qualities of our products.**
  我們會致力於產品的品質。
- **We focus on making our company family-friendly.**
  我們會致力於成為一個關心員工家庭生活的公司。
  ＊family-friendly 適合家庭的

1 對話 **A** Where should we place this product?
B 我們會鎖定年輕人的市場。
A That seems like a good plan.

A 我們該如何定位這個產品？
B We focus on the youth market.
A 這主意好像還不錯。

2 練習 我們會鎖定女性流行市場。(women)
We focus on ______________________.

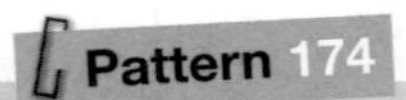

Market research shows...
市場調查顯示，…

要跟客戶、同事報告市場調查結果時，只要在 market research 或 market survey 後面接上動詞 show 就行了。

- **Market research shows** that there are 300,000 teens living in the area.
  市場調查顯示，有三十萬的青少年居住在這個區域。 ＊teen 青少年
- **Market research shows** most homes now have a smart phone.
  市場調查顯示，現在大部分的家庭都擁有一支智慧型手機。
- **Market research shows** that demand for this product will be high.
  市場調查顯示，這項產品的需求將會提高。 ＊demand 需求
- **Market research shows** the average income for this region to be quite high.
  市場調查顯示，該地區的平均薪資相當高。

1 對話
A What kind of strategy should we pursue?
B 市場調查顯示，該地區的平均薪資相當高。
A Then perhaps we should focus on high-end magazines.

A 我們應該要採取什麼樣的策略呢？
B Market research shows the average income for this region to be quite high.
A 那麼我們或許可以將宣傳重點放在高檔雜誌上。

2 練習 市場調查顯示，男性比較少購買道路地圖。
(less likely to, road maps)
Market research shows ______________________________.

Pattern 175

We'll advertise...
我們將會…打廣告。

想要說明行銷和宣傳的方式和手法的話，就可以使用這個句型。動詞 advertise 後面可接 local radio, online, on the subway, in all the major papers 等宣傳地點，是非常好用的句型。

- **We'll advertise in several different newspapers and magazines.**
  我們將會在數家不同的報紙和雜誌打廣告。
- **We'll advertise on local radio.**
  我們將會在當地的廣播電台打廣告。
- **We'll advertise online and at the shopping mall.**
  我們將會在網路和購物中心打廣告。
- **We'll advertise at the technology expo.**
  我們將會在科技展覽會打廣告。　　＊expo 博覽會，展覽會

1 對話
A 我們將會在數家不同的報紙和雜誌打廣告。
B National or local?
A National.

A We'll advertise in several different newspapers and magazines.
B 是地方性的，還是全國性的？
A 是全國性的。

2 練習 我們將會在地鐵上打廣告。(on)
We'll advertise ________________.

7-1~7-5

黃金複習 15 分鐘！

前面這 25 個句型和 125 個句子全都記熟了嗎？
來驗收一下學習成果吧！如果不能充滿自信地用英文說出以下 40 個句子，請翻到前面再重新複習一次！

01 我們公司是世界上最大的企業之一。

____

02 我們將會在數種不同的報紙和雜誌打廣告。

____

03 我們是專門從事紡織品的公司。

____

04 市場調查顯示，有三十萬的青少年居住在這個區域。

____

05 我們公司位於底特律。

____

06 我們會致力於最大化商品的曝光度。

____

07 我們在家電製品市場有百分之十五的市佔率。

____

08 我們主要的目標客戶是家庭主婦。

____

解答 01. Our company is one of the largest in the world.
02. We'll advertise in several different newspapers and magazines.
03. We specialize in textiles.
04. Market research shows that there are 300,000 teens living in the area.
05. We're based in Detroit. 06. We focus on maximizing the exposure of the product.
07. We have a 15 percent share of the home appliances market.
08. Our main target is housewives.

09 我們有三家在時尚產業的關係企業。

____

10 訴求對象是十幾歲的青少年。

____

11 這是最新的型號。

____

12 不知道您能否告訴我這項產品跟其他產品比起來如何。

____

13 這項產品使用太陽能發電。

____

14 請詳細說明一下這項產品的細節。

____

15 這項產品擁有許多功能。

____

16 我們想知道關於性能的資訊。

____

17 這是防水的設計。

____

18 我在找不同顏色的筆記型電腦。

____

解答 09. We have three affiliate companies in the fashion business.
10. This will appeal to teenagers. 11. This is the latest version.
12. I was wondering if you could tell me about how this product compares to others.
13. This product uses solar power to get electricity.
14. Please explain the details of the product. 15. This item has a lot of versatility.
16. We'd like to get information on performance. 17. This is designed to repel water.
18. I'm looking for a laptop in a different color.

19 這項商品會附贈電池。

____

20 我們對貴公司手提包的最低價格有興趣。

____

21 我們保固這項產品五年的時間。

____

22 我們有訓練完備的客戶支援小組24小時營運。

____

23 有限的保固包括六個月期間的修理費用。

____

24 這可以提供顧客 24 小時的服務。

____

25 我們公司是業界最具有競爭力的公司之一。

____

26 我們將會在當地的廣播電台打廣告。

____

27 我們專門從事出口貨品。

____

28 我們公司的業務範圍是日用品市場。

____

29 我們每天執行一次備份電子郵件的動作。

____

解答 19. It comes with batteries. 20. We're interested in your best deal on handbags.
21. We can guarantee this product for five years.
22. We run a trained customer support team on a 24-hour basis.
23. The limited warranty covers the cost of repairs for six months.
24. This will provide a 24-hour service to customers.
25. Our company is one of the strongest performers in the industry.
26. We'll advertise on local radio. 27. We specialize in exports.
28. We're based in the commodities market. 29. We run daily backups of our email activity.

30 我們在軟體市場有百分之二的市佔率。

____

31 我們會鎖定年輕人的市場。

____

32 我們有五家購買我們產品的聯營公司。

____

33 我們主要的目標客戶是老年人。

____

34 這是最新的趨勢。

____

35 訴求對象是單身男性。

____

36 這項產品使用四個二號電池提供系統動力。

____

37 不知道您能否告訴我貴公司的新價格。

____

38 這項產品擁有最佳性能表現的規格。

____

39 請詳細說明一下付款方式的細節。

____

40 保固已經過期了。

____

解答 30. We have a 2 percent share of the software market.
31. We focus on the youth market. 32. We have five affiliate companies that buy our products.
33. Our main target is the elderly. 34. This is the latest trend.
35. This will appeal to single men.
36. This product uses four AA batteries to power its systems.
37. I was wondering if you could tell me about your new rates.
38. This item has the best performance specifications.
39. Please explain the details of the payment plan. 40. The warranty has expired.

Unit 8
協商
談成一筆好生意

8-1

開始協商

I'd like to begin by...	176	我想先從…開始。
We hope to reach...	177	我們希望達成…
We can offer you...	178	我們可以提供您…
What about + 價格 + per...?	179	每…，如何？
We have a special offer for...	180	對於…，我們有特別的優惠。

Pattern 176

I'd like to begin by...
我想先從…開始。

雙方會面後，想要正式進入協商階段時，就可以使用這個句型。本句型中的 by 後面必須要接 V-ing 形式的單字。類似的句型有 I'd like to begin with a few words about... 等。

- **I'd like to begin by demonstrating the product.**
  我想先從展示這項產品開始。　　＊demonstrate 展示，示範操作
- **I'd like to begin by outlining our proposal.**
  我想先從簡要說明我們的提案開始。
- **I'd like to begin by describing our operation.**
  我想先從說明我們的營運狀況開始。　　＊operation 運行；營運
- **I'd like to begin by going over the agenda for today's negotiation.**
  我想先從今天的協商議程開始審查。

1 對話
A 我想先從簡要說明我們的提案開始。
B Go right ahead.
A We'd like to enter into an exclusive agreement with you.

A I'd like to begin by outlining our proposal.
B 請開始吧！
A 我們想跟貴公司簽訂獨占合約。

2 練習 我想先從簡述我們雙方目前都同意的部分開始。
(summarize, agree)
I'd like to begin by ______________________________.

Pattern 177

We hope to reach...
我們希望達成…

當你想跟對方提出需要協議的內容時，就可以先使用 We hope to... / We wish to... / We'd like to... 等句型，後面再接上 reach an agreement on, reach a compromise, reach an agreement 等內容，表達要跟對方達成共識的意願。

- **We hope to reach an agreement soon.**
  我們希望盡快達成協議。
- **We hope to reach an agreement on price.**
  我們希望在價格上達成協議。
- **We hope to reach a compromise on the issue.**
  我們希望在這個爭議上達成妥協。　＊compromise 妥協，折衷方案
- **We hope to reach an agreement on the final design.**
  我們希望在最後的設計上達成協議。

1 對話
A 我們希望在價格上達成協議。
B What is your first offer?
A We think $10,000 is fair.

A We hope to reach an agreement on price.
B 你們最多可以出多少？
A 我們認為一萬美元是個很合理的價格。

2 練習 我們希望能達成一個令人滿意的結論。(satisfactory)
We hope to reach ______________________.

Pattern 178

178

We can offer you...
我們可以提供您⋯

在協商過程中，當你想告知對方他將可以獲得優惠價格或特別的好處時，就可以單刀直入地使用 We can offer you... 的句型。雖然本句型是使用 can 這個助動詞，但並不帶有強勢，而是肯定的意味，所以在談生意過程中請放心使用這個句型吧！

- **We can offer you a huge discount.**
  我們可以提供您大量的折扣。
- **We can offer you 30% off.**
  我們可以提供您七折的折扣。
- **We can offer you a money-back guarantee.**
  我們可以提供您退費保證。 ＊money-back guarantee 退費保證
- **We can offer you payment in installments.**
  我們可以提供您分期付款。 ＊installment 分期付款

1 對話
A I'm looking for the best deal.
B 我們可以提供您七折的折扣。
A I like it.

A 我希望能得到最好的優惠。
B We can offer you 30% off.
A 太好了。

2 練習 我們可以提供您這世界上最好的價格。(best price)
We can offer you ______________________.

Pattern 179

What about + 價格 + per...?
每…，如何？

當你想要報價給對方時，就可以使用這個簡單的句型。本句型中的 per 後面可以接上 bushel, shipment 等單位量詞。

What about 100 dollars per bushel?
每蒲式耳一百美元，如何？

＊bushel 蒲式耳（農產品的容量單位），1 蒲式耳＝8 加侖

What about 50 dollars per day?
每天五十美元，如何？

What about 32 dollars per order?
每張訂單三十二美元，如何？

What about 20 dollars per hour?
每小時二十美元，如何？

1 對話
A We need to come up with a fair price.
B 每張訂單三十二美元，如何？
A Explain how you came up with that amount.

A 我們希望能拿到一個好價格。
B What about 32 dollars per order?
A 請說明一下這個金額的計算方式。

2 練習 每次運費 1,250 美元，如何？(shipment)
What about ________________ per ________________?

Pattern 180

180

We have a special offer for...
對於…，我們有特別的優惠。

句型中的 special offer 表示「特別的優惠方案」。當對方購買數量較多，你想給客戶優惠時，就可以使用這個句型。

- **We have a special offer for first-time buyers.**
  對於首次購買的顧客，我們有特別的優惠。
- **We have a special offer for our best customers.**
  對於我們的忠實顧客，我們有特別的優惠。
- **We have a special offer on large orders.**
  對於大筆的訂單，我們有特別的優惠。
- **We have a special offer on financing right now.**
  對於立刻付款的客戶，我們有特別的優惠。 ＊finance 提供資金

1 對話
A 對於我們的忠實顧客，我們有特別的優惠。
B What is it?
A 10% off on more than 10,000 orders.

A We have a special offer for our best customers.
B 什麼樣的優惠？
A 一次購買超過一萬個的話，就可以打九折。

2 練習 今天我們對於所有的顧客都有特別的優惠。(customers)
We have a special offer for ______________________.

8-2

出現反對的聲音

I don't believe it's...	181	我不認為…是個…
I'm afraid we can't...	182	很抱歉，我們無法…
I don't think I can... on my own	183	我想我無法自己…
I don't understand why...	184	我不懂為什麼…
I'm sorry I can't...	185	很抱歉，我無法…

Pattern 181

I don't believe it's...
我不認為…是個…

當你不同意對方的提議時，就可以使用這個句型。本句型後面可以接 good idea, effective way, simple way 等字彙。

- **I don't believe it's a good idea to increase the investment.**
  我不認為增加投資是個好主意。 ＊investment 投資（費用）
- **I don't believe it's a good idea to renew our contract.**
  我不認為續約是個好主意。 ＊renew 更新，續簽
- **I don't believe it's an effective way to do as you said.**
  我不認為照你說的去做是個有效的方法。
- **I don't believe it's a simple way to merge with a big-name company.**
  我不認為跟一家有名的公司合併有那麼簡單。 ＊big-name 知名的

1 對話
A Do you agree with me?
B Hmm, 我不認為續約是個好主意。
A Oh, that's too bad.

A 你贊成我的提議嗎？
B 嗯…，I don't believe it's a good idea to renew our contract.
A 喔，那真是太遺憾了。

2 練習 我不認為開一家分店是個好主意。(branch)
I don't believe it's ______________________.

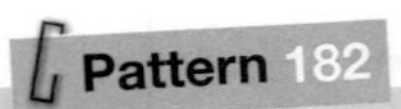

I'm afraid we can't...
很抱歉，我們無法⋯

當你想要委婉地拒絕對方提出的要求時，就可以使用這個句型。同義的句型為之前學過的 We regret to say we have to... 和 We regret to inform you we can't...，可以交替使用。

- **I'm afraid we can't meet your demands.**
  很抱歉，我們無法滿足你們的要求。 ＊meet 滿足，符合
- **I'm afraid we can't go quite that low.**
  很抱歉，我們無法接受這麼低的價錢。
- **I'm afraid we can't work on the project without our CEO's agreement.**
  很抱歉，沒有總裁的同意，我們無法進行這個計畫。
- **I'm afraid we can't go that high unless you offer us something extra.** ＊extra 追加的
  很抱歉，我們無法接受這麼高的價錢，除非您提供更優惠的折扣。

1 對話

A We can't give you 50% down.
B Why not?
A 很抱歉，我們無法接受這麼低的價錢。

A 我們不能給你五折價。
B 為什麼不行？
A I'm afraid we can't go quite that low.

2 練習 很抱歉，在沒有取得客戶的同意下，我們無法支付10美元以上的金額。(go beyond)
I'm afraid we can't ______________________.

Pattern 183

I don't think I can...on my own
我想我無法自己…

在協商過程中，如果遇到自己無法決定的重大提案時，就可以使用這個句型，暫時先保留這個提案。本句型中的 on my own 表示「靠自己（的力量）」的意思，在這種情況下與 alone 或 by myself 有著微妙的差異。

- **I don't think I can make that decision on my own.**
  我想我無法自己決定這件事。
- **I don't think I have the authority to answer on my own.**
  我想我自己沒有權力回答這個問題。　＊authority 權力，職權
- **I don't think I can take that responsibility on my own.**
  我想我無法自己承擔這個責任。
- **I don't think I can act on my own.**
  我想我無法自己行動。

1 對話
A Shall we seal the deal?
B I don't know.
A What's the problem?
B 我想我無法自己決定這件事。

A 我們現在要簽約了嗎？
B 我不知道。
A 有什麼問題嗎？
B I don't think I can make that decision on my own.

2 練習 我想我無法自己決定是否要接受貴公司的提議。(accept)
I don't think I can ______________________ on my own.

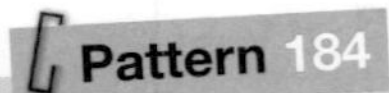

I don't understand why...
我不懂為什麼…

在協商或是開會過程中，當你無法理解對方說的話或不能接受對方的說法時，就可以使用這個句型。本句型雖然是帶著否定意味，但是目的卻不是為了讓對方感到不愉快，而是為了追求當下情況的利益。

- **I don't understand why your estimate is so high.**
  我不懂為什麼你的估價這麼高。　＊estimate 估價
- **I don't understand why we can't work together.**
  我不懂為什麼我們無法共事。
- **I don't understand why we will only take 25% profit.**
  我不懂為什麼我們只獲得 25% 的利潤。
- **I don't understand why you can't come down in price.**
  我不懂為什麼你無法降價。

1 對話
A 我不懂為什麼我們為什麼無法共事。
B Let me give you my perspective on this.
A Please.

A I don't understand why we can't work together.
B 針對這點，容我跟你說一下我的個人看法。
A 請說。

2 練習 我不懂為什麼一定要在今天完成這筆交易。(must be, finish)
I don't understand why ______________________.

185

Pattern 185

I'm sorry I can't...
很抱歉，我無法…

當你實在無法同意協議內容時，就可以使用這個句型，讓你既不會傷害到對方，又可以直接地拒絕對方。

- **I'm sorry I can't offer you a better deal.**
  很抱歉，我無法提供你更好的條件了。
- **I'm sorry I can't give you what you want.**
  很抱歉，我無法給你想要的。
- **I'm sorry I can't sign the agreement today.**
  很抱歉，我今天無法簽訂這份協議。
- **I'm sorry I can't agree to this partnership.**
  很抱歉，我無法同意這次的合作。

1 對話 **A** 很抱歉，我無法提供你更好的條件了。
B I understand. Times are tough.
A Perhaps we can do business with you when the economy improves.

A I'm sorry I can't offer you a better deal.
B 我了解，最近的景氣不太好。
A 也許等到經濟變好時，我們還會有機會合作。

2 練習 很抱歉，我無法跟貴公司做生意。(do business with)
I'm sorry I can't ______________________.

8-3

進入價格協商階段

Pattern 186

Can you offer me...?
你可以給我…嗎？

這是在討論協商條件時常常會用到的句型，解釋成「你可以…給我嗎？」會比較自然。在看英文句子時，有時與其按字面意思來解讀，倒不如配合前後語意來解釋會更好。

- **Can you offer me your best deal?**
  你可以給我你最好的價格嗎？
- **Can you offer me a discount?**
  你可以給我折扣嗎？
- **Can you offer me a break in the price?**
  你可以給我優惠價嗎？　　＊break（價格）調整
- **Can you offer me financing?**
  你可以提供我資金嗎？　　＊financing 資金

1 對話
A 你可以給我折扣嗎？
B We have a little flexibility on price. How about 5%?
A That's good.

A Can you offer me a discount?
B 我們在價格上有些微的彈性空間。九五折如何?
A 好的。

2 練習 你可以算我便宜一點嗎？(reduction)
Can you offer me ____________________?

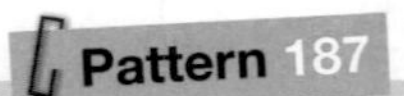

187

Can you reduce the price if we...?
如果我們…的話，價格可以再低一點嗎？

在協商價格時，雙方你來我往、互相討價還價的過程中，有很多機會使用到這個句型。本句型中的 reduce 是表示「減少、降低」的意思，希望對方可以給你更多優惠。

- **Can you reduce the price if we pay in cash?**
  如果我們付現的話，價格可以再低一點嗎？
- **Can you reduce the price if we place our order today?**
  如果我們今天就下訂單的話，價格可以再低一點嗎?
- **Can you reduce the price if we agree to a longer contract?**
  如果我們同意簽訂長期合約的話，價格可以再低一點嗎？
- **Can you reduce the price if we cover shipping?**
  如果我們負擔運費的話，價格可以再低一點嗎？

1 對話 **A** 如果我們負擔運費的話，價格可以再低一點嗎？
B We might be able to work something out.
A Let's look at the numbers.

A Can you reduce the price if we cover shipping?
B 也許我們能夠找到什麼辦法。
A 看一下數據資料吧。

2 練習 如果我們保證以後還會跟貴公司做生意的話，價格可以再低一點嗎？(commit to)
Can you reduce the price if ______________________?

Pattern 188

Is there a discount on...?
…有優惠嗎？

在詢問報價時常常會使用到這個句型。如果是在 repeat customer（老顧客）或 bulk order（大宗訂單）等情況下，句型中的介系詞 on 可以用 for 或 if 等單字替代。在做生意時，討價還價是很常見的事，熟記這些相關單字將會有助於提升商務英語會話能力。

- **Is there a discount on bulk orders?**
  大量訂購有優惠嗎？　　＊bulk 大量的
- **Is there a discount for repeat customers?**
  老顧客有優惠嗎？
- **Is there a discount for first-time customers?**
  首次購買的顧客有優惠嗎？
- **Is there a discount if I buy the whole set?**
  如果我買整套的話有優惠嗎？

1 對話
A 老顧客有優惠嗎？
B Yes, we can take 10% off on your next order.
A That'll probably apply to all future orders.

A Is there a discount for repeat customers?
B 有的，下次訂貨時將享有九折的優惠。
A 往後下訂單應該都能享有這項優惠吧？

2 練習 運費方面有優惠嗎？(shipping costs)
Is there a discount on ______________________________?

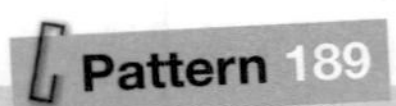

Would it cost less if we...?
如果我們⋯的話，可以算便宜一點嗎？

當你想詢問費用是否能再減少，卻發現自己不知道如何表達時，是不是感到束手無策呢？其實這個時候你只要使用 Would it cost less if we...? 這個句型就行了。相反的句型為 Would it cost more if we...?

- **Would it cost less if we buy last year's model?**
  如果我們購買去年的型號的話，可以算便宜一點嗎？
- **Would it cost less if we assemble it ourselves?**
  如果我們自行組裝的話，可以算便宜一點嗎？ ＊assemble 組合，組裝
- **Would it cost less if we are committed to future purchases?**
  如果我們保證將來會繼續購買的話，可以算便宜一點嗎？
- **Would it cost less if we order these in bulk?**
  如果我們大量訂購這些產品的話，可以算便宜一點嗎？ ＊bulk 大量的

1 對話
A Here is the total.
B 如果我們大量訂購這些產品的話，可以算便宜一點嗎？
A We could take off 10% for orders over 5,000.

A 這是總價。
B Would it cost less if we order these in bulk?
A 一次訂購五千個以上的話，可以享有九折優惠。

2 練習 如果我們付現的話，可以算便宜一點嗎？(in cash)
Would it cost less if we ____________________?

Pattern 190

Is there a charge for...?
需要支付…費嗎？

charge 雖然是表示針對服務或商品「索取費用」的動詞，但也常常當作名詞，在這個句型中，charge 用來表示商品的「價格」或服務的「費用」。

- **Is there a charge for delivery?**
  需要支付配送費嗎？ ＊delivery 配送，寄送
- **Is there a charge for gift wrapping?**
  需要支付禮物包裝費嗎？ ＊gift wrapping 包裝禮物
- **Is there a charge for returning an item?**
  需要支付退貨手續費嗎？
- **Is there a charge for shipping?**
  需要支付運費嗎？

1 對話
A We can have the products shipped anywhere in the world.
B 需要支付運費嗎？
A No. It's included in the price.

A 我們公司提供配送到世界各地的服務。
B Is there a charge for shipping?
A 不需要，價格包含運費。

2 練習 需要支付開戶的費用嗎？(open, account)
Is there a charge for ______________________________?

8-4

協商其他條件

What we're looking for is...	191	我們期待的是…
A small fee is charged for...	192	…會酌收一筆手續費。
Payment is due...	193	…應付款。
Do you think it's possible...to...?	194	你覺得有可能…嗎？
Would it be okay if...?	195	假如…，可以嗎？

Pattern 191

What we're looking for is...
我們期待的是⋯

如果能夠接受對方提出的要求，就輪到我方提出要求了，這種時候就可以使用這個句型。除此之外，一樣能用來表達我方要求的句型還有 Let me make a suggestion...。

- **What we're looking for is the best price.**
  我們期待的是最好的價錢。
- **What we're looking for is a long-term deal.**
  我們期待的是長期的合作計畫。
- **What we're looking for is some new distribution channels.**
  我們期待的是一些新的銷售通路。　＊distribution 銷售，經銷
- **What we're looking for is easier payment terms on the financing.**
  我們期待的是在資金調度上有更方便的付款方式。

1 對話
A What's the most important aspect of the contract?
B 我們期待的是長期的合作計畫。
A Okay. We can be flexible about the length.

A 這份合約書中最重要的一點是什麼？
B What we're looking for is a long-term deal.
A 我知道了，合約的時間長度是可以調整的。

2 練習 我們期待的是快速交貨。(delivery)
What we're looking for is ______________________.

Pattern 192

192

A small fee is charged for...
…會酌收一筆手續費。

用來表達「價格」的單字有很多，但你知道這些單字的相異之處嗎？ price 是商品的價格，cost 是金錢方面的結算，fee 是各種手續費或公共費用，fare 是運費或船車費，charge 是各式各樣的服務費用，fine 是罰金，expense 則是雜項費用或開銷，可以將這些字彙的差異記起來，之後加以分辨。

- **A small fee is charged for late payments.**
  延遲付款會酌收一筆手續費。
- **A small fee is charged for changes in orders.**
  更改訂單會酌收一筆手續費。
- **A small fee is charged for loading and unloading.**
  裝卸貨會酌收一筆手續費。　＊loading and unloading 裝卸貨
- **A small fee is charged for delivery.**
  配送會酌收一筆手續費。

1 對話
A What is the penalty if our payment is late?
B 延遲付款會酌收一筆手續費。
A How much is the fee?
B $250 per day.

A 延遲付款的話會有罰金嗎？
B A small fee is charged for late payments.
A 費用是多少呢？
B 一天 250 美元。

2 練習 我們的服務會酌收一筆手續費。(services)
A small fee is charged for ______________.

Payment is due...
…應付款。

due 一般來說有三種意思，表示「因為…」、「為了…而…」和「付款」的意思，所以當你想表達「什麼時候應該付款」時，就可以使用這個句型。

- **Payment is due on delivery.**
  貨品寄達時應付款。
- **Payment is due on the fifth of each month.**
  每個月的五號應付款。
- **Payment is due on time, or a late fee is charged.**
  應準時付款，否則將會索取延遲付款的費用。　　＊charge 索價，收費
- **Before the shipment can be sent, 50% of the payment is due.**
  在貨品運送之前，應支付 50% 的款項。

1 對話
A 每個月的五號應付款。
B How much flexibility is there?
A We allow a 24-hour grace period.

A Payments are due on the fifth of each month.
B 付款日有任何彈性嗎？
A 有二十四小時的寬限時間。

2 練習 寄送貨物前應該要先付款。(before, shipment)
Payment is due ______________________.

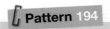

Pattern 194

Do you think it's possible...to...?
你覺得有可能…嗎？

當你提出條件或建議後，想要向對方小心試探是否可行時，就可以使用這個句型。意義相近的句型有 Would it be possible to...?。

Do you think it's possible to push the deadline back?
你覺得有可能把截止日期延後嗎？ ＊push~back 把…延後

Do you think it's possible to add a new clause?
你覺得有可能增加一項新條款嗎？ ＊clause 條款

Do you think it's possible for us to get overnight delivery? ＊overnight delivery 當天寄送（隔夜寄達）
你覺得有可能幫我們當天寄出嗎？

Do you think it's possible for us to get free shipping?
你覺得有可能給我們免運費嗎？

1 對話

A Is there anything else?
B 你覺得有可能增加一項新條款嗎？
A It's a little late in the negotiations for that.

A 還有其他事嗎？
B Do you think it's possible to add a new clause?
A 協商中現在才提可能有點太遲了。

2 練習 你覺得有可能換掉這個字眼嗎？(change, word)
Do you think it's possible to ______________________?

Pattern 195

Would it be okay if...?
假如…，可以嗎？

在協商過程中，如果想要尋求對方諒解或是讓對方給予方便時，就可以使用這個句型。本句型中的 okay 可以用 all right, possible 等單字替代，請試著靈活運用。

- **Would it be okay if we adjusted the numbers?**
  假如我們想調整數量，可以嗎？ ＊adjust 調整
- **Would it be okay if we pay in Taiwanese dollars?**
  假如我們想用台幣付款，可以嗎？
- **Would it be possible if payment is made after 60 days?**
  假如在 60 天後付款，可以嗎？
- **Would it be all right if we changed this part of the contract?**
  假如我們更改合約書上這部分的內容，可以嗎？

1 對話
A 假如我們更改合約上這部分的內容，可以嗎？
B How do you want to change it?
A We just want to make the delivery date a little later.

A Would it be all right if we changed this part of the contract?
B 你想要怎麼修改？
A 我們只是想將寄送日期稍微延後一些。

2 練習 假如我們晚一天簽名，可以嗎？(wait, sign)
Would it be okay if ____________________?

8-5

確認對方的心意

Pattern 196

Are you saying...?
您是說…嗎？

當你想要確認對方提出的提議或條件內容時，就可以使用這個句型，讓對方跟你重新說明。類似的句型有 Are you requesting...? 或 Are you asking us to...? 等。

Are you saying this price is too high?
您是說價錢太高了嗎？

Are you saying you don't agree on the delivery date?
您是說你不同意寄送日期嗎？

Are you saying our quality is not good enough?
您是說我們的品質不夠好嗎？ ＊quality 品質

Are you saying our minimum order size is too small?
您是說我們的最小訂購量太少了嗎？ ＊minimum 最小量

1 對話
A I'm unhappy with the purses we purchased from you.
B What is the problem?
A They fall apart, and the leather fades quickly.
B 您是說我們的品質不夠好嗎？

A 我很不滿意我跟你們買的那些皮包。
B 有什麼問題嗎？
A 皮包會裂開，而且皮革很快就褪色了。
B Are you saying our quality is not good enough?

2 練習 您是說您已經準備好要簽名了嗎？(be ready to)
Are you saying ______________________?

Pattern 197

What do you mean by...?
您說的…是什麼意思？

在協商過程中，如果不明白對方的意思時，就要使用這個句型仔細問清楚才行。意義相近的句型有 I don't know what you mean by...。

- **What do you mean by "minimum order"?**
  您說的「最小訂購量」是什麼意思？
- **What do you mean by this clause?**
  您說的那項條款是什麼意思？
- **What do you mean by "additional charges"?**
  您說的「附加費用」是什麼意思？
- **What do you mean by "seller accepts liability"?**
  您說的「賣家承擔法律責任」是什麼意思？

* liability 法律責任

1 對話
A 您說的這項條款是什麼意思？
B We simply want to add a guarantee.
A I'm not sure we can agree on that.

A What do you mean by this clause?
B 我們只是希望增加一個保障。
A 我不確定我們是否能夠同意那項條款。

2 練習 您說的「流動價格」是什麼意思？(flexible)
What do you mean by ____________________?

Pattern 198

What are you asking us to...?
你要求我們…什麼呢？

當你想要詢問對方所要求的事項內容時，就可以使用這個句型。意義相似的句型為 What do you want us to do about...? 本句型中的 ask 是表示「請求、要求」的意思，也可用 request, demand 等單字替代。

- **What are you asking us to provide?**
  你要求我們提供什麼呢？
- **What are you asking us to pay?**
  你要求我們支付什麼款項呢？
- **What exactly are you requesting us to do about quality control?**
  關於品質控管，你究竟要求我們做些什麼呢？
- **What exactly are you demanding us to do about the packaging design?**
  關於產品包裝，你究竟要求我們做些什麼呢？

1 對話
A 關於品質控管，你究竟要求我們做些什麼呢？
B We want you to provide us with guarantees.
A In what form?

A What exactly are you requesting us to do about quality control?
B 我們希望你們能提供商品擔保。
A 採用什麼樣的形式？

2 練習 關於行銷，你究竟要求我們做些什麼呢？(about, marketing)
What exactly are you asking us to ____________________?

Pattern 199

Can I ask...?
我想請教一下，…？

當你想向對方公司的負責人小心地提問時，就可以使用這個句型。本句型中的 can 若用 could 替代時，語氣會較正式。

- **Can I ask when the product will be ready?**
  我想請教一下，貨品什麼時候會準備好呢？
- **Can I ask who you spoke with before?**
  我想請教一下，您之前跟誰談過呢？
- **Can I ask how you heard about us?**
  我想請教一下，您從哪裡得知我們公司的呢？
- **Could I ask if you've negotiated with anyone else?**
  我想請教一下，您之前是否跟任何人洽談過呢？　＊negotiate 交涉，洽談

1 對話
A We have your order for 5,000 tires.
B Can I change that to 6,000?
A Sure. That's not a problem.
B Then 我想請教一下，貨品什麼時候會準備好呢?

A 您向我們訂購了五千個輪胎。
B 我可以改成訂六千個嗎？
A 當然可以，沒問題。
B 那麼，can I ask when the product will be ready?

2 練習 我可以向你請教一下業務方面的經驗嗎？(in sales)
Could I ask ______________________________?

Pattern 200

200

Let me hear...
請說一下…

當你希望對方說明時，就可以使用這個句型。本句型中的動詞 let 只要簡單地想成「請你…」的意思就行了。

- **Let me hear what you think about this proposal.**
  請說一下你對這個提案有什麼想法。
- **Let me hear your ideas on this project.**
  請說一下你對這個計畫的意見。
- **Let me hear what my boss has to say about this.**
  我想知道我的主管會怎麼評論這件事。
- **Let me hear how this merger will work.**
  我想知道這次的合併會如何運作。

＊work 運作

1 對話
A Hi, Jim. Did you open the packet I sent you?
B Yes. I read through the papers this morning.
A 請說一下你對這個提案有什麼想法。

A 你好，吉姆。你有收到我寄給你的包裹了嗎？
B 收到了。我今天早上已經看過那些資料了。
A Let me hear what you think about this proposal.

2 練習 請說一下你認為對公司來說最重要的是什麼。(what, important)
Let me hear ______________________.

8-1~8-5

黃金複習 15 分鐘！

前面這 25 個句型和 125 個句子全都記熟了嗎？
來驗收一下學習成果吧！如果不能充滿自信地用英文說出以下 40 個句子，請翻到前面再重新複習一次！

01 我想先從簡要說明我們的提案開始。

02 請說一下你對這個計畫的意見。

03 我們希望在價格上達成協議。

04 我想請教一下，貨品什麼時候會準備好呢？

05 我們可以提供您七折的折扣。

06 你要求我們提供什麼呢？

07 每天五十美元，如何？

08 您說的「最小訂購量」是什麼意思？

09 對於我們的忠實顧客，我們有特別的優惠。

解答 01. I'd like to begin by outlining our proposal.
02. Let me hear your ideas on this project. 03. We hope to reach an agreement on price.
04. Can I ask when the product will be ready? 05. We can offer you 30% off.
06. What are you asking us to provide? 07. What about 50 dollars per day?
08. What do you mean by "minimum order"?
09. We have a special offer for our best customers.

10 您是說你不同意寄送日期嗎？

11 我不認為續約是個好主意。

12 假如我們想用台幣付款，可以嗎？

13 很抱歉，我們無法接受這麼低的價錢。

14 你覺得有可能把截止日期延後嗎？

15 我想我自己沒有權力回答這個問題。

16 每個月的五號應付款。

17 我不懂為什麼我們無法共事。

18 裝卸貨會酌收一筆手續費。

19 很抱歉，我無法給你想要的。

20 我們期待的是長期的合作計畫。

解答 10. Are you saying you don't agree on the delivery date?
11. I don't believe it's a good idea to renew our contract.
12. Would it be okay if we pay in Taiwanese dollars? 13. I'm afraid we can't go quite that low.
14. Do you think it's possible to push the deadline back?
15. I don't think I have the authority to answer on my own.
16. Payment is due on the fifth of each month.
17. I don't understand why we can't work together.
18. A small fee is charged for loading and unloading.
19. I'm sorry I can't give you what you want. 20. What we're looking for is a long-term deal.

21 你可以給我折扣嗎？

22 我想先從展示這項產品開始。

23 如果我們付現的話，價格可以再低一點嗎？

24 我們希望盡快達成協議。

25 大量訂購有優惠嗎？

26 我們可以提供您大量的折扣。

27 每蒲式耳一百美元，如何？

28 如果我們購買去年的型號的話，可以算便宜一點嗎？

29 需要支付退貨手續費嗎？

30 我想知道這次的合併會如何運作。

31 我不認為增加投資是個好主意。

解答 21. Can you offer me a discount? 22. I'd like to begin by demonstrating the product. 23. Can you reduce the price if we pay in cash? 24. We hope to reach an agreement soon. 25. Is there a discount on bulk orders? 26. We can offer you a huge discount. 27. What about 100 dollars per bushel? 28. Would it cost less if we buy last year's model? 29. Is there a charge for returning an item? 30. Let me hear how this merger will work. 31. I don't believe it's a good idea to increase the investment.

32 我們期待的是最好的價錢。

33 很抱歉，我們無法滿足你們的要求。

34 更改訂單會酌收一筆手續費。

35 我想我無法自己決定這件事。

36 貨品寄達時應付款。

37 我不懂為什麼你的估價這麼高。

38 你覺得有可能幫我們當天寄出嗎？

39 很抱歉，我無法提供你更好的條件了。

40 假如我們想調整數量，可以嗎？

解答 32. What we're looking for is the best price. 33. I'm afraid we can't meet your demands.
34. A small fee is charged for changes in orders.
35. I don't think I can make that decision on my own. 36. Payment is due on delivery.
37. I don't understand why your estimate is so high.
38. Do you think it's possible for us to get overnight delivery?
39. I'm sorry I can't offer you a better deal. 40. Would it be okay if we adjusted the numbers?

Unit 9
協議・合約・購買
打動對方的心

9-1

意見協調 (1)

How about we...?	201	我們…如何？
May I suggest...?	202	我可以提出…嗎？
Would you consider...?	203	你是否考慮…？
We'll reconsider...	204	我們會重新考慮…
I'd rather have... than...	205	比起…，我更想要…

How about we...?
我們…如何？

當你想詢問對方這樣做是否可行時，就可以使用這個句型，後面接你想要的方案內容，十分常見於雙方在協商過程中協調條件的對話內容。

- **How about we do it for 5,000 dollars?**
  我們用五千美元成交如何？
- **How about we meet half way?**
  我們各退一步如何？
- **How about we compromise on the price?**
  我們在價格上妥協如何？
  * compromise 妥協
- **How about we agree on a price somewhere in between?**
  我們將售價訂在介於我們兩個同意的價格之間如何？

1 對話
A I can sell this smart phone to your company for $250.
B That seems a little high. How about $180？
A I can't do it. 我們將售價訂在介於我們兩個同意的價格之間如何？

A 我能將這支智慧型手機以 250 美元賣給你們公司。
B 這價格好像有點高，180 美元，如何？
A 不行，How about we agree on a price somewhere in between?

2 練習 我們各退一步，將價格定在一萬美元左右如何？
(find, somewhere around)
How about we ________________________________?

202

Pattern 202

May I suggest...?
我可以提出…嗎？

當你面對需要小心處理的情況，如對方要求你打折或產品發生問題時，若你想要恭敬地提出解決方案的話，就可以使用這個句型。本句型中的 suggest 可以用 offer, recommend 等動詞替代。

- **May I suggest a few possible solutions?**
  我可以提出一些可能的解決辦法嗎？
- **May I suggest that we discuss a small discount?**
  我可以提議我們協商出一些折扣嗎？
- **May I offer you a chance to file a formal complaint?**
  可以請你提出正式的抗議申請文件嗎？

  ＊file 提出申請　＊complaint 不滿，抗議
- **May I recommend that we discuss them at our next meeting?**
  我可以建議我們下次開會再討論那些事嗎？

1 對話
A Please tell me what the problem is.
B I'm very unhappy with my purchase.
A I understand. 我可以提出一些可能的解決辦法嗎？

A 請告訴我問題出在哪。
B 我非常不滿意我這次的消費。
A 我知道了，May I suggest a few possible solutions?

2 練習 我可以建議您去跟我們的會計師談談嗎？(accountant)
May I suggest ______________________________?

Pattern 203 203

Would you consider...?
你是否考慮…？

本句型的 consider 指的不是單純的看法，而是表示經過慎重考慮後的決定。在協商或會議過程中，當你想要說服對方和協調意見時，就可以使用這個句型。

203 詢問對方的想法

- **Would you consider a full refund?**
  你是否考慮全額退費？　　* full refund 全額退費
- **Would you consider rewriting the contract?**
  你是否考慮修改這份合約？
- **Would you consider combining our resources?**
  你是否考慮結合我們的資源？　　* combine 結合
- **Would you consider inviting a third partner to join us?**
  你是否考慮邀第三者加入？

1 對話

A Are you ready to sign the contract?
B I have a problem with the language in Part C.
A 你是否考慮修改這份合約？

A 您可以簽約了嗎？
B 我覺得 C 部分的文字表達有點問題。
A Would you consider rewriting the contract?

2 練習 如果是大批訂單的話，你是否考慮給予折扣？
(discount, large orders)
Would you consider ______________________?

Pattern 204

We'll reconsider...
我們會重新考慮…

在英文單字前面加上 re- 的話，是表示「再…」的意思，所以 reconsider 是表示「再考慮」的意思。當對方提出提案或提議，你想要再考慮一下時，就可以使用這個句型，為自己增加考慮的時間。

- **We'll reconsider our decision.**
  我們會重新考慮我們的決定。
- **We'll reconsider your idea.**
  我們會重新考慮你的意見。
- **We'll reconsider your offer.**
  我們會重新考慮你的提議。
- **We'll reconsider a discount if you order by Friday.**
  如果您在禮拜五前下訂，我們會重新考慮給您折扣。

1 對話 **A** I can't see any good points in your idea.
B Really?
A But 我們會重新考慮你的意見。

A 我看不出來你的提案有任何優點。
B 真的嗎？
A 但是 we'll reconsider your idea.

2 練習 我們會重新考慮是否要降價。(lower)
We'll reconsider ______________________.

205

Pattern 205

I'd rather have... than...
比起…，我更想要…

當你衡量過兩方事物的輕重好壞才做出選擇時，就可以使用這個句型。句型中若出現 rather 的話，後面 99% 會出現 than，兩者結合構成比較型態的句型，表示「…比…更好」的意思。

- **I'd rather have a quick delivery than a lower price.**
  比起更低的價格，我更想要快速的運送。
- **I'd rather have a high-quality product than a cheap one.**
  比起便宜的產品，我更想要高品質的產品。
- **I'd rather have a money-back guarantee.**
  我比較想要不滿意包退的保證。
- **I'd rather have a handmade scarf than a designer label.**
  比起著名設計師品牌的產品，我更想要一條手工圍巾。

* **designer label** 著名設計師品牌的產品
* **handmade** 手工的

1 對話
A You can save a little on the total by using a slower delivery method.
B 比起更低的價格，我更想要快速的運送。
A Okay. We have several express options.

A 選擇配送時間較長的寄送方式的話，總費用會減少一些。
B I'd rather have a quick delivery than a lower price.
A 我知道了，我們這邊提供了幾種快遞方式。

2 練習 比起那項服務，我更想要能夠取消訂單的選擇權。(option, cancel)
I'd rather have ________________ than ________________.

9-2

意見協調 (2)

 206

Pattern 206

You can't find better...
你找不到比這更好的…了。

俗話說「貨比三家不吃虧」，當你想確切地告訴對方沒有比這更好的選擇時，請充滿自信地使用這個句型！本句型的語意和「我們是你的最佳選擇」之間有著些微的差異。

- **You can't find better quality.**
  你找不到比這更好的品質了。
- **You can't find better deals.**
  你找不到比這更好的條件了。
- **You can't find better suppliers.**
  你找不到比這更好的供應商了。 ＊supplier 供應商
- **You can't find better prices anywhere.**
  你到任何地方都找不到更好的價格了。

1 對話 **A** How does this price compare to that of other suppliers?
B 你到任何地方都找不到更好的價格了。
A This is probably the best.

A 你們公司的報價比起其他供應商又如何呢？
B You can't find better prices anywhere.
A 看來這是最好的價格了！

2 練習 你找不到比這更好的服務了。(service)
You can't find better ______________________.

Pattern 207

We could be willing to...
我們可以…

be willing to 表示「樂意、願意」，所以 could be willing to 表示「可以…」的意思。因此在協商的過程中，當你想跟對方釋出空間表達「我可以…」的意思時，就可以使用這個句型。

- **We could be willing to go a little lower.**
  我們可以降低一些價格。
- **We could be willing to accept a counteroffer.**
  我們可以接受你們的出價。　　＊counteroffer 討價還價，買方的出價
- **We could be willing to hold your order for a few days.**
  我們可以幫您先保留訂單幾天。
- **We could be willing to include a clause limiting your liability.**
  我們可以增加一條限制貴公司法律責任的條款。　　＊liability 法律責任

1 對話
A Will you place an order today?
B I'd like to think about it some more.
A 我們可以幫您先保留訂單幾天。

A 您今天要下訂單嗎？
B 我想要再多考慮一下。
A We could be willing to hold your order for a few days.

2 練習 我們可以一起工作。(work)
We could be willing to ______________________.

Pattern 208

That's acceptable if you...
如果您…的話，我們可以接受。

在簽約或協商過程中，如果你在某條件下願意體諒對方的立場或開出的條件時，就可以使用這個高階的句型。本句型可以用在文書往來、講電話或電子郵件上，用途十分廣泛。

- **That's acceptable if you insist upon it.**
  如果您堅持的話，我們可以接受。
- **That's acceptable if you find it to be an essential clause.** ＊essential clause 必要的條款
  如果您認為有這必要的話，我們可以接受在合約裡加入此條款。
- **That's acceptable if you want to go in that direction.**
  如果您想要往那個方向進行的話，我們可以接受。
- **That's not acceptable if you aren't willing to compromise.**
  如果您不願意妥協的話，我們就無法接受。

1 對話 **A** How would you like to amend the contract?
B I want it to address "potential new partnership".
A 如果您認為有這必要的話，我們可以接受在合約裡加入此條款。

A 您希望怎麼修改這份合約書？
B 我希望可以在上面寫上「潛在新夥伴」。
A That's acceptable if you find it to be an essential clause.

2 練習 如果您和我們有生意往來的話，我們可以接受。(account, with)
That's acceptable if you ______________________.

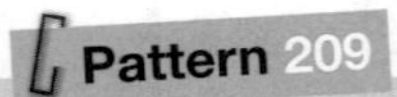

It looks like we're...
看來我們…

協商進入收尾的階段，當你想跟對方提及已經完成協議的部分，或是想要暗示這次協商可以告一段落時，就可以使用這個句型。

- **It looks like we're in agreement about the terms.**
  看來我們在條件上都達成協議了。
- **It looks like we're in agreement about everything.**
  看來我們所有事項都達成協議了。
- **It looks like we're ready to sign.**
  看來我們已經準備好簽約了。
- **It looks like we're about ready to wrap things up.**
  看來我們已經準備好結束這件事了。　　＊**wrap up** 完成，結束

1 對話
A 看來我們所有事項都達成協議了。
B Then let's wrap it up.
A Our lawyer will look over the contract, and then we'll sign it.

A It looks like we're in agreement about everything.
B 那就結束這場會議吧。
A 等我們的律師檢查過這份合約書的內容後，我們就會簽約。

2 練習　看來我們大部分的議題都已經取得共識。(most of, issue)
It looks like we're ______________________.

Pattern 210

We've made... progress
我們已經有…進展。

如果 progrees 是表示「進展、發展」的意思，一定會和動詞 make 同時出現，make...progress 表示「取得進展、有進步」。當你想表達「我們取得了重要的進展」時，只要如下面例句一樣說 We've made significant progress 就行了。

- **We've made significant progress.**
  我們已經有重大的進展。　　＊**significant** 重要的，重大的
- **We've made steady progress.**
  我們已經有穩定的進展。
- **We've made no progress.**
  我們沒有任何進展。
- **We've made rapid progress.**
  我們已經有快速的進展。

1 對話
A How is the deal with our buyers coming?
B 我們沒有任何進展。
A What? I need to report to our boss by tomorrow.

A 和客戶的生意談的怎麼樣？
B We've made no progress.
A 什麼？看來我明天必須跟老闆報告一下才行。

2 練習 我們已經有很大的進展。(major)
We've made ______________________ progress.

9-3

簽訂合約

This deal is only good...	211	這份合約只…有效。
We're ready to...	212	我們準備好要…
Please sign...	213	請…簽名。
We'll provide...	214	我們會提供…
The contract can be revoked if...	215	假如…，合約就會終止。

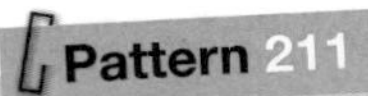

This deal is only good...
這份合約只…有效。

當你想要告知對方此次交易的有效期限，就可以使用這個句型。本句型中的 deal 指的是業務上的「交易、合約」而 good 則是「有效的」意思。

- **This deal is only good for one year.**
  這份合約只在一年內有效。
- **This deal is only good for a limited time.**
  這份合約只在限定期間內有效。
- **This deal is only good if you buy online.**
  這份合約只在線上購買的情況下有效。
- **This deal is only good on these specific products.**
  這份合約只對特定的商品有效。

＊specific 特定的

1 對話 **A** What is the duration of the contract?
B 這份合約只在一年內有效。
A Okay, I see.

A 這份合約的有效期限是多久？
B This deal is only good for one year.
A 好，我了解。

2 練習 這份合約一定要在今天簽訂才有效。(if, sign)
This deal is only good ________________.

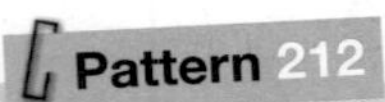

We're ready to...
我們準備好要…

當你想告知對方自己已準備好要做某些事，就可以使用這個句型。通常這個句型是用在已經接受對方公司的提案或條件的情況下。

- **We're ready to sign the contract.**
  我們準備好要簽約了。
- **We're ready to accept your offer.**
  我們準備好要接受你的提案了。
- **We're ready to wrap our negotiation up.**
  我們準備好要結束我們的協商了。
- **We're ready to implement it right now.**
  我們準備好要立刻執行了。

* **implement** 實施，執行

1 對話

A Have you made a decision on the purchase?
B Yes. 我們準備好要簽約了。
A Excellent.

A 請問您決定要購買了嗎？
B 嗯，We're ready to sign the contract.
A 太好了。

2 練習 我們準備好要著手進行這筆交易了。(move forward, deal)
We're ready to ______________________.

Pattern 213

Please sign...
請…簽名。

這個句型用在要求對方在合約書上簽名的時候。在命令句中加上 please 才更能表達出尊重的意思，也顯得更禮貌。

- **Please sign after you've read this.**
  請你在閱讀完後簽名。
- **Please sign where indicated.**
  請在指示的地方簽名。 ＊indicate 指示，指出
- **Please sign on both pages.**
  請在雙方的頁面上都簽名。
- **Please sign on behalf of him.**
  請代表他簽名。

1 對話
A Is this everything?
B Yes. 請你在閱讀完後簽名。
A Here?

A 就這些嗎？
B 是的，Please sign after you've read this.
A 簽在這裡嗎？

2 練習 請在虛線處簽名。(dotted line)
Please sign ______________________.

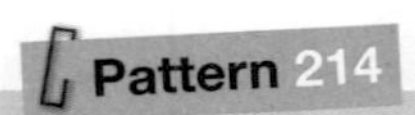

We'll provide...
我們會提供⋯

當你要提供對方公司需要的資料或文件時，就可以使用這個句型。本句型中的動詞 provide 是表示「提供、供給」的意思。

- **We'll provide copies of the necessary documents.**
  我們會提供必要文件的影本。
- **We'll provide all of the required materials.**
  我們會提供所有必要的資料。 ＊required 必要的
- **We'll provide samples of our entire product line.**
  我們會提供我們所有產品的樣本。
- **We'll provide any support you may need.**
  我們會提供你可能會需要的任何幫助。

1 對話
A 我們會提供必要文件的影本。
B When can I get those?
A They should be ready by tomorrow.

A We'll provide copies of the necessary documents.
B 我什麼時候可以拿到？
A 您明天就能拿到了。

2 練習 我們會提供所有員工的就職資料。(references, employees)
We'll provide ______________________.

Pattern 215

The contract can be revoked if...
假如…，合約就會終止。

當你想說明哪些行為或情況會造成合約終止或違約時，就可以使用這個句型。本句型中的 revoke 表示「廢除、撤銷」，所以前面加上 can be 時即表示「有可能廢除、撤銷」的意思。

- **The contract can be revoked if the terms are violated.**
  假如有違反條約的情況，合約就會終止。
- **The contract can be revoked in the event of a violation.**
  假如有違反的情況，合約就會終止。　＊violation 違反行為
- **The contract can be revoked if delivery is not made promptly.**
  假如寄送不準時，合約就會終止。
- **The contract can be revoked if payment is not received promptly.**
  假如沒有如期收到款項，合約就會終止。

1 對話
A When can we expect delivery?
B It'll be another few days.
A Remember. 假如寄送不準時，合約就會終止。

A 什麼時候可以收到東西？
B 還要花上幾天的時間。
A 請記得，The contract can be revoked if delivery is not made promptly.

2 練習 假如雙方都同意的話，合約就會終止。(both parties)
The contract can be revoked if ______________________.

下訂單與接訂單

Pattern 216

216

Are...available?
…有貨嗎？

不論是在英語會話或寫作中，available 都是一個讓我們常感到頭痛不已的單字。一般來說，available 在提及時間或能力方面時，表示「可以…」，在下訂單的情況下則是表示「有貨」的意思。

- **Are these items available?**
  這些品項有貨嗎？ ＊item 品項，物品
- **Are these smart phones available?**
  這些智慧型手機有貨嗎？
- **Are other colors available?**
  其他顏色有貨嗎？
- **Are the napkins in Egyptian cotton available?**
  埃及棉的的餐巾有貨嗎？

1 對話
A 其他顏色有貨嗎？
B Yes. We also have white.
A What about red?

A Are other colors available?
B 有的，還有白色。
A 有紅色嗎？

2 練習 這些泳鏡有貨嗎？(goggles)
Are ______________________ available?

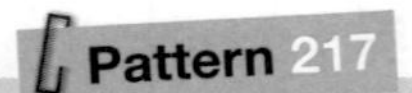

Does it come in...?
有…嗎？

Does it come in...? 是一個看似簡單，卻無法直接從字面上翻譯的句型。當你想詢問某產品是否有其他顏色、大小、版本等時，就可以這麼問。

- **Does it come in red?**
  有紅色嗎？
- **Does it come in any other styles?**
  有別的樣式嗎？
- **Does it come in a larger size?**
  有大一點的尺寸嗎？　　＊larger 大一點的（large 的比較級）
- **Does it come in different sizes?**
  有不同的尺寸嗎？

1 對話　A Any questions?
B 有大一點的尺寸嗎？
A Yes, I believe it does.

A 有什麼問題嗎？
B Does it come in a larger size?
A 有的，我想應該有。

2 練習　有大盒裝的嗎？(large)
Does it come in ______________________?

Pattern 218

Do you have something that...?
你們有…的產品嗎？

英語系國家常常會使用 something 這個單字來代稱想找的東西，當你想要找某樣東西時，就可以說 Do you have something that...?。這個句型的 something 是表示「產品」。

- **Do you have something that has a long shelf life?**
  你們有倉儲壽命比較長的產品嗎？ ＊shelf life 倉儲壽命
- **Do you have something that can be delivered quickly?**
  你們有可以比較快寄出的產品嗎？
- **Do you have something that we can sell in multiple markets?**
  你們有可以讓我們在多個市場販賣的產品嗎？ ＊multiple 複合的，多樣的
- **Do you have something that isn't too expensive?**
  你們有沒這麼貴的產品嗎？

1 對話
A What are you looking for?
B 你們有可以比較快寄出的產品嗎？
A Sure. This item can be delivered by the 15th.

A 請問您在找什麼？
B Do you have something that can be delivered quickly?
A 當然有，這個產品在15號就能寄給您。

2 練習 你們有不容易碎裂的產品嗎？(fall apart, easily)
Do you have something that ______________________?

Pattern 219

We'd like to order...
我們想要訂購…

我們常常用 place an order 來表示「訂購」，但其實可以和這個句型一樣，只用 order 就行了。而字首 re 加上 order 即可表示「添購」或「再次訂購」的意思。

- **We'd like to order the latest model.**
  我們想要訂購最新的款式。 ＊latest 最新的
- **We'd like to order item number 5 in the catalog.**
  我們想要訂購目錄上的五號商品。
- **We'd like to reorder this fabric in a different pattern.**
  我們想要追加訂購這種布料的另一個花色。
- **We'd like to reorder this product in a different shape.**
  我們想要追加訂購這個商品的另一個形狀。 ＊shape 外形，形狀

1 對話
A Are you interested in placing an order?
B 我們想要訂購最新的款式。
A Anything particular you have in mind?

A 請問你們要訂購嗎？
B We'd like to order the latest model.
A 心目中有任何特別想要的款式嗎？

2 練習 我們想盡可能地多訂購一些。(as much as)
We'd like to order ____________________.

 220

Pattern 220

I'd like to purchase...
我想要購買…

這是當你表達購買意願時可以使用的句型。訂購產品時要用 order，購買產品時則是用 buy 或 purchase，而 purchase 比 buy 更適合用在商務場合中。

- **I'd like to purchase 7,000 coffee cups.**
  我想要購買七千個咖啡杯。
- **I'd like to purchase your Singapore operation.**
  我想要購買你們新加坡的工廠。 ＊operation 工廠
- **I'd like to purchase the rights to use your logo.**
  我想要購買你們的商標使用權。
- **I'd like to purchase more of your products.**
  我想要購買貴公司更多的商品。

1 對話
A Hello, Ms. Constance. How can I help you?
B I'm interested in placing a large order.
A Terrific! What would you like?
B 我想要購買七千個咖啡杯。

A 你好，康斯坦斯小姐。有什麼可以幫忙的地方嗎？
B 我想下一筆大量訂單。
A 太好了！你想要買什麼呢？
B I'd like to purchase 7,000 coffee cups.

2 練習 我想要購買貴公司時尚線的產品。(fashion)
I'd like to purchase ______________________.

變更訂單內容與退貨

We'd like to change...	221	我們想要更改…
I'm sorry, but I have to cancel...	222	很抱歉，我必須取消…
We'd like to return...	223	我們想要退掉…
If we return this,...	224	如果我們把這個退掉的話，…
What's your policy on...?	225	貴公司關於…的規定是什麼？

Pattern 221

We'd like to change...
我們想要更改…

這是在想變更訂單內容時可以使用的句型。當你想要更改訂單的數量、送貨日期或收件地址時，就可以說 We'd like to change...。

- **We'd like to change our order.**
  我們想要更改我們的訂單。
- **We'd like to change the delivery date.**
  我們想要更改寄送日期。
- **We'd like to change the shipping address.**
  我們想要更改寄送地址。　＊shipping address 寄送地址
- **We'd like to change the amount we ordered.**
  我們想要更改訂購數量。

1 對話
A Could I change the order I placed today?
B Certainly. What would you like to change?
A 我們想要更改寄送日期。

A 我可以修改今天的訂單內容嗎？
B 當然可以。你想要修改哪個部分？
A We'd like to change the delivery date.

2 練習 我們想要更改帳單地址。(billing)
We'd like to change ____________________.

Pattern 222

222

I'm sorry, but I have to cancel...
很抱歉，我必須取消…

這是使用在想要取消訂單時的句型。此外，取消訂單或解約這類緊急的情況要用 urgent，如果是用電子郵件聯絡對方時，信件的標題要用 We request your immediate attention，請求對方盡快處理。

- **I'm sorry, but I have to cancel the order that I made this morning.**
  很抱歉，我必須取消今天早上下的訂單。
- **I'm sorry, but I have to cancel the order because I no longer need it.**
  很抱歉，因為我已經不需要了，我必須取消這筆訂單。
- **I'm sorry, but I have to cancel the order because I mistakenly made it.**
  很抱歉，因為我誤訂了，我必須取消這筆訂單。 ＊mistakenly 錯誤地
- **I'm sorry, but I have to cancel your order as it's out of stock.**
  很抱歉，因為沒有庫存，我必須取消你的訂單。

1 對話 A 很抱歉，我必須取消今天早上下的訂單。
B May I ask why?
A We've reassessed our needs and we don't need it at this time.

A I'm sorry, but I have to cancel the order that I made this morning.
B 可以請教一下取消的原因嗎？
A 我們重新評估了一下我們的需求，發現這次並不需要這項物品。

2 練習 很抱歉，我必須取消貴公司一部分的訂單。(portion of)
I'm sorry, but I have to cancel ______________________.

Pattern 223

223

We'd like to return...
我們想要退掉…

當你收到有瑕疵或損傷的產品而想要退貨時，就可以使用這個帶有動詞 return 的句型。

- **We'd like to return these items.**
  我們想要退掉這些商品。
- **We'd like to return a defective product.**
  我們想要退掉一個瑕疵品。 ＊ defective 有瑕疵的
- **We'd like to return half of our order.**
  我們想要退掉一半的訂單。
- **We'd like to return the incorrect items that you sent us.**
  我們想要退掉你寄給我們的錯誤商品。

1 對話 **A** How can I help you?
B 我們想要退掉這些商品。
A May I ask why?
B The quality was not up to our standards.

A 有什麼可以幫忙的地方嗎？
B We'd like to return these items.
A 可以請教一下退貨的理由嗎？
B 這個產品的品質不符合我們的標準。

2 練習 我們想要退掉所有的訂貨。(entire)
We'd like to return ______________________.

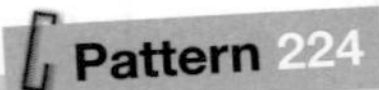

If we return this,...
如果我們把這個退掉的話，…

在退貨時，如果想要詢問更具體的細節內容，就可以使用這個由 if 子句組成的假設語氣句型。

- **If we return this, can we get a refund?**
  如果我們把這個退掉的話，可以全額退費嗎？
- **If we return this, can we exchange it?**
  如果我們把這個退掉的話，可以換貨嗎？
- **If we return this, will there be a charge?**
  如果我們把這個退掉的話，需要付費嗎？
- **If we return this, will we need a receipt?**
  如果我們把這個退掉的話，需要收據嗎？

＊**receipt** 收據

1 對話
A 如果我們把這個退掉，可以全額退費嗎？
B We only allow a partial refund on this product.
A How much can we get back?

A If we return this, can we get a refund?
B 此產品只允許部分退費。
A 我們可以拿回多少呢？

2 練習
如果我們現在把這筆訂單退掉的話，以後還可以再下訂單嗎？
(reorder)
If we return this order now, ______________________________?

Pattern 225

225

What's your policy on...?
貴公司關於…的規定是什麼？

當你想了解訂購方面的相關規定時，就用這個句型來詢問對方。以個人或公司名義購買產品，想知道退款、換貨、退貨等資訊時，只要利用 policy 這個單字來表達就行了。

- **What's your policy on returns?**
  貴公司關於退貨的規定是什麼？
- **What's your policy on refunds?**
  貴公司關於退款的規定是什麼？
- **What's your policy on order cancellations?**
  貴公司關於取消訂單的規定是什麼？　　＊ cancellation 取消
- **What's your policy for exchanges?**
  貴公司關於換貨的規定是什麼？

1 對話
A Do you have any questions?
B Yes. 貴公司關於取消訂單的規定是什麼？
A We charge a small fee for cancellations.

A 請問還有其他問題嗎？
B 有的，What's your policy on order cancellations?
A 取消訂單時需要支付一點手續費。

2 練習 貴公司關於顧客滿意度的規定是什麼？(satisfaction)
What's your policy on ______________________?

9-1~9-5

黃金複習 15 分鐘！

前面這 25 個句型和 125 個句子全都記熟了嗎？
來驗收一下學習成果吧！如果不能充滿自信地用英文說出以下 40 個句子，請翻到前面再重新複習一次！

01 我們用五千美元成交如何？

02 貴公司關於退貨的規定是什麼？

03 我可以提議我們協商出一些折扣嗎？

04 如果我們把這個退掉的話，可以換貨嗎？

05 你是否考慮修改這份合約？

06 我們想要退掉一個瑕疵品。

07 我們會重新考慮你的意見。

08 很抱歉，因為我誤訂了，我必須取消這筆訂單。

解答 01. How about we do it for 5,000 dollars? 02. What's your policy on refunds?
03. May I suggest that we discuss a small discount? 04. If we return this, can we exchange it?
05. Would you consider rewriting the contract? 06. We'd like to return a defective product.
07. We'll reconsider your idea.
08. I'm sorry, but I have to cancel the order because I mistakenly made it.

09 比起更便宜的產品，我更想要高品質的產品。

10 我們想要更改寄送日期。

11 你找不到比這更好的條件了。

12 我想要購買七千個咖啡杯。

13 我們可以接受你們的出價。

14 我們想要訂購目錄上的五號商品。

15 如果您認為有這必要的話，我們可以接受在合約裡加入此條款。

16 你們有可以比較快寄出的產品嗎？

17 看來我們所有事項都達成協議了。

18 有別的樣式嗎？

解答 09. I'd rather have a high-quality product than a cheap one.
10. We'd like to change the delivery date. 11. You can't find better deals.
12. I'd like to purchase 7,000 coffee cups. 13. We could be willing to accept a counteroffer.
14. We'd like to order item number 5 in the catalog.
15. That's acceptable if you find it to be an essential clause.
16. Do you have something that can be delivered quickly?
17. It looks like we're in agreement about everything. 18. Does it come in any other styles?

19 我們已經有穩定的進展。

______

20 這些智慧型手機有貨嗎？

______

21 假如有違反的情況，合約就會終止。

______

22 我們在價格上妥協如何？

______

23 我們會提供所有必要的資料。

______

24 我可以提出一些可能的解決辦法嗎？

______

25 請在指示的地方簽名。

______

26 你是否考慮全額退費？

______

27 我們準備好要接受你的提案了。

______

28 我們會重新考慮我們的決定。

______

29 這份合約只在限定期間內有效。

______

解答 19. We've made steady progress. 20. Are these smart phones available?
21. The contract can be revoked in the event of a violation.
22. How about we compromise on the price? 23. We'll provide all of the required materials.
24. May I suggest a few possible solutions? 25. Please sign where indicated.
26. Would you consider a full refund? 27. We're ready to accept your offer.
28. We'll reconsider our decision. 29. This deal is only good for a limited time.

30 我比較想要不滿意包退的保證。

31 這些品項有貨嗎？

32 你找不到比這更好的品質了。

33 有紅色嗎？

34 我們可以降低一些價格。

35 你們有倉儲壽命比較長的產品嗎？

36 如果您堅持的話，我們可以接受。

37 我們想要訂購最新的款式。

38 看來我們在條件上都達成協議了。

39 我想要購買你們新加坡的工廠。

40 我們已經有重大的進展。

解答 30. I'd rather have a money-back guarantee. 31. Are these items available?
32. You can't find better quality. 33. Does it come in red?
34. We could be willing to go a little lower.
35. Do you have something that has a long shelf life?
36. That's acceptable if you insist upon it. 37. We'd like to order the latest model.
38. It looks like we're in agreement about the terms.
39. I'd like to purchase your Singapore operation. 40. We've made significant progress.

Unit 10
送貨・付款
提高顧客滿意度

10-1

要求送貨

When can I expect...?	226	預計什麼時候會…？
How soon...?	227	要過多久才…？
We need these by...	228	我們必須在…以前拿到。
Will you deliver...?	229	你可以寄送…嗎？
Can you send that by...?	230	你可以用…寄送嗎？

226

Pattern 226

When can I expect...?
預計什麼時候會…？

當你想確認貨品什麼時候可以寄出，寄出後又會多久後才能收到等相關事項，就可以使用這個十分正式的句型 When can I expect...?。

- **When can I expect delivery?**
  預計什麼時候會寄達？
- **When can I expect to receive the shipment?**
  預計什麼時候會收到貨品？
  * shipment 貨運，貨品
- **When can I expect to hear from you?**
  預計什麼時候會有你的消息？
- **When can I expect your next order?**
  你下次訂購預計是什麼時候？

1 對話
A We will ship your order out tomorrow.
B Great. 預計什麼時候會寄達？
A Within 3 to 5 days.

A 我們明天會將您的貨品寄出。
B 太好了！When can I expect delivery?
A 三到五天內。

2 練習 預計什麼時候會收到款項？(payment)
When can I expect ______________________?

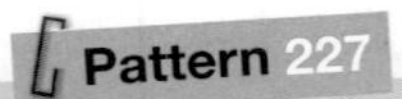

How soon...?
要過多久才⋯？

227 詢問出貨時間

這是一個由 how 和 soon 結合組成的句型，表示「要再過多久才⋯」的意思。這個句型的文法完全不同於中文，所以我們在剛開始使用時會覺得不習慣，但只要將這句型常掛在嘴邊練習的話，就會發現這個句型非常好用。

- **How soon will the product ship?**
  物品要過多久才會寄出？
- **How soon can we expect it to arrive?**
  預計要過多久才會抵達？
- **How soon will the shipment be ready?**
  貨品要過多久才會準備好？
- **How soon can you get us our order?**
  要過多久才會把貨品給我們？

1 對話 **A** 物品要過多久才會寄出？
B The product has already shipped.
A That's perfect!

A How soon will the product ship?
B 已經出貨了。
A 太好了！

2 練習 那些東西要過多久才會寄出？(those, deliver)
How soon ______________________________?

Pattern 228

228

We need these by...
我們必須在…以前拿到。

當你在產品上市前等特定時間點需要取得某項產品，就可以使用這個句型，單刀直入地用 We need 表達就行了。

- **We need these by the end of the week.**
  我們必須在本週末以前拿到。
- **We need these by our meeting this afternoon.**
  我們必須在今天下午的會議以前拿到。
- **We need these by November, when we will launch the new product.**
  我們必須在 11 月新產品上市以前拿到。
- **We need these by Wednesday in order to start the project.**
  為了開始那個企畫，我們必須在週三以前拿到。　＊in order to 為了…

1 對話
A Can you provide express delivery?
B Sure. When do you need them by?
A 我們必須在本週末以前拿到。

A 您可以用快遞寄出嗎？
B 當然可以，您什麼時候要收到東西呢？
A We need these by the end of the week.

2 練習 我們必須在關店前拿到。(closing)
We need these by ________________.

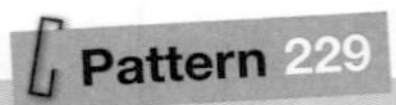

Will you deliver...?
你可以寄送…嗎？

有些人容易搞混 deliver 和 delivery 兩個單字，delivery（遞送、傳送）的動詞是 deliver，所以當我們想表達「可以寄…嗎？」時，不能用 Will you delivery...? 使得句子沒有動詞，而是應該要用本句型 Will you deliver...?。

- **Will you deliver to our area?**
  你可以寄送到我們這一區嗎？
- **Will you deliver outside of the region?**
  你可以寄送到這一區之外嗎？ ＊outside of …的範圍之外
- **Will you deliver to Asia?**
  你可以寄送到亞洲嗎？
- **Will you deliver them all at once?**
  你可以立刻寄送那些物品嗎？ ＊all at once 立刻

1 對話

A Let's discuss shipping.
B 你可以寄送到我們這一區嗎？
A Certainly. Just give me the shipping address.

A 現在來談一下送貨的事宜。
B Will you deliver to our area?
A 當然可以，請告訴我您的地址。

2 練習 你可以免費寄送嗎？(of, charge)
Will you deliver ____________________?

Pattern 230

Can you send that by...?
你可以用…寄送嗎？

當你想要指定貨物寄送的方式時，就可以使用這個簡單的句型 Can you send that by...?。

- **Can you send that by airmail?**
  你可以用航空信件寄送嗎？
- **Can you send that by FedEx?**
  你可以用 FedEx 寄送嗎？　　＊FedEx = Federal Express（聯邦快遞）
- **Can you send that by the fastest available option?**
  你可以用最快的方法寄送嗎？　　＊fastest 最快的（fast 的最高級）
- **Can you send that as soon as possible?**
  你可以盡快寄送嗎？

1 對話
A 你可以用 FedEx 寄送嗎？
B Or... Would UPS be acceptable?
A I would prefer FedEx.

A Can you send that by FedEx?
B 嗯…可以用 UPS 嗎？
A 我比較喜歡 FedEx 耶。

2 練習 你可以用 DHL 寄送嗎？(DHL)
Can you send that by ______________________?

10-2

送貨與收貨

Your order will arrive...	231	貴公司訂購的貨品將會…送達。
The shipment didn't...	232	寄送來的貨品沒有…
I'm sorry that the shipment will be delayed...	233	我很抱歉，貨品將會延遲…
The product is supposed to...	234	產品應該…
We were told...	235	我們聽說…

Pattern 231 231

Your order will arrive...
貴公司訂購的貨品將會…送達。

當你想告知對方何時可以收到東西時，就可以使用這個句型。有時會看到 Your order will be arrived... 這樣的句子，這是錯誤的表達方式，要用 will arrive 才是正確的。

- **Your order will arrive within 24 hours.**
  貴公司訂購的貨品將會在 24 小時內送達。
- **Your order will arrive by the end of the week.**
  貴公司訂購的貨品將會在本週末前送達。
- **Your order will arrive overnight.**
  貴公司訂購的貨品將會在隔日送達。 ＊overnight 隔日（送達的）
- **Your order will arrive within five business days.**
  貴公司訂購的貨品將會在五個工作天內送達。 ＊business day 工作天

1 對話
A When can we expect delivery?
B 貴公司訂購的貨品將會在五個工作天內送達。
A Is there any way to speed that up?
B We have an express delivery option.

A 我什麼時候可以收到東西？
B Your order will arrive within five business days.
A 有辦法再早一點收到嗎？
B 我們也有提供快遞的服務。

2 練習 貴公司訂購的貨品將會在禮拜五送達。(Friday)
Your order will arrive ______________________.

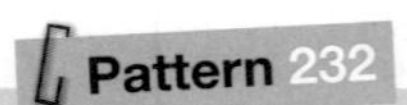

The shipment didn't...
寄送來的貨品沒有…

232 寄送來的貨品有缺陷

當寄送來的貨品有誤、已損毀，或是缺了 packing slip（包裝單，表明出口貨物的包裝形式、包裝內容、數量、質量、體積與件數的單據）等資料時，就可以使用這個句型。本句型中的 shipment 指的是「（寄送來的）貨品」。

The shipment didn't arrive on time.
寄送來的貨品沒有準時送達。

The shipment didn't arrive in good condition.
寄送來的貨品沒有以完好的狀態送達。

The shipment didn't include all of the items.
寄送來的貨品沒有包含全部的品項。

The shipment didn't meet our specifications.
寄送來的貨品不符合我們所要求的規格。

＊meet 符合，滿足　＊specification（詳細的）規格

1 對話
A What is your complaint?
B 寄送來的貨品沒有包含全部的品項。
A Could you send us a list of the missing products?

A 您不滿意的地方是什麼呢？
B The shipment didn't include all of the items.
A 可以請您將缺少物品的清單寄給我們嗎？

2 練習 寄送來的貨品沒有包含包裝單。(packing slip)
The shipment didn't ______________________________.

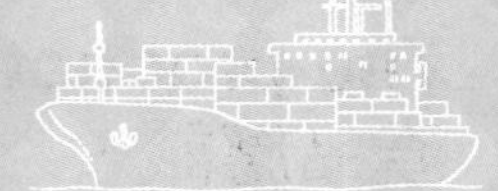

Pattern 233

233

I'm sorry that the shipment will be delayed...
我很抱歉，貨品將會延遲…

遇到因為颱風或水災等天災，或是貨運公司罷工和庫存不足等因素而無法如期出貨時，就可以使用這個句型向顧客表達歉意。

- **I'm sorry that the shipment will be delayed for several days.**
  我很抱歉，貨品將會延遲幾天。
- **I'm sorry that the shipment will be delayed due to a strike at UPS.** ＊strike 罷工
  我很抱歉，由於 UPS 罷工，貨品將會延遲。
- **I'm sorry that the shipment will be delayed as it's currently out of stock.** ＊currently 目前 ＊out of stock 沒有現貨
  我很抱歉，由於目前沒有庫存，貨品將會延遲。
- **I'm sorry that the shipment will be delayed until after Christmas.**
  我很抱歉，貨品將會延遲到耶誕節之後。

1 對話

A How can I help you?

B The product was supposed to be delivered later this week.

A 我很抱歉，貨品將會延遲到耶誕節之後。

A 有什麼可以幫忙的地方嗎？

B 之前說好這個週末就可以收到貨。

A I'm sorry that the shipment will be delayed until after Christmas.

2 練習 我很抱歉，由於暴風雨的關係，貨品將會延遲。(due to, storm)

I'm sorry that the shipment will be delayed ______________.

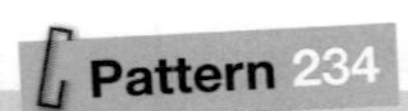

The product is supposed to...
產品應該…

片語 be supposed to... 常用來表示「應該…」的意思，所以當你想要詢問對方產品的相關資訊時，就可以使用這個句型。

- **The product is supposed to come with a warranty.**
  產品應該附有保證書。
  * warranty 保證書
- **The product is supposed to arrive on Monday.**
  產品應該會在禮拜一送達。
- **The product is supposed to come in two boxes.**
  產品應該會分成兩箱送達。
- **The product was supposed to come with a carrying case.**
  產品應該附有收納提箱。

1 對話
A The CEO wants an update on our shipment to Guam.
B 產品應該會在禮拜一送達。
A He wanted it there by today.

A 執行長想知道要寄去關島那批貨的最新情況。
B The product is supposed to arrive on Monday.
A 執行長希望能在今天就寄到。

2 練習 產品應該會在這個週末送到。(deliver, later)
The product is supposed to ____________________.

Pattern 235

We were told...
我們聽說…

I was told... 表示「我聽說…」，這個句型是它的延伸型態 We are told...，表示「我們聽說…」，用來確認貨品寄送的相關訊息。

- **We were told that there would be no delays.**
  我們聽說寄送不會有延遲。 ＊delay 延遲，延誤
- **We were told that the product had already shipped.**
  我們聽說貨品已經寄出了。
- **We were told to expect delivery no later than the 15th.**
  我們聽說貨品最遲會在 15 號寄出。
- **We were told that the price was the same for express shipping.**
  我們聽說快速件是相同的價錢。

1 對話
A There's been a delay with your shipment.
B 我們聽說寄送不會有延遲。
A Unfortunately, the delivery truck was in an accident.

A 您的包裹將會晚一點送到。
B We were told that there would be no delays.
A 很不幸地，貨運車遇到事故。

2 練習 我們聽說明天就會收到包裹。(that, make)
We were told ________________________________.

10-3

確定貨品寄送資訊

I'd like to check the status of...	236	我想要確認一下…狀況。
Could I get a tracking number...?	237	可以給我…的追蹤號碼嗎？
We shipped them via...	238	我們用…將貨品寄出了。
Did you get...?	239	您是否收到…？
The invoice number is...	240	發票號碼…

236

Pattern 236

I'd like to check the status of...
我想要確認一下…狀況。

當你想要確認目前訂單或產品的出貨狀態時，就可以使用這個句型。本句型中的 status 是表示「情況、狀態」的意思。意義相似的句型為 Please check on the progress of...。

- **I'd like to check the status of my order.**
  我想要確認一下我的訂單狀況。
- **I'd like to check the status of my delivery.**
  我想要確認一下我的寄件狀況。
- **I'd like to check the status of my account.**
  我想要確認一下我的帳戶狀況。
- **I'd like to check the status of the order I made yesterday.**
  我想要確認一下我昨天下訂的訂單狀況。

1 對話
A What can I do for you?
B 我想要確認一下我的訂單狀況。
A Sure. What is your confirmation number?

A 您需要協助嗎？
B I'd like to check the status of my order.
A 好的，請問您的訂單編號是？

2 練習 我想要確認一下包裹目前的出貨狀況。(package)
I'd like to check the status of ______________________.

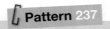

Pattern 237

Could I get a tracking number...?
可以給我…的追蹤號碼嗎？

為了確認貨品的下落，我們常常必須詢問貨物寄出時的追蹤號碼，使用這個句型來詢問就行了。

- **Could I get a tracking number for my order?**
  可以給我訂單的追蹤號碼嗎？
- **Could I get a tracking number on the shipment?**
  可以給我寄送貨品的追蹤號碼嗎？
- **Could I get a tracking number from UPS?**
  可以給我 UPS 的追蹤號碼嗎？
  ＊UPS ＝ United Parcel Service（美國郵政）
- **Could I get a tracking number sent to me by email?**
  可以將追蹤號碼用電子郵件寄給我嗎？
  ＊by email 用電子郵件

1 對話
A 可以給我訂單的追蹤號碼嗎？
B Sure. I'll email it to you as soon as the item ships.
A How soon will that be?
B By the end of the day.

A Could I get a tracking number for my order?
B 當然可以，等東西出貨時，我會立刻將包裹的追蹤號碼用電子郵件寄給您。
A 要再過多久才會出貨？
B 今天結束以前。

2 練習 可以將追蹤號碼傳到我的手機嗎？(send, cell phone)
Could I get a tracking number ______________________?

238

Pattern 238

We shipped them via...
我們用…將貨品寄出了。

via 是表示「經由、通過」某個場所或系統的介系詞。常見的寄件方式包括郵局快捷 EMS 或聯邦快遞 FedEx 等，如果因為貨品數量較大而必須採用集箱運送時，可以選擇 FCL / LCL base 來送件。FCL 是 Full Container Load（整裝貨櫃）的縮寫，LCL 則是 Less than Container Load（併裝貨櫃）的縮寫。

We shipped them via UPS.
我們用 UPS 將貨品寄出了。

We already shipped them via express air.
我們已經用航空快遞將貨品寄出了。　＊express air 空運快遞

We shipped them with FCL base.
我們用整裝貨櫃將貨品寄出了。

We shipped them with LCL base.
我們用併裝貨櫃將貨品寄出了。

1 對話
A I'd like a guarantee that these will arrive by tomorrow.
B 我們已經用航空快遞將貨品寄出了。
A Oh, really? Okay.

A 我希望你們能保證東西明天就會送到。
B We already shipped them via express air.
A 喔，真的嗎？我知道了。

2 練習 我們已經用 EMS 將貨品寄出了。(EMS)
We shipped them via ____________________.

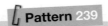

239

Pattern 239

Did you get...?
您是否收到⋯？

當你想確認對方是否已準時收到貨品或發票時，就可以使用這個以 do 的過去式 did 開頭的疑問句來向對方詢問。

- **Did you get the products on time?**
  您是否如期收到貨品？
  ＊on time 準時，如期
- **Did you get the item you ordered?**
  您是否收到您訂購的商品？
- **Did you get the invoice I sent you?**
  您是否收到我寄給您的收據？
- **Did you get the entire shipment on the same day?**
  您是否在同一天內收到全部的貨品？

1 對話

A Hello. This is a follow-up call about your recent order.
B Yes. I received everything in good shape.
A Great. 您是否如期收到貨品？
B Yes. In fact, it arrived earlier than expected.

A 您好，我是打來追蹤確認您近期的訂單情況。
B 是的，我已經全部都收到了。
A 太好了！Did you get the products on time?
B 有，其實還比想像中更早送到。

2 練習 您是否收到您想要的商品？(items, expect)
Did you get ______________________?

240

Pattern 240

The invoice number is...
發票號碼…

「發票號碼」的英文是 invoice number，本句型 The invoice number is... 是以 invoice number 為主題的代表句型之一，可以用來跟對方確認發票的資訊。

The invoice number is 67439.
發票號碼是 67439。

The invoice number is printed at the bottom.
發票號碼印在最下方。　＊at the bottom 最下方

The invoice number should be on your receipt.
發票號碼應該在您的收據上。

The invoice number doesn't match up.
發票號碼不吻合。　＊match up 吻合，一致

1 對話
A I'm having a problem with a delivery.
B Let me check it out. What's your invoice number?
A 發票號碼是 67439。

A 貨物寄送方面出了問題。
B 讓我幫你確認一下，發票號碼是多少？
A The invoice number is 67439.

2 練習 發票號碼在右上角。(top, corner)
The invoice number is ______________________.

10-4

要求付款

I want to remind you...	241	我想提醒您…
Payment must be made...	242	一定要…付款。
If you fail to pay...	243	假如你無法…付款，…
Your account is...	244	你的記帳戶頭…
We'll be forced to...	245	我們只能…

Pattern 241

I want to remind you...
我想提醒您…

當你想提醒客戶某件事時，就可以使用這個句型。remind 是「提醒」的意思，在這個句型裡，remind 的後面先接「人」，然後再接 of 或 that，之後加上要提醒的「事件」。

- **I want to remind you of your payment due date.**
  我想提醒您付款截止日。 ＊payment due date 付款截至日
- **I want to remind you that your payment is two days late.**
  我想提醒您您的付款已經逾期兩天了。
- **I want to remind you that your payment has not been received.**
  我想提醒您我們尚未收到您的付款。
- **I just want to inform you that we'll pursue legal action.**
  我只是想要通知您我們將會採取法律行動。 ＊pursue 實行，採取

1 對話
A What seems to be the problem?
B 我想提醒您我們尚未收到您的付款。
A What? I sent the payment last week.

A 有什麼事嗎？
B I want to remind you that your payment has not been received.
A 什麼？我上個禮拜就已經付款了。

2 練習 我想提醒您昨天是付款的最後期限。(payment due date)
I want to remind you ______________________.

Pattern 242

Payment must be made...
一定要…付款。

當你想告訴對方付款條件時，就可以使用這個句型。這是合約書中最重要的內容，所以一定要跟對方說明清楚。本句型中的 must 是為了加強語氣，表示強調。

- **Payment must be made promptly.**
  一定要準時付款。
  * payment 支付，支付的款項
- **Payment must be made in full.**
  一定要全額付款。
  * in full 全部的，全額
- **Payment must be made in U.S. dollars.**
  一定要用美元付款。
- **Payment must be made before delivery.**
  一定要在寄送之前付款。

1 對話

A Let me explain our terms of business.
B Yes, go ahead.
A 一定要準時付款。If your account is overdue, we have the right to suspend your service.

A 我想向您說明交易條件內容。
B 好的，請說吧！
A Payment must be made promptly. 假如沒有在期限內付款的話，我們有權利中止服務。

2 練習

這個月底前一定要付款。(end of the month)
Payment must be made ______________.

243

Pattern 243

If you fail to pay...
假如你無法…付款，…

當你想告知對方沒有支付款項時會出現什麼情況時，就可以使用這個句型，句型中的 fail to 可解釋為「無法…」。

- **If you fail to pay within the week, we will have to cancel your order.**
  假如你無法在一週內付款，我們必須取消你的訂單。
- **If you fail to pay on time, we can no longer do business.**
  假如你無法準時付款，我們無法再跟你做生意。
- **If you fail to pay on time, your account will be frozen.**
  假如你無法準時付款，你的帳戶將會被凍結。 ＊frozen 凍結
- **If you fail to pay promptly, the remainder of your order will not be shipped.** ＊remainder 其餘的，剩餘的
  假如你無法如期付款，你其餘的貨物將不會被寄出。

1 對話
A 假如你無法準時付款，你的帳戶將會被凍結。
B For how long?
A Until payment is received.

A If you fail to pay on time, your account will be frozen.
B 會凍結多久？
A 直到我們收到你的款項為止。

2 練習 假如你無法準時付款，就會增加 5%的服務費。
(service charge, add)
If you fail to pay ______________________________.

Pattern 244

Your account is...
你的記帳戶頭…

當你想告知付款現況時，就可以使用這個句型。account 除了可以表示銀行帳戶，也能表示公司之間往來交易情況下，客戶方的「記帳戶頭」（客戶記帳購物，定時付款的戶頭）。

- **Your account is past due.**
  你的記帳戶頭已經逾期了。
  * past due 逾期
- **Your account is overdue.**
  你的記帳戶頭已經超過期限了。
  * overdue 超過期限
- **Your account is frozen.**
  你的記帳戶頭已經被凍結了。
- **Your account is not in good standing.**
  你的記帳戶頭使用狀況不佳。

1 對話
A Ms. Nelson, we have a problem.
B I know.
A 你的記帳戶頭已經逾期了。

A 尼爾森小姐，我們遇到問題了。
B 我知道。
A Your account is past due.

2 練習
你的記帳戶頭還沒更新。(up-to-date)
Your account is ____________________.

Pattern 245

We'll be forced to...
我們只能…

當送貨已完成，對方卻遲遲不肯付款且屢勸不聽時，最後只能凍結對方的帳戶或取消這筆交易，這時最常用到的句型就是 be forced to（被迫…／只能…）。

- **We'll be forced to freeze your account.**
  我們只能凍結你的帳戶。
- **We'll be forced to close your account.**
  我們只能關閉你的帳戶。
- **We'll be forced to discontinue our services.**
  我們只能中斷我們的服務。 ＊discontinue 停止，中斷
- **We'll be forced to turn your account over to a collection agency.**
  我們只能把你的帳戶轉給催收公司。 ＊collection agency 催收／討債公司

1 對話

A Your payment is long overdue.
B We're trying to arrange payment.
A If we don't receive it soon, 我們只能把你的帳戶轉給催收公司。

A 您的應付款項已經逾期太久了。
B 我們正在努力安排付款事宜。
A 假如在近期內仍收不到這筆款項，we'll be forced to turn your account over to a collection agency.

2 練習 我們只能聯絡我們的法律顧問。(contact, lawyer)
We'll be forced to ______________________.

付款方式

Pattern 246

Can we pay...?
我們可以…付款嗎？

當你正和客戶討論付款方式時，就可以使用這個句型。另外，現金付款的英文是 in cash，開公司支票或個人支票付款的英文是 by check，分期付款的英文則是 in installments。

- **Can we pay in cash?**
  我們可以用現金付款嗎？
- **Can we pay by check?**
  我們可以用支票付款嗎？
- **Can we pay in installments?**
  我們可以分期付款嗎？
- **Can we pay some now and some later?**
  我們可以先付一部分，之後再全部付清嗎？ ＊later 之後，以後

1 對話
A How would you like to pay?
B 我們可以用支票付款嗎？
A That would be fine.

A 你想要用什麼方式付款？
B Can we pay by check?
A 沒問題。

2 練習 我們可以用匯票付款嗎？(order)
Can we pay ______________________?

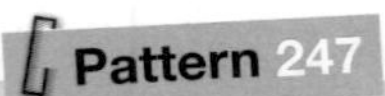

247

Is there a fee for...?
…會收手續費嗎？

這是用來詢問各種手續費的句型。跟付款有關的單字有 price, fare, charge, fee 等，其中 fee 就是「手續費」的意思。因此當你想詢問是否有手續費時，就可以使用這個句型。

- **Is there a fee for late payments?**
  延遲付款會收手續費嗎？
- **Is there a fee for overseas orders?**
  海外的訂單會收手續費嗎？　　* overseas 海外的
- **Is there a fee for payment by check?**
  用支票付款會收手續費嗎？
- **Is there a fee for express delivery?**
  用快遞寄送會收手續費嗎？

1 對話
A I see that payment has not yet been made.
B No, it hasn't. 延遲付款會收手續費嗎？
A We add a 5% fee per week on late payments.

A 我看到您好像還沒付清款項。
B 嗯，我還沒付。Is there a fee for late payments?
A 每延遲一個禮拜我們就會加收 5%的手續費。

2 練習 寄送和處理會收手續費嗎？(shipping, handling)
Is there a fee for ____________________?

Pattern 248

248

Our payment is...
我們的付款…

正如前面提到過的，公司之間在進行金錢交易時，會互相開設帳戶來處理款項，因此本句型中的 payment 即表示「應付款項」。這是一個用途很廣泛的句型，請參考下列的例句。

- **Our payment is on its way.**
  我們的付款正在處理中。 ＊on one's way 正…中
- **Our payment is a little late.**
  我們的付款有點延遲。
- **Our payment is already listed on the account.**
  我們的付款已經列在帳戶上了。
- **Our payment is for the last two months.**
  這是我們過去兩個月的款項。

1 對話 A 我們的付款有點延遲。
B When can we expect it?
A It should arrive by tomorrow.

A Our payment is a little late.
B 我們什麼時候能收到款項呢？
A 明天就會收到了。

2 練習 我們的付款期限快到了。(be going to, due)
Our payment is ______________________.

Pattern 249

249

We've remitted...
我們已經匯了…

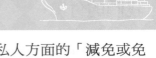

句型中的動詞 remit 除了可以表示私人方面的「減免或免除債務」之外，在商務英語中主要用來表示「匯款」；因此當你想要表達「我們已匯款」時，就可以使用這個句型。

- **We've remitted payment.**
  我們已經匯款了。
- **We've remitted deposit.**
  我們已經匯了訂金。

  ＊deposit 訂金，保證金
- **We've remitted $5,000 to your account.**
  我們已經匯了五千美元到你的帳戶。
- **We've remitted the second installment.**
  我們已經匯了第二期的分期付款。

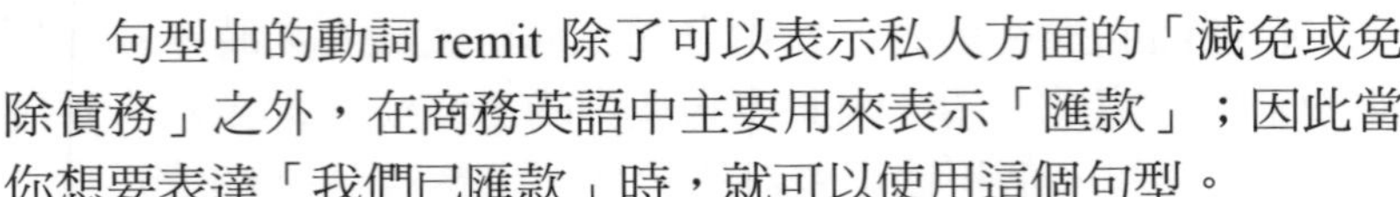

1 對話

A Our records show you are late with this month's check.
B 我們已經匯款了。
A When did you send it?
B Two days ago.

A 根據我們的紀錄，你們這個月的款項好像遲了。
B We've remitted payment.
A 什麼時候匯的呢？
B 兩天前。

2 練習 我們已經匯了全部的款項。(full)

We've remitted ______________________________.

250

Pattern 250

We've confirmed...
我們已經確認…

跟付款有關的單字中，最常見到的就是前面提過的 account, remit 以及本句型中的 confirm。當你想跟對方確認付款情況時，就可以使用這個句型。

- **We've confirmed your payment.**
  我們已經確認您的付款。
- **We've confirmed receipt of your deposit.**
  我們已經確認收到您的保證金了。
- **We've confirmed the agreed-upon fee to be $100,000.**
  我們已經確認貴公司同意的十萬元費用。 ＊agreed-upon （貴公司）同意的
- **We've confirmed that your payment has gone through.**
  我們已經確認您已成功付款。 ＊go through 通過，成功

1 對話 **A** I'm returning your call from this morning.
B Oh, yes. Have you located my deposit?
A Yes. 我們已經確認收到你的保證金了。

A 我要回覆您今天早上的來電。
B 喔，對，你確認過我的保證金了嗎？
A 有的，We've confirmed receipt of your deposit.

2 練習 我們確認過最後一批貨已經抵達了。
(that, the last of the packages)
We've confirmed ________________________.

10-1~10-5

黃金複習 15 分鐘！

前面這 25 個句型和 125 個句子全都記熟了嗎？
來驗收一下學習成果吧！如果不能充滿自信地用英文說出以下 40 個句子，請翻到前面再重新複習一次！

01 你下次訂購預計是什麼時候？

02 我們已經確認收到您的保證金了。

03 預計要過多久才會抵達？

04 我們已經匯了訂金。

05 我們必須在今天下午的會議以前拿到。

06 我們的付款有點延遲。

07 你可以寄送到這一區之外嗎？

08 海外的訂單會收手續費嗎？

09 你可以用最快的方法寄送嗎？

解答 01. When can I expect your next order? 02. We've confirmed receipt of your deposit. 03. How soon can we expect it to arrive? 04. We've remitted deposit. 05. We need these by our meeting this afternoon. 06. Our payment is a little late. 07. Will you deliver outside of the region? 08. Is there a fee for overseas orders? 09. Can you send that by the fastest available option?

10 我們可以用支票付款嗎？

____

11 貴公司訂購的貨品將會在本週末前送達。

____

12 我們只能關閉你的帳戶。

____

13 寄送來的貨品沒有以完好的狀態送達。

____

14 你的記帳戶頭已經超過期限了。

____

15 我很抱歉，由於 UPS 罷工，貨品將會延遲。

____

16 假如你無法準時付款，你的帳戶將會被凍結。

____

17 產品應該會在禮拜一送達。

____

18 一定要全額付款。

____

19 我們被告知寄送不會有延遲。

____

20 我想提醒您您的付款已經逾期兩天了。

____

解答 10. Can we pay by check? 11. Your order will arrive by the end of the week.
12. We'll be forced to close your account. 13. The shipment didn't arrive in good condition.
14. Your account is overdue.
15. I'm sorry that the shipment will be delayed due to a strike at UPS.
16. If you fail to pay on time, your account will be frozen.
17. The product is supposed to arrive on Monday. 18. Payment must be made in full.
19. We were told that there would be no delays.
20. I want to remind you that your payment is two days late.

21 發票號碼印在最下方。

22 預計什麼時候會寄達？

23 您是否收到您訂購的商品？

24 物品要過多久才會寄出？

25 我們已經用航空快遞將貨品寄出了。

26 我們必須在本週末以前拿到。

27 可以給我寄送貨品的追蹤號碼嗎？

28 你可以寄送到我們這一區嗎？

29 我想要確認一下我的寄件狀況。

30 你可以用航空信件寄送嗎？

31 我們已經確認您的付款。

解答 21. The invoice number is printed at the bottom. 22. When can I expect delivery? 23. Did you get the item you ordered? 24. How soon will the product ship? 25. We already shipped them via express air. 26. We need these by the end of the week. 27. Could I get a tracking number on the shipment? 28. Will you deliver to our area? 29. I'd like to check the status of my delivery. 30. Can you send that by airmail? 31. We've confirmed your payment.

32 貴公司訂購的貨品將會在 24 小時內送達。

33 我們已經匯款了。

34 寄送來的貨品沒有準時送達。

35 我們的付款正在處理中。

36 我很抱歉，貨品將會延遲幾天。

37 延遲付款會收手續費嗎？

38 產品應該附有保證書。

39 我們可以用現金付款嗎？

40 我們聽說貨品已經寄出了。

解答 32. Your order will arrive within 24 hours. 33. We've remitted payment.
34. The shipment didn't arrive on time. 35. Our payment is on its way.
36. I'm sorry that the shipment will be delayed for several days.
37. Is there a fee for late payments? 38. The product is supposed to come with a warranty.
39. Can we pay in cash? 40. We were told that the product had already shipped.

Unit 11
合約糾紛
展現解決問題的能力

11-1

提出問題

Unfortunately, we haven't received...	251	很遺憾地，我們還沒有得到…
We found out that...	252	我們發現…
Your product failed to...	253	貴公司的產品沒有…
You promised...	254	你承諾過…
The quality of your service is...	255	貴公司的服務品質…

Pattern 251

251

Unfortunately, we haven't received... 很遺憾地，我們還沒有得到…

當你想告訴對方沒收到電子郵件的回信或寄來的包裹時，就可以使用這個句型。意義相似但語氣較為隨意輕鬆的句型為 We didn't get... 和 I didn't get...。

- **Unfortunately, we haven't received your response to our offer.**
  * response 回應，答覆
  很遺憾地，我們還沒有得到貴公司對我們提案的回覆。
- **Unfortunately, we haven't received approval.**
  很遺憾地，我們還沒有得到批准。
  * approval 贊成，許可
- **Unfortunately, we haven't received the contract.**
  很遺憾地，我們還沒有收到合約。
- **Unfortunately, we haven't received the price list yet.**
  很遺憾地，我們還沒有收到價目表。

1 對話 We would like to begin the project. 很遺憾地，我們還沒有獲得批准。It would be helpful if you sent an email to our vice president. He is still not convinced. Giving him more details is essential.

我們想開始進行那個計畫，Unfortunately, we haven't received approval. 如果您能寄信給我們公司的副總裁，將能幫上我們的大忙。副總裁目前還不相信這個計畫，所以跟他報告更多細節內容是非常重要的。

2 練習 很遺憾地，我們還沒有得到您的答覆。(answer, yet)
Unfortunately, we haven't received ____________________.

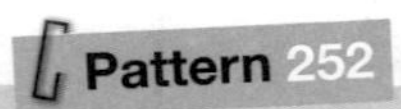

We found out that...
我們發現…

當你發現產品有瑕疵或損傷，想要跟對方明確地表達不滿，就可以使用這個句型。因為是第一次抱怨時使用的句型，所以語氣較輕微。

- **We found out that the product was flawed.**
  我們發現產品有瑕疵。 ＊flawed 有缺陷的
- **We found out that the product did not match your description.**
  我們發現產品跟您所描述的不符。
- **We found out that we had been overcharged.**
  我們發現我們被多收了費用。 ＊overcharge 對…索價太高
- **We found out that this item is out of stock.**
  我們發現這項產品缺貨中。 ＊out of stock 沒有庫存，缺貨

1 對話 我們發現產品有瑕疵。We need a replacement immediately. If it is not in better condition, we will have to take our business elsewhere.

We found out that the product was flawed. 我們要求立刻換貨，如果還是沒改善的話，我們就會去購買別家公司的產品。

2 練習 我們發現這個產品不符合我們公司的需求。(meet one's needs)
We found out that ______________________.

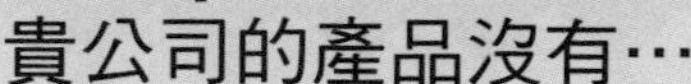

253

Your product failed to...
貴公司的產品沒有…

當你發現對方寄來的產品並不符合公司的標準或期待，就可以使用這個句型。本句型中的 fail to 如前面所提過的意思一樣，是表示「無法…」的意思。

- **Your product failed to meet our standards.**
  貴公司的產品沒有達到我們的標準。
- **Your product failed to live up to our expectations.**
  貴公司的產品辜負了我們的期待。 ＊live up to 不辜負（期待）
- **Your product failed to do what it promised.**
  貴公司的產品無法執行之前所承諾的（性能等）。
- **Your product failed to meet regulations.**
  貴公司的產品沒有達到規定。 ＊regulation 規定，基準

1 對話 A 貴公司的產品辜負了我們的期待。
B In what way?
A The size and shape are not what we want.

A Your product failed to live up to our expectations.
B 您指的是哪方面呢？
A 貴公司產品的大小跟形狀都不是我們想要的。

2 練習 貴公司的產品沒有市場。(sell, market)
Your product failed to ______________________.

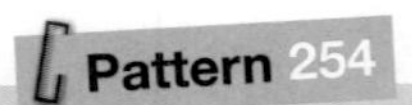

254

You promised...
你承諾過⋯

當購買者發現產品有瑕疵時，可以理直氣壯地跟賣方理論，尤其是在對方沒有依照約定行事時，你就可以使用這個句型來質問對方。

- **You promised we'd have your payment today.**
  你承諾過我們今天就會收到貴公司的付款。
- **You promised the shipment would arrive next week.**
  你承諾過貨品下週就會寄達。
- **You promised a 24-hour service.**
  你承諾過會提供 24 小時的服務。
- **You promised the same product for less money.**
  你承諾過用較低的價格賣相同的產品給我們。 ＊less 較少的

1 對話
A Help! My new refrigerator is leaking!
B I'm sorry, but we can't repair this until tomorrow.
A 你承諾過會提供 24 小時的服務。

A 請幫幫我！我的新冰箱漏水了！
B 很抱歉，我們要到明天才能修理它。
A You promised a 24-hour service.

2 練習 你承諾過會更換任何壞掉的零件。(replace, broken)
You promised ______________________.

255

Pattern 255

The quality of your service is...
貴公司的服務品質…

這個句型用在對客服或窗口表達強烈不滿，特別是針對服務方面提出規勸忠告時。下面例句中出現的單字都是商務英語的必備單字，希望大家可以熟記起來。

- **The quality of your service is unacceptable.**
  貴公司的服務品質令人無法接受。　＊unacceptable 不能接受的
- **The quality of your service is, frankly, subpar.**
  老實說，貴公司的服務品質在標準之下。　＊subpar 在標準之下
- **The quality of your service is worse than your competitor's.**　＊worse 更糟的（bad 的比較級）
  貴公司的服務品質比您的競爭對手還要糟。
- **The quality of your service leaves a lot to be desired.**　＊leave～to be desired 還有很多改善空間
  貴公司的服務品質還有很多改善的空間。

1 對話
A 貴公司的服務品質令人無法接受。
B What can we do to improve your experience?
A You can start by finding my shipment!

A The quality of your service is unacceptable.
B 我們要怎麼做才能改善呢？
A 先想辦法去把我的包裹找回來再說吧！

2 練習
貴公司的服務非常糟糕。(appalling)
The quality of your service is ______________________.

11-2

索償

I have some complaints about... 256 關於…，我有一些不滿。

I'm very disappointed in... 257 我對…感到失望。

We're unhappy with... 258 我們對…很不滿意。

This is the worst... 259 這是最糟糕的…

I must insist that... 260 我堅決要求…

Pattern 256 256

I have some complaints about...
關於⋯，我有一些不滿。

當你想向賣方抱怨或抗議時，就可以使用這個句型。意義相似的句型有 I find it difficult to understand... 和 This is not the first time that...，也都很常用。

- **I have some complaints about the delays in shipping.**
  關於寄送延遲，我有一些不滿。
- **I have some complaints about your product quality control.** ＊quality control 品質控管
  關於貴公司的產品品質控管，我有一些不滿。
- **I have some complaints about the quality of the item I ordered.**
  關於我訂購的商品品質，我有一些不滿。
- **I have some complaints about one of your employees' behavior last week.** ＊behavior 行為，態度
  關於上週貴公司其中一位員工的態度，我有一些不滿。

1 對話 關於寄送延遲，我有一些不滿。We depend on this product for our business. We cannot wait so long for it to arrive. In the future, please ensure that the product is shipped swiftly.

I have some complaints about the delays in shipping. 這個產品對我們公司很重要。所以我們無法像這樣久等貨物送達，希望未來你們能迅速地將產品寄出。

2 練習 關於處理問題方面，我有一些不滿。(handling)
I have some complaints about ______________.

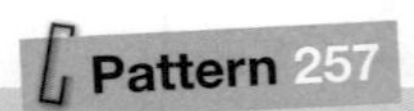

I'm very disappointed in...
我對…感到失望。

當你對產品的服務或品質感到失望時，就可以使用這個句型。雖然本句型是現在式，但是在解讀時要視為「我對（過去發生過的某件事）感到失望」。

- **I'm very disappointed in your level of service.**
  我對你們的服務水準感到失望。
- **I'm very disappointed in the quality of your product.**
  我對你們的產品品質感到失望。
- **I'm very disappointed with your response to the problem.**
  我對貴公司對該問題的回應感到失望。
- **I'm very disappointed my order was cancelled.**
  我對我的訂單被取消感到失望。

* cancel 取消

1 對話
A 我對你們的產品品質感到失望。
B Could you be more specific?
A The construction was substandard.

A I'm very disappointed in the quality of your product.
B 你可以說得再具體一點嗎？
A 這產品的結構在水準之下。

2 練習
我對我的包裹損毀一事感到相當失望。(shipment, damaged)
I'm very disappointed ______________________.

Pattern 258

258

We're unhappy with...
我們對…很不滿意。

舉例來說，因為對方公司的網頁設計太過複雜難以使用，或是對產品的包裝方式、顏色、品質等感到不滿時，就可以使用這個句型來表達。

- We're unhappy with **your return policy.**
  我們對貴公司的退費政策很不滿意。 ＊policy 政策，方針
- We're unhappy with **your complicated website.**
  我們對貴公司複雜的網站很不滿意。
- We're unhappy with **the gift-wrapping.**
  我們對貴公司的禮物包裝方式很不滿意。 ＊wrapping 包裝，包裝材料
- We're unhappy with **your delivery service.**
  我們對貴公司的寄送服務很不滿意。

1 對話 A 我們對貴公司的禮物包裝方式很不滿意。
B What seems to be the problem?
A Several of the items broke quite easily.

A We're unhappy with the gift-wrapping.
B 是出了什麼問題嗎？
A 有好幾樣物品很容易就會被打破。

2 練習 我們對品質很不滿意。(quality)
We're unhappy with ______________________.

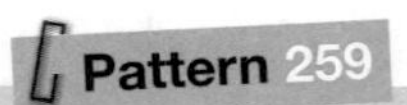

This is the worst...
這是最糟糕的⋯

當你想要強調自己非常不滿意，就可以使用這個帶有 the worst 的句型。這個句型表達出強烈的不滿，主要使用在希望對方能有後續處理的情況。

- **This is the worst packing job.**
  這是最糟糕的打包方式。
- **This is the worst experience I've had with an online distributor.**
  這是我在網路購物最糟糕的一次經驗。　＊distributor 販賣業者
- **This is the worst customer service I've ever had to deal with.**
  這是我處理過最糟糕的客戶服務。　＊deal with 應付，處理
- **This is the worst response I've ever gotten to a complaint.**
  這是我投訴以來，收到最糟糕的回應。

1 對話
A 這是我在網路購物最糟糕的一次經驗。
B I'm sorry you feel that way.
A Solve the problem!

A This is the worst experience I've had with an online distributor.
B 很抱歉讓您有這種感覺。
A 解決問題！

2 練習 這是我們收到最糟糕的一個報價。(price quote, receive)
This is the worst ________________________.

Pattern 260

260

I must insist that...
我堅決要求⋯

當你想強烈要求對方立即做處理時，就可以使用這個句型。本句型中的動詞 insist 可以用 correct, resolve, fix, solve, compensate, remedy, replace 等其他動詞替代。如果要用溫和一點的語氣，可以使用句型 I'd appreciate it if... 或 We'd be pleased if...。

- **I must insist that you issue a refund.**
  我堅決要求您退費給我。
- **I must insist that this blouse be replaced with a new one.**
  我堅決要求您換一件新的上衣給我。
- **I must insist that you apologize for being rude.**
  我堅決要求你對你的無禮道歉。 ＊rude 粗魯的，無禮的
- **I must insist that you take immediate action to replace the damaged product.** ＊immediate 立即的
  我堅決要求貴公司立即採取行動，更換這個損壞的產品。

1 對話 我堅決要求貴公司立即採取行動，更換這個損壞的產品。We need your product for a project we are currently working on. If you cannot get it to us, we will take our business to another supplier.

I must insist that you take immediate action to replace the damaged product. 我們公司現在進行的計畫需要你們的產品。如果你們不將產品寄過來的話，我們會改找其他供應商。

2 練習 我堅決要求你們全額退費。(return, in full)
I must insist that ______________________.

11-3

道歉

We're very sorry that... 261 我們很抱歉，…

We apologize for... 262 我們對…感到抱歉。

Please accept our apologies for... 263 對於…，請接受我們的道歉。

We should have + p.p. ... 264 我們應該要…才對。

We'll make sure...not... 265 我們會確保…不會…

261

Pattern 261

We're very sorry that...
我們很抱歉，…

在跟對方進行生意上的往來過程中，當我方出錯時，就要馬上向對方道歉，唯有如此才能繼續順利進行下一階段的交易，因此可以用本句型來向對方表達歉意。

- **We're very sorry that you are not satisfied.**
  我們很抱歉，讓您感到不滿意。
- **We're very sorry that the product was lost in transit.**
  我們很抱歉，貨品在運送過程中遺失了。 ＊**transit** 運輸，運送
- **We're very sorry that the product was damaged during shipping.**
  我們很抱歉，產品在運送過程中受損了。
- **We're very sorry to have caused you any inconvenience.**
  我們很抱歉，造成貴公司的不便。 ＊**inconvenience** 不便

1 對話 真的很抱歉，貨品在運送過程中遺失了。We try to provide the best service possible, but we must rely on outside companies for shipping. We will send out a replacement immediately.

We are very sorry that the product was lost in transit. 雖然我們努力想要提供您最好的服務，但是運送業務卻一定要委外辦理。我們會馬上再重寄一次產品給您。

2 練習 我們很抱歉，無法配合您的需求。(be able to, needs)
We're very sorry that ____________________.

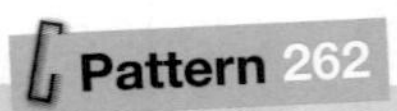

We apologize for...
我們對…感到抱歉。

用來表達歉意的句型可以依照鄭重程度分成好幾種，其中 We apologize for... 會比 I am sorry... 更為正式。此外，本句型中的介系詞 for 後面一定要接名詞或動名詞。

- **We apologize for the mix-up in your order.**
  我們對弄錯貴公司的訂單感到抱歉。 ＊mix-up 混亂，錯誤
- **We apologize for inconveniencing you.**
  我們對造成您的不便感到抱歉。
- **We apologize for the delay in shipping you the items.**
  我們對延遲寄送貴公司的貨品感到抱歉。
- **We apologize for not realizing there was a problem.**
  我們對沒意識到問題所在感到抱歉。 ＊realize 意識到，了解

1 對話 我們對弄錯貴公司的訂單感到抱歉。Sometimes errors are made, but we are working to solve the problem immediately. We ask for your patience in this matter.

We apologize for the mix-up in your order. 我們偶爾也會出錯，但是我們會立即努力修正這個錯誤。希望您對此事能給予我們更多耐心。

2 練習 我們對超收您產品費用一事感到抱歉。(overcharge, product)
We apologize for ______________________.

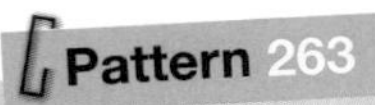

Please accept our apologies for...
對於…，請接受我們的道歉。

這是比上個句型更有禮貌的道歉句型。介系詞 for 後面要接道歉的原因，並且必須使用名詞或動名詞。

- Please accept our apologies for **our tardy payment.**
  對於我們的延遲付款，請接受我們的道歉。 ＊**tardy** 延遲的，遲到的
- Please accept our apologies for **receiving a broken set.**
  對於收到壞掉的套組，請接受我們的道歉。 ＊**broken** 破碎的，損壞的
- Please accept our apologies for **the damaged furniture.**
  對於損壞的家具，請接受我們的道歉。
- Please accept our apologies for **not getting back to you.** ＊**get back to** 回覆，後續聯絡
  對於沒能立刻跟您聯絡，請接受我們的道歉。

1 對話 對於沒能立刻跟您聯絡，請接受我們的道歉。We receive a large number of inquiries, so it is difficult to respond in a timely fashion. We have reviewed your case and are ready to help you.

Please accept our apologies for not getting back to you. 因為我們接到太多的諮詢，所以無法即時回覆您。我們已經看過您的案件，並準備好要協助您了。

2 練習 對於產品的運送狀況不佳，請接受我們的道歉。(bad condition)
Please accept our apologies for ____________________.

Pattern 264

We should have + p.p. ...
我們應該要…才對。

本句型是我們熟悉的 “should have + p.p.” 句型，用來表示「應該要…，但是卻沒這樣做」的意思。當你想為自己犯下的錯反省時，就可以使用這個句型。

- **We should have *predicted* that the product would be delayed.**
  我們應該要預料到貨品會延遲才對。 ＊predict 預測，預料
- **We should have *taken* your concerns more seriously.**
  我們應該要更嚴肅一點看待您所擔心的事才對。 ＊concern 擔心的事
- **We should have *been* prepared for such an eventuality.** ＊eventuality 可能會發生的事件
  我們應該要對這種可能會發生的事件做好準備才對。
- **We should have *anticipated* such a problem.**
  我們應該要預料到這樣的問題才對。

1 對話 I heard three of the photos are offensive! Our customers are boiling mad! 我們應該要預料到這樣的問題才對。

我們聽說其中三張照片冒犯了大家！我們的客戶都非常生氣！
We should have anticipated such a problem.

2 練習 我們應該要更早一點回信給您才對。(more)
We should have answered ______________________.

Pattern 265

265

We'll make sure...not...
我們會確保…不會…

這是使用片語 make sure 所組成的句型。當你想跟對方承諾不會再犯下同樣的錯時，就可以這麼說。

- **We'll make sure this will not occur again.**
  我們會確保這種事不會再發生。
- **We'll make sure this mistake is not repeated.**
  我們會確保同樣的錯不會再犯。
- **We'll make sure this problem will not arise in the future.**
  ＊arise 產生，出現
  我們會確保未來不會再出現這個問題。
- **We'll make sure this delay does not happen next time.**
  我們會確保這樣的延遲下次不會再發生。

1 對話 Sometimes during our busy season, mistakes are made. 我們會確保同樣的錯不會再犯。We hope that you will forgive this error and continue to do business with us.

我們在旺季時偶爾會犯下這樣的失誤。We'll make sure this will not occur again. 希望您能原諒我們，繼續跟我們做生意。

2 練習 我們會確保這種不幸的錯誤不會再發生。(unfortunate error)
We'll make sure ______________________.

11-4

解釋

The problem was caused by...	266	這個問題是因為…所引起的。
The reason is that...	267	理由是…
I've been...	268	我最近…
I was so...that...	269	我因為太…而…
I have no good excuse for...	270	對於…，我責無旁貸。

Pattern 266

266

The problem was caused by...
這個問題是因為…所引起的。

公司之間在談生意過程中出現了問題，你想說明問題發生的原因時，就可以使用這個句型。本句型中的 be caused by... 表示「因為…而引起的」的意思。

- **The problem was caused by a miscommunication.**
  這個問題是因為溝通不良所引起的。 ＊miscommunication 溝通不良
- **The problem was caused by the flood of last summer.**
  這個問題是因為去年夏天的淹水所引起的。
- **The problem was caused by a power outage.**
  這個問題是因為停電所引起的。 ＊power outage 停電
- **The problem was caused by an outside contractor.**
  這個問題是因為外部承包商所引起的。 ＊contractor 承包商

1  對話

A I ordered 1,000 clocks but received 1,000 socks!
B I'm so sorry. I will try to fix this.
A I knew the sales clerk misunderstood me.
B Clearly, 這個問題是因為誤解所引起的。

A 我訂了一千個時鐘，卻收到了一千雙襪子！
B 很抱歉，我們會馬上修正這個錯誤。
A 可能是你們業務員誤解我說的話了。
B 顯然是這樣的，the problem was caused by a miscommunication.

2 練習 這個問題是因為沒接到電話所引起的。(missed)
The problem was caused by ________________.

267

Pattern 267

The reason is that..
理由是…

當對方公司向你提出你無法照辦的要求，你想說明不能遵循的原因時，就可以使用這個句型來拒絕對方的要求。

- **The reason is that we must protect our copyright on this ad copy.**
  理由是我們必須保護我們這個廣告的著作權。 * copyright 著作權
- **The reason is that we are contractually forbidden from revealing this information.**
  理由是在合約上有註明我們不能洩漏這項資訊。
  * contractually 按照合約 * reveal 洩漏，接露
- **The reason is that we are not contractually obligated to exchange a product.**
  理由是在合約上我們沒有交換商品的義務。
- **The reason is that our security protocols do not allow us to give out receipts.** * protocol 協議，草案
  理由是我們的安全協議不允許我們將收據向外部人士流出。

1 對話 I'm sorry we cannot answer your questions regarding our company's interests in Taiwan. 理由是在合約上有註明我們不能洩漏這項資訊。

很抱歉，關於你問我們公司是否對台灣有興趣一事，恕我們無法回答。The reason is that we are contractually forbidden from revealing this information.

2 練習 理由是我們不能公開合作廠商的資訊。(partners, disclose)
The reason is that ______________________.

268

I've been...
我最近…

這個句型是使用在你因為太忙而無法即時回覆對方，想尋求對方的諒解的時候。這是利用現在完成式來表達目前忙碌狀態的句型。

- **I've been busier than usual lately.**
  我最近比平常還要忙。
- **I've been overwhelmed at the office.**
  我最近在公司忙翻了。 ＊overwhelmed 淹沒的，壓倒的
- **I've been working on a big project.**
  我最近在進行一個大案子。
- **I've been sorting out some issues.**
  我最近在整理一些問題。 ＊sort out 整理，分類

1 對話 我最近比平常還要忙，I just finished a major project, so I am finally catching up on my email. I promise that you now have my full attention.

I have been busier than usual lately. 我剛完成一個大案子，直到現在才有時間確認我的電子信箱。我保證從現在會把全部心思都放在你身上。

2 練習 我最近剛完成一筆大生意。(finish up, major)
I've been ______________.

Pattern 269　269

I was so...that...
我因為太…而…

這是使用 so... that...（太…所以…）組成的句型。本句型中的 so 後面要接 busy 等與狀態有關的形容詞，意義相似的句型為 too... to...（太…以至於無法…）。

- **I was so busy that I couldn't respond to any emails.**
  我因為太忙而無法回覆任何電子郵件。
- **I was so preoccupied that I forgot to respond.**
  我因為想得太出神而忘記回答。　＊preoccupied 全神貫注的，出神的
- **I was so overworked that I didn't have time to write you.**
  我因為工作太多而沒有時間寫信給你。　＊overworked 工作過度的
- **I was so involved in this project that I couldn't do anything else.**
  我因為太專注於這個企畫而無法分神做其他事情。

1 對話 I'm sorry for the delay. 我因為太專注於這個企畫上而無法分神做其他事情。Now that it's finished, I'll be available to talk to you about your issue. Perhaps, we could arrange a conference call.

很抱歉那麼晚才回信。I was so involved in this project that I couldn't do anything else. 現在終於結束了，我可以跟你談談你的問題，也許我們可以安排時間開視訊會議。

2 練習 我因為太專注在工作上，所以沒有跟你聯絡。(backlog, contact)
I was so ____________________ that ____________________.

Pattern 270

270

I have no good excuse for...
對於…，我責無旁貸。

當我們在尋求諒解或辯解時，常常會使用 excuse 這個單字，在商務場合也一樣。當你想對目前的情況表示「無話可說／沒有藉口／責無旁貸」時，就可以使用這個句型。

- **I have no good excuse for the delay.**
  對於延誤出貨，我責無旁貸。
- **I have no good excuse for having failed to find your record of purchase.**
  對於無法找到您的購買紀錄，我責無旁貸。
- **I have no good excuse for not having delivered your product on time.**
  對於沒有將貴公司的商品準時寄出，我責無旁貸。
- **I have no good excuse for our failure to provide you with adequate service.** ＊adequate 足夠的，適當的
  對於敝公司沒能提供您完善的服務，我責無旁貸。

1 對話 I have looked into your missing order and found that it was never sent from our corporate warehouse. 關於延誤出貨一事，我們責無旁貸。I deeply apologize for this error.

我們確認過您的訂貨遺失一事，發現那是因為貨品還在倉庫裡，尚未出貨。I have no good excuse for the delay. 在此向您深表歉意。

2 練習 對於未能將追蹤號碼告知您一事，我責無旁貸。
(fail to, tracking number)
I have no good excuse for ______________.

11-5

處理合約糾紛

We'll try to...	271	我們會設法…
If you're not satisfied,...	272	如果您還是不滿意的話，…
You can exchange...	273	您可以交換…
We'll do our best to...	274	我們會盡全力…
We'll compensate you for...	275	我們會補償您…

 271

Pattern 271

We'll try to...
我們會設法…

當客戶發現訂貨或發票不見時，一定會感到十分慌張，如果你在這種情況下想安撫客戶的話，就可以使用這個句型。

- **We'll try to find a way to satisfy you.**
  我們會設法找到讓您滿意的方法。
- **We'll try to find out what happened.**
  我們會設法查清楚發生了什麼事。
- **We'll try to remedy the situation.**
  我們會設法補救這個狀況。　　＊**remedy** 補救
- **We'll try to replace the defective item.**
  我們會設法替換有缺陷的商品。　　＊**defective** 有缺陷的

1 對話
A 我們會設法補救這個狀況。
B How?
A We're looking for the missing invoices right now.

A We'll try to remedy the situation.
B 你們要怎麼做？
A 我們正在尋找遺失的發票。

2 練習 我們會設法盡快退費給您。(refund, as soon as)
We'll try to ______________________________.

Pattern 272

If you're not satisfied, ...
如果您還是不滿意的話，…

當你收到來自客戶或顧客的抱怨，向對方鄭重道歉後還是無法安撫對方的話，就可以使用這個句型提供後續方案，採取正面進攻。

- **If you're not satisfied, we can offer a full refund.**
  如果您還是不滿意的話，我們可以全額退費給您。
- **If you're not satisfied, you can choose another product.**
  如果您還是不滿意的話，您可以選擇另一項產品。
- **If you're not satisfied, we'll give you double your money back.**
  如果您還是不滿意的話，我們會退還兩倍的金額給您。
- **If you're not satisfied, you should write a letter of complaint.**
  * letter of complaint 投訴信
  如果您還是不滿意的話，您應該寫投訴信。

1 對話
A 如果您還是不滿意的話，我們可以全額退費給您。
B I don't have time to find a replacement product elsewhere.
A Then we will look for a replacement from our suppliers.

A If you're not satisfied, we can offer a full refund.
B 我沒時間再去其他地方購買替代產品。
A 那麼我們幫您從供應商方面找替代產品。

2 練習 如果您還是不滿意的話，可以跟我們的經理談談。
(speak, manager)
If you're not satisfied, ______________________.

Pattern 273

273

You can exchange...
您可以交換…

當產品有瑕疵或送錯貨，就會遇到需要換貨的情況。當你告知對方換貨的相關資訊時，可以使用這個內含 exchange（交換）的句型。

- **You can exchange it for another item.**
  您可以交換另一項商品。
- **You can exchange the item for one of equivalent value.**
  您可以交換其他等值商品。　　＊equivalent 等值的
- **You can exchange your order for up to 60 days after purchase.**
  您可以在購買後六十天內調換您的貨品。
- **You can exchange everything but the swimsuits.**
  除了泳裝，您可以交換任何商品。　　＊but 除了…之外（＝except）

1 對話
A This product simply doesn't work.
B 您可以交換其他等值商品。
A Can I see the catalogue?

A 這個產品完全不能用。
B You can exchange the item for one of equivalent value.
A 可以讓我看一下目錄嗎？

2 練習 您可以交換另一項跟這個類似的產品。(comparable)
You can exchange ______________________.

Pattern 274

We'll do our best to...
我們會盡全力…

274
安撫客戶

我們想跟對方表達會盡全力時，最常說的話正是 We'll do our best to...。產品在出貨過程中發生問題，例如沒有確實送達或中途遺失，這是一件非常難堪的事，這時候就可以用本句型來安撫客戶。

- **We'll do our best to locate your lost shipment.**
  我們會盡全力找出您遺失的貨品。
- **We'll do our best to remedy the situation very quickly.**
  我們會盡全力盡快補救這個狀況。
- **We'll do our best to ensure prompt delivery.**
  我們會盡全力確保準時交貨。　＊ensure 保證，擔保
- **We'll do our best to find a replacement product that satisfies you.**
  我們會盡全力找到讓您滿意的替代商品。　＊replacement 替代品

1 對話
A The product should be there in two weeks.
B Are you sure?
A 我們會盡全力確保準時交貨。

A 產品將在兩週後送到。
B 你確定嗎？
A We'll do our best to ensure prompt delivery.

2 練習 我們會盡全力滿足您的要求。(satisfy)
We'll do our best to ______________________.

Pattern 275

We'll compensate you for...
我們會補償您⋯

動詞 compensate 表示「賠償、補償」。當發生合約糾紛而必須賠償客戶或公司時，就可以使用這個句型。

- **We'll compensate you for your lost time and wages.**
  我們會補償您損失的時間和報酬。　＊wage 薪水，報酬
- **We'll compensate you for your trouble.**
  我們會補償對您造成的麻煩。
- **We'll compensate you for any damages you may have sustained.**
  我們會補償您遭受到的任何損失。　＊sustain 遭受，蒙受
- **We'll compensate you for any wasted time.**
  我們會補償您損失的時間。

1 對話
A I'm so frustrated by dealing with your company.
B I apologize.
A It's just that I've wasted so much time on this issue!
B I understand. 我們會補償您損失的時間。

A 和你們公司的做生意讓我感到非常沮喪。
B 對不起。
A 我浪費了太多時間在這個問題上面了！
B 我了解，We'll compensate you for any wasted time.

2 練習　我們會補償這項產品對您造成的問題。(problem, cause)
We'll compensate you for ______________________.

11-1~11-5

黃金複習 15 分鐘！

前面這 25 個句型和 125 個句子全都記熟了嗎？
來驗收一下學習成果吧！如果不能充滿自信地用英文說出以下 40 個句子，請翻到前面再重新複習一次！

01 很遺憾地，我們還沒有得到批准。

02 我們會補償對您造成的麻煩。

03 我們發現我們被多收了費用。

04 我們會盡全力盡快補救這個狀況。

05 貴公司的產品辜負了我們的期待。

06 您可以交換其他等值商品。

07 你承諾過貨品下週就會寄達。

08 如果您還是不滿意的話，您可以選擇另一項產品。

09 貴公司的服務品質比您的競爭對手還要糟。

解答 01. Unfortunately, we haven't received approval.
02. We'll compensate you for your trouble. 03. We found out that you were overcharged.
04. We'll do our best to remedy the situation very quickly.
05. Your product failed to live up to our expectations.
06. You can exchange the item for one of equivalent value.
07. You promised the shipment would arrive next week.
08. If you're not satisfied, you can choose another product.
09. The quality of your service is worse than your competitor's.

10 我們會設法補救這個狀況。

11 關於寄送延遲，我有一些不滿。

12 對於延誤出貨，我責無旁貸。

13 我對你們的產品品質感到失望。

14 我因為想得太出神而忘記回答。

15 我們對貴公司複雜的網站很不滿意。

16 我最近在辦公室忙翻了。

17 這是我投訴以來，收到最糟糕的回應。

18 理由是在合約上有註明我們不能洩漏這項資訊。

19 我堅決要求您換一件新的上衣給我。

解答 10. We'll try to remedy the situation.
11. I have some complaints about the delays in shipping.
12. I have no good excuse for the delay.
13. I'm very disappointed in the quality of your product.
14. I was so preoccupied that I forgot to respond.
15. We're unhappy with your complicated website.
16. I've been overwhelmed at the office.
17. This is the worst response I've ever gotten to a complaint.
18. The reason is that we are contractually forbidden from revealing this information.
19. I must insist that this blouse be replaced with a new one.

20 這個問題是因為去年夏天的淹水所引起的。

______

21 我們會確保這種事不會再發生。

______

22 很遺憾地，我們還沒有得到貴公司對我們提案的回覆。

______

23 我們應該要更嚴肅地看待您所擔心的事才對。

______

24 我們發現產品有瑕疵。

______

25 對於收到壞掉的套組，請接受我們的道歉。

______

26 貴公司的產品沒有達到我們的標準。

______

27 我們對造成您的不便感到抱歉。

______

28 你承諾過我們今天就會收到貴公司的付款。

______

29 我們很抱歉，貨品在運送過程中遺失了。

______

30 貴公司的服務品質令人無法接受。

______

解答 20. The problem was caused by the flood of last summer.
21. We'll make sure this will not occur again.
22. Unfortunately, we haven't received your response to our offer.
23. We should have taken your concerns more seriously.
24. We found out that the product was flawed.
25. Please accept our apologies for receiving a broken set.
26. Your product failed to meet our standards. 27. We apologize for inconveniencing you.
28. You promised we'd have your payment today.
29. We're very sorry that the product was lost in transit.
30. The quality of your service is unacceptable.

31 這個問題是因為溝通不良所引起的。

32 關於貴公司的產品品質控管，我有一些不滿。

33 我對你們的服務水準感到失望。

34 理由是我們必須保護我們這個廣告的著作權。

35 我們對貴公司的退費政策很不滿意。

36 我最近比平常還要忙。

37 這是我在網路購物最糟糕的一次經驗。

38 我因為太忙而無法回覆任何電子郵件。

39 我堅決要求您退費給我。

40 對於無法找到您的購買紀錄，我責無旁貸。

解答 31. The problem was caused by a miscommunication.
32. I have some complaints about your product quality control.
33. I'm very disappointed in your level of service.
34. The reason is that we must protect our copyright on this ad copy.
35. We're unhappy with your return policy. 36. I've been busier than usual lately
37. This is the worst experience I've had with an online distributor.
38. I was so busy that I couldn't respond to any emails.
39. I must insist that you issue a refund.
40. I have no good excuse for having failed to find your record of purchase.

Part 3

職場生活

Unit 12
辦公室交流
與同事打好關係

12-1

同儕關係

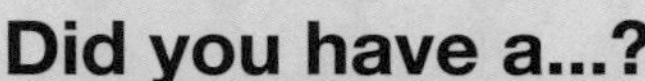

276

Did you have a...?
你有個愉快的…嗎？

早晨上班時，許多上班族會拿著一杯咖啡，互相打招呼，這時候最常使用的問候句型就是 Did you have a...?。本句型中的形容詞 nice 可以用 good, wonderful, great 等單字替代。

- **Did you have a good weekend?**
  你有個愉快的週末嗎？
- **Did you have a wonderful time last night?**
  昨晚你度過了美好的時光嗎？
- **Did you have a nice date?**
  你有個愉快的約會嗎？
- **Did you have a nice lunch?**
  你有個愉快的午餐嗎？

1 對話 **A** Hi, Alex.
B Hi, Alice. 午餐愉快嗎？
A Yes, we went to that new restaurant.

A 你好，艾力克斯。
B 你好，艾麗絲，Did you have a nice lunch?
A 嗯，我們去了那間最近新開的餐廳。

2 練習 旅行愉快嗎？(trip)
Did you have a ______________________?

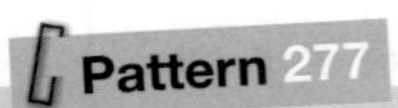

277

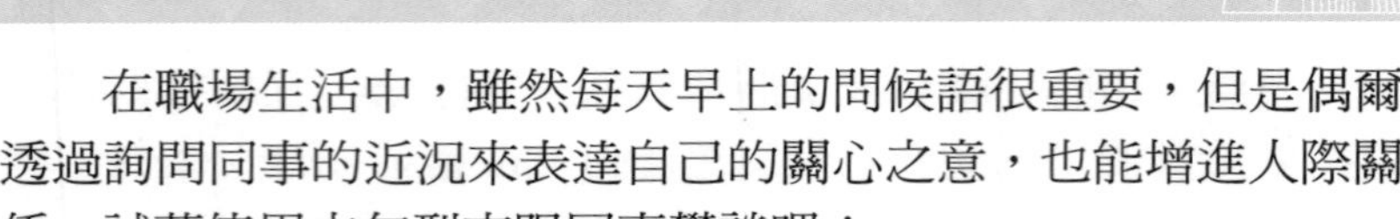

How's...?
…如何？

在職場生活中，雖然每天早上的問候語很重要，但是偶爾透過詢問同事的近況來表達自己的關心之意，也能增進人際關係。試著使用本句型來跟同事攀談吧！

- **How's it going?**
  最近如何？
- **How's the new staff member?**
  新同事如何？ ＊staff member 同事
- **How's your project coming along?**
  你的企畫進展如何？ ＊come along 發展
- **How's your new office?**
  你的新公司如何？

1 對話
A 新同事如何?
B We all love him.
A Really? That surprises me.

A How's the new staff member?
B 我們都很喜歡他。
A 真的嗎？真令我意外。

2 練習 盈利報告看起來如何？(profit report, look)
How's ______________________________?

Pattern 278

278

You look...
你看起來…

這個句型的意義相似於 You look like...，表示「你看起來…」的意思。當對方看起來很疲累或心情不好時，就可以使用這個句型來跟對方搭話。

You look tired.
你看起來很累。

You look stressed out.
你看起來壓力很大。 ＊stressed out 承受很大的壓力

You look nervous.
你看起來很緊張。 ＊nervous 緊張的

You look relaxed.
你看起來很放鬆。 ＊relaxed 放鬆的

1 對話
A What's wrong?
B Why do you think something's wrong?
A 你看起來壓力很大。

A 怎麼了嗎？
B 你為什麼會這樣問？
A You look stressed out.

2 練習 你看起來很棒。(terrific)
You look ________________.

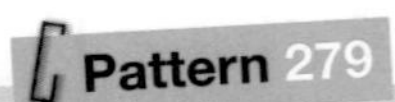

I like your...
我喜歡你⋯

這是用來稱讚對方的句型，稱讚能成為你和職場同事或上司之間的潤滑劑，讓大家每天早上都能有一個好的開始。聽到別人稱讚你時，立刻回覆對方 Thank you 或是再用此句型稱讚同事，才是有禮貌的表達。

- **I like your hair.**
  我喜歡你的髮型。
- **I like your shoes.**
  我喜歡你的鞋子。
- **I like your writing style in this report.**
  我喜歡你這篇報告的寫作風格。
- **I like your attention to detail.**
  我喜歡你注意細節（的做事方法）。

＊detail 細節

1 對話 **A** You're all dressed up today!
B Yes, I have a meeting with the CEO.
A 我喜歡你的鞋子。

A 你今天打扮得很漂亮！
B 對啊，因為我今天要跟執行長開會。
A I like your shoes.

2 練習 我喜歡你的外套。(jacket)
I like your ______________.

Pattern 280

280

Let's grab...
我們去吃（喝）…吧。

我們知道 grab 用來表示「抓、握」，但其實美國人更常用它來表示「吃、喝」的意思。當你想邀約同事一起喝杯咖啡或吃飯時，就可以使用這個句型。

- **Let's grab some lunch.**
  我們去吃午餐吧。
- **Let's grab a bite to eat.**
  我們去吃點東西吧。 ＊bite 便餐，少量的食物
- **Let's grab something to drink.**
  我們去喝個東西吧。
- **Let's grab a cup of coffee.**
  我們去喝杯咖啡吧。

1 對話

A I need to talk to you.
B Sure. What about?
A Employee concerns.
B Okay. 我們去喝個東西吧。

A 跟我聊聊吧。
B 好啊，你想聊什麼？
A 關於職員的事。
B 好的。Let's grab something to drink.

2 練習 我們去喝杯東西吧！ (drink)
Let's grab ______________________.

12-2

指派工作

I need you to...	281	我需要你⋯
The boss wants...	282	老闆要⋯
Don't forget to...	283	別忘了⋯
There will be...	284	⋯將會有⋯
Do you want me to...?	285	需要我⋯嗎？

Pattern 281

281

I need you to...
我需要你⋯

當上司想指派工作給下屬員工或同事時，最簡單的句型正是 I need you to...。本句型中的 you 後面要接 to 不定詞，並說出交辦事項的動詞詞組。

- **I need you to complete your report by 3:00.**
  我需要你在三點前完成你的報告。
- **I need you to give today's presentation.**
  我需要你執行今天的口頭發表。
- **I need you to organize a meeting of our investors.**
  我需要你為我們的投資者安排一場會議。
  ＊organize 安排　＊investor 投資者
- **I need you to go over the budget with me.**
  我需要你跟我一起來檢討預算。　＊go over 檢討，確認　＊budget 預算

1 對話
A Can we meet around 2:00 today?
B I think so. I'll check my calendar.
A 我需要你跟我一起來檢討預算。

A 我們今天兩點左右可以見個面嗎？
B 應該可以，我會確認一下我的行事曆。
A I need you to go over the budget with me.

2 練習 我需要你飛到邁阿密一趟。(fly to)
I need you to ＿＿＿＿＿＿＿＿＿＿＿＿＿＿＿＿.

Pattern 282

The boss wants...
老闆要…

英文中的 boss 指的是「直屬上司」，換句話說副社長的 boss 是社長，職員的 boss 是課長，以此類推。當你想要跟同事轉達直屬上司說過的話，就可以使用這個句型。

- **The boss wants you in her office.**
  老闆要你進她的辦公室。
- **The boss wants this done ASAP.**
  老闆要這件事盡快完成。　＊ASAP 盡快（＝as soon as possible）
- **The boss wants us to increase our pace.**
  老闆要我們加快腳步。
- **The boss wants to see some progress.**
  老闆要看到一些進展。　＊progress 進展，進步

1 對話

A　Is the shipment to Belgium ready yet?
B　No. We're still packing the boxes.
A　老闆要我們加快腳步。

A　要寄到比利時的那批貨品都準備好了嗎？
B　還沒，我們還在包裝這些箱子。
A　The boss wants us to increase our pace.

2 練習　老闆要我們去收拾殘局。(mess, clean up)
The boss wants ______________________.

Pattern 283

283

Don't forget to...
別忘了…

本句型中的不定詞 to 後面可以接 send, bring, notify 等原形動詞，其中在公司對話裡最常用的動詞是 send 和 notify，請把這幾個單字跟本句型一起記住。

- **Don't forget to make copies for everyone.**
  別忘了幫每個人影印一份。
- **Don't forget to send Victoria a copy of your memo.**
  別忘了將備忘錄的影本寄給維多莉亞。
- **Don't forget to notify Hong Kong of the merger.**
  別忘了通知香港辦公室合併一事。 ＊merger 合併
- **Don't forget to review the contract one more time.**
  別忘了再檢查一次合約。

1 對話
A Some staff members don't know the regulations.
B I'll notify Accounting, Acquisitions, and Sales.
A Okay. And 別忘了將備忘錄的影本寄給維多莉亞。

A 有些職員不太清楚公司的規定。
B 我會通知會計部門、採購部門和業務部門。
A 好的，還有 don't forget to send Victoria a copy of your memo.

2 練習 別忘了把這件事寫在你的行事曆上。(put something on)
Don't forget to ______________________.

Pattern 284

There will be...
…將會有…

當你想告知對方往後會有那些會議、活動或研討會時，就可以使用這個句型。本句型中的 will 是助動詞，所以後面要接原形 be 動詞。

- **There will be a marketing workshop on the 18th.**
  18 號將會有一場行銷研討會。
- **There will be a business forum in Los Angeles in the fall.**
  秋天在洛杉磯將會有一場商務研討會。
- **There will be a short meeting on Friday.**
  禮拜五將會有一個簡短的會議。
- **There will be an informal get-together after lunch.**
  午餐後將會有一個非正式的聚會。 ＊get-together 聚會，聯歡會

1 對話
A 18 號將會有一個行銷研討會。
B Are you going to the workshop?
A I'm planning on it.

A There will be a marketing workshop on the 18th.
B 你要參加這場研習嗎？
A 我有打算要去。

2 練習 下個月將會有一場跟推銷能力有關的研討會。
(salesmanship, next month)
There will be ______________________.

Pattern 285

285

Do you want me to...?
需要我…嗎？

本句型的組成結構為「Do you want + 名詞 + to 不定詞」，在上司或同事開口要你幫忙之前，不妨先主動開口使用這句型來詢問，藉此展現你對工作的積極態度吧！

- **Do you want me to give you a hand?**
  需要我幫忙嗎？ ＊give～a hand 幫…的忙
- **Do you want me to call him and ask for you?**
  需要我幫你打給他詢問嗎？
- **Do you want me to arrange ground transportation?**
  需要我安排陸上交通嗎？ ＊ground transportation 陸上交通
- **Do you want me to sit in on the conference call?**
  電話視訊會議時，需要我在場嗎？

1 對話
A You're giving a presentation, right?
B Yes, and I'm preparing the agenda and taking notes.
A 需要我幫忙嗎？

A 你今天有個發表會對嗎？
B 對啊，我正在準備議程和作筆記。
A Do you want me to give you a hand?

2 練習 需要我幫忙檢查他的紀錄嗎？(records)
Do you want me to ______________________________?

12-3

確認工作內容

How's...going?	286	…進行得怎麼樣了？
Are you ready for...?	287	你準備好…了嗎？
What are you V-ing?	288	你現在正在…？
I'm working on...	289	我正在製作…
Let me know when...	290	當…時，跟我說一聲吧。

Pattern 286

286

How's...going?
…進行得怎麼樣了？

本句型是利用疑問詞 How + going 來確認進度或情況，所以當你想詢問計畫或報告目前的狀況時，就可以使用這個句型跟對方確認。

- **How's your project going?**
  你的計畫進行得怎麼樣了？
- **How's the office renovation going?**
  你的辦公室整修進行得怎麼樣了？ ＊renovation 整修，翻新
- **How's the staff training going?**
  職員的教育訓練進行得怎麼樣了？ ＊staff training 在職人員教育訓練
- **How's your grant writing going?**
  你的補助金申請文件進行得怎麼樣了？ ＊grant 補助金

1 對話
A 你的計畫進行得怎麼樣了？
B It's going well. Thanks.
A Do you think you'll be done by Christmas?
B I hope so!

A How's your project going?
B 很順利，謝謝。
A 你在聖誕節前可以完成這個計畫嗎？
B 希望可以。

2 練習 協商進行得怎麼樣了？(negotiation)
How's ______________________ going?

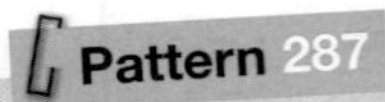

287

Are you ready for...?
你準備好…了嗎？

當你想問對方「準備好了沒？」時，雖然可以簡單地說 Are you ready?，但是如果想問得更具體、詳細一點時，就可以在後面加上 for，表示「準備好…了嗎？」的意思。

- **Are you ready for the meeting?**
  你準備好要開會了嗎？
- **Are you ready for staff evaluations?**
  你準備好職員業績評估了嗎？
  ＊ **evaluation** 評估，評價
- **Are you ready for the boss' speech?**
  你準備好社長的演講了嗎？
- **Are you ready for our office move?**
  你準備好我們辦公室搬遷的事了嗎？

1 對話

A Here are your handouts.
B Thanks.
A 你準備好要開會了嗎？
B Sure.

A 這是你的講義。
B 謝謝。
A Are you ready for the meeting?
B 當然。

2 練習 你準備好口頭報告了嗎？(presentation)
Are you ready for ______________________________?

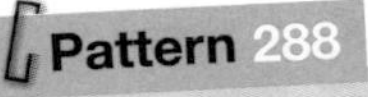

288

What are you V-ing?
你現在正在…？

當你想詢問對方目前正在做什麼事時，就可以使用這個現在進行式的句型。除此之外，這也是同事間常用來互相問候的其中一種句型。

- **What are you currently working on?**
  你現在正在忙些什麼？
- **What are you doing with regard to the Murphy account?**
  關於莫非的帳戶，你現在正在做些什麼？ ＊with regard to 關於…
- **What are you trying to accomplish with this project?**
  你現在正在努力用這個計畫實現什麼？ ＊accomplish 完成，實現
- **What are you spending your time on?**
  你現在正在花時間做些什麼？

1 對話
A I need your help with an emergency project.
B I can't. I have too much to do.
A 你現在正在忙些什麼？
B Fiscal reports.

A 我有個緊急計畫需要你的幫忙。
B 我不行啦，我還有很多事要忙。
A What are you currently working on?
B 財務報告。

2 練習 你現在正在計畫什麼？(plan)
What are you ______________________?

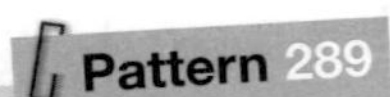

289

I'm working on...
我正在製作…

work on 常見於商務英語中，是用來表示正在進行某件事的萬能字彙，例如「辦公、製作」等，因此看到本句型 I'm working on... 時，應該根據前後文來解釋片語的意義。

I'm working on my monthly status report.
我正在製作我的每月業務報告。 ＊monthly status report 每月業務報告

I'm working on increasing my production.
我正在努力增加我的生產量。 ＊production 生產額，生產量

I'm working on building a team.
我正在構想組建一個團隊。

I'm working on my client's account.
我正在看我客戶的帳目。 ＊account （會計）帳目

1 對話
A Are you busy, Tina?
B 我正在製作我的每月業務報告。
A I forgot to do mine!

A 蒂娜，你在忙嗎？
B I'm working on my monthly status report.
A 我忘了要做我的！

2 練習 我正在編列年度預算。(annual)
I'm working on ________________.

Pattern 290

290

Let me know when...
當…時，跟我說一聲吧。

利用使役動詞 let 組成的句型為「Let + me + 原形動詞」，表示「讓我…」的意思。本句型是搭配動詞 know，所以是表示「讓我知道…／…跟我說」的意思。

- **Let me know when you have time to talk.**
  當你有時間談談時，跟我說一聲吧。
- **Let me know when you finish the project.**
  當你的企畫案結束時，跟我說一聲吧。
- **Let me know when you've sent the email.**
  當你寄出電子郵件時，跟我說一聲吧。
- **Let me know when you finish the urgent phone call.**
  當你講完這通緊急電話時，跟我說一聲吧。 ＊urgent 緊急的

1 對話
A We should get a cup of coffee some time.
B I'd love to, but this project is consuming all of my time.
A Okay. 當你的企畫案結束時，跟我說一聲吧。

A 我們找個時間一起喝杯咖啡吧！
B 我也很想，但這個企畫案消耗了我所有的時間。
A 好吧！Let me know when you finish the project.

2 練習 客戶跟你聯絡時，跟我說一聲吧。(hear from, client)
Let me know when ______________________.

12-4

管理行程

You have to finish... 291 你必須完成…

Can I have...by...? 292 …以前可以…嗎？

I'll be done... 293 我會…（做）好…

Before you go,... 294 在你下班之前，…

The meeting starts... 295 …開始開會。

Pattern 291

You have to finish...
你必須完成…

當上司在管理員工的工作日程時，就可以使用這個帶有 have to 的命令句型。此外，請記得本句型中的 finish 後面要接上名詞以及 by, before 等限定時間的介系詞，使用方法請參考以下的例句。

- **You have to finish this report by tomorrow.**
  你必須在明天以前完成這份報告。
- **You have to finish the project by the end of the quarter.**
  你必須在這一季結束以前完成這個企畫案。 ＊quarter 季度
- **You have to finish the deal before the end of the week.**
  你必須在這週結束以前完成這項交易。
- **You have to finish the work as soon as possible.**
  你必須盡快完成這項工作。

1 對話 A I think I'm going to leave a little early.
B But 你必須在明天以前完成這份報告。
A I know. I'm going to work on it at home.

A 我想要早點下班。
B 但是 you have to finish this report by tomorrow.
A 我知道，我打算帶回家做。

2 練習 你必須在下班前完成這些數據加總的工作。(add up, leave)
You have to finish ______________________.

Pattern 292

Can I have...by...?
…以前可以…嗎？

當你想詢問在某個時間點前是否可完成某項工作時，就可以使用這個句型。此外，本句型中的 by 後面要接上跟時間有關的字彙。

Can I have those tables by Friday?
禮拜五以前可以拿到那些桌子嗎？

Can I have 60 copies by 9:00?
九點以前可以影印六十份給我嗎？

Can I have your answer by this afternoon?
今天下午以前可以給我你的答覆嗎？

Can I have the contract signed by 11:00?
11 點以前可以拿到簽好的合約嗎？

1 對話
A Is that the new instruction manual?
B Yes, it was just released.
A 九點以前可以影印六十份給我嗎？

A 這就是新的使用說明書嗎？
B 對，剛發行的。
A Can I have 60 copies by 9:00?

2 練習 今天結束以前可以簽好名嗎？(signature)
Can I have ______________ by ______________?

Pattern 293 293

I'll be done...
我會…（做）好…

be done 是表示「完成、結束」，想要表達「我完成了」的意思時，可以說 I'm done，或者也可以使用本句型 I'll be done...。

- **I'll be done revising this contract within the hour.**
  我會在一個小時內修正好這份合約。 ＊revise 修訂，修正
- **I'll be done organizing my presentation by next Wednesday.**
  我會在下週三前整理好我的口頭發表。
- **I'll be done with this report by the end of the day.**
  我會今天結束以前做好這份報告。
- **I'll be done organizing my files by 5:00.**
  我會在五點以前整理好我的資料。

1 對話
A It looks like you're ready to go to court tomorrow.
B Yes, I'm trying to put all of my documents together.
A Do you need any help?
B No. 我會在五點以前整理好我的資料。

A 看來你已經準備好參加明天的法庭了。
B 嗯，我正在整合我所有的資料。
A 需要幫忙嗎？
B 不用，I'll be done organizing my files by 5:00.

2 練習 我會在午餐時間前準備好我的報告。(prepare for, lunchtime)
I'll be done ______________________.

Pattern 294

294

Before you go,...
在你下班之前，…

在公司裡提到工作日程時，最常使用到的字彙就是 before 和 after。本句型 Before you go,... 可依照當時的情況解釋為離開之前、下班之前或外出之前等意思。

- **Before you go, please turn in your report.**
  在你下班之前，請先交出你的報告。 ＊turn in 交上，交出
- **Before you go, I'd like to talk to you.**
  在你離開之前，我想跟你談談。
- **Before you go, turn off the lights.**
  在你下班之前，把電燈都關掉。 ＊turn off 關掉（電器等）
- **Before you go, see if Kim needs anything.**
  在你外出之前，跟金先生確認一下他是否需要任何東西。

1 對話
A I'm leaving at 4:00 today. I have to stop at the bank.
B 在你下班之前，請先交出你的報告。
A Okay.

A 我今天四點就要離開，因為必須要去銀行一趟。
B Before you go, please turn in your report.
A 知道了。

2 練習 在你外出之前，先將電腦登出。(log off)
Before you go, ______________________.

Pattern 295

The meeting starts...
…開始開會。

我們會用動詞 start 或 begin 來表達會議或研討會等的「開始」。很多人會好奇 start 和 begin 之間的差異在哪裡，其實不需要想那麼多，只要隨意挑一個使用就行了。

- **The meeting starts at 10:00.**
  十點開始開會。
- **The meeting starts in a half hour.**
  半小時後開始開會。 ＊a half hour 半小時
- **The meeting starts after lunch.**
  午餐後開始開會。
- **The meeting starts when Mr. Gates arrives.**
  等蓋茲先生一來就開始開會。

1 對話
A When does the meeting start?
B 等蓋茲先生一來就開始開會。
A We've been waiting for fifteen minutes.

A 會議幾點開始？
B The meeting starts when Mr. Gates arrives.
A 我們已經等了十五分鐘了。

2 練習 等大家都到了以後就開始開會。(once, here)
The meeting starts ______________________.

12-5

辦公室百態

Pattern 296

296

I feel terrible that...
…我真的很抱歉。

本句型中的 terrible 只是用來強調，表示「真的」很抱歉的意思，所以不需要以過於負面的角度看待。當你因為忘了參加會議或上班缺勤而感到不好意思時，就可以使用這個句型。

I feel terrible that I missed the meeting.
沒有出席會議，我真的很抱歉。 ＊miss 錯過，未出席

I feel terrible that I can't make it to the office party.
不能參加辦公室的慶祝會，我真的很抱歉。 ＊office party 辦公室聚會

I feel terrible that I forgot the paperwork.
忘記處理書面文件，我真的很抱歉。 ＊paperwork 文書工作

I feel terrible that I was out yesterday.
昨天外出了，我真的很抱歉。

1 對話
A Where were you this morning?
B I was at my desk.
A The boss was asking for you at our regular meeting.
B Oh, no! 沒有出席會議，我真的很抱歉。

A 你今天早上人在哪？
B 我在我的座位上工作。
A 老闆不是要你參加我們的定期會議嗎？
B 喔，天啊！I feel terrible that I missed the meeting.

2 練習 沒打電話給您，我真的很抱歉。(have, call)
I feel terrible that ______________________.

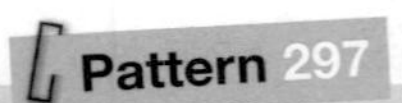

297

Can you cover...?
可以請你代理…嗎？

297 請別人代理工作

當你想拜託某人代替你去做某項工作時，就可以使用這個句型。動詞 cover 可以用來表示「覆蓋、遮掩、掩護、付錢」等多種涵義，但在本句型中是表示「代替…工作」的意思。

- **Can you cover for me?**
  可以請你代理我的工作嗎？
- **Can you cover my shift today?**
  今天可以請你幫我代班嗎？ ＊shift 輪班時間
- **Can you cover for me while I'm away?**
  我外出的時候可以請你代理我的工作嗎？ ＊away 不在，外出
- **Can you cover Amber's region?**
  可以請你代理安柏的（工作）範圍嗎？ ＊region 領域，範圍

1 對話
A You're leaving early?
B Yes. 今天可以請你幫我代班嗎？
A Sure.

A 你今天要早退嗎？
B 嗯，Can you cover my shift today?
A 沒問題。

2 練習 可以請您代我們招呼紐約的客戶嗎？(clients)
Can you cover ______________________________?

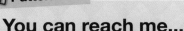

Pattern 298

298

You can reach me...
你可以…跟我聯絡。

當你想告知對方方便聯絡的時間與方式時，就可以使用這個句型。動詞 reach 常用來表示「聯絡」的意思。此外，當你想詢問在哪裡才聯絡得上某人時，只要說 Do you know where I can reach him / her? 就行了。

- **You can reach me this afternoon.**
  你可以在今天下午跟我聯絡。
- **You can reach me by phone or email.**
  你可以用電話或電子郵件跟我聯絡。
- **You can reach me in my office after 3:00.**
  三點以後，你可以在我的辦公室找到我。
- **You can reach me through my secretary.**
  你可以透過我的祕書跟我聯絡。

* **through** 透過，經由

1 對話
A I'm working from home this afternoon.
B What if I need to get a hold of you?
A 你可以用電話或電子郵件跟我聯絡。

A 我今天下午會在家裡工作。
B 如果我有事需要聯絡你呢？
A You can reach me by phone or email.

2 練習 你可以在家裡或辦公室找到我。(at, or)
You can reach me ______________________.

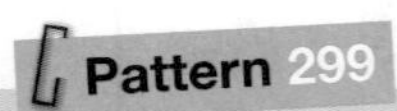

299

Would you help me...?
可以請你幫我…嗎？

當你在公司想拜託同事或屬下幫忙時，就可以使用這個句型。本句型語氣十分謙恭有禮，意義相似的句型為 Could you help me...?

- **Would you help me file these papers?**
  可以請你幫我將這些文件歸檔嗎？
- **Would you help me create a list of employees?**
  可以請你幫我製作一份員工清單嗎？ ＊employee 員工
- **Would you help me move my desk near the window?**
  可以請你幫我將我的書桌搬到窗戶附近嗎？
- **Would you help me find his telephone number?**
  可以請你幫我找出他的電話號碼嗎？

1 對話

A The boss wants to hold a meeting with the entire office.
B I suppose you have to organize it.
A Yes. 可以請你幫我製作一份員工清單嗎？

A 老闆想跟全部的員工一起開個會。
B 我想你應該負責安排這個會議。
A 沒錯，Would you help me create a list of employees?

2 練習 可以請你幫我安排一個約會嗎？(schedule)
Would you help me ________________________________?

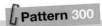

Pattern 300

300

I heard...
我聽說…

當你想提起自己聽說的事時，就可以使用這個句型。此外，本句型中的 heard 後面要不要接 that 都可以。heard 的發音為 [hɝd]，請仔細聽本書音檔的發音，多加練習吧！

- **I heard Jim is up for a promotion.**
  我聽說吉姆快要升職了。 ＊promotion 升職
- **I heard we'll have our salaries raised 5% this year.**
  我聽說今年我們的薪資會調漲 5%。
- **I heard Lisa is getting a big bonus this year.**
  我聽說今年麗莎會得到很多分紅。 ＊bonus 獎金，分紅
- **I heard Mr. Kim is going to be our new manager.**
  我聽說金先生即將成為我們的新經理。

1 對話
A There's a lot of gossip over this year's promotions.
B I haven't heard any.
A 我聽說吉姆快要升職了。

A 有很多跟今年升遷有關的傳聞。
B 我完全沒聽過耶。
A I heard Jim is up for a promotion.

2 練習 我聽說有人快被炒魷魚了。(fire)
I heard ________________.

12-1~12-5

黃金複習 15 分鐘！

前面這 25 個句型和 125 個句子全都記熟了嗎？
來驗收一下學習成果吧！如果不能充滿自信地用英文說出以下 40 個句子，請翻到前面再重新複習一次！

01 昨晚你度過了美好的時光嗎？

02 我聽說今年我們的薪資會調漲 5%。

03 新同事如何？

04 可以請你幫我製作一份員工清單嗎？

05 你看起來壓力很大。

06 你可以在今天下午跟我聯絡。

07 我喜歡你的鞋子。

08 今天可以請你幫我代班嗎？

09 我們去喝個東西吧。

解答 01. Did you have a wonderful time last night?
02. I heard we'll have our salaries raised 5% this year. 03. How's the new staff member?
04. Would you help me create a list of employees? 05. You look stressed out.
06. You can reach me this afternoon. 07. I like your shoes. 08. Can you cover my shift today?
09. Let's grab something to drink.

10 不能參加辦公室的慶祝會，我真的很抱歉。

11 我需要你為我們的投資者安排一場會議。

12 半小時後開始開會。

13 老闆要這件事盡快完成。

14 在你離開之前，我想跟你談談。

15 別忘了幫每個人影印一份。

16 我會在下週三前整理好我的口頭發表。

17 秋天在洛杉磯將會有一場商務研討會。

18 九點以前可以影印六十份給我嗎？

19 需要我幫你打給他詢問嗎？

20 你必須在這一季結束以前完成這個企畫案。

解答 10. I feel terrible that I can't make it to the office party.
11. I need you to organize a meeting of our investors. 12. The meeting starts in a half hour.
13. The boss wants this done ASAP. 14. Before you go, I'd like to talk to you.
15. Don't forget to make copies for everyone.
16. I'll be done organizing my presentation by next Wednesday.
17. There will be a business forum in Los Angeles in the fall. 18. Can I have 60 copies by 9:00?
19. Do you want me to call him and ask for you?
20. You have to finish the project by the end of the quarter.

21 你有個愉快的週末嗎？

22 當你寄出電子郵件時，跟我說一聲吧。

23 最近如何？

24 我正在努力增加我的生產量。

25 你看起來很累。

26 關於莫菲的帳戶，你現在正在做些什麼？

27 我喜歡你的髮型。

28 你準備好職員業績評估了嗎？

29 我們去吃點東西吧。

30 你的辦公室整修進行得怎麼樣了？

31 沒有出席會議，我真的很抱歉。

解答 21. Did you have a good weekend? 22. Let me know when you've sent the email. 23. How's it going? 24. I'm working on increasing my production. 25. You look tired. 26. What are you doing with regard to the Murphy account? 27. I like your hair. 28. Are you ready for staff evaluations? 29. Let's grab a bite to eat. 30. How's the office renovation going? 31. I feel terrible that I missed the meeting.

32 我需要你在三點前完成你的報告。

33 可以請你代理我的工作嗎？

34 老闆要你進她的辦公室。

35 你可以用電話或電子郵件跟我聯絡。

36 別忘了將備忘錄的影本寄給維多莉亞。

37 可以請你幫我將這些文件歸檔嗎？

38 18 號將會有一場行銷研討會。

39 我聽說吉姆快要升職了。

40 需要我幫忙嗎？

解答 32. I need you to complete your report by 3:00. 33. Can you cover for me?
34. The boss wants you in her office. 35. You can reach me by phone or email.
36. Don't forget to send Victoria a copy of your memo.
37. Would you help me file these papers?
38. There will be a marketing workshop on the 18th. 39. I heard Jim is up for a promotion.
40. Do you want me to give you a hand?

Unit 13
海外出差

自己一個人也
沒問題！

13-1

在機場與飛機上

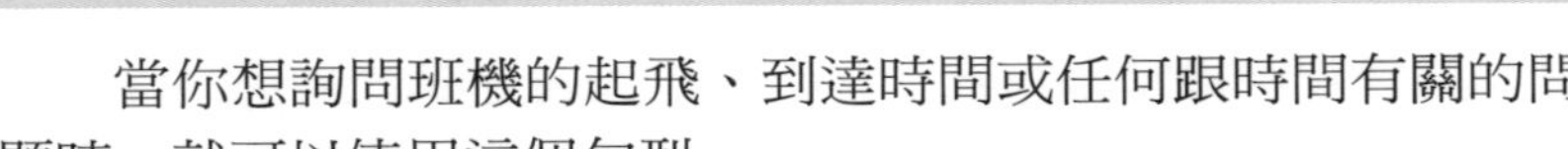

Pattern 301

What time does...?
什麼時候…？

301 詢問時間

當你想詢問班機的起飛、到達時間或任何跟時間有關的問題時，就可以使用這個句型。

- **What time does boarding begin?**
  什麼時候開始登機？ ＊board 登機
- **What time does your plane land?**
  你的飛機什麼時候抵達？ ＊land 降落
- **What time do they serve the meal?**
  他們什麼時候開始送餐？
- **What time does the airport shuttle pick you up?**
  機場接駁車什麼時候會來？ ＊pick~up（車子）搭載（人）

1 對話
A I'm going to Seoul tomorrow, Bob.
B 你的飛機什麼時候抵達？
A At 10:00 in the morning.

A 鮑伯，我明天要飛去首爾。
B What time does your plane land?
A 早上十點。

2 練習 什麼時候開始登機？(boarding)
What time does ________________?

Pattern 302

Where do I...?
我要在哪裡⋯？

雖然我們常常會認為本句型跟 Where can I...? 可以替換使用，但其實這兩個句型存在微妙的差異。Where do I...? 是表示「我要」在⋯做⋯呢？，Where can I...? 則是表示「我可以」在⋯做⋯呢？的意思。

Where do I check in?
我要去哪裡辦理登機手續？

Where do I check my baggage?
我要在哪裡托運行李？ ＊baggage 行李

Where do I put my carry-on bag?
我要把隨身行李放在哪裡？ ＊carry-on bag 提上飛機的隨身行李

Where do I wait to board?
我要在哪裡等候登機？

1 對話
A 我要去哪裡等候登機？
B You can go to the KAL lounge.
A Where is it?
B Near the departure gates.

A Where do I wait to board?
B 你可以先到大韓航空貴賓室等候。
A 那是在哪裡呢？
B 就在登機口附近。

2 練習 我要去哪裡取得登機證？(pass)
Where do I ______________________________?

Pattern 303

Could you bring me...?
可以請你給我…嗎？

在搭乘飛機時，當你需要水或毛毯，就可以使用這個句型詢問空服員。如果是想索取額外的物品，只要在名詞前面加上 extra 就行了，例如 extra blanket, extra pillow 等。

- **Could you bring me a blanket?**
  可以請你給我一條毛毯嗎？
- **Could you bring me some water?**
  可以請你給我水嗎？
- **Could you bring me a pair of headphones?**
  可以請你給我一副耳機嗎？
- **Could you bring me a pillow, please?**
  可以請你給我一個枕頭嗎？

* pillow 枕頭

1 對話
A Excuse me, 可以請你給我一條毛毯嗎？
B Certainly, sir. Would your colleague like one?
A She's in the restroom, but I'm sure she would.

A 對不起，could you bring me a blanket?
B 當然可以，客人。您旁邊這位也要一件嗎？
A 她現在在化妝間，但我相信她也需要。

2 練習 可以請你給我暈機藥嗎？(airsickness)
Could you bring me ______________________?

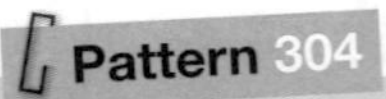

I'm here for...
我來這裡是為了…

出國通過入境檢查時，偶爾會遇到比較嚴格的海關，就會被問到比較多的問題。當你想簡單明瞭地告訴對方來此處的目的時，就可以使用這個句型。本句型中的 for 後面除了可以接目的，也可以接目的地或時間。

- **I'm here for the tourist attractions.**
  我來這裡是為了參觀觀光景點。　＊tourist attraction 觀光景點
- **I'm here for a meeting with one of our clients.**
  我來這裡是為了跟我們公司的一位客戶碰面。　＊client 委託人，客戶
- **I'm here for the national sales conference.**
  我來這裡是為了全國行銷會議。
- **I'm here for less than a week.**
  我在這裡的時間少於一週。

1 對話

A What brings you here?
B 我來這裡是為了跟我們公司的一位客戶碰面。
A Have a good time.

A 您為什麼來這裡？
B I'm here for a meeting with one of our clients.
A 祝您玩得愉快。

2 練習 我來這裡是為了拜訪親戚。(visit with)
I'm here for ______________________.

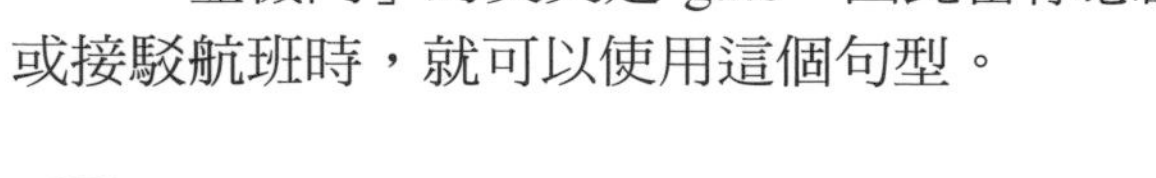

Which gate do we...?
我們在哪一個登機門⋯？

「登機門」的英文是 gate，因此當你想詢問班機的登機門或接駁航班時，就可以使用這個句型。

- **Which gate do we depart from?**
  我們在哪一個登機門出發？　　＊depart 出發
- **Which gate should we wait at?**
  我們應該在哪一個登機門等候？
- **Which gate does his flight leave from?**
  他的班機在哪一個登機門出發？
- **Which gate should I go to for my connecting flight?**
  我應該去哪一個登機門轉機？

1 對話
A 我們在哪一個登機門出發？
B 26B.
A Is it a long walk?
B I don't think so.

A Which gate do we depart from?
B 26B。
A 要走很久嗎？
B 應該不會。

2 練習 他們剛剛是說哪一個登機門？(say)
Which gate did ________________________________?

13-2

交通

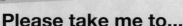

306

Pattern 306

Please take me to...
請載我到…

搭計程車時，司機多半會用 Where to...? 的句型詢問你要去哪，這時候你只要使用這個含有動詞 take 的簡單句型 Please take me to... 就可以了。本句型中的 Please 也可以放在句尾。

- **Please take me to the conference center.**
  請載我到會議中心。 ＊conference 會議
- **Please take me to the airport.**
  請載我到機場。
- **Please take me to this place.**
  請載我到這個地方。
- **Take me to the Sheraton Hotel, please.**
  請載我到喜來登飯店。

1 對話
A 請載我到機場。
B Which airport?
A It's John F. Kennedy Airport.

A Please take me to the airport.
B 哪一個機場？
A 甘迺迪國際機場。

2 練習 請載我到暢貨中心。(outlet mall)
Please take me to ______________________.

Could you pull over...?
可以請你在…讓我下車嗎？

當你在搭乘計程車的途中突然想在某處下車時，就可以使用這個句型。如果不知道 pull over 這個基本片語的話，你就永遠只能說 stop，所以請多利用下面的例句來練習這個句型吧！

Could you pull over at the corner?
可以請你在轉角讓我下車嗎？

Could you pull over in front of that building?
可以請你在那棟大樓的前面讓我下車嗎？

Could you pull over on the next block?
可以請你在下一個街區讓我下車嗎？

Could you pull over now?
可以請你現在讓我下車嗎？

1 對話
A The conference center is up ahead.
B 可以請你在轉角讓我下車嗎？
A No problem. That'll be $8.

A 會議中心就在前面。
B Could you pull over at the corner?
A 沒問題，車資是八美元。

2 練習 可以請你在經過那棟建築物之前讓我下車嗎？(before, pass)
Could you pull over ____________________?

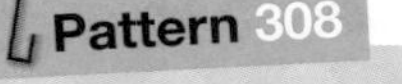

308

Where should I...?
請問我應該在哪裡⋯？

到海外出差時會有很多機會搭乘巴士、地鐵或計程車等交通工具，所以你一定要記住這個句型。注意，「攔」計程車的英文說法是 hail，請一定要牢記。

- **Where should I change subway lines?**
  請問我應該在哪裡轉乘地鐵？ ＊subway line 地下鐵路線
- **Where should I go to take the number 12 bus?**
  請問我應該到哪裡搭 12 號巴士？
- **Where should I hail a taxi?**
  請問我應該到哪裡攔計程車？ ＊hail 攔（計程車，巴士等）
- **Where should I get off the bus?**
  請問我應該在哪裡下車？ ＊get off 下車

1 對話

A Excuse me. Could you possibly help me?
B I'll be happy to try.
A 請問我應該到哪裡搭乘 12 號巴士？
B You are in luck. Right here!

A 不好意思，可以幫幫我嗎？
B 我很樂意幫忙。
A Where should I take the number 12 bus?
B 你很幸運，就在這裡！

2 練習 請問我應該到哪裡搭地鐵？(look for, station)
Where should I ______________________________?

Pattern 309

Which bus goes to...?
要去…的話，應該要搭幾號巴士？

雖然本句型的直譯為「哪一線巴士是往…？」，但是我們應該解讀成「要去…的話，應該要搭幾號巴士？」比較通順。此外，雖然地鐵的英文是 subway，但是在詢問要搭乘幾號線這種情況下，使用 line 這個字彙比較恰當。

- **Which bus goes to the airport?**
  要去機場的話，應該要搭幾號巴士？
- **Which bus goes to the theater?**
  要去劇院的話，應該要搭幾號巴士？
- **Which line goes to my hotel?**
  要去我的飯店的話，應該要搭幾號線？
- **Which line goes to the business district?**
  要去商業區的話，應該要搭幾號線？

* district 地區，區域

1 對話 **A** Is there something I can help you find?
B Yes. 去劇院應該要搭幾號巴士？
A From here, you should take the number 3 bus.

A 有什麼我可以幫上忙的地方嗎？
B 嗯，Which bus goes to the theater?
A 你可以在這裡搭乘三號巴士。

2 練習 要去醫院的話，應該要搭幾號線？(hospital)
Which line goes to ______________________?

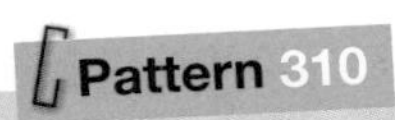

What would happen if I...?
萬一我…的話，會怎麼樣嗎？

這個句型是假設句型，可以使用在國外租車的時候。想問「萬一我…的話，會怎麼樣嗎？」時，就可以使用這個句型。這是懂得未雨綢繆的聰明人必背的其中一個句型，讓你提前做好準備。

- **What would happen if I got in an accident?**
  萬一我出了什麼意外的話，會怎麼樣嗎？ ＊accident 意外
- **What would happen if I were late returning the car?**
  萬一我延遲還車的話，會怎麼樣嗎？
- **What would happen if I needed to return it early?**
  萬一我必須提早還車的話，會怎麼樣嗎？
- **What would happen if I lost the keys?**
  萬一我遺失了鑰匙的話，會怎麼樣嗎？ ＊lose 遺失

1 對話
A 萬一我必須提早還車的話，會怎麼樣嗎？
B Just call ahead.
A Do I have to pay for the days I don't use?

A What would happen if I needed to return it early?
B 直接打電話給我就行了。
A 那我還需要支付那之後的租車費用嗎？

2 練習 萬一我讓另一個人開車的話，會怎麼樣嗎？(let, someone else)
What would happen if I ______________________________?

13-3

尋找目的地

Are there any places to...?	311	有什麼…的地方嗎？
How can I get to...?	312	…該怎麼去？
Which way is it to...?	313	到…要往哪個方向？
How long will it take to get to...?	314	請問到…要花多少時間？
Where is the best place to...?	315	…的最佳地點是哪裡？

Are there any places to...?
有什麼⋯的地方嗎？

當你到海外出差時，一定會想買紀念品、土產，又或者是想去逛逛購物中心；但是因為對地理環境不熟悉，所以常常想向路人或飯店櫃檯詢問地點，這時就可以使用這個句型。

- **Are there any places to buy souvenirs?**
  有什麼購買紀念品的地方嗎？
  * souvenir 紀念品
- **Are there any places to find good bargains?**
  有什麼可以找到價格划算的物品的地方嗎？
  * good bargain 價格划算的物品
- **Are there any places that are good for photographs?**
  有什麼適合拍照的地方嗎？
- **Are there any places that you recommend that I see while in town?**
  市區內有什麼你建議我去看看的地方嗎？

1 對話
A 有什麼購買紀念品的地方嗎？
B There are some souvenirs stores at the mall.
A How far away is it?
B It's just a few blocks away.

A Are there any places to buy souvenirs?
B 在購物中心裡面有幾家紀念品店。
A 購物中心離這裡多遠？
B 只有幾條街的距離。

2 練習 有什麼可以買書的地方嗎？(buy)
Are there any places to ______________________________?

Pattern 312

How can I get to...
…該怎麼去？

這是當你在問路時最常使用的其中一個句型，可以和上一課的句型一起搭配使用。

- **How can I get to the subway station from here?**
  從這裡該怎麼去地鐵站？
- **How can I get to the nearest drugstore?**
  最近的藥局該怎麼去？ ＊drugstore 藥局
- **How can I get to the convention center from here?**
  從這裡該怎麼去會議中心？ ＊convention 會議
- **How can I get to Washington Square?**
  華盛頓廣場該怎麼去？

1 對話
A I'd like to see the Statue of Liberty.
B The best way to get there is to take the subway.
A 從這裡該怎麼去地鐵站？
B Walk three blocks north and take a left.

A 我想要去看自由女神像。
B 最方便的交通方式就是搭地鐵過去。
A How can I get to the subway station from here?
B 往北走三個街道，然後往左轉。

2 練習 金融街該怎麼去？(financial)
How can I get to ________________________?

Pattern 313

Which way is it to...?
到…要往哪個方向？

當你想詢問方向或目的地位置時，就可以使用這個句型，可翻譯為「到…該走哪條路？」或「到…要往哪個方向？」的意思。

- **Which way is it to the center?**
  到市中心要往哪個方向？
- **Which way is it to the Lolo Hotel?**
  到羅羅飯店要往哪個方向？
- **Which way is it to the taxi stand?**
  到計程車招呼站要往哪個方向？　　＊taxi stand 計程車招呼站
- **Which way is it to the shopping district?**
  到購物商圈要往哪個方向？

1 對話

A I don't feel like walking back to the hotel.
B Neither do I. 到計程車招呼站要往哪個方向？
A I saw one two blocks over.

A 我不想走路回飯店。
B 我也是，Which way is it to the taxi stand?
A 我剛剛在離這兩個街道處有看到一個。

2 練習

到禮品店要往哪個方向？(gift shop)
Which way is it to ______________________?

Pattern 314

How long will it take to get to...?
請問到…要花多少時間？

當你想知道來往兩地之間所需的通勤時間時，就可以使用這個 How long 開頭的問句。特別常用於詢問計程車司機或飯店櫃檯到達特定地點的時間長度。

- **How long will it take to get to the bus station?**
  請問到公車站要花多少時間？
- **How long will it take to get to the train station?**
  請問到火車站要花多少時間？
- **How long will it take to get to the airport?**
  請問到機場要花多少時間？
- **How long will it take to get to the theater on foot?**
  請問步行到劇院要花多少時間？

* on foot 步行，走路

1 對話
A Excuse me. 請問到機場要花多少時間？
B About 20 minutes.
A I hope I don't miss my flight.

A 對不起，How long will it take to get to the airport?
B 差不多二十分鐘。
A 希望我不會錯過班機。

2 練習
請問到那家公司要花多少時間？(company)
How long will it take to get to ____________________?

Pattern 315

315

Where is the best place to...?
…的最佳地點是哪裡？

當你想向人詢問某方面的最佳地點在哪裡時，使用這個以 Where 開頭的問句就行了。以下例句分別是在詢問無線上網、享用晚餐等的最佳地點。

- Where is the best place to **get free Wi-Fi?**
  使用免費無線網路的最佳地點是哪裡？
- Where is the best place to **get a steak dinner?**
  享用牛排晚餐的最佳地點是哪裡？
- Where is the best place to **buy shoes?**
  買鞋的最佳地點是哪裡？
- Where is the best place to **have my hair done?**
  做髮型的最佳地點是哪裡？ ＊ have + 名詞 + p.p. 使（某事物）被完成

1 對話
A How do you like Montreal so far?
B I love it. I do have a question though.
A What is it?
B 使用免費無線網路的最佳地點是哪裡？

A 到目前為止你還喜歡蒙特婁嗎？
B 我很喜歡，雖然我有一個疑問。
A 是什麼？
B Where is the best place to get free Wi-Fi?

2 練習 觀賞夕陽的最佳地點是哪裡？(sunset)
Where is the best place to ______________________?

13-4

在飯店

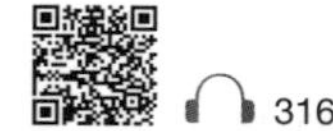
316

Pattern 316

I've reserved...
我已經預訂了…

抵達預約好的飯店辦理入住手續時，雖然可以簡單地說 I reserved...，但最正確的用法是用完成式 I've reserved...。當你想告知對方自己事前已先預定好飯店、車輛或餐廳時，都可以使用這個句型。

- **I've reserved a room with a queen-sized bed.**
  我已經預訂了一間附雙人床的房間。
- **I've reserved a table for two in the hotel restaurant.**
  我已經在飯店的餐廳預訂了兩個人的位子。
- **I've reserved lodging for two nights.**
  我已經預訂了兩晚的住宿。 ＊lodging 投宿，住宿
- **I've reserved an extra room for the children.**
  我已經幫小孩另外預訂了一間房。

1 對話
A I'm glad we could join you on your business trip.
B Me too. It'll be nice and romantic.
A Romantic? But we have all three kids with us.
B 我已經幫小孩另外預訂了一間房。

A 真高興能跟你一起來出差。
B 我也是，一定會既美好又浪漫。
A 浪漫？但是我們的三個小孩也一起來了。
B I've reserved an extra room for the children.

2 練習 我已經幫我們房間預訂了一瓶紅酒。(a bottle of)
I've reserved ______________________.

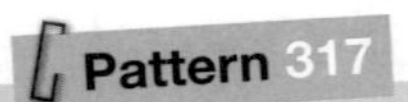

Can I get a room with...?
可以給我有…的房間嗎？

當你在飯店登記入住時，若想提出一些特殊需求，例如有網路的房間或景觀好的房間時，就可以說 Can I get a room with...? 或 Could I get a room with...?。

- **Can I get a room with a balcony?**
  可以給我有陽台的房間嗎？
- **Can I get a room with a nice view?**
  可以給我景色不錯的房間嗎？
  ＊nice view 美景
- **Can I get a room with two beds?**
  可以給我有兩張床的房間嗎？
- **Can I get a room with Internet access?**
  可以給我有網路的房間嗎？

1 對話
A Do you have any special requests?
B 可以給我有網路的房間嗎？
A Certainly. All of our rooms have Internet connections.

A 請問您有特別的需求嗎？
B Can I get a room with Internet access?
A 當然沒問題，我們飯店的所有客房都可以上網。

2 練習 可以給我有咖啡機的房間嗎？(coffee maker)
Can I get a room with ______________________?

 318

Pattern 318

Could you send...to...?
可以請你送…到…嗎？

在飯店住宿時，當你想要求飯店多送被子或毛巾過來，就可以使用這個句型。此外，也可以使用句型 I need...（我需要…）或 Let me get... 來表達「請拿…給我」的意思。

- **Could you send an extra pillow to room 512?**
  可以請你多送一個枕頭到 512 號房嗎？
- **Could you send some ice to my room, please?**
  可以請你送一些冰塊到我的房間嗎？麻煩你。
- **Could you send a clean towel to room 304?**
  可以請你送一條乾淨的毛巾到 304 號房嗎？
- **Could you send the housekeeper to room 101?**
  可以請你派清潔員到 101 號房嗎？ ＊housekeeper 房務管理員，清潔員

1 對話
A Can I help you?
B 可以請你送一些冰塊到我的房間嗎？麻煩你。
A There is an ice machine down the hall.

A 請問有需要幫忙的地方嗎？
B Could you send some ice to my room, please?
A 房間外的走道上有一台製冰器。

2 練習 可以請你送一份客房服務菜單到我的房間嗎？
(room service menu)
Could you send to ______________________________?

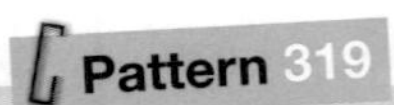

I'm having a problem with...
我…有些問題。

進入飯店房間後，可能會遇到一些使用上的問題，例如冷氣溫度不正常、網路無法連線等，這個句型就是用在當你想打電話去跟飯店櫃台反應的時候。

- I'm having a problem with **my air conditioner.**
  我的冷氣有些問題。
- I'm having a problem with **the TV in my room.**
  我房間裡的電視有些問題。
- I'm having a problem with **my Internet connection.**
  我的網路連線有些問題。
- I'm having a problem with **the lock on my door.**
  我的門鎖有些問題。

1 對話
A Could you send up a repairman?
B Certainly. What is the trouble?
A 我的網路連線有些問題。

A 可以請你們叫一位修理人員過來嗎？
B 我們會的，請問是什麼問題呢？
A I'm having a problem with my Internet connection.

2 練習 我房間裡的廁所有些問題。(toilet)
I'm having a problem with ____________________.

320

Pattern 320

I'd like to extend...
我想要將…延長…

當你想在飯店多住一兩天或延長飯店的預約天數時，就可以使用這個含有動詞 extend 的句型。

- **I'd like to extend my reservation for another day.**
  我想要將我的預約延長一天。
- **I'd like to extend my stay for a few days.**
  我想要將我的住宿延長幾天。 ＊stay 停留期間
- **I'd like to extend my stay until this coming Sunday.**
  我想要將我的住宿延長到這個週日。
- **I'd like to extend my check-out time until 6:00 this evening.**
  我想要將退房時間延長到晚上六點。

1 對話
A Hello. This is room 513.
B How can I be of assistance?
A 我想要將退房時間延長到晚上六點。

A 您好，這裡是 513 號房。
B 有什麼需要幫忙的地方嗎？
A I'd like to extend my check-out time until 6:00 this evening.

2 練習 我想要再多停留幾天。(duration of)
I'd like to extend ______________________.

13-5

在餐廳

We have a reservation for... 321 我們已經預約好…

Could I get a table...? 322 可以給我…的座位嗎？

I'll have... 323 我要點…

How long will we have to...? 324 我們還要…多久？

Could you get me..., please? 325 請你給我…，好嗎？

Pattern 321

321

We have a reservation for...
我們已經預約好…

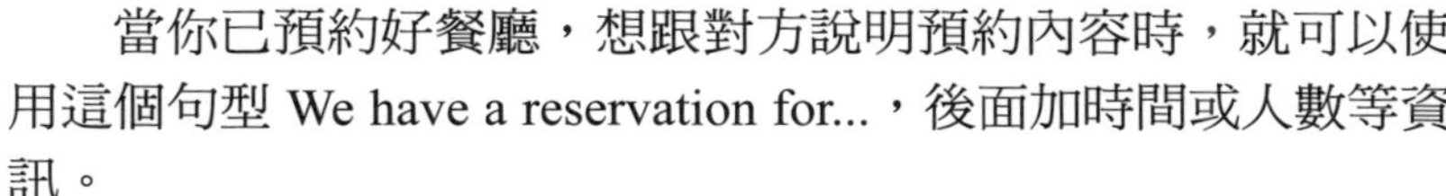

當你已預約好餐廳，想跟對方說明預約內容時，就可以使用這個句型 We have a reservation for...，後面加時間或人數等資訊。

- **We have a reservation for dinner.**
  我們已經預約好晚餐。
- **We have a reservation for 8:00.**
  我們已經預約好八點。
- **We have a reservation for six people.**
  我們已經預約好六個人。
- **We have a reservation for a private room.**
  我們已經預約好一個私人房間。

* **private** 私人的

1 對話

A 我們已經預約好六個人了。
B I think Johnson wants to come, too.
A I'll call the restaurant and add one more.

A We have a reservation for six people.
B 我覺得強森也會想來。
A 我會打電話到餐廳再多加一個人。

2 練習 我們已經預約好四個人的座位了。(table for)
We have a reservation for ________________.

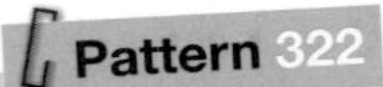

322

Could I get a table...?
可以給我…的座位嗎？

在餐廳詢問服務生「是否有…的位子」的英文是 get a table...?，因此當你到餐廳想要指定座位時，在 get a table 的後面加上所要求的內容即可。

- **Could I get a table by the window?**
  可以給我窗邊的座位嗎？
- **Could I get a table for three?**
  可以給我三個人的座位嗎？
- **Could I get a table in the non-smoking area?**
  可以給我禁煙區的座位嗎？
  ＊non-smoking area 禁煙區
- **Could I get a table in the back?**
  可以給我後面的座位嗎？

1 對話
A 可以給我窗邊的座位嗎？
B Yes, but it will be about 15 minutes.
A That's no problem.

A Could I get a table by the window?
B 好的，但您可能要等十五分鐘。
A 沒問題。

2 練習 可以給我角落的座位嗎？(corner)
Could I get a table ______________________?

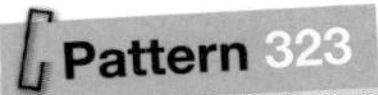

323

I'll have...
我要點…

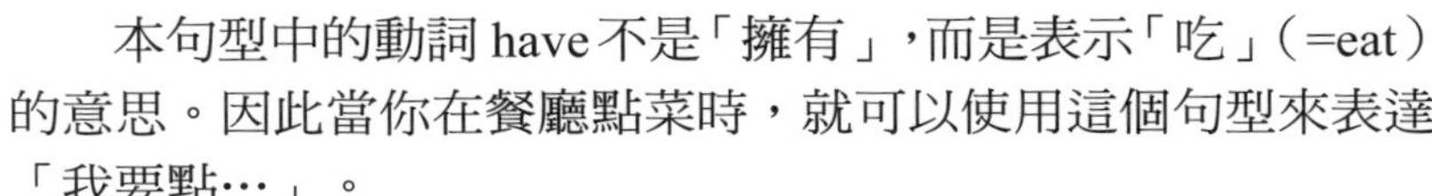

本句型中的動詞 have 不是「擁有」，而是表示「吃」（=eat）的意思。因此當你在餐廳點菜時，就可以使用這個句型來表達「我要點…」。

- **I'll have a jelly roll for dessert.**
  我要點果凍捲當作甜點。
- **I'll have a bottle of wine.**
  我要點一瓶酒。
- **I'll have the pasta without vegetables.**
  我要點沒有蔬菜的義大利麵。　＊without 沒有…
- **I'll have what she's having.**
  我要點她正在吃的那個。

1 對話
A 我要點一瓶酒。
B That sounds good.
A Do you prefer white or red?
B I like red.

A I'll have a bottle of wine.
B 聽起來不錯。
A 你喜歡喝紅酒還是白酒？
B 我喜歡紅酒。

2 練習　我要點一套全餐。(complete)
I'll have ______________________.

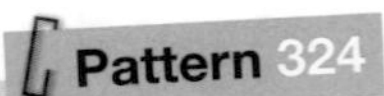

How long will we have to...?
我們還要…多久？

人氣高的餐廳因為生意很好，所以上菜時間通常都較長，當你已經忍耐不住飢餓，想知道還要再等多久餐點才會上菜時，就使用這個句型問問服務人員吧！

- **How long will we have to wait?**
  我們還要等多久？
- **How long will we have to wait for the food?**
  我們還要等多久，餐點才會做好？
- **How long will we have to wait for the check?**
  我們還要等多久，帳單才會準備好？ ＊check 帳單
- **How long will we have to sit at the bar?**
  我們還要坐在吧檯多久？

1 對話
A It's one of the finest restaurants in the city.
B 我們還要等多久，餐點才會做好？
A I don't know, but they're usually quick.

A 這間是這座城市裡其中一間最棒的餐廳。
B How long will we have to wait for the food?
A 我也不清楚，但通常都很快。

2 練習 我們還要待在這裡多久？(stay)
How long will we have to ______________________?

325

Pattern 325

Could you get me..., please?
請你給我⋯，好嗎？

本句型中的動詞 get 不是「得到」的意思，而是跟 bring 同義。當你在餐廳吃飯，想要求對方送叉子、餐巾紙或一杯水時，就可以使用這個句型。

- **Could you get me another fork, please?**
  請你給我另一支叉子，好嗎？
- **Could you get me a dessert menu, please?**
  請你給我甜點類的菜單，好嗎？
- **Could you get me a receipt, please?**
  請你給我收據，好嗎？ ＊receipt 收據
- **Could you get me a refill, please?**
  請你幫我續杯，好嗎？ ＊refill 續杯

1 對話
A Do you need anything else?
B 請你給我一份甜點菜單，好嗎？
A No problem.

A 請問您還需要些什麼？
B Could you get me a dessert menu, please?
A 沒問題。

2 練習 請你給我另一條餐巾，好嗎？(another)
Could you get me ______________________, please?

13-1~13-5

黃金複習 15 分鐘！

前面這 25 個句型和 125 個句子全都記熟了嗎？
來驗收一下學習成果吧！如果不能充滿自信地用英文說出以下 40 個句子，請翻到前面再重新複習一次！

01 你的飛機什麼時候抵達？

02 請你給我一份甜點菜單，好嗎？

03 我要在哪裡托運行李？

04 我們還要等多久，餐點才會做好？

05 可以請你給我水嗎？

06 我要點一瓶酒。

07 我來這裡是為了跟我們公司的一位客戶碰面。

08 可以給我三個人的座位嗎？

09 我們應該在哪一個登機門等候？

解答 01. What time does your plane land? 02. Could you get me a dessert menu, please?
03. Where do I check my baggage? 04. How long will we have to wait for the food?
05. Could you bring me some water? 06. I'll have a bottle of wine.
07. I'm here for a meeting with one of our clients. 08. Could I get a table for three?
09. Which gate should we wait at?

10 我們已經預約好六個人。

11 請載我到機場。

12 我想要將我的住宿延長幾天。

13 可以請你在那棟大樓的前面讓我下車嗎？

14 我房間裡的電視有些問題。

15 請問我應該在哪裡轉乘地鐵？

16 可以請你送一些冰塊到我的房間嗎？麻煩你。

17 要去劇院的話，應該要搭幾號巴士？

18 可以給我有兩張床的房間嗎？

19 萬一我延遲還車的話，會怎麼樣嗎？

20 我已經預訂了兩晚的住宿。

解答 10. We have a reservation for six people. 11. Please take me to the airport. 12. I'd like to extend my stay for a few days. 13. Could you pull over in front of that building? 14. I'm having a problem with the TV in my room. 15. Where should I change subway lines? 16. Could you send some ice to my room, please? 17. Which bus goes to the theater? 18. Can I get a room with two beds? 19. What would happen if I were late returning the car? 20. I've reserved lodging for two nights.

21 使用免費無線網路的最佳地點是哪裡？

22 什麼時候開始登機？

23 請問到公車站要花多少時間？

24 我要在哪裡辦理登機手續？

25 到羅羅飯店要往哪個方向？

26 可以請你給我一條毛毯嗎？

27 從這裡該怎麼去地鐵站？

28 我來這裡是為了參觀觀光景點。

29 有什麼購買紀念品的地方嗎？

30 我們在哪一個登機門出發？

31 我已經預訂了一間附雙人床的房間。

解答 21. Where is the best place to get free Wi-Fi? 22. What time does boarding begin?
23. How long will it take to get to the bus station? 24. Where do I check in?
25. Which way is it to the Lolo Hotel? 26. Could you bring me a blanket?
27. How can I get to the subway station from here? 28. I'm here for the tourist attractions.
29. Are there any places to buy souvenirs? 30. Which gate do we depart from?
31. I've reserved a room with a queen-sized bed.

32 請載我到會議中心。

______

33 可以給我景色不錯的房間嗎？

______

34 可以請你在轉角讓我下車嗎？

______

35 可以請你多送一個枕頭到 512 號房嗎？

______

36 請問我應該在哪裡下車？

______

37 我的冷氣有些問題。

______

38 要去機場的話，應該要搭幾號巴士？

______

39 我想要將我的預約延長一天。

______

40 萬一我發生了什麼意外的話，會怎麼樣嗎？

______

解答 32. Please take me to the conference center. 33. Can I get a room with a nice view? 34. Could you pull over at the corner? 35. Could you send an extra pillow to room 512? 36. Where should I get off the bus? 37. I'm having a problem with my air conditioner. 38. Which bus goes to the airport? 39. I'd like to extend my reservation for another day. 40. What would happen if I got in an accident?

Unit 14
人資檢討
自信說出自己的好表現

14-1

進行年中／年末檢討

You'll need to fill out... 326 你需要填寫…

It is time for your... 327 輪到你的…

Are you available to meet...? 328 你在…有空可以面談嗎？

Let's schedule... 329 我們來安排…

Have you completed...? 330 你已經完成…了嗎？

Pattern 326

You'll need to fill out...
你需要填寫…

有些公司在每年的年中或年末需要填寫評估報告，當你要提醒其他同事該填寫評估相關的文件時，就可以用這個句型。可以跟同事說 You'll need to fill out your review paperwork. 來提醒他們在會議前要先填寫考核的表格，以作為人資的參考。

- **You'll need to fill out a self-evaluation form for your review.** ＊self-evaluation 自我評價
  你需要為你的考核填寫一份自我評價的表格。
- **You'll need to fill out a survey.**
  你需要填寫一份調查。 ＊survey 調查
- **You'll need to fill out a reflection form.**
  你需要填寫一份反思表格。
- **You'll need to fill out your annual sales numbers.**
  你需要填寫你的年度銷售數字。

1 對話 **A** Is there anything I need to prepare for our meeting?
B 你需要填寫一份反思表格。
A Can I get a copy of it?

A 有任何我需要為我們會議準備的事項嗎？
B You'll need to fill out a reflection form.
A 我可以拿一份影本嗎？

2 練習 你需要填寫一份線上表單。(online form)
You'll need to fill out ______________________.

Pattern 327

It is time for your...
輪到你的…

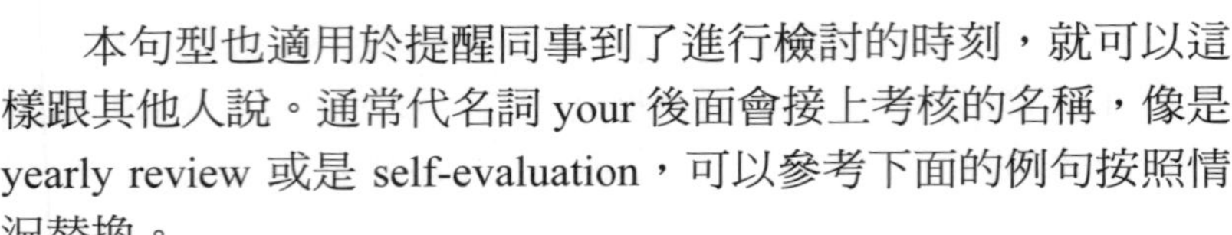

本句型也適用於提醒同事到了進行檢討的時刻，就可以這樣跟其他人說。通常代名詞 your 後面會接上考核的名稱，像是 yearly review 或是 self-evaluation，可以參考下面的例句按照情況替換。

- **It is time for your mid-year review.**
  輪到你的年中考核了。
- **It is time for your meeting with HR.**
  輪到你與人事部的面談了。　＊HR＝hunan resource 人事部門
- **It is time for your performance evaluation.**
  輪到你的表現評估了。
- **It is time for your sales review.**
  輪到你的銷售考核了。

1 對話
A 輪到你的年中評估了。
B When would you like to meet?
A Will tomorrow work for you?

A It's time for your mid-year review.
B 你想要什麼時候面談呢？
A 明天你可以嗎？

2 練習
輪到你的評估了。
It is time for your ____________________.

Pattern 328

Are you available to meet...?
你在…有空可以面談嗎？

本句型的目的是要詢問同事什麼時候有空可以面談，因此動詞 meet 後面可以接上時間，像是 sometime next week 或是 before year-end，或是加上介系詞 for 來表示面談的目的，例如 for your year-end review。

- **Are you available to meet next week for your year-end review?**
  你在下禮拜有空可以針對你的年終考核面談嗎？
- **Are you available to meet this afternoon?**
  你在今天下午有空可以面談嗎？
- **Are you available to meet before the end of the week?**
  你在這週末之前有空可以面談嗎？
- **Are you available to meet for your evaluation?**
  你有空可以針對你的評估面談嗎？

1 對話

A We need to finish your review.
B 你在下周的某一天可以面談嗎？
A Does Tuesday work for you?

A 我們需要完成你的考核。
B Are you available to meet sometime next week?
A 你星期二有空嗎？

2 練習 你可以當面面談你的考核嗎？ (review)
Are you available to meet ______________________?

Let's schedule…
我們來安排…

當你要跟其他同事或員工安排時間面談，就可以使用這個句型，不只可以用在人事考核上，也可以用在其他情境上，例如安排會議時間、客戶見面等等。動詞 schedule 後面可以加上時間，來表示要約什麼時段，或是名詞表示要約什麼事項。

- **Let's schedule your review.**
  我們來安排你的考核。
- **Let's schedule your annual review.**
  我們來安排你的年度考核。
- **Let's schedule time next week.**
  我們來安排下禮拜的時間。
- **Let's schedule that ASAP.**
  我們來盡快安排。

1 對話
A 我們來安排時間談談。
B I'm free now.
A That works for me!

A Let's schedule a time to talk.
B 我現在有空。
A 我也可以！

2 練習 我們來安排你的年中評估。(mid-year)
Let's schedule your ______________________________.

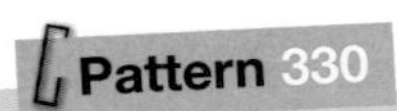

Have you completed...?
你已經完成…了嗎？

本句型是跟其他人確認他們有沒有完成一些人資檢討的文件，因此時態會使用完成式，並且動詞 complete 的後面會加上一些事項的英文，像是 paperwork、questionnaire 或是 evaluation 等單字。

- **Have you completed your review yet?**
  你已經完成你的考核了嗎？
- **Have you completed the self-assessment?**
  你已經完成自我評價了嗎？ ＊self-assessment 自我評價
- **Have you completed the meeting with HR?**
  你已經完成和人事部的會議了嗎？
- **Have you completed your self-evaluation?**
  你已經完成你的自我評估了嗎？

1 對話 A Your review is this afternoon.
B Is there anything I need to do about it?
A 你已經完成自我評估了嗎？

A 你的考核是這個下午。
B 有任何事項是我需要做的嗎？
A Have you completed the self-assessment?

2 練習 你已經完成每件你需要做的事項了嗎？
Have you completed ______________________?

14-2

說出自己的好表現

I'm doing well in...	331	我在…做得很好。
There are some areas that...	332	有幾個領域是…
I had a record...	333	我…破紀錄。
I'm proud of...	334	我對…感到驕傲。
I'm happy with...	335	我對…感到開心。

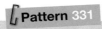

Pattern 331

I'm doing well in...
我在…做得很好。

本句型是用在回答主管或人資專員的問題，如果被問你對自己這段時間的表現有什麼想法，就可以說你自己的優點，I'm doing well in my role. 或者是 I'm doing well in the sales department.，來表達自己在工作崗位上做得很好，幫自己說好話加分。

- **I'm doing well in this position.**
  我在這個職位做得很好。
- **I'm doing well in hitting my sales target.**
  我在達到銷售業績做得很好。
  ＊sales target 銷售目標
- **I'm doing well in building relationships.**
  我在建立關係做得很好。
- **I'm doing well in connecting with clients.**
  我在與客戶聯繫做得很好。

1 對話 **A** What do you feel you're doing well?
B 我在建立關係做得很好。
A I agree with you.

A 你覺得你哪方面做得很好呢？
B I'm doing well in building relationships.
A 我同意你說的。

2 練習 我在建立業務做得很好。 (business)
I'm doing well in ______________________.

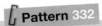

 332

Pattern 332

There are some areas that...
有幾個領域…

本句型是用在評論表現的時候，如果同事問你對於他的表現有什麼看法時，就可以說他在哪些部份需要加強，例如：There are some areas that need some work.。除了評論別人的表現，也可以用這個句型表達自己要改進的地方，像是 There are some areas that I should improve.。

- **There are some areas that need your attention.**
  有幾個領域需要你的專注力。
- **There are some areas that could use improvement.**
  有幾個領域可能需要改進。
- **There are some areas that we are concerned about.**
  有幾個領域是我們在擔心的。
- **There are some areas that you need to work on.**
  有幾個領域需要你去改善。 ＊work on 修理；改善

1 對話
A How do you think I'm doing?
B 有些領域可能需要改進。
A Can you give me an example?

A 你覺得我做得如何？
B There are some areas that could use improvement.
A 你可以給我一個例子嗎？

2 練習 有些領域是我很失望的。 (disappointed about)
There are some areas that ______________________.

Pattern 333

I had a record...
我…破紀錄。

在接受人資檢討考核的時候，可以盡量說出自己這段時間的好表現，這時就要提到自己最亮眼的成績，可以說自己的業績有破紀錄，是公司表現最好的人，例如：I had a record quarter，來表示自己這個季度的成果最亮眼。

- **I had a record number of sales last month.**
  我在上個月銷售數字破紀錄。
- **I had a record profit last quarter.**
  我上個季度破紀錄。
- **I had a record breaking year.**
  我有個破紀錄的一年。
- **I had a record number of new clients.**
  我新客戶的數量破紀錄。

1 對話
A What are you most proud of this past year?
B 我在上個季度獲利破紀錄。
A That's impressive!

A 過去這一年你最驕傲的是什麼？
B I had a record profit last quarter.
A 那令人印象深刻！

2 練習 我新進客戶的數量破紀錄。(incoming customers)
I had a record ______________________________.

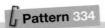

Pattern 334

I'm proud of...
我對…感到驕傲。

本句型一樣是用在表達自己亮眼的地方，跟人資或主管說自己驕傲的地方在哪個方面，像是 I'm proud of my role in the company.。當然你也可以很謙虛地說，你對團隊感到驕傲，稱讚大家的團隊合作能力，例如：I'm proud of my sales team.。

- **I'm proud of my sales numbers.**
  我對我的銷售數字感到驕傲。
- **I'm proud of how much I've learned this year.**
  我對我今年所學到的事情感到驕傲。
- **I'm proud of the projects I worked on.**
  我對我執行過的計畫感到驕傲。
- **I'm proud of the changes I made.**
  我對我做的改變感到驕傲。

1 對話

A What is something you feel you're doing well in your role?
B 我對我的銷售數字感到驕傲。
A You are doing well with that.

A 在你的職位中，什麼事項是你做得好的？
B I'm proud of my sales numbers.
A 你在那方面表現得很好。

2 練習 我對我們達成的成就感到驕傲。
I'm proud of ________________________.

Pattern 335

I'm happy with...
我對…感到開心。

這也是表示自己對表現或成績而感到開心的句型，可以跟人資或主管說這段時間最讓自己開心的事情是什麼，例如：I'm happy with my success.，或是對考核結果感到滿意，也可以說 I'm happy with my review.。

- **I'm happy with my accomplishments.**
  我對我的成就感到開心。　　＊accomplishment 成就；實現
- **I'm happy with your feedback.**
  我對你的回饋感到開心。
- **I'm happy with everything I've done this year.**
  我對今年做得每件事感到開心。
- **I'm happy with my evaluation.**
  我對我的評估感到開心。

1 對話
A How do you feel your review went?
B 我對我的評價感到開心。
A I'm glad!

A 你覺得你的考核進展如何呢？
B I'm happy with my evaluation.
A 我很高興！

2 練習 我對我的加薪感到開心。
I'm happy with ______________________.

14-3

檢討自己的缺點

Pattern 336

I struggle to...
我對…感到困難

工作上有做得很好的事情，當然也就有不擅長的項目，這個句型就是讓你跟人資或主管提出你認為自己的弱點在哪邊，並一起討論要怎麼改善。可以說 I struggle to make a sale. 或是 I struggle to develop relationships.，檢討自己需要加強的方面在哪邊，並在未來朝這個方向進步。

I struggle to meet my weekly goals.
我對達到我每週目標感到困難。

I struggle to close a sale.
我對完成銷售感到困難。

I struggle to work on a team.
我對團隊工作感到困難。

I struggle to plan a budget.
我對計畫預算感到困難。

1 對話
A What's something you need to work on?
B 我對團隊工作感到困難。
A I see that as a weak point too.

A 什麼方面是你需要改善的？
B I struggle to work on a team.
A 我也認為這是個弱點。

2 練習 我對使用新軟體有困難。
I struggle to ______________________.

337

Pattern 337

I think the sales target is...
我認為銷售目標…

當人資或主管提到你這段時間的銷售目標時，就可以用這個句型來表達自己的銷售表現如何，例如：I think the sales target is perfect.，表示自己的銷售目標很完美，或是 I think the sales target is tough to reach.，提出這樣的銷售目標很難達成，需要調整一下。

- **I think the sales target is too high.**
  我認為銷售目標太高了。
- **I think the sales target is demanding.**
  我認為銷售目標太苛刻了。 ＊demanding 苛刻的
- **I think the sales target is tough to reach.**
  我認為銷售目標很難達到。
- **I think the sales target is too much.**
  我認為銷售目標太超過了。

1 對話 **A** Why haven't you hit your sales goal?
B 我認為這個銷售目標太超過了。
A I disagree with that.

A 為什麼你還沒達到你的銷售目標呢？
B I think the sales target is too much.
A 我並不同意那樣的說法。

2 練習 我認為銷售目標不足。
I think the sales target is ______________________.

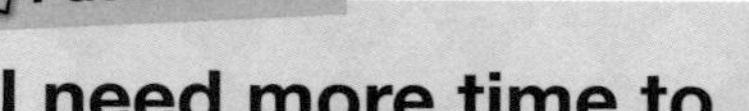

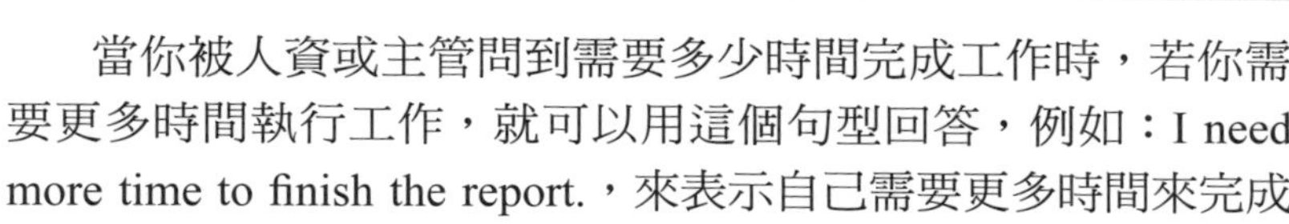

I need more time to...
我需要更多時間…

當你被人資或主管問到需要多少時間完成工作時，若你需要更多時間執行工作，就可以用這個句型回答，例如：I need more time to finish the report.，來表示自己需要更多時間來完成報告。

上班族萬用句

- **I need more time to hit my sales goal.**
  我需要更多時間達到我的銷售目標。
- **I need more time to complete the work.**
  我需要更多時間完成這項工作。
- **I need more time to finalize the plan.**
  我需要更多時間完成這個計畫。
- **I need more time to finish the paperwork.**
  我需要更多時間完成這份文件。

1 對話
A 我需要時間完成這個報告。
B How much time do you need?
A Can I have another day?

A I need more time to finish the report.
B 你需要多少時間？
A 我可以再多一天嗎？

2 練習 我需要更多時間完成這筆銷售。(wrap up)
I need more time to ______________________.

Pattern 339

339

I have a hard time...
我對…有困難。

本句型用於自己在工作上有沒有遇到困難的時候，可以提出自己的弱點在哪邊，並且討論該怎麼調整工作的模式，例如當你說 I have a hard time meeting new clients.，人資與主管可以給你更多建議，讓你在工作上做出改進。

- **I have a hard time reaching the sales goal.**
  我對達到銷售目標有困難。
- **I have a hard time finding customers.**
  我對尋找客戶有困難。
- **I have a hard time with the software.**
  我對這個軟體有困難。
- **I have a hard time staying on schedule.**
  我對按照時間表有困難。

1 對話 A What's your biggest challenge?
B 我對尋找客戶有困難。
A I can help you with that.

A 你最大的挑戰是什麼？
B I have a hard time finding customers.
A 我可以幫你那件事。

2 練習 我對遵循指示有困難。 (instruction)
I have a hard time ______________________________.

My sales numbers aren't...
我的銷售數字沒有…

本句型是在你被問到銷售情況如何的時候使用，如果這段期間你的銷售數字不太理想，可以回答 My sales numbers aren't very good.，來表達這段期間的業績並沒有達標，或是達到自己預期的數字，可以用下面的例句交換使用。

- **My sales numbers aren't very good this quarter.**
  我的銷售數字在這個季度沒有很好。
- **My sales numbers aren't as good as they could be.**
  我的銷售數字沒有達到最好的狀態。
- **My sales numbers aren't what they need to be.**
  我的銷售數字沒有達到該有的水準。
- **My sales numbers aren't where I want them.**
  我的銷售數字沒有達到我期望的地步。

1 對話
A 我的銷售數字沒有達到最好的狀態。
B I don't think they're that bad.
A Are you sure?

A My sales numbers aren't as good as they could be.
B 我不認為有這麼糟糕。
A 你確定嗎？

2 練習 我的銷售數字不夠好。
My sales numbers aren't ______________________.

14-4

制度可以改善的地方

Pattern 341

I have an idea to...
我有個…的想法。

大多數的公司會定期檢討制度是否適合所有員工，因此有些公司會徵詢員工的意見，來做為之後改善制度的依據。當你對公司有一些意見時，可以這樣跟人資或主管說 I have an idea to improve sales. 或是 I have an idea to grow the business. 等例句。

- **I have an idea to increase profit.**
  我有個增加獲利的想法。
- **I have an idea to bring in clients.**
  我有個吸引客戶的想法。　　* bring in 引入
- **I have an idea to increase weekly sales.**
  我有個增加每週銷售額的想法。
- **I have an idea to improve productivity.**
  我有個增進生產力的想法。

1 對話
A 我有個增加獲利的想法。
B Can you share it with me?
A Let's talk in my office.

A I have an idea to increase profit.
B 你可以跟我分享這個想法嗎？
A 來我的辦公室聊聊吧。

2 練習 我有個促進銷售的想法。(boost)
I have an idea to ____________________.

Pattern 342

I believe my suggestion will help...
我相信我的建議會幫助…

本句型也是在建議公司的制度改進時使用，若主管和人資向你詢問關於公司制度有什麼需要變動的地方，你就可以說出你的建議，並且在後面補上一句 I believe my suggestion will help boost sales.，以加深建議的可信度。

- **I believe my suggestion will help us make more money.**
  我相信我的建議會幫助我們賺更多錢。
- **I believe my suggestion will help improve our bottom line.** ＊bottom line 損益表底線
  我相信我的建議會幫助增進我們的損益表底線。
- **I believe my suggestion will help bring in new customers.**
  我相信我的建議會幫助吸引新顧客。
- **I believe my suggestion will help grow our profit.**
  我相信我的建議會幫助我們的獲利成長。

1 對話 **A** I have an idea for work.
B What kind of idea?
A 我相信我的建議會幫助我們賺更多錢。

A 我有個關於工作的想法。
B 是什麼樣的想法呢？
A I believe my suggestion will help us make more money.

2 練習 我相信我的建議會幫助促進生意。 (boost)
I believe my suggestion will help ______________.

Pattern 343

I'd like to suggest...
我想要建議…

本句型用於提供建議給人資或主管的時候，如果被問到工作上有什麼需要調整的地方，就可以說 I'd like to suggest something. 或是 I'd like to suggest we make a change.，來提出你自己的想法給其他人參考，作為日後改變的參考。

- **I'd like to suggest a change that could increase our profit.**
  我想要建議一個可以增進我們獲利的改變。
- **I'd like to suggest a policy change.**
  我想要建議一項政策改變。
- **I'd like to suggest a change in our process.**
  我想要建議一項針對我們流程的改變。
- **I'd like to suggest some ideas I came up with.**
  我想要建議幾個我想到的點子。

1 對話
A 我想要建議一項政策的改變。
B Why would we do that?
A It will save us money.

A I'd like to suggest a policy change.
B 為什麼我們要那樣做呢？
A 那會讓我們省錢。

2 練習 我想要建議一個小小的改變。
I'd like to suggest ______________________.

Pattern 344

This switch will improve...
這種轉變會增進…

當你提出建議後，可以再用這個句型強調你提出的建議會帶來什麼樣的成效。例如你可以說 This switch will improve profits. 來表達這樣會增進獲益，或是其他抽象的事物，像是 culture、morale 等單字。

- **This switch will improve our progress.**
  這種轉變會增進我們的進展。
- **This switch will improve our company's culture.**
  這種轉變會改善我們公司的文化。
- **This switch will improve the team's morale.**
  這種轉變會增進團隊的士氣。　＊morale 士氣
- **This switch will improve our bottom line.**
  這種轉變會增進我們的損益表底線。

1 對話
A 這種轉變會增進我們的進展。
B How will it do that?
A Let me show you.

A This switch will improve our progress.
B 那樣要怎麼做呢？
A 讓我展示給你看。

2 練習 這種轉變會增進我們的銷售數字。
This switch will improve ______________________.

 345

Pattern 345

I can double our profit...
我可以…讓我們獲利雙倍

本句型是更直接、自信的表達，目的在說服對方按照你的方式改變可以獲利雙倍。後面可以加上時間或是用什麼方法，例如 this month、in no time 或是 with this idea。

- **I can double our profit this year.**
  我可以讓我們今年獲利雙倍。
- **I can double our profit with this change.**
  我可以用這項改變讓我們獲利雙倍。
- **I can double our profit with my idea.**
  我可以用我的想法讓我們獲利雙倍。
- **I can double our profit by making a few changes.**
  我可以藉由執行幾項改變讓我們獲利雙倍。

1 對話
- **A** 我可以讓我們今年獲利雙倍。
- **B** I don't believe you.
- **A** Wait and see!

- **A** I can double our profit this year.
- **B** 我不相信你。
- **A** 等著看吧。

2 練習 我可以用這個替代方案讓我們獲利雙倍。 (substitution)
I can double our profit ______________________.

14-5

總結這段時間的表現

I hit my goals…	346	我…達到目標。
I had record sales…	347	我銷售額破紀錄…
I fell short of…	348	我未達到…
I didn't meet my sales…	349	我沒有達到我的銷售…
I had an outstanding…	350	我有個傑出的…

Pattern 346

346

I hit my goals...
我…達到目標。

最後談完年中或年終檢討時，可以用這個句型再次總結自己這段時間的表現。句型的後面加上時間會讓表達更確切，例如 this quarter 或是 every month this year 等。

- **I hit my goals last month.**
  我上個月達到目標。
- **I hit my goals this week.**
  我這週達到目標。
- **I hit my goals last quarter.**
  我上個季度達到目標。
- **I hit my goals again this year.**
  我今年再次達到目標。

1 對話

A How are you doing with your sales?
B 我今年每個月都達到目標。
A That's awesome!

A 你的銷售狀況如何呢？
B I hit my goals every month this year.
A 那真是太好了！

2 練習 我今年每一週都達到目標。
I hit my goals ______________________________.

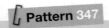

Pattern 347

I had record sales...
我⋯銷售額破紀錄。

本句型用於強調自己在銷售上有好看的成績，句型的後面可以加上時間點，說明自己是在什麼時候銷售額破了紀錄，像是 this quarter 或是 every month 等時間，讓你的論述更有依據。

- **I had record sales this month.**
  我這個月銷售額破紀錄。
- **I had record sales this year.**
  我今年銷售額破紀錄。
- **I had record sales for the first time.**
  我第一次銷售額破紀錄。
- **I had record sales again this year.**
  我今年再次銷售額破紀錄。

1 對話

A 我第一次銷售額破紀錄。
B That's great! Nice work!
A Thank you.

A I had record sales for the first time.
B 太好了！做得好！
A 謝謝您。

2 練習

我上個月銷售破紀錄。
I had record sales ________________________.

Pattern 348

I fell short of...
我未達到…

本句型是在總結自己這段時間未達到的事項，並使用 fall short 這個片語，意思是「不符合標準」的意思，後面加上介系詞 of 就可以接 target sales、goal 等相關單字。

- **I fell short of my sales goal this year.**
  我今年未達到我的銷售目標。
- **I fell short of the standard.**
  我未達到這個標準。
- **I fell short of the required sales.**
  我未達到需要的銷售額。 ＊required 需要的
- **I fell short of the target.**
  我未達到這個目標。

1 對話 **A** 我未達到這個目標。
B I need you to catch up this month.
A I'll try my best.

A I fell short of the target.
B 我需要你在這個月趕上。
A 我會盡力的。

2 練習 我未達到我的整體銷售目標。 (sales goal)
I fell short of ______________________.

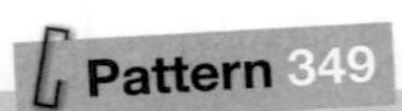

I didn't meet my sales...
我沒有達到我的銷售…

本句型也跟銷售的結果有關，如果這段時間狀況不太好，就可以用這個句型。sales 後面可以加上其他單字，表示不同的銷售單位，例如：sales goal、sales quota 和 sales target 等單字，並且接上明確的時間 this month 或 this year 等。

- **I didn't meet my sales quota this period.**
  我這段時間沒有達到我的銷售配額。　＊quota 配額；定額
- **I didn't meet my sales goal this month.**
  我這個月沒有達到我的銷售目標。
- **I didn't meet my sales benchmark.**
  我沒有達到我的銷售基準點。　＊benchmark 基準點
- **I didn't meet my sales deadline.**
  我沒有達到我的銷售期限。

1 對話
A 我沒有達到我的銷售目標。
B Don't worry about it.
A I'll hit it next month.

A I didn't meet my sales goal.
B 不用擔心這件事。
A 我在下個月會達到的。

2 練習 我沒有達到我的銷售數字。
I didn't meet my sales ______________________.

Pattern 350 350

I had an outstanding...
我有個傑出的…

這個句型是用在稱讚自己的好表現，作為檢討的總結。outstanding 是形容詞，表示「傑出的」意思，後面可以加上時間 month、week、quarter 等，或是一般的銷售相關名詞，例如：sales number、profit 等單字。

- **I had an outstanding year.**
  我有個傑出的一年。
- **I had an outstanding sales number.**
  我有個傑出的銷售數字。
- **I had an outstanding profit.**
  我有個傑出的獲益。
- **I had an outstanding sales period.**
  我有個傑出的銷售期間。

1 對話

A How are sales going?
B 我有個傑出的一年。
A That's great news!

A 銷售狀況如何呢？
B I had an outstanding year.
A 那真是好消息！

2 練習

我有個傑出的考核。 (review)
I had an outstanding ______________.

14-1~14-5

黃金複習 15 分鐘！

前面這 25 個句型和 125 個句子全都記熟了嗎？
來驗收一下學習成果吧！如果不能充滿自信地用英文説出以下 40 個句子，請翻到前面再重新複習一次！

01 我未達到這個標準。

02 我對達到銷售目標有困難。

03 我有個傑出的銷售數字。

04 我可以讓我們今年獲利雙倍。

05 我對我今年所學到的事情感到驕傲。

06 輪到你的銷售考核了。

07 我第一次銷售額破紀錄。

08 我對今年做得每件事感到開心。

09 我有個傑出的獲益。

解答 01. I fell short of the standard. 02. I have a hard time reaching the sales goal.
03. I had an outstanding sales number. 04. I can double our profit this year.
05. I'm proud of how much I've learned this year.
06. It is time for your sales review.
07. I had record sales for the first time.
08. I'm happy with everything I've done this year.
09. I had an outstanding profit.

10 我對尋找客戶感到困難。

11 我需要更多時間完成這個計畫。

12 我這週達到目標。

13 我今年再次銷售額破紀錄。

14 我有個增加獲利的想法。

15 我相信我的建議會幫助我們賺更多錢。

16 我對完成銷售感到困難。

17 我想要建議幾個我想到的點子。

18 我認為銷售目標太高了。

19 我在與客戶聯繫做得很好。

20 我對團隊工作感到困難。

解答 10. I have a hard time finding customers. 11. I need more time to finalize the plan.
12. I hit my goals this week. 13. I had record sales again this year.
14. I have an idea to increase profit.
15. I believe my suggestion will help us make more money.
16. I struggle closing a sale. 17. I'd like to suggest some ideas I came up with.
18. I think the sales target is too high. 19. I'm doing well in connecting with clients.
20. I have a hard time working on a team.

21 我想要建議一個可以增進我們獲利的改變。

____

22 我需要更多時間完成這份文件。

____

23 我有個吸引客戶的想法。

____

24 我這個月沒有達到我的銷售目標。

____

25 我對你的回饋感到開心。

____

26 我在建立關係做得很好。

____

27 我對這個軟體有困難。

____

28 我認為銷售目標太苛刻了。

____

29 我想要建議一項政策改變。

____

30 我對達到每週目標感到困難。

____

解答 21. I'd like to suggest a change that could increase our profit.
22. I need more time to finish the paperwork. 23. I have an idea to bring in clients.
24. I didn't meet my sales goal this month. 25. I'm happy with your feedback.
26. I'm doing well in building relationships.
27. I have a hard time with the software.
28. I think the sales target is demanding.
29. I'd like to suggest a policy change.
30. I struggle meeting my weekly goals.

31 我需要更多時間達到我的銷售目標。

32 我對按照時間表有困難。

33 我對我做的改變感到驕傲。

34 我想要建議一項在我們流程的改變。

35 我可以用我的想法讓我們獲利雙倍。

36 我這個月銷售額破紀錄。

37 我可以用這項改變讓我們獲利雙倍。

38 我有個增進生產力的想法。

39 我有個傑出的銷售期間。

40 我對我的銷售數字感到驕傲。

解答 31. I need more time to hit my sales goal.
32. I have a hard time staying on schedule. 33. I'm proud of the changes I made.
34. I'd like to suggest a change in our process. 35. I can double our profit with my idea.
36. I had record sales this month.
37. I can double our profit with this change.
38. I have an idea to improve productivity.
39. I had an outstanding sales period.
40. I'm proud of my sales numbers.

練習題解答

Part 1
Unit 1 ~ Unit 5

1-1

001 Good afternoon. This is the warehouse.
002 I'd like to speak with his secretary.
003 Can I speak to someone who is in charge of overseas sales?
004 Is this the headquarters?
005 This is a colleague of Dan's from California.

1-2

006 I'm sorry, but I'm going out now.
007 Can I call you when I have more information?
008 I'm afraid she's on a business trip.
009 I think he just left the meeting room.
010 When do you expect he'll have time to take a call?

1-3

011 Would you like to leave another message?
012 Please tell him that I have a question for him.
013 Could you tell him to push back the meeting one hour?
014 Can I have your fax number?
015 I'll tell him that you're anxious to speak with him.

1-4

016 I'm calling to schedule a lunch meeting.
017 I'm calling about your late payment.
018 Is this a good time to talk about this?
019 When do you need the estimates?
020 Let me check if the manager has arrived.

1-5

021 This connection isn't very good.
022 I have trouble hearing due to the copy machine.
023 Could you speak more clearly?
024 Did you say you agree on that?
025 My phone battery is old.

2-1

026 I am Frank Miller from the Max Corp.
027 I am in charge of all imports.
028 Let me start off by introducing our operation.
029 Thank you for sending us some free samples.
030 I'm sorry for sending out the wrong catalog.

2-2

031 We met at the presentation last week.
032 I was referred to you by Murray Smith of the Ace Bank.
033 I got your email address from your company's website.
034 I am the person who called you about collaborating on a project.
035 I am responding to your proposal.

2-3

036 I'm writing to invite you to join our committee.
037 I'm contacting you because I think we can help each other.
038 We are pleased to inform you that we have found your lost product.
039 It's great to hear that you're making progress.
040 We regret to tell you that we have decided not to participate in the meeting.

2-4

041 We'd like to meet you more often.
042 Could you send me an outline of your proposal?
043 I'd be grateful if you could make a quick decision.
044 As requested, we will mail you a free sample.
045 I'm attaching a copy of our brochure.

2-5

046 It will take a week to get approval.
047 I'll get back to you after my meeting with the brokers.
048 I am still considering your offer with my boss.
049 Please feel free to call me with the wording of this document.
050 We look forward to your prompt response.

3-1

51 Thank you for the invitation.
52 We see this meeting as our last chance to come to an agreement.
53 Before we begin, shall we establish some guidelines?
54 Let's start with some introductions.
55 At our last meeting, we agreed on pricing.

3-2

56 We're here today to review the budget.
57 The purpose of this meeting is to improve our marketing strategy.
58 I'll brief you on last week's symposium.
59 I'll update you on the status of the project.
60 Allow me to take a few minutes to outline the plan.

3-3

61 Let me give you time to think it over.
62 I suggest that we be more aggressive in our negotiation.
63 Why don't we make a list of ideas?
64 What we really need is a tougher sales team.
65 We're expecting to see a loss on this product line.

3-4

66 That's a fine suggestion.
67 I support that in theory, but I'm not sure it's practical.
68 I can partly agree to that, but we'll need to amend the contract.
69 Let me think about the ideas from today's meeting.
70 I must have misunderstood that part of our agreement.

3-5

71 Does anyone object to my suggestion?
72 I'm sorry to interrupt, but could I ask a question?
73 I feel sorry to say this, but I don't think it's going to work out.
74 I don't think we can help you with that.
75 I'm against that because it isn't practical.

4-1

76 Here is the login details for the meeting.
77 Did you send the meeting invitation to Ryan?
78 Use this call-in number to access the online meeting.
79 I'll forward you all the documents for the meeting.
80 Please find the meeting invitation in the group email.

4-2

81 Can you mute yourself during the presentation?
82 I'm here! I was on mute and didn't realize it.
83 Your camera keeps shutting down.
84 Is anyone else hearing that noise?
85 Everyone needs to click the join link.

4-3

86 Can you see what I'm doing?
87 Could you share how you created the meeting?
88 I'll share that keynote during our Teams meeting.
89 How do I share my questions during the meeting?
90 Can you see what I'm asking you to do?

4-4

91 Let's try to stick to the schedule.
92 This item wasn't in the lineup for today's meeting.
93 Can I add a point that needs to be discussed?
94 I think we should stay on this topic for a minute.
95 We're getting off to a good start.

4-5

96 Does anyone have anything to bring up?
97 Are there any questions about the presentation?
98 Did we cover your idea?
99 Thank you for setting this meeting up!
100 Is there anything else we had to figure out?

5-1

101 My name is Tim and I'm responsible for global communications.
102 The topic of today's presentation is our new Tokyo office.
103 Please interrupt me if you need assistance.
104 After my presentation, there will be time for networking.
105 I'd like to begin with our last earning rate.

5-2

106 Please take a look at the image on page 5 of the handout.
107 This slide shows that our market share could shrink again this year.
108 As you can see from this chart, our company is in trouble.
109 Let's move on to the next picture.
110 For the next five minutes, I'll talk about investments.

5-3

111 What is really important is how to become a global leader.
112 It's essential to understand where to focus our resources.
113 I should repeat that these are prototypes, not the final products.
114 I'm sure everyone in this room can identify with this difficulty.
115 I think it might be worthwhile to listen to his proposal.

5-4

116 Let's briefly go over the questions raised by this.
117 I'd like to finish by saying that I'm available anytime if you have questions.
118 I'd recommend that you not wait long before making an order.
119 In closing, I want you to remember the purpose of this presentation.
120 Thank you all for your patience.

5-5

121 Now, I'll answer only questions relating to the procedure.
122 Are there any additional comments?
123 Could you tell us more about your concerns?
124 That's a bold question!
125 As I said earlier, that shouldn't be an issue.

Part 2
Unit 6 ~ Unit 11

6-1

126 Is next week okay with you?
127 Can we meet later in the month?
128 I can make it this afternoon.
129 Could you arrange a team meeting?
130 If it's all right, I'd like to meet tomorrow.

6-2

131 I'm sorry, but I need to cancel this appointment.
132 I don't think I'll be able to be there.
133 Can we reschedule the deadline?
134 Is there another way we can connect this week?
135 Call me if anything changes before then.

6-3

136 I'm calling to confirm our appointment schedule.
137 I just want to make sure I'm bringing the appropriate papers.
138 Can you still make the 10:00 meeting?
139 If you need to arrive a little late, okay.
140 Please bring your status report to the third quarter meeting.

6-4

141 Let me pick our speaker up at the hotel.
142 I'll be waiting outside.
143 You must be Mr. Midler's wife.
144 This is my lawyer, Mr. Anderson.
145 I'll show you our factory at work.

6-5

146 What would you like to talk about?
147 Have you ever tried bubble tea?
148 This restaurant is popular for its steak.
149 Let me show you how to chop the kimchi.
150 Did you enjoy the conversation?

7-1

151 Our company is one of the leaders in imports.
152 We specialize in audio equipment.
153 We're based in women's clothing.
154 We have a 50 percent share of the domestic market in that business.
155 We have affiliate companies that have exclusive agreements with us.

7-2

156 This is the latest in communication devices.
157 This product uses water as a coolant.
158 This item has the best durability.
159 This is designed to assist disabled people.
160 It comes with a free charger.

7-3

161 We can guarantee your satisfaction.
162 The warranty is non-transferable.
163 The limited warranty covers the product for one year.
164 This will provide a huge time savings to customers.
165 We run the best customer service center in Europe.

7-4

166 We're interested in your latest leather fashions.
167 I'm looking for a powerful cleaning solution.
168 We'd like to get some information on this car's gas mileage.
169 Please explain the details on how to lock the computer.
170 I was wondering if you could tell me about the bike's durability.

7-5

171 This will appeal to mothers.
172 Our main target is young professionals.
173 We focus on women's fashions.
174 Market research shows men are less likely to buy road maps.
175 We'll advertise on the subway.

8-1

176 I'd like to begin by summarizing the points we have agreed on so far.
177 We hope to reach a satisfactory conclusion.
178 We can offer you the best price in the world.
179 What about 1,250 dollars per shipment?
180 We have a special offer for all customers today.

8-2

181 I don't believe it's a good idea to open a branch.
182 I'm afraid we can't go beyond 10 dollars without the approval of our clients.
183 I don't think I can accept your offer on my own.
184 I don't understand why the deal must be finished today.
185 I'm sorry I can't do business with your company.

8-3

186 Can you offer me a price reduction?
187 Can you reduce the price if we commit to future deals?
188 Is there a discount on shipping costs?
189 Would it cost less if we pay in cash?
190 Is there a charge for opening an account?

8-4

191 What we're looking for is quick delivery.
192 A small fee is charged for our services.
193 Payment is due before shipment can be made.
194 Do you think it's possible to change the word?
195 Would it be okay if we waited a day to sign?

8-5

196 Are you saying you're ready to sign?
197 What do you mean by "flexible pricing"?
198 What exactly are you asking us to do about marketing?
199 Could I ask about your experience in sales?
200 Let me hear what's most important to your company.

9-1

201 How about we find a number somewhere around 10,000 dollars?
202 May I suggest you talk to our accountant?
203 Would you consider giving a discount for large orders?
204 We'll reconsider lowering the price.
205 I'd rather have the option to cancel than the service.

9-2

206 You can't find better service.
207 We could be willing to work together.
208 That's acceptable if you have an account with us.
209 It looks like we're in agreement about most of the issues.
210 We've made major progress.

9-3

211 This deal is only good if it's signed today.
212 We're ready to move forward with the deal.
213 Please sign on the dotted line.
214 We'll provide the references of all the employees.
215 The contract can be revoked if both parties agree on that.

9-4

216 Are these swimming goggles available?
217 Does it come in a large box?
218 Do you have something that won't fall apart easily?
219 We'd like to order as much as possible.
220 I'd like to purchase your fashion line.

9-5

221 We'd like to change the billing address.
222 I'm sorry, but I have to cancel a portion of your order.
223 We'd like to return the entire order.
224 If we return this order now, can we reorder later?
225 What's your policy on customer satisfaction?

10-1

226 When can I expect payment?
227 How soon can those be delivered?
228 We need these by closing time.
229 Will you deliver free of charge?
230 Can you send that by DHL?

10-2

231 Your order will arrive by Friday.
232 The shipment didn't include a packing slip.
233 I'm sorry that the shipment will be delayed due to a storm.
234 The product is supposed to be delivered later this week.
235 We were told that delivery would be made by tomorrow.

10-3

236 I'd like to check the status of my package.
237 Could I get a tracking number sent to my cell phone?
238 We shipped them via EMS.
239 Did you get the items you expected?
240 The invoice number is in the top right corner.

10-4

241 I want to remind you that yesterday was your payment due date.
242 Payment must be made by the end of the month.
243 If you fail to pay on time, a 5% service charge will be added.
244 Your account is not up-to-date.
245 We'll be forced to contact our lawyers.

10-5

246 Can we pay by money order?
247 Is there a fee for shipping and handling?
248 Our payment is going to be due.
249 We've remitted the full amount.
250 We've confirmed that the last of the packages has arrived.

11-1

251 Unfortunately, we haven't received your answer yet.
252 We found out that the product did not meet our needs.
253 Your product failed to sell on the market.
254 You promised to replace any broken parts.
255 The quality of your service is appalling.

11-2

256 I have some complaints about the handling of the problem.
257 I'm very disappointed my shipment was damaged.
258 We're unhappy with the quality.
259 This is the worst price quote we've received.
260 I must insist that you return our payment in full.

11-3

261 We're very sorry that we were not able to meet your needs.
262 We apologize for overcharging you for the product.
263 Please accept our apologies for the bad condition of the shipment.
264 We should have answered your email more quickly.
265 We'll make sure this unfortunate error doesn't happen again.

11-4

266 The problem was caused by a missed phone call.
267 The reason is that our partners do not disclose information.
268 I've been finishing up a major deal.
269 I was so backlogged that I couldn't contact you.
270 I have no good excuse for having failed to give you the tracking number.

11-5

271 We'll try to refund your money as soon as possible.
272 If you're not satisfied, you may speak with the manager.
273 You can exchange it for a comparable item.
274 We'll do our best to satisfy your needs.
275 We'll compensate you for the problems the product caused you.

Part 3

Unit 12 ~ Unit 14

12-1

276 Did you have a great trip?
277 How's the profit report looking?
278 You look terrific.
279 I like your jacket.
280 Let's grab a drink.

12-2

281 I need you to fly to Miami.
282 The boss wants this mess cleaned up.
283 Don't forget to put this on your calendar.
284 There will be a seminar about salesmanship next month.
285 Do you want me to check his records?

12-3

286 How's the negotiation going?
287 Are you ready for your presentation?
288 What are you planning?
289 I'm working on the annual budget.
290 Let me know when you've heard from the client.

12-4

291 You have to finish adding up these numbers before you leave.
292 Can I have your signature by the end of the day?
293 I'll be done preparing for my presentation by lunchtime.
294 Before you go, log off your computer.
295 The meeting starts once everyone is here.

12-5

296 I feel terrible that I haven't called you.
297 Can you cover our clients in New York?
298 You can reach me at home or at the office.
299 Would you help me schedule an appointment?
300 I heard someone will be fired.

13-1

301 What time does boarding start?
302 Where do I get my boarding pass?
303 Could you bring me something for airsickness?
304 I'm here for a visit with relatives.
305 Which gate did they say?

13-2

306 Please take me to the outlet mall.
307 Could you pull over before we pass that building?
308 Where should I look for a metro station?
309 Which line goes to the hospital?
310 What would happen if I let someone else drive the car?

13-3

311 Are there any places to buy books?
312 How can I get to the financial district?
313 Which way is it to the gift shop?
314 How long will it take to get to the company?
315 Where is the best place to watch the sunset?

13-4

316 I've reserved a bottle of wine for our room.
317 Can I get a room with a coffee maker?
318 Could you send a room service menu to my room?
319 I'm having a problem with my toilet.
320 I'd like to extend the duration of my stay.

13-5

321 We have a reservation for a table for four.
322 Could I get a table in the corner?
323 I'll have a complete dinner.
324 How long will we have to stay here?
325 Could you get me another napkin, please?

14-1

326 You'll need to fill out an online form.
327 It is time for your evaluation.
328 Are you available to meet in person for your review?
329 Let's schedule your mid-year evaluation.
330 Have you completed everything you needed to do?

14-2

331 I'm doing well in building the business
332 There are some areas that I'm disappointed about.
333 I had a record number of incoming customers.
334 I'm proud of how much we accomplished.
335 I'm happy with my raise.

14-3

336 I struggle to use the new software.
337 I think the sales target is not enough.
338 I need more time to wrap up the sale.
339 I have a hard time following the instructions.
340 My sales numbers aren't good enough.

14-4

341 I have an idea to boost sales.
342 I believe my suggestion will help boost business.
343 I'd like to suggest a small change.
344 This switch will improve our sales numbers.
345 I can double our profit with this substitution.

14-5

346 I hit my goals each week this year.
347 I had record sales last month.
348 I fell short of my total sales goal.
349 I didn't meet my sales numbers.
350 I had an outstanding review.

台灣廣廈 國際出版集團
Taiwan Mansion International Group

國家圖書館出版品預行編目（CIP）資料

全新！外國人天天在用上班族萬用英文 / 白善燁著；許竹瑩譯.
-- 初版. -- 新北市：國際學村, 2024.03
面； 公分
ISBN 978-986-454-339-7（平裝）
1.CST: 商業英文 2.CST: 會話

805.188 113000817

國際學村

全新！外國人天天在用上班族萬用英文

只要會這350句，就能拿下每筆生意，成為年年升職加薪的職場菁英！

作　　者／白善燁
譯　　者／許竹瑩
編輯中心編輯長／伍峻宏・**編輯**／陳怡樺
封面設計／何偉凱・**內頁排版**／菩薩蠻數位文化有限公司
製版・印刷・裝訂／東豪・紘億・秉成

行企研發中心總監／陳冠蒨
媒體公關組／陳柔彣
綜合業務組／何欣穎
線上學習中心總監／陳冠蒨
產品企製組／顏佑婷、江季珊、張哲剛

發 行 人／江媛珍
法 律 顧 問／第一國際法律事務所 余淑杏律師・北辰著作權事務所 蕭雄淋律師
出　　版／國際學村
發　　行／台灣廣廈有聲圖書有限公司
地址：新北市235中和區中山路二段359巷7號2樓
電話：（886）2-2225-5777・傳真：（886）2-2225-8052
讀者服務信箱／cs@booknews.com.tw

代理印務・全球總經銷／知遠文化事業有限公司
地址：新北市222深坑區北深路三段155巷25號5樓
電話：（886）2-2664-8800・傳真：（886）2-2664-8801
郵 政 劃 撥／劃撥帳號：18836722
劃撥戶名：知遠文化事業有限公司（※單次購書金額未達1000元，請另付70元郵資。）

■出版日期：2024年03月
ISBN：978-986-454-339-7